the DEMON PRINCE

USA TODAY BESTSELLING AUTHOR

EMMA HAMM

emma hamm

ALSO BY EMMA HAMM

The Otherworld
Heart of the Fae
Veins of Magic
The Faceless Woman
The Raven's Ballad
Bride of the Sea
Curse of the Troll

Of Goblin Kings
Of Goblins and Gold
Of Shadows and Elves
Of Pixies and Spells
Of Werewolves and Curses
Of Fairytales and Magic

Dragon of Umbra
Fire Heart
Bright Heart
Brave Heart
Torn Heart

and many more...

Let this book be an escape from the world.

Sink into its pages, luxuriate in the misty moors, and wrap yourself in some red silk.

Tempt the vampire. You never know what you might get in return.

emma hamm

the demon prince

PRIDE

GREED

LUST

GLUTTONY

ENVY

SLOTH

WRATH

Chapter 1

When had the scent of blood in the evening become so comforting?

Katherine sat with a bag of ice pressed against her hip, leaning against the outside wall of the almshouse. They mostly treated the wounded who had gotten in Gluttony's way. Whether their patients had angered him or sparked his insatiable appetite, every victim ended up in the same place. Here.

She was covered in grime from the day. Sweat had slithered down her back as she worked to close wounds and heal injuries. And then there were the various—and copious—amounts of blood that she hadn't scrubbed completely off.

Though today, they had a bit of a reprieve from their illustrious leader. A mining operation from another town had encountered a rather large hiccup. Three kelpies and twin vodyanoy had attacked their camp. Katherine expected they might have been fine if it had only been the vodyanoy. Sixteen men could easily fight a few water spirits who looked like overgrown toads. But kelpies? No one could fight them.

The water horses were wily and cruel. She still shuddered when she thought of the men's injuries. So many broken limbs, flesh chewed through by sharp teeth that had scissored through muscle with ease. Deep furrows showed how wide the kelpie's jaw could open. Some large enough to sink a man's head into the darkness while they chewed his chest and shoulders. She'd had to remove so many limbs today, and there were still more in there. Each of them hoped someone would have time to save their lives, and few would receive that help.

Most of her crew were getting ready to leave. The second shift had arrived and that meant her coworkers were all about to stagger home through the muck and the fog. The safe planks were marked with yellow paint so no one would fall through rotting wood. Soon they would get to their floating town that was already sinking back into the swamplands. But for now, they were safe as long as they stayed on the path.

She nodded as three of them walked by her, everyone with dark hollows under their eyes and a staggering gait that suggested they might already be asleep on their feet.

One of them paused beside her seat outside, staring into the fog for a few moments before her eyes slanted down. "Do you need help getting home?"

Grace was a lovely young woman with blonde hair, a slight frame, and surprising strength at holding someone down by the shoulders while someone sawed through their mangled leg. She was also one of the most thoughtful companions Katherine had ever met.

However, she wasn't in the habit of taking help from her friends. So she smiled tightly and shook her head. "Just have to rest it for a few moments, and then I'll be on my way. Get started or I'll catch up to you."

It was meant to be a joke, but Grace just winced.

They all knew Katherine was at a disadvantage. Her hip couldn't take long hours like today. Standing was one of the many things that exacerbated the fused bone that gave her a rather awkward limp and made her slower than the others. It didn't help that Grace and Katherine lived in the same boarding house in town, and Grace had likely seen the scars that covered Katherine's side.

Her cheeks flushed bright red with embarrassment, but she still flashed a grin at her friend. Hoping, please, don't mention it.

Grace gave her another tight nod and moved on.

So it went with the few others who were still inside the almshouse. The ones who lingered were always the ones who offered their help. And Katherine appreciated it. She really did. But also she wanted them to see her as a woman who could take care of herself.

She'd lived with this injury for fifteen years just fine. They didn't have to look at her with that pity anymore. She knew what her life was. She'd made it better through practice and...

She had to get going.

The moors were no place to walk after dark. Will-o'-the-wisps were very convincing when they wanted to be, and all manner of swamp creatures unearthed themselves from the muck. Awkwardly getting to her feet, she reached for the railing.

The worn wooden railing fit into the palm of her hand like an old friend. When she was little, she'd pretended it was a hand she held to get from place to place, and those memories still lingered as warmth bloomed in her chest. The walk home would be long, but maybe it would get rid of the stiffness that plagued her.

She started off, ignoring the creaking wood beneath her and the echoing moans that always filled the air around the building. It was why they'd built the almshouse so far from the town. No one enjoyed hearing the sick and the dying.

These walkways extended all throughout their kingdom. Wood that constantly had to be replaced because the ever prevalent rot would sink in. But this was a well-maintained path, considering the injuries that happened in this kingdom, so she knew the boards were steady under her feet.

Katherine let her gaze wander over the moors themselves. So pretty. So deceiving. As night settled in, everything came to life around her. The willow trees, with their long hanging tendrils, made a hushed sound as the wind blew through them. The bog water smelled like peat and greenery, decorated with lily pads, bright flowers, and emerald patches of algae that suddenly glowed in the darkness. Fireflies burst to life, swirling around her and blinking in every direction. Will-o'-the-wisps hid among them, but one would never know.

If her eyes cast downward, she might see the souls of the fallen. Those who had died in the mud always stayed where they were. Their ghostly features glowed a sickly green in the nighttime as they waited for someone to fall into the depths.

There were, of course, creatures to fear other than the kelpie and the vodyanoy. Rusalki with their beautiful calls, loup garou who haunted the land, näkki who only hunted children brave enough to stray from their mother's sides. They were all there.

But Katherine had never been afraid in the moors. Not once. She'd always seen the beauty in the wild.

Her shuffling steps were uneven, the clunking sounds followed by silent footsteps until she saw the town reveal itself in the mist. She hadn't realized how swallowed she'd been by the swamp until she could see civilization again. Home, and it was pretty, although some didn't agree with her.

They had to wash the walls constantly to get rid of mold and algae, but it had given the entire town a soft green hue. Vines grew from the rooftops, burying the buildings into the swamp. None were over two stories, and even that was rare. Small walkways reached out to each house, all the individual homes spread out across the water and blinking fireflies. Quaint. Quiet. It was a beautiful little town full of people that were kind in their own way.

The boarding house was the largest building in her town and had good reason to be. A monolith of its own, and one of the few two-story buildings, she lived on one side with all the other women and the men lived on the opposite end. Rather archaic, considering they were all in the boarding house for the same reason. If they couldn't afford a home on their own, how could they afford marriage?

Sighing, she walked up to the front door and headed in. Her room was on the first floor, which meant she was frequently woken by people passing by. Tonight? She was so tired that she doubted she would wake for anything. Even a fire wouldn't get her to leave the dreaming realm.

The interior wasn't much. Just a dusty entryway that they were supposed to clean, but rarely did, considering all the mud others tracked in. Dim lights hung above her head, blinking and clicking, considering their electricity was spotty. The rug used to be red, she thought, but now it was just a frayed rag that laid on the floor to collect more mud. Hadn't there been a desk here at one point as well? Someone usually was here to greet people in case they needed lodging...

There hadn't been a free room in ages, she remembered. No one ever left the boarding house.

Pausing in the doorway, she gently shut it behind her as she tried to massage out the spasm in her glute. Just two minutes. Two minutes to pause and she'd start down the long hallway that led to her lumpy bed. It was better than what it could be, she reminded herself. She was so close to rest, even if it was an uncomfortable rest.

Until Grace came careening down the other hall. Her blonde hair was streaked with blood, red and fresh. Eyes wild and fear making her shake, Grace pointed behind her.

"I'm sorry," she wheezed. "There's another one, Katherine. She couldn't make it to the almshouse. Said she couldn't pay, but it's... it's so bad."

Sleep would have to wait, she supposed. Or at the very least, she could maybe sleep on her feet for a few moments while she stitched.

Gritting her teeth through the pain in her hip that now seared down to her knee, she plodded down the hall toward the kitchens. They all shared the room, and this wasn't the first time they'd all banded together to patch up one of their own. But it was the first time she'd seen this much blood.

It was everywhere. Slicking the floor, leading in a trail up to the massive table where most of them ate. Katherine batted a hanging bundle of drying basil out of her way as she stomped toward the crowd of people clustered where the benches usually were. At this point, she was dragging her leg rather than walking on it. She put all her weight on her cane as she shoved people out of her way.

"Get me light," she scolded. "Just the flames from the fire won't help. Move."

A few people parted and revealed the young woman on the table and everything froze as Katherine took it all in. Grace was already setting up her tools on the opposite side of the table. Twin, raking wounds slashed across the woman's neck so deep she could see muscle. Blood sluggishly rolled down her neck, dripping onto the table and creating a small river. Wet plops hit the stone floor, dripping like the ticking of a clock. Counting down until the moment where Katherine had wasted too much time.

She recognized her.

The woman's dark brunette hair had always looked so sleek and clean, but right now it was filled with brambles and prickers. Wide eyes locked with hers, and then she heard Grace snap her name.

Everything came back in a rush. The sound of the others moving around them, the murmur of "what happened?", and the scent of blood so strong it was like someone had slapped her.

Katherine reached silently for the needle and thread. Placing her hand on the woman's chest, she breathed in and out slowly. Mimicking the movements so the woman would start to follow her.

"Breathe," she said quietly. "This will hurt, but no more than what caused this, yes?"

Her calm tones hushed everyone in the room. A young man in the back, his face far too pale, quietly asked, "Is she going to make it?"

Maybe.

Perhaps.

Katherine wasn't a magic practitioner, and she certainly was no witch. Healing took time and energy and effort. That's how it worked. There was no magical way to snap her fingers and say yes, this woman would live. She'd lost a lot of blood and that would be tiring to remake.

But she'd also seen so many young women in the same state as this, and they survived. So she could say, while staring into the woman's eyes, "Yes."

And so she worked. Hunched over the table with Grace at her side, both of them silently stitching and holding the skin together. Katherine hadn't started doing this job. She'd been cleaning the almshouse at night when she first got in there, but then their boss had seen how neat her stitches were and he'd thrown her into it.

Now, she almost found the work soothing. She knew how skin wanted to be tucked in, folded, held together by thread and pierced by needle. Nothing startled her anymore. Almost as though her mind now recognized injuries and went numb the moment she got her hands on the patient.

Sighing, she finally tied the last knot in the skin and let Grace bandage the young woman up.

Rose. That was her name.

They'd met at one of the dinners. She was particularly good at making lemon tarts, even though the fruit was so rare to find here in Gluttony's kingdom. Perhaps she hadn't been born here. She'd been carted off like cattle, discarded in a kingdom of nightmares.

Someone had brought her a seat. Katherine hardly even noticed it while she worked, but she sank down onto it as she watched Grace's fingers put salve over what must be a searing wound. But Rose's eyes were on Katherine.

"What happened?" Katherine asked, her voice little more than a whisper.

"They said he'd give me money," Rose croaked. Her voice didn't sound like its normally beautiful lilt. It was hoarse and rough, so filled with pain it was almost difficult to understand what she said. "My ma is sick."

"Who?"

The young woman's eyes went wild and wide again. "Him."

Everyone in the room sucked in a breath, because they all knew who him was. Gluttony. Their king. The man who feasted upon their women and sent them home bleeding like he didn't care if they died on the walkway home or if the scent drew creatures to the one he'd wounded.

The pale young man lurched forward, gripping Rose's hand in his. "I'll kill him."

"No," Rose rasped.

Even Katherine felt the need to step in after that declaration, and she wasn't the type to care what someone said at the bed of an injured loved one. "Attacking Gluttony will only end in your own death. You know this."

He glared at her. "He's going to keep doing this to our women. He's going to keep hurting people if someone doesn't stop him."

"And you think that person should be you?" Katherine had to look away from him before he saw the pity in her eyes. "No one can stop him. He's a demon, remember? He rules us all."

And her words rang true throughout the room. Others drifted out of the kitchen, heading who knows where. Perhaps just finding a quiet space where they could process what had happened to one of their own.

As Grace finished up, she helped Rose upright and then handed her off to the young man who handled her like she was precious. He cast a glare in Katherine's direction, of course. Why should he thank her for saving Rose's life when he could be mad at her for pointing out the obvious?

Everyone left until it was just Grace and Katherine, like always. Then Grace looked at her and shook her head. "You have to work on your bedside manner. Really, Katherine?"

"What?"

"The boy just wants to help."

"By throwing his life away the moment he steps foot near Gluttony and tells him... what? To stop feasting upon women? He's been doing that for the better part of a year, other than those few months when he disappeared." Katherine shook her head and tried to stand, but her hip locked up. "Someone has to be the voice of reason. That boy will get himself killed."

"So? If he wants to be the hero, let him. Even if he wants to just be a fictional hero to make her feel better, let him." Grace shook her head. "That big mouth of yours is going to get you in trouble someday, Katherine."

Then she left. Not offering to help this time, Katherine noted.

Sitting by the firelight, pain lancing up and down her spine, all the way to her toes, Katherine wondered if her big mouth had already gotten her into trouble. It sure felt like this loneliness was the definition of it.

Wincing, she used the table as leverage and forced herself to limp back to her room. Alone. Covered in blood.

Life never seemed to change here.

Chapter 2

Gluttony wiped his mouth with the back of his hand, wincing at the acidic bite of gypsum that he'd somehow smeared on his lips. He'd thought he had washed his hands enough, but his senses had always been a little too strong to use the substance.

The alchemical book in his hands suggested that gunpowder happened to have a reaction to copper, but so far, he'd seen no such reaction. He could leave them both in the beaker until the morning... What if they exploded, though? He'd already had enough mishaps in his laboratory to last a lifetime.

And his lifetimes were rather long. Infinite, really.

Sighing, he leaned back in his chair and stared down at the book. This was supposed to be written by one of the best alchemists of their time. The man had quite literally created an elixir of life, or so the legends told.

He had a hard time believing it if the man couldn't even turn copper blue.

Hissing out a frustrated breath, he tore the page out of the rather priceless book and threw it into the fire. Let the flames consume this fool's work because clearly it wasn't as impressive as the man thought it was.

Gluttony stared around his workroom and wondered when it had degraded into such chaos. Used beakers were littered everywhere and on every surface. The room was massive, large enough to be an entertaining area if he'd ever had anyone come to his kingdom. Instead, he had filled it with tables and vials and giant, looping tubes that twisted around each other and into other beakers. Burners covered every corner, along with dust and all manner of objects that were supposed to help him in his quest.

He had to figure out what the substance was that had somehow knocked his brother unconscious. He had to know what weapon the mortals had created that was so dangerous to him and his brothers.

This was his job. His reason for existence.

His apology for disappointing so many of them.

Already he could hear Wrath's voice in his head. "You've fucked up one too many times, Gluttony. You're eating your own subjects now? What kind of monster have you become?"

And there it was again. The rage. The anger that burned in his chest because he knew they were judging him for it. He almost wanted them to judge him for his desires, because he knew they were wrong. Wrath was correct in saying that he was a monster or that he'd become one. He certainly had. Gluttony was everything that people in this kingdom feared. He was the monster waiting at the foot of their bed, slavering over the scent of their blood.

Maybe he liked it a bit. The judgment. The disgust. The hatred for everything that he wanted, and so he continued to be a monster because it tasted so fucking good on his tongue.

Already it burned again. The need to devour, consume, and to feel their very life force trickling down his throat. His brothers didn't understand this need, but how could they? They couldn't put it in perspective that they all had their faults.

Lust fucked himself into oblivion. Greed stole every priceless object that he could. Envy took from others just because he had to, and Sloth lingered in his castle without ever leaving it.

They were all flawed monsters. He had just accepted it about himself long before his brothers.

Running a hand down his face again, he felt the prickles of his beard and the general unkempt nature of his form. When was the last time he'd bathed? He smelled like a lab. Like chemicals and sulfur had sunk so deep into his skin that he'd never be able to get them out.

This wasn't him. Gluttony had always at least kept himself clean, and he'd been presentable. But right now, he'd been so engrossed in punishing himself for all that he was that he'd forgotten to even eat.

Or had he?

He felt the crust of dried blood on his mouth and licked at it. Too savory. He winced at the faint, smokey flavor that now covered his tongue again. Gluttony had forgotten about the woman who had come to his keep, begging for coins, and offering her neck like it was a prize to be bought.

He'd been weak. Tired. Hating himself so much that it only felt right to throw a bag of coins at her and sink his teeth into that neck offered so freely. But the blood had tasted wrong, tainted with a thick layer of alcohol that streamed through her body and years of misuse. Too much like pork and red meat and not enough of a healthy diet.

She'd tasted like poison. He'd wrenched himself away from her, gagging, and trying so hard not to vomit on what he knew was an open wound. And without another word, she'd fled.

He couldn't remember much else, only his self loathing that always threatened to swallow him up.

Sighing, he stood from his desk and staggered toward his bedroom. He needed to change. Scrub himself from top to bottom to get the flavor of her out of his mouth.

He gagged again, the memories suddenly blooming up from his stomach until every exhalation tasted like her. He barely made it to his bathing room before he fell to his knees in front of the toilet and threw up what only felt like a mouthful of blood. But it was still the same taste, and he spent hours gagging, trying to get the taste of her out of his mouth.

Exhaustion settled in a half hour later, but he still needed to get clean. Now he was coated in her blood and vomit and a mixture of what he guessed was probably red wine, but couldn't be certain at this point. So he dragged himself to the tub and filled it.

He sank deep, ducking his head underneath the water and watching the ripples warp the candlelight. Nothing would happen if he just stayed under here. He couldn't die, and he'd tried every creative way to make that happen. So he could just stay here for hundreds of years, until someone eventually found him and tried to reanimate his body.

Maybe they'd succeed. And all he would have done is left his entire kingdom to deal with six other demons who would absolutely go to war over a kingdom none of them wanted.

He came back out of the water, shaking his head like a dog. Water droplets sprayed from his long, dark hair, soaking into the peeling wallpaper that covered the bathroom. He'd forgotten about it, honestly. So much of this castle had been decorated by other people, and it had all just turned to dust in his mind. He rarely even noticed the finer details of his home. But this wallpaper was shredding. It used to be a scene of the sunny moors, only rarely seen a few times a year. And now there were pieces torn and faded.

Perhaps he should fix the castle up. He could hire some of the townsfolk from the area nearby, and could even hire people from the outer reaches to come to his castle. It would get more money for them. Money that apparently they were now willing to get through offering their blood.

Gagging again, he pulled himself out of the tub and got dressed.

When was the last time he'd slept? He couldn't remember. Sleep wasn't really all that necessary these days. All he did was have nightmares, anyway. It seemed like a waste.

By the time he'd staggered back through his dark bedroom, he realized there was a shadow at the base of his door. An open door, so he should have been able to see what cast that shadow. But it was... nothing. A dark mass stood in front of him, about knee high, and it waited. As though it wanted him to see it.

And then, strangely enough, it rolled into the hall.

Was he hallucinating? Had that woman taken drugs before she'd gotten to his house and was that why he was feeling like this? Surely not. Surely she wasn't so foolish as to poison him by poisoning herself? It wouldn't be the first time someone had tried to do so.

But no, that made little sense.

Trailing along behind the mass, he saw it roll through his candlelit hall and down the massive spiral stairwell. Frowning, he continued to follow it all the way to his door. Was it a spirit?

He couldn't remember what a black spirit was. They all had some sort of color or shade to them. He knew there weren't any white ones, so why was there a black one?

Maybe he shouldn't be following it, but he'd long ago lost any sense of self preservation. So he followed the mass out of his castle, down through the ancient gardens that used to be filled with countless plants that grew with no light at all. Now, they were all dead. He hadn't taken care of them in years, or centuries was it? His castle looked rather like a mausoleum surrounded by a graveyard these days. The mass continued down the boardwalk, though, so he kept going.

It was long into the night. Nothing would bother him, anyway, although many of the creatures grumbled as he strode past them. A rather lovely blonde rusalka even touched her hand to his boot. He didn't pause to see what she wanted, nor did he really care to know. His kingdom was full of more magical creatures than any other. They flocked here, knowing that he saw them as his people, as equal to the humans. And yet, he still didn't know how to help them.

Not really.

Gluttony was a rather lousy king. Always had been. But his kingdom wasn't exactly set up for success.

Finally, the mass reached the village, and he thought it must be some kind of spirit. Few humans could see them, most didn't even try, and there were plenty of emotions for spirits to exist off of in his kingdom. But what was this emotion, and why had it come to his castle at all?

Disgruntled, he trailed it through the empty streets until it floated up to the boarding house. Of course. The cesspit for all emotions. Gluttony tried to stay far away from it. But when the little spirit slipped through an open window, he couldn't stop himself from striding up to the window and peering into the room.

Perhaps he feared the spirit would try to possess someone, not that it was all that easy to do. But then a scent drifted through the opening and he found his entire body locking in place.

Blood in the air, savory, thick, and smoky. It made bile rise in his throat again, but then there was another scent underneath it. He inhaled deeply, ignoring the sudden rush of vomit in his throat.

Because there was something more. Something underneath it all that captivated him.

Honey.

That's what it was. Sweet honey mixed with ginger and spice, like the tea he'd drink on a cold winter's day. Soothing, like a balm, it poured down the aching muscles of his throat and filled his lungs with a sense of peace that he hadn't felt in years.

What was this scent? How did it smell like a warm crackling fire and a cozy blanket tossed over his shoulders?

He stepped closer, knowing this wasn't his place or his right. That anyone could walk by and see him looming as he peered through an open window. They would scream if they saw him. They would try to throw him out of the town, and he would have to fight back. Blood would spill and flow into the moors until creatures came and attacked with him.

But he would take this risk if only to fill his lungs with that scent until he could taste it on his tongue.

The spirit was nowhere to be found. But the room was a bedroom. Filled with so many trinkets, he could hardly tell where to cast his eyes first. Countless books were strewn about the room, some open, some with folded edges, others that were laying on the pages themselves as if to keep track of where the owner had left off. Vases full of dead flowers and clothing tossed everywhere covered every surface he could see.

But his eyes found a small mound on the bed, rising and falling with her breath in sleep. And he had to look twice, because at first glance it appeared as though blood had spilled across her pillow.

It was her hair, he realized. Long, curly red hair that was the center of that scent he could smell. He was certain of it. Honey and sweet things, and it made his mouth water while that hunger rose from the bottom of his being. He wanted to slip into her room. He wanted to crawl through the shadows and bury his face in those curls.

There was no need to bite her. Not yet. He would soon have her blood. Whenever he wanted, really, he was the demon king. He could order her to give him whatever he desired and yet... Right now, all he wanted to do was curl up on that bed with her and draw whatever comfort he could from her scent.

Leaning against her windowsill, he watched as she rolled over in her sleep. She was strange, he would admit. Her features were slightly broad. Her eyes were spaced too far apart. A faint discoloration marred the right side of her face as well, hardly noticeable, but he'd spent centuries looking at her kind. Freckles dusted her nose. Where she'd gotten them, he had no idea. There was no sun here to give her the little marks that he found he might actually like.

Freckles always reminded him of Lust, and he didn't particularly like that brother of his. But he could forgive the marks if she continued to smell like that.

Gluttony knew this was foolish. The longer he stayed, the more likely he was to form an attachment to the little creature. He'd already

20

promised himself that he would no longer feed from people who did not first offer themselves. Lingering in the shadows, violating her privacy, wouldn't lead to her giving herself over to him.

And yet, he couldn't pull himself away. He wanted to look at her. Just look. He wanted to watch as the dreams moved behind her eyelids and her breathing kicked up a notch. She shifted underneath the covers, and they drew down her lovely neck. Swan-like, he thought. So pale and already throbbing with her pulse.

Perhaps she was having a nightmare, because he was living in one. His claws slowly extended, pushing out through the tips of his fingers like giant needles and he needed to get control over himself or he would bust into her room like an animal enraged.

He wanted...

No.

Needed to taste her.

And when he felt saliva pooling in his mouth, he forced himself to turn away. He had to go. The monster was coming out, and he refused to let it prey upon her.

But something deep in his core knew he'd be back.

Chapter 3

Katherine's hip was on fire. The pain and stiffness had become a familiar companion in the long days she'd put in at the clinic. But a bad case of lung rot had spread throughout her town, and everyone else had called out sick.

Katherine had already had lung rot when she was a child. Most of these townsfolk hadn't traveled through the kingdom in the earlier years of their life, and unfortunately, that meant they were very unlikely to have been exposed to it.

So there was no one else to work in the clinic. Her boss had nearly coughed up a lung, telling her that she would get paid double if she came in. He hadn't needed to offer the money. Katherine only had her work, after all. If they closed the almshouse, she'd have ended up in people's homes trying to treat them, anyway.

Otherwise, she'd be sitting in her room. Alone, while the pain slowly drove her mad. At least when she was standing and moving, her mind had something to do other than focus on the pain.

But now it was nighttime, and that made everything so much worse. Like now, lying in her bed and staring up at the ceiling. The pain spiked at night, so she tried to distract herself with the numerous cases that came in today. Cases outside of lung rot, even.

A little girl had walked in covered in red bumps. Her mother was coughing into her sleeve, trying to explain that the bumps had appeared overnight. They didn't know how to treat them. They weren't itchy, but they were spreading and getting worse.

Then there had been the young man who had food poisoning for the last three days. He'd thought he had lung rot as well, but no one else in his house was vomiting quite so profusely. Then he'd vomited in her trash can and promised to drink more water.

She didn't know how to help them. Katherine had been trained for stitches and surgeries, not... this. General ailments weren't her speciality, nor had she ever been trained. After all, she wasn't a healer. She was a stitcher, good at closing wounds and mending clothing.

Even now, anger bloomed in her chest. How dare her boss throw her to the kelpies like that? What did he think would happen?

He didn't want to invest the time or energy into making her a real healer, but he was perfectly fine treating her like one. She didn't even need the money. Katherine was well aware that the trained healers were paid more. And she didn't mind it. What would she do with money?

Move into her own house?

There weren't any buildings to buy. The swamps were already threatening their small town that was sinking into the muck. Monstrous creatures waited just below the walkways and they were certain to eventually drag someone into the deep. She couldn't ask someone to build a home for her in those conditions.

Not to mention she'd be alone. At least here she could yell and someone would tell her to quiet down.

At least here she could pretend she was alive.

Rolling onto her side, she let the cool breeze play over her face. Though outside was getting colder, the boarding house was always ridiculously warm this time of year. She didn't know if the owner started up the fires in the basement early, but if he did, the man needed to reconsider the resources he was wasting.

Not that they didn't have a surplus of peat to use whenever they needed it. They were drowning in the stuff.

Her scratchy wool blanket was too warm. Sweat slicked down her back, but she'd never been able to sleep without a blanket covering her toes and back. Annoyed, she sat straight up and shoved her rioting curls away from her face.

This was ridiculous. She was exhausted. Her heart was already racing to keep up with her movements, her entire body ached from standing all day, and all she wanted was a little sleep. But her mind wouldn't let her, and the zinging ache at her hip only made everything seem worse.

Katherine would go insane if she tried to sleep like this. But if she didn't sleep, she'd go insane as well.

"Damn it," she muttered, rolling out of bed and taking a few hesitant steps forward. Her leg dragged behind her, useless now that the nerves were exploding with sensation.

She staggered to the window and threw it all the way open. Bracing herself on the windowsill, she stuck her torso out. Neighbors be damned. If they got an eye full of her in her dingy gray nightgown, then so be it. They could look for all she cared, but she was too damn hot.

"Thank the gods," she whimpered as the air chilled the sweat on her skin. At the very least, she could cool herself down. Her hip might hurt. Her mind might worry that she'd accidentally murdered someone today, but at least she was no longer sweltering.

She ran her fingers along the smooth wood, the sensation of it as familiar to her as every step of this town. How many times had she stood here in the winter just like this? Too many to count. Years upon years after her father had died and her mother had disappeared into the moors. Though she'd been alone as a child, she'd had enough money to buy her first year here after selling all her parents' things.

And then she'd worked. Oh, she had worked herself to the bone day after day, because there was nothing else in this kingdom but that.

A sharp spike of pain stabbed her in the pointer finger. Frowning, she looked down at the windowsill to see that small splinters had been carved into the wood. Almost as though something sharp had cut through it.

It took her a second to see in the dim moonlight, but she realized it wasn't just one mark on her windowsill. There were ten of them. Ten marks gouged into her windowsill that looked rather like where someone would put their hands.

"What—" She tried to think of any words, but nothing would come to her.

She didn't know of any creature that could make marks like this. And if it had been some monstrous being, they'd have woken her trying to get through the window. Besides, none of the creatures had ever gotten up onto the wooden walkways. The silent truce between human and swamp monster had always been followed for countless years.

So if they weren't trying to attack her, then what had made these marks?

A sound echoed across the moors. Not something she usually would have noticed. It was like someone had kicked a stone into the water. The wet plop could have been anything from a bubble popping as gas leaked between the layers of peat, or it could have been a frog leaping into the shallows.

But her heart stilled in her chest. Katherine felt icy tendrils of fear trailing between her shoulder blades like water dripping down her spine and she knew—she knew—something was watching her.

She could feel their eyes. She could sense their breath that was coming faster now as it realized how defenseless she was. It would be so easy for something to race at her open window and yank her out of it.

No one would even realize that she'd been taken until they needed her at the almshouse. Then someone would ask, "Where in the world did Katherine get off to?"

And it would be too late. They'd never find a trace of her and the entire town would think she'd wandered off with the wisps. Just like that mad mother of hers who had muttered about spirits and ghostly creatures living in the moors.

Breathing hard, she tried to control the panic that told her to run. It whispered through her mind, dragging claws inside her skull as it told her that something terrible would happen if she stayed here. She needed to bolt. To hide. To put herself somewhere that no one would ever find her because a predator watched her from the shadows.

But this wasn't her. Katherine didn't believe in superstitions and she knew how the real world worked. No creature was going to yank her out of her house. That had never happened before.

People didn't just disappear in the middle of the night. Even one person going missing would put the entire town up in arms and she would have heard about any incidents. The only reason anyone disappeared was because they had sought out Gluttony's castle and they had offered themselves up in dire circumstances.

Sometimes those people didn't make it home. But there was a reasonable explanation for why they didn't make it. She was a woman of science and logic. If she felt like something was staring at her, then she was strong enough to look back.

Still, her fingers curled around the chipped wood and she had to push herself to be brave. Her heart raced, her breathing quickened, but she lifted her eyes to the darkness and peered into it.

At first, she saw nothing. Just the shadows and the mist and the strange shapes the moon cast in between buildings and railings. It was her town, the same as it always was and never all that surprising.

Until she saw him.

The shape of a man waited in that darkness, almost impossible for her to see. He was standing perfectly in the shadow of a willow tree right in the center of town. It wasn't anyone she recognized, because she knew the shape of every person.

Jimmy Tompkins had one shoulder higher than the other. Andrew Riley was much more round than this man. Even Bruce Calloway had a distinctly coifed haircut that billowed around his head like a dandelion puff. This man was none of them.

His silhouette was tall and lean, a powerful figure that seemed almost otherworldly. Not a creature like any she'd seen before, so at least she was certain nothing had crawled up out of the muck to attack her home. But there was an air of danger around this man. Almost as though it vibrated around his form.

And she felt that vibration deep in her core. A sudden heat flushed throughout her entire body, coiling through her being in an entirely unfamiliar way. Suddenly, she wanted… something. She needed it. But what she needed, Katherine had no idea, and still she wanted to beckon him closer. She wanted to know what he looked like beyond the outline of his body.

They were dastardly, foolish thoughts of a woman who had read too many romantic stories. No one was waiting outside her window because she'd beguiled them with her beauty.

Katherine had lost that future long ago. She had never been the blushing young woman who had countless men at her doorstep, hoping that she'd let them inside to visit. The fire had taken everything from her. Her grace, her looks, even the feeling in much of the right side of her body. It was ridiculous to think this man was here for any reason other than the nefarious ones.

And still, she leaned a little further out of the window. Just to catch a glimpse of this tall, dark, stranger who stood outside her window without moving even a single step.

She opened her mouth, about to call out to ask who he was, or if he needed lodging for the night. Though the thought fluttered through her mind that she was a foolish girl indeed if she thought to invite a stranger into her bed.

Then it happened.

For just a split second, she thought she saw gleaming red eyes in that shadow. But surely not. They were gone just as soon as she saw them.

Katherine took a deep breath and her hands flexed on the wood. The slivers dug into her fingers again and this time the pain startled her so much that she ripped her hands away. One of the slivers cut through the pad of her thumb all the way to the first joint. Hissing out a breath, she found her gaze on those red eyes that glowed from the darkness. Not staring back at her eyes, but watching her thumb with all too much interest.

The madness that had possessed her disappeared. Shocked at herself, angry that she'd ever make such a foolish decision, Katherine lunged away. She slammed her window shut so hard it shook the wall as she locked it. She smeared blood all over the glass, but she didn't care.

Whatever was out there, even if it was just a conjuring of her exhausted mind, she wanted nothing to do with it.

She was logical. She was intelligent. She knew when there was danger right in front of her and that man, whoever it was, risked her very life.

Stepping back from the glass, Katherine stared at the meager shield between herself and whatever monster waited for her there. It wasn't enough. If it wanted to come into her room, it would. It would be so easy for it to break through the glass and snag her long before anyone else had heard her screaming.

Breathing hard, she found she couldn't move. Katherine had backed up into the very corner of the room with her gaze locked on the window. She held her bleeding thumb to her chest, pressing frantically on the wound as though the creature outside could smell her.

And when a shadow passed in front of the window, she thought she might faint in fear. It had come for her. Whatever it was, it wanted her blood.

It wanted her.

She had no idea how long she stayed frozen in that corner.

Katherine wasn't even sure she blinked before she flinched at the sound of knocking on her door.

"Katherine?" Grace asked through the wood. "Aren't you supposed to be at the clinic?"

"I—" She could hardly speak. Her voice sounded like she'd been screaming all night, but she hadn't. Had she?

Her door creaked open and Grace stepped inside. Katherine watched as Grace looked around, only to find her huddled on the other side of the door, still clutching her hand to her chest.

Grace's eyes widened before she burst into action. "Katherine! What happened?"

She didn't know what to say, even as the other woman crouched beside her and placed a hand on her forehead. "You're burning up. Have you been here all night?"

Katherine tried her best to unlock her legs, but they just... wouldn't. Every bone in her body felt like it had stuck in place. How long had she been crouched here?

With that thought, the rush of pain came as well. Wincing, she tried her best to straighten her body, but the creaking and clicking sounds gave her away. Grace ducked underneath her arm, gently easing her upright and taking all of Katherine's weight when she couldn't stand on her own.

"You know better," Grace scolded as she put Katherine to bed. "What in the world has gotten into you? Too many hours at that almshouse, I reckon. I told Alexander to not put so many hours on you while the rest of us were sick. I told him that hip of yours couldn't take it, but why listen to the trained healer? I'm not the one who runs the almshouse, he is."

She finally found her tongue. "Grace, I'm fine. It was a nightmare, that's all."

"You're not fine, and you're staying here today." Grace pointed at her with a rather severe look. "If you move, that hip of yours will stop you from doing it. So I know I don't have to tell you to stay put. However, the only reason you're allowed to get up today is to get more ice. Do I make myself clear?"

Though she hated to admit Grace was right, Katherine wasn't certain it would take her weight at all.

So sullenly, she nodded. Grace flitted around her for a while, scolding her for a few more minutes until Katherine was as comfortable as she was going to get and then Grace left for work.

Leaving Katherine alone, staring at the window and wondering how much of last night her mind had conjured up.

And how much of it had been real.

Chapter 4

This need was an addiction. Gluttony knew the word for it, at least the word his brothers used. He had a better one.

Obsession.

Gluttony didn't have to drink blood. He could exist without it and had for many years of his life. And it wasn't just anyone's blood that called to him. Sure, he would take whatever was offered, but that didn't mean he enjoyed it. But sometimes there was a certain blood that was just so divine that it swallowed up all rational thought. He could smell it, suck it into his nose and in his throat until he tasted a bit of that elixir.

Addiction. Obsession. The same meaning but one word made him feel slightly better about himself.

Leaning back at his desk, a rarely used piece of furniture in his home, he pinched the bridge of his nose and tried to convince himself that he was all right. Gluttony didn't need blood. He didn't need to go back to that poor woman's window, where he could scent her on the breeze.

He wasn't a stalker. This was just any other night where he had to look into the substance that could be used to attack both him and his brothers. He needed to figure out the reasoning for it, or maybe there was another alchemical recounting that could tell him where to go from here.

And yet, no matter how far he tried to guide his mind, he always landed back in the same place.

Her.

"Get a hold of yourself," he growled. The sound of his own voice did nothing, however, and he finally snapped.

Slamming his palm down on his desk, he conjured up the small disk that could connect him to any of his brothers. A simple call would help. Maybe. He'd always called the same brother, who always answered no matter how many times he called in the middle of the night.

The magic zinged, fraying through the realms until it delved underneath the stone of the second kingdom. Envy's home was a pile of rock, after all. His people had tunneled deep into the earth, creating a mountainous home worthy of the dwarven legends of old. Envy had burrowed so deep that it was difficult for even magic to get through it.

And then there he was. His brother. Shimmering to life in a blue light, glowing on the other side of the desk and seated just as Gluttony had expected him to be.

Envy was strange compared to all the rest of them. More human, if that was even possible. Perhaps because he had one of the baser emotions, like Lust, who also appeared almost human at first glance.

Envy had dark inky hair like Gluttony, but he was infinitely more broad. Square faced, strong featured, his eyes cut through everything and anything that stood before him. Top that with his shoulders that were so wide he barely fit in a chair, and the thousands of tattoos that covered every area of his body other than his face, neck, and hands? The man was terrifying and otherworldly. It fit his kingdom, though, and his people knew better than to test their terrifying king.

Tonight, however, Envy didn't look as intimidating as usual. He had a glass of something in his hand, probably mead, knowing his brother, and his eyes were a little foggy.

"Late night for you, Gluttony," Envy said, his words slightly slurred. "I thought you were supposed to be fixing our problem."

"It's no small problem to fix."

"And yet, you were the one who grabbed the task." A bright flash of emerald made his brother's eyes glow even through the projection. And there it was. Envy.

Of course, his brother had likely thought he would get the esteemed role of figuring out what this new weapon was. Envy, after all, was more in touch with magic than the rest of them. Even Pride, although his eldest brother, wouldn't ever admit it.

His brother's downfall was that Envy wanted what he didn't have. He didn't care what it was, like Greed, who collected rare objects and artifacts. Envy wanted what others had, period. If it was just a speck of dirt on their shoe, he would take it.

Both Greed and Envy hated each other. Perhaps because they saw their own flaws in each other.

"That's not why I'm calling," Gluttony grumbled. He wished he had a glass of good wine, but then he remembered that red wine looked like blood.

His brother's drink did not. Amber and glistening, made of honey, no doubt. He could almost smell it. The honey that would pour down his throat, burning along the way down like fingernails scratching at him. Begging him to stop... No, that wasn't what he wanted. Begging him to continue—

"Ah," Envy said, sitting forward in his chair and eyeing Gluttony like the project he was. "A bad night, then."

"The worst in a long time." Gluttony raked his hands through his hair, shocked when he couldn't even get his fingers through the tangled snarls.

His hair was down to his ribs in a waterfall of darkness. He had to brush it often, or it would snarl like this. When was the last time he'd brushed it? When was the last time he'd even thought about what he looked like while he stood outside her window, like the animal he had become?

"Gluttony," Envy said, his voice breaking through the thoughts. "Tell me."

The words rushed out of him. "There is a woman in the village. I've never seen her before, but I don't go there anymore, now do I? I know how I make them all nervous. It's not fair for me to wander amongst them when I know what I am. A monster. The beast who torments and feeds off his people. I understand their hesitation, but I can't stop. No matter how hard I try. I can't... I can't..."

"Take a deep breath. You're spiraling, brother." Envy leaned forward again, tapping his hand on his own desk, but the sound still came through. Steady thuds. One, two, three, in time with the breath that Gluttony was supposed to be taking.

But every time he breathed in, it was like her scent was stuck in his nose. He could smell her. Taste her on the back of his tongue. Just the slightest hint of flavor that wasn't the true bloom of how she'd really taste and he knew it would be so much better if he could just sink his teeth into the side of that lovely, swan-like neck and draw everything of her deeply into his mouth. Would she even let him?

"What did you do?" Envy's voice broke through again.

"Nothing." Gluttony blew out a long breath, drawing himself back to his lonely office with his brother, who wasn't even here. "I haven't done anything with her, to her, or around her. She's just... there. In her room. And I stand as far back as I can without waking her."

He let the words trail off, though, because they weren't entirely true. She had woken. Just a few nights ago, she'd seen him standing there, and she'd reacted like a hellhound had come to hunt her soul.

Envy's eyes narrowed, and he knew his brother had seen the thought pass in front of his eyes. "So you did something, then."

"She saw me a few nights ago, and I've been here ever since." He lifted his arms and let them fall limp back onto the chair. "I can't seem to move. If I stand, my feet take me to the door and if I sit here, at least I'm not bothering her."

"It's been a long time since you've been this obsessed."

"I know," he snarled. "That's why I called you."

Perhaps it was something in his tone that finally got through to his brother. Envy seemed to shake off the effects of his alcohol and nodded. "So this one is different, then. Tell me why."

"I don't know. I haven't said a word to her before, nor do I know what she does in the town. She always smells like blood, though." Perhaps she worked at the almshouse. It wasn't animal blood that followed her around like the ghost of another person. It was human blood. "The other blood isn't the temptation. If anything, it's a good mask, because I hate the smell of them on her skin. Hers though...

It's underneath all of it. It's honey and wine, a mixture of scents that I cannot seem to banish from my thoughts."

"When was the last time you fed?"

"Not long ago." Gluttony could feel his cheeks pale at the memory. Even now, his stomach rolled at the flavor that remained when he burped. "It was less than satisfactory. I spent hours vomiting afterward."

"And she had freely given herself to you?" Where was his brother going with this?

"Of course she did," he snapped. "I haven't taken anyone unwillingly since the first, and even then, you know she had... she'd..."

His dear Larissa. The only young woman who had ever looked at him and seen something other than a monster. She'd been so kind and sweet to him for the two months that she wandered up to his castle. She was the first he'd ever fed from, completely unwilling at the time, and she'd been terrified of him afterwards. But he'd gotten a taste for the forbidden and suddenly she hadn't... minded.

Oh, she hadn't sought him out to feed from her. Of course. No woman in her right mind enjoyed the sensation of someone sucking out their life blood, but she had endured it. For him.

Until she'd shown up on his doorstep that fateful night and then everything had gone to shit.

Dragging a hand down his mouth, Gluttony shook his head. "No reason to bring that up now. You know the story."

Some of his brothers believed him, others didn't. Wrath didn't care what the actual story was. All he cared about was that a woman was dead and it was Gluttony's fault.

And it had been. In a way.

Envy pursed his lips, tilting his head back to the ceiling as he thought. One of his tattoos writhed underneath his skin. The four snakes usually rested above his heart in a knitted pattern, but sometimes they moved. This time, one slithered up to encircle his neck and hovered above the pulse there. "Forgive me for suggesting this, brother, but do you believe the consent is the problem?"

Icy cold dread settled hard in his belly like he'd swallowed cement. "What do you mean?"

"All the women since La—since the first—have offered themselves to you. Freely given. Blood that they wanted you to have in exchange for something else, yes?"

He nodded.

"Then perhaps the issue is that you want to take it. I understand the feeling, and trust me, I've had my fair share of enjoyment in taking what isn't mine to take." Envy's eyes flashed before he settled. "So. Perhaps that is your problem."

He rolled the thought around in his mind. But it wasn't the right one. He could feel that it didn't fit, like he was trying to thrust an explanation into the puzzle of this problem. "No, I don't believe it's that. My vice has never been about taking, but consuming."

"And yet you are consuming and nothing is satisfying." Envy tossed his hands up in the air. "Unless, perhaps, you are toying with the thought of actually eating this one? I've heard human flesh tastes particularly different from anything else."

The thought was also wrong. No, he didn't want to chew through the muscles and sinew of this woman's body. There were parts of it he wanted to discover. He'd really only seen the general outline of her shape.

Gluttony wanted to leave bite marks between her thighs, upon her breasts, throughout her entire body. He wanted to claim and mark and ruin for her anyone else because he had consumed every part of her body, but that wasn't the same as eating.

He could devour her whole and still leave her breathing.

Gluttony shook his head with a frustrating sigh. "I don't know what it is about this one. Nothing has changed in my life. She is just another villager who wants nothing to do with me, and is well within her right to not want that, so I don't understand the need. I don't understand any of this."

His brother shrugged again. "You will have to figure it out, though, won't you? Wrath made it very clear. You can no longer take what isn't freely offered, and you've been getting enough offerings to keep your strength up. If you snap, you know the threat."

Yes, they all knew the threat that Wrath had barked out in angry words unlike any Gluttony had ever heard out of his brother.

If he stepped out of line again, endangering all of their brothers by provoking his own kingdom into mutiny, then Wrath would return. He had killed spirits before, though never one as strong as Gluttony. They would battle to the death and no one questioned who would win in that situation.

Gluttony didn't think death for them was anything like the humans. For spirits like himself, it was simply extinguishing a candle. There one moment, gone the next.

He swallowed hard. He knew the risk he took in focusing on this woman. If he kept tormenting the little human, then maybe he would incite another riot. Wrath would return, even though Gluttony had yet to do anything wrong.

Fangs tingling, claws stretching as though they were ready to defend him, Gluttony nodded again. "I know, brother. The risk will always be there for me, no matter how many necks I bite."

"Then keep everything to yourself. Find a way to get this woman to offer herself to you and slake your thirst." Envy set his drink down hard, a gleam in his eyes. "Prove to her and yourself that you can get whatever you want. You're the king of your kingdom, Gluttony! Command her to your castle. Woo her if you must, but get rid of this obsession and quickly."

"You're right." He lied. Lied straight through his teeth while looking his brother in the eyes, as if this wasn't a problem at all. "I'll set this all to rights. Thank you for speaking with me this late at night."

"Next time call when you have an answer about that damned weapon the mortals built."

Envy disappeared and Gluttony was left alone with his thoughts and the lies that swirled around him.

He would get control of himself? He'd told his brother he could, but... he wasn't convinced.

Gluttony didn't know if he had that ability. If he did, he wouldn't end up at her window every single night. Looking forlornly into her room while she quaked in her bed.

He just... needed.

Damn it, he needed, and he didn't know what that need was or why it had suddenly appeared. But he desperately wanted to crawl underneath those covers with her and bury his face in that honey scent for just a few moments. Just enough so that this damned ache in his body would stop for two seconds so he could go back to himself.

He feared this obsession would drive him to ruin.

Chapter 5

Hunched over a glass of what tasted like wine mixed with sweat, Katherine stared into the red substance and tried very hard not to think about her day. So many people had come in with wounds. So many.

If she closed her eyes, she still saw their skin and the stitches that she wove over and over again. The parting of the flesh and red blood dripping down their sides as she tried her best to stitch them closed again.

Skin shouldn't look like that. No one should experience standing in a line waiting for people to stitch them closed after they were attacked.

Grace sat on the opposite side of the table, breathing out a long sigh as she stretched her neck from side to side. "Never seen anything like today in all my days of working at the almshouse."

"Me either."

"You did good work today, though. Those stitches were neat and tidy."

Katherine lifted her mug and tried to smile, but the expression felt rather hollow on her face. "Thanks. And to think, I used to spend my days mending dresses and ripped hems."

"Who would want that job?" Grace clinked their mugs together, and both of them shook their heads.

No one else would spend hours on end at their job. They were useful to the town, that much was certain. But spending the entire day covered in blood and everyone else's problems? Not something that people really wanted to do.

Only the desperate ended up in her situation and Katherine was well aware of that.

"How many people did we see today?" she asked, her face halfway in the mug as she tried very hard to stay awake.

"Oh, I don't know. At least thirty."

"Felt like more."

"That's because no one came in with just one wound." Grace rolled onto her side and then laid down on the bench, disappearing from view. "What did they say it was?"

"Kelpies."

"Again?"

Katherine shrugged, then remembered her friend couldn't see her. "Something like that. They didn't see the creature, so they thought it must be a kelpie considering all the injuries."

A quiet silence stretched between them before Grace quietly asked, "How much longer are we going to stay here?"

The question hovered in the air. It was the same question almost everyone in the boarding house asked every day. This kingdom wasn't just hard to live in, it was dangerous. Every day they risked life and limb, and for what?

For the moors, Katherine thought. For the mornings she woke up and saw the mist blanketing the ground like a magic spell. Wisps would dance through it, blinking with the fireflies as the willows wept a sad song in the breeze.

She stayed because she loved it. Because a few hard days at work would never take away from the magic that living here provided. Every day she was greeted with beauty, even if some people didn't see it in the gray and rainy days that would soon follow.

Swallowing another gulp of wine, she finally said, "No money means no travel, Grace. Or did you forget that?"

Her friend sat up, her hair a dandelion puff around her head. "I know of a way to get money."

Katherine frowned. "No you don't."

"I do." Grace nodded, her eyes slightly unfocused. Was she drunk? "Look, I know you won't like the idea of it. Gluttony isn't anyone's favorite person, but it's such a small price to pay if we can get enough money to get out of here."

What?

What was her friend even talking about? They couldn't... No one should go up to that castle. Hadn't she seen what happened to the last girl?

Katherine hooked her finger over her shoulder, pointing as though the castle was right behind her. "You want him to rip out your throat? And did that girl we just treated on this table..." She thumped her finger down, missing the table but then trying again and getting the satisfying thud. "Did she look like she had any money? She's still here. Still working in the... the..."

Grace was already nodding with every word. "At the mill. She's one of the seamstresses."

"A seamstress," Katherine repeated, drawing out the word as though it was a dream job. "That's what I wanted to be."

"No, you didn't. They don't get paid half as much as we do and you're right, she didn't have any money. But the girl probably dropped it after she realized she was bleeding out at the neck."

Grace stood, weaving slightly before she grabbed onto the table for balance. She meandered out of the room like she was going to go to Gluttony's castle right now, and Katherine couldn't have that.

Lurching up after her friend, the two very drunk women made their way down the hall to Grace's bedroom. Katherine set her up on the bed, tucking her in maybe a little tight with chops of her hand on every side of her body before attempting to point at Grace's face. "You're going to stay right here all night. And we're going to talk about this in the morning. You got it?"

But Grace was already asleep. So she really didn't have to worry about her friend sneaking off in the middle of the night.

Grace's room was so nice, Katherine thought as she stumbled to the door. Her friend was so clean and orderly. Everything was in its right place, and everything had a purpose to be where it was. Bright flowers that were still alive decorated the pretty windowsills. A rug on the floor in rainbow colors, not sun bleached and hazy.

It was all so nice. So cozy. So safe.

All that alcohol didn't help as she stepped out into the hall. Katherine closed the door behind her and thudded her forehead against it before turning to the long, long hallway that led to her own door.

The door that was her only barrier between herself and the situation that she had told no one else about. The situation that showed up, without fail, every single night.

Blowing out a breath, she made her way to her bedroom. When was the last time she'd gotten a good night's sleep? It had been ages. A week maybe?

That shadow always showed up outside her window. Sometimes early, sometimes late. But Katherine always woke when it was there.

She could feel it. The lurking, looming danger of someone watching her while she slept. A part of her brain knew when he was out there, and it always made her heart thunder in her chest and her lungs suddenly squeeze as if preparing for her to run. But she didn't. She couldn't run anymore with this damn hip, so she was stuck where she was, hoping like hell that whatever monster stood outside her window wouldn't come inside.

Putting her hand on the doorknob, she had to fight through her fear to enter her room.

The problem was that it had been getting closer. Every night she didn't scream or cry out for someone to help her, it got a few steps closer. Last night, it had been in the hidden shadows of the next building. So close it would only take a few steps for her to lunge forward and touch it.

Why was it coming closer? Why was it coming anywhere near her at all?

These were questions she couldn't ask. Every time she tried to open her mouth when she saw it, to either scream for help or to shout at it to leave, she ended up frozen. Incapable of speech.

Why?

She had no idea. But some hidden fear inside of her worried it was because she wasn't brave at all. That she'd spent her entire life pretending she was so much more than she actually was. And that feeling burned through her chest so heavily that it turned her fear into anger.

Or maybe that was the alcohol. Katherine wanted to pretend it was because she was brave, so she was going with that.

Instead of bolting underneath the covers like she'd been doing every night since she first saw it, Katherine took her time. If her peeping tom wanted a show, then she'd give him a show.

Katherine took her time undressing. She let her overdress fall to the ground, then stood in nothing but her shift. The chilly wind coming in through her open window brushed against her skin and it felt so good. So good to just stand there and let it cool her warm cheeks. Her bare arms soon were speckled with goosebumps, but it didn't matter. She wanted to feel the touch of the wind.

The touch of... a gaze.

He was here.

Her breath caught for a few moments before she let it wheeze out of her. She'd wanted this. This was the point of what she was doing. She wanted him to see her standing here, and...

All her nerves roared back to life. What was she doing? She had someone who stood outside her window every night, trying to either scare her or manipulate her. He was probably some murderer or the magical creature that was attacking all those people she had just stitched back up. The last thing she needed was to show him all the pearly white skin he could ruin with a sharp knife and creativity.

At least her shift didn't show many of her scars. Stiff, she walked over to her small table with a mirror and started brushing out the tangles in her hair. She hadn't done it in a while, but the slow strokes had always eased her mind.

Of course, it was better when someone else was doing it. She didn't enjoy ripping through the knots and her arms got so tired.

Still, the lulling sensation of the brush eased that tension that had gathered at the base of her spine. She could almost pretend that there wasn't someone out her window, watching her, waiting to see what she would do next.

And the sensation of those eyes on her had stirred something else. Something darker that coiled in her belly and made her grow slick between her thighs.

The forbidden, she thought. Perhaps it was that she was doing the wrong thing right now, and they both knew it. She was tempting him. Tempting the monster just outside her windowsill.

In the mirror she caught a shifting of darkness and again, that spike of fear made her freeze.

He was right outside her window. So close that if she leaned even a little bit, she would be able to see who it was. And it was definitely a man. That frame, those features, the shape of the shadow, all of it.

And oh, that heat burned ever hotter.

She was stupid. This was playing with fire, and she knew better. Slamming her brush down on the table, she felt a small amount of satisfaction as the shadow moved away.

Let him be afraid. He was the one who was stalking her, and he had no right to do it.

But still, she could feel how embarrassingly wet she was as she made her way over to her bed. Ignoring the window. Ignoring the man who thought he could watch her and she wouldn't even notice.

She slithered underneath the cool covers and threw the blanket up to her neck. Rolling onto her side, she stared at the window for a few minutes longer before a plan rose in her mind.

If he was this close, maybe he would get even closer if she pretended to be asleep. Maybe she could actually see who it was that thought he had a right to linger in the darkness.

Was it Jackson? He'd been overly friendly at the almshouse lately, but they shared the same shift and she'd been taking on a lot of work for him. She'd always thought he had a thing for Grace, so why would he be... here? Wouldn't he be at Grace's door?

Alcohol induced choices continued to run her evening. So instead of doing the smart thing and calling for help, Katherine stayed awake and pretended to drift into sleep.

She measured her breaths, even and quiet and oh so delicate. She let her hand fall limp by her face, just enough to cover her slitted gaze if she had to. Enough so that anyone would likely think she was asleep.

And then...

Oh, and then.

A hand reached through her window. Long fingers, graceful in their movements, tipped with neat black claws that were so sharp she could see the little wood curls they left as he clenched her windowsill. Almost as though he was angry. Doing the same thing he'd done all those nights ago.

And by all the seven kingdoms, she really was an idiot because she felt an answering gush between her legs. She wanted those fingers to touch her. To stroke her skin and to part her thighs and do all those wicked things that Katherine wanted someone to do. Desperately.

Clenching her thighs together, she forced herself to remain still and silent as her shadow lifted himself through the window and then crouched on her floor. But when he rose to his great height, her breath stuttered.

Taller than most men she'd ever seen, lean and muscular, the man now standing in her living room was clearly a god. He'd stepped out of a portrait painted by one of the greats, with a face that would send any woman onto her knees as she begged for a taste of him. Chiseled, clean lines, red eyes that saw too much. A full mouth, with kissable lips just below a long nose. And his hair, oh, his hair. Long and dark, like a waterfall of ink that fell just below his ribcage.

He wore all black, and his button-down shirt had been opened to reveal pale muscles that were likely hard as rocks.

He was... glorious.

Handsome.

No, that wasn't the right word. It wasn't enough to describe the beauty that made her eyes sting with tears because he was perfection personified and it hurt to even look at him.

And then he took a step forward, and she remembered to be afraid. He was in her room.

He was in her room.

He'd never given her the impression that he would come all the way inside, and if he had, then she wouldn't have put on that stupid show for him. She wouldn't have tempted him to step all the way up to her bed.

Those gleaming red eyes reminded her, horrifically, of what so many of her patients had said. He was handsome, but his eyes were that of a demon. He hadn't looked at all dangerous until he had met their eyes and then suddenly they remembered he was the demon king.

Was this... Gluttony?

Was the king himself in her room?

And then her heart thundered in her chest because the mattress just beside her head dipped as he braced himself against it. With one smooth movement, slow and calculated, he leaned down and...

Sniffed her? Inhaled her scent deep into his lungs and then suddenly, he was gone again.

She sat straight up in her bed, clutching the blankets to her chest as she wildly looked around in the moonlight.

But he was gone. Like he'd never been here at all.

Chapter 6

One inhalation of her scent was all he needed. That's what he told himself for nights upon nights until he finally cracked. Because who was he kidding? One night where he sniffed that lovely hair didn't mean a damn thing.

She'd been so beautiful. So tempting as she let her gown drop and stood there in nothing but a gray shift. She had likely thought she was being brave, tempting him like that when she thought he wouldn't enter her private room.

And she knew he was there. Oh, his little pet knew exactly where he was at all times.

Gluttony would never forget the grace of her arms as she dragged that brush through her hair. How she hadn't even needed candlelight to move through her room. She lived in the darkness, just like he did. And he had known those pale limbs would look so beautiful wrapped around his neck, his waist, anywhere he could get her to touch.

She'd become a living, breathing obsession that he couldn't get out of his head.

And he'd taken the risk. Leaning onto her bed when he damn well knew she was awake. His pet certainly had no idea how easy it was for him to read her. He didn't even know if she'd realized who he was just yet. Her heart had thundered in her throat, a temptation that was almost impossible to ignore as his lips were so close to that throbbing beat.

But he had held himself back. Somehow. Perhaps because he enjoyed the chase, just as his brother had suggested. Maybe he did need to just take what he wanted, because that was when the blood tasted sweetest.

Yet, he had the feeling her blood would taste sweet no matter how he had it. No matter when she gave it to him, willingly or not. She would taste like honey and all the glowing, bright things that he'd never had in his life.

He needed to get himself together.

She'd sunk her little claws into him and he couldn't be a good ruler, or at least stay out of the way, if he was obsessed with yet another of his subjects. Once she knew who was outside her window, she'd slam it shut. Bar it with metal and close him off from the only thing he wanted right now.

And yet...

Her window was open tonight.

He stood outside as he had the nights before, staring into the room and telling himself to leave. He didn't need to be here. She deserved to have her privacy, but he'd already well and truly broken through that dream, hadn't he?

Her name was Katherine. Gluttony had taken the time to figure out who lived in the boarding house, and what rooms they were in. It took surprisingly little effort to find, considering the front door was rarely locked.

After he'd left that night, with her scent filling his lungs, he'd snuck into the manager's office. Also unlocked. The paperwork wasn't difficult to find, although it was lacking in detail. Just a room number, a name, and the last time they paid.

This place was ridiculously expensive for what it was. He enjoyed Katherine's room because it was pretty and it smelled like her, but that didn't mean it was worth the price. The walls were peeling; the floor was warped and likely would rot through after the swamp finally touched the bottom of the building. He wouldn't have it. His newest obsession would not live in such a dangerous place.

She'd need to leave the moment she bent to him, and he wouldn't have it any other way.

Leaning into the window, he peered around her room. There was no tell-tale lump on her bed tonight. No rising and falling of sweet breaths that filled his lungs with sunshine and flashes of red hair.

But he could smell her. Not just that her room was full of her scent, but because she was in the room. He could feel her looking at him too and hear the thundering beat of her heart.

What had his little pet planned? Was she finally going to fight back against him because he was a strange man who had entered her room?

The thought was strangely exciting.

Gluttony climbed through her window as he pondered the thought of her attacking him. He didn't want to taste fear in her blood, but he also liked the idea of her little claws coming out to play. What if she scratched him? Would she draw blood?

Ah, the thought was enough to send a man to his knees. Already stiffening, pressing against the buttons of his pants, he wandered through her room. Touching everything he could.

Some primal part of himself wanted to leave his scent here. Even though he knew mortals couldn't smell anything like he could, it made him feel a little better. Any mortal man could walk in here. He could step through those doors because she invited him in, and Gluttony could do nothing about it.

He'd have to stand outside that window, watching another man fall upon her like an animal, knowing only he could feast upon her the way she so desperately wanted.

A low growl echoed in the depths of his throat, and he heard her heart stutter. It kicked back into a quick beat, likely so hard that she could feel it beating against her ribs.

Now, where was she?

He turned, his eyes skating around the room as he tried to plan out their first meeting. He hadn't expected it to go like this, of course. Gluttony had already been planning how he would introduce himself to her. First, he would bump into her on the street. She'd be surprised to see him, the demon king of their kingdom, out and about.

He would suggest that he was going to the market. And perhaps she would like to join him. After all, he had no idea where he was going and it had been a long time since he'd been into the town.

Then, of course, he'd flash a disarming grin. She'd blush, and he would have to take a moment because the scent of her shyness would likely make him mad with want and desire. But he'd get himself under control and guide her to the market with her hand on his arm.

They'd spend a wonderful day together. He'd invite her back to his castle, and then they would have a moment in his great hall where he bent her over his arm and feasted upon her neck.

He could already see the twin beads of blood that would drip down that lovely swan neck of hers. But that was so far ahead of himself, and obviously wouldn't happen now.

Instead of the gentleman she met on the boardwalk, he was the intruder who had let himself into her room in the middle of the night. And he knew she was here. He knew exactly where she was, because her heartbeat gave her away.

His pet had hidden herself under the bed. What did she think she was going to do from under there?

Now, Gluttony knew he should leave. The reasonable part of his mind said he had to get out of there because she was very much awake and she knew he was here. But he also knew she'd already seen him.

So why would he leave?

While the reasonable part of his brain screamed at him to get out of her room, the monstrous part of him sat down on her bed. He smoothed his hand over the blankets that smelled so much like her. His fingers danced over the depression on her pillow where she had certainly been laying just a few moments before.

He wanted to spread himself out on these sheets. Damn it, he wanted to smell like her.

Envy was right. He had gone too far with this woman and he wasn't going to apologize for it. He wanted her so badly it hurt.

Fuck. Looking up at the ceiling, he realized he had no idea what he was going to do. She was pinned under the bed. He wouldn't be able to get her out of there. And now she was going to be afraid of him. What woman in her right mind wouldn't be?

Biting his lip, he went for the soft approach. "Katherine?"

There was no response from the woman underneath her own bed. He wondered if it was as dirty under there as it was up here. He could only imagine she was the woman who kicked clothing underneath her bed, so she didn't have to see everything she had to pick up.

Adorable. Really, it was. He found everything about her so adorable that it hurt.

But he'd have to hire maids when she moved to the castle.

And yes, he was moving her to the castle. This obsession needed to be worked out from his body. He wouldn't kill this one. He would be good and not bite her too hard, so she would stay alive for a long time. And he'd have the perfect little pet.

"I know you're in here," he breathed, trying to keep his voice to a smooth, reassuring cadence. "And I know you can hear me."

Her heart rate slowed just slightly. There was no way he'd somehow eased her mind, so he had to assume she was holding her breath.

"I assume you know who I am." Gluttony chuckled, running a hand through his hair. "This isn't normally how I meet people. I suppose I should admit this entire circumstance is rather unusual for the both of us."

Still nothing.

But then he noticed he could see his reflection in the mirror she'd brushed her hair in. And underneath the bed was the slightest hint of red hair. She was watching him, of that he was certain.

She stared into the mirror and he looked back at her with his head tilted to the side. Gluttony didn't look terrifying. It was one of the best parts of the physical form he'd taken. While his brothers were intimidating, he was very easy to look at. Thin, wiry, handsome to a fault. He lulled humans into a false sense of security because they didn't know what lurked underneath his skin.

He met her gaze and smiled. "Hello, Katherine."

Apparently, that was the wrong thing to say. That red hair disappeared like she thought she could hide from him still. But he wasn't letting her get away like a little mouse finding her way into the wall.

"Oh, come now. You have always been so brave with me just outside of your window. What about this makes you feel like you're unsafe?"

Was that the slightest snort he heard?

He grinned, likely a mistake. The long canines in his mouth flashed in the moonlight. "You find that funny. Why?"

She had to talk. He knew exactly where she was. He'd seen her! And he'd never once heard the sound of her voice and he found himself desperate to know what she sounded like.

Was her voice melodic? Burbling like a clear watered brook? Perhaps she sounded like Varya, loud and opinionated as she took up an entire room with the power of her words alone. He could see that. She had always seemed a little brash when he watched her through the window.

But when she spoke, her voice was unlike anything he'd ever heard before. "I find it funny because you've broken into my room."

His eyes rolled back in his head. Ah, but her voice. Raspy, like she'd inhaled too much smoke, deeper than he'd expected and without an ounce of fear in those words. She said what she wanted without even the slightest bit of hesitation.

Beautiful. So incredibly beautiful, and he was certain she had no idea how lovely she sounded.

Finally, he had to open his eyes again and focused on the room. If he drifted through that obsession, then he was far too likely to let her run.

And if she ran, he had no idea what he would do to her.

Clearing his throat, he leaned back on his palms. The scratchy texture of her blanket abraded his hands. Her scent drifted up around him, so pretty and light. It eased the squeezing pain in his chest and soothed the desire to toss the bed aside and grab her. "I did break into your room."

"Why are you here?"

"If I knew that, I don't think I'd be here, pet." He wished he knew. Oh, he wished he had an answer for why he was sitting on her bed, terrorizing her. "I thought you might have the answer to that."

Another soft snort. "I don't even know who you are."

His eyes flashed as he looked back to the mirror, back underneath the dark softness that hid between his feet. "Is that so? You don't even have a guess?"

A small shift, perhaps as though she was trying to get even further away from him. "Whatever guess I have comes from a place of madness."

"Ah, and evil. A darkness that haunts the land with long reaching claws and red eyes." He let his powers flex through him, those eyes glowing as they surely had when he stood outside her window. Even his claws grew longer, although those were buried in her mattress right now. "Guess, pet. I wish to hear you say it."

She swallowed hard, and the click of her throat was a sweet release. "I don't want to."

"Why not?"

"Saying the words makes this feel less like a dream and more... reality." The way she paused before saying the word made him wonder if she thought this wasn't actually happening.

"This isn't a dream, Katherine." He leaned forward, bracing his elbows on his knees so he was slightly closer to the mirror. "I'm right here, sitting on your bed while you are cowardly hiding underneath it."

"I'm not hiding," she hissed.

"Oh, did you have a plan?" He raised a dark brow. "You were perhaps going to burst out and attack me? With what weapon?"

To his utter shock, she threw something out from underneath the bed. A knife from the kitchen skittered between his feet, sliding to a halt just out of his reach. Moonlight played along the rather dull edges.

He chuckled. "Did you think that would really hurt me?"

The soft little growl from underneath the mattress went straight to his cock. "I didn't know who you were for certain. And if you were Jackson, then I intended to stab you in the thigh and refuse to stitch you back up."

He bared his teeth in the mockery of a smile. "Who's Jackson?"

Oh, the jealousy that burned through him showed in the sudden tension of his shoulders and the long claws that elongated through his fingertips. He saw her hesitate. He could feel the nerves that made her freeze.

But she didn't back down from him. His pet wouldn't do that, after all. She was too perfect for him.

Instead, he heard her confidently reply, "Not anyone you need to know about, Gluttony."

It made him want to scream. He would feast upon anyone who tempted her away from him, and he suddenly didn't want to continue having this conversation with a shadow underneath the bed. But hearing his name spoken in those raspy tones? Ah, it was more than enough to soothe that angry wound.

Lunging upright, he spun toward the bed and reached a long arm underneath it. Claws caught on the back of her shirt, tangling her in his grip even as she struggled like an angry kitten.

"Come on, pet," he said with a laugh at her hisses. "Let's hear you say that to my face."

Chapter 7

She thought perhaps she should have fought a little harder. But considering he grabbed her by the back of the shirt and yanked her out from underneath the bed like a kitten, Katherine rather thought it was a better idea to not fight at all.

She dangled in his grip for a few moments, hanging there staring at him and wondering what he intended to do with her. It gave Katherine a few moments to really look at him up close.

Until now, she'd only seen him from the window. The distance had made him seem significantly less intimidating. She'd thought his form was slighter than she'd expected, thinner, easier for her to fight back.

This was not necessarily an intimidating man in front of her. At least, in theory. He stood there, lean and long and all too handsome. But with her eyes open, not pretending that she wasn't looking at him, all she could see was how powerful he was.

Those red eyes stared back at her with too much interest. Fangs glinted where they poked out through his lips and made tiny divots on his full bottom lip. Not a single strand of hair was out of place, although she had no idea how that was even possible considering how much he'd moved just to get her out. Claws scraped along her back, not enough to be a threat, but more as a warning.

He was so clearly inhuman. Not even remotely close to anything she'd ever seen, and she'd been a few feet from kelpies before with their frog like skin and fanged mouths.

Then she blinked, and she was floating. No, falling. Tumbling back onto her bed where she landed in the wrong direction. Her head almost hung off the edge while her hip twinged as her feet dangled over the opposite side.

Gluttony prowled up her body on his hands and knees as he joined her on the bed. Looming over her. His fangs flashing in a full smile as he stared down into her shocked expression.

"Well?" he asked, his voice deep and low. "Now that you've really seen me, pet, what do you think?"

She swallowed hard. "I saw you a few nights ago when you came into my room the first time."

"Ah, that is no surprise. But you were trying so hard to hide that you were awake." His face dipped down, nose trailing between her breasts. "You didn't want me to know, but your heart was thundering in your chest. I can hear it, you know. I can see the way your little pulse flutters in your neck like a bird just waiting to flee its cage."

Poetry for such terrifying words. Although she had to grit her teeth as a sudden blush turned her cheeks red hot. "You cannot enter a woman's room without permission."

"Oh, but I can. And I do. Regularly." He snorted against her nightgown, and then drew himself up her body until his breath fanned across her throat. "Now, why don't you tell me who this Jackson is?"

A slight huff of a laugh escaped her. "We're back to that, are we?"

"Apparently so."

"You have no right to know who anyone is in my life. I don't even know you."

But then he settled his weight onto her and oh, her hip might not move very well, but it moved enough to accommodate him. He settled between her thighs, hot and hard and so masculine that it made her stomach clench.

Katherine couldn't remember the last time a man had lain with her like this. Had it been years? She didn't have time to think of anything but her job and the pain that was a constant battle. No man wanted to hear her complaining about it, and no one wanted to be thoughtful enough to be aware of her old injury. It had been so long... So long since she'd twined her arms around a broad back or felt narrow hips pressed against her own.

Sighing, she tried very hard to focus when he was all but grinding himself against her.

"I have no right?" Gluttony murmured, his voice so deep she could feel the vibrations of it against her neck. "I have whatever rights I desire. I'm the king of this kingdom. I could command you to tell me."

"And I still wouldn't tell you." Mostly because she didn't want poor Jackson to lose his head. "Why do you care so much?"

He reared back, those red eyes staring into hers, and she swore she saw something flicker in the depths. As though he wanted to tell her the truth, even though he feared what the truth actually was. Or maybe he hadn't considered why he was in her room, acting like a jealous lover when this was the first time they'd ever spoken with each other.

And strangely enough, she didn't mind it all that much. Katherine should have been screaming for someone to help her, but a small part of her soul whispered for her to pause.

He was... familiar to her. Or perhaps that wasn't the right way to say it, but in a strange way, he was. Her heart knew him, or perhaps she knew him in another life. Because it felt as though they'd lain on this bed a hundred times before, him asking her about a man that she mentioned and her having to sooth his aching ego.

Which was a problem in itself, but still. It was as though they'd done this before, and that feeling made her hesitate. Just for a moment.

It was apparently the wrong thing to do. Again.

With a groan, he tilted his head down and buried it in her throat. Katherine had to make space for him, just so he didn't touch her more, but that only made more room for his lips against her pulse.

"I don't know why it matters," he whispered against her skin, inhaling so deeply she wondered if he was trying to keep her scent in his lungs. "I cannot seem to keep myself away from you, and we'd never even spoke. Now? Oh, now you are more than just an obsession, pet."

Katherine didn't like that.

She did not like that even if her stomach clenched and her thighs shook with a need she hadn't felt in years. She didn't want to be his pet, and she certainly didn't want to be an obsession.

Katherine had gone mad. That was the only answer for what was happening right now in her head. She'd lost all sense of reason and in doing so, she was convincing a murderous tyrant that she was interested.

"I—" What was she going to say?

Warm and slick, his tongue glided up her neck. Just that brief touch scattered all her thoughts to the wind. She tilted her hips up toward his, as much as she could with her bad one, and he groaned against her. The sound shook through her throat and went straight to her core.

If he could smell her blood, surely he could smell her interest?

Another groan. Another rocking of his hips against hers, and she could feel how hard he was. This was getting so far out of hand and she needed to get control over the situation or she'd be yet another woman he'd fed from.

But would that be so bad?

Suddenly she had flashing images of his teeth sinking into her neck as he drove himself deep inside her. The pulsing sensation of him feeding upon her while she milked him dry below. And oh, it was as divine an imagination as it was obscene. She shouldn't be interested in that, and she certainly shouldn't dream it up, and yet...

His lips touched her neck now, pausing to suck lightly at that artery he'd pointed out before. "So sweet," he groaned against her skin.

And then she remembered all the women she'd treated before. All the necks that were torn open so horrifically that the women almost didn't survive. She'd spent hours, even today, meeting with people who struggled after the blood loss, and advised them on what to eat and how to replenish the blood their body needed.

This man was the problem. Again, he laved her neck with his tongue that had been so tantalizing just moments before, but now she felt the scrape of his teeth with it.

She was not a weak woman. She would not fall under his spell just because he kissed her a few times and expected her to fall at his feet.

Perhaps he had some demonic magic she was unaware of and that she was only just breaking free from. Whatever madness had overtaken her, this was ill advised.

Hissing out a long breath, she used her good knee and shoved him off her.

Katherine was surprised at how easy it was. She hadn't expected him to be quite so light. But perhaps she was aided by the element of surprise as his eyes flew open in shock and he fell onto his knees at the edge of the bed. Though she had little time to waste, she noticed that he'd seemed a little stunned by his own reaction.

That expression was the last one she saw before she grabbed her lamp and bashed him over the head with it.

Really, she hadn't expected it to do anything. He was a demon king, and therefore stronger than any man she might have met before him. He had an innate ability to simply be more than people like her. But he dropped like a stone the moment she hit him over the head, his eyes rolling back into his skull and his graceful body somehow wilting like he'd intended to fall.

Katherine froze, the lamp still lifted in her grip and her breath heaving in her lungs.

She hadn't just done that. Had she?

Surely she was smart enough to not attack the demon king of Gluttony who ruled their kingdom through blood and vengeance?

"Oh, no," she whispered when he didn't move at all. "Oh, no. Katherine, what have you done?"

He laid on her floor, a little blood trickling out of the wound on his head. He was breathing, at least. She hadn't killed him, and that was a very good thing. Now, she just had to get out of bed and... what? Run?

There was nowhere she could go in this entire kingdom where he wouldn't be able to find her. She didn't have the money for the bridge fees to leave to another kingdom, although maybe one of his brothers would take pity on her. Unlikely, but she'd heard Lust really didn't like this brother.

Katherine had no plan. No escape. She had to face this head on and accept the fact that she'd attacked him in a momentary lapse of judgment and maybe, just maybe, she could use his obsession against him.

Yes. This was a good plan.

Sliding off her bed, she limped over to her closet and searched for anything that would help. Right now? Ropes. Which she didn't have, of course. But she had plenty of thin shifts she could twist into a rope. Which... wasn't ideal, really, but it was something.

Turning on her heel, she approached him with slow, measured steps. His chest rose and fell, but he didn't so much as stir when she walked up to him. And if he was close to gaining consciousness, he would have stirred. Her floor was thin and bent with every step, like she was on a springy mattress rather than solid wood.

Katherine knelt behind him and nudged him onto his side. He really was thin. Too easy for someone to move, even though she had gotten a lot stronger the more she worked at the almshouse. Katherine could lift anyone necessary if they needed to get onto a bed or somewhere else. But this man was far too light for his frame.

Focusing, she put all her effort into making knots that were difficult for anyone to wiggle out of. He was stronger than she was, or at least, that's what the rumors said. So she tied four of her shifts up and down his arms, making sure he was completely bound.

And then she sat down on the bed again, leaning forward as far as her hip would let her, and settled down to watch.

It gave her more time to study the demon king, who didn't look that terrifying while he was unconscious. Was he as strong as people said? Surely he must be. There were plenty of people she'd treated who were wounded beyond recognition that he'd attacked.

But now that she was looking at him, they all claimed he'd bitten them. Twenty times, some had said, with raking teeth that ripped and tore.

Unless he had another form, that would be rather impossible. He had the same size jaw as she did. He wouldn't even be able to make the wounds that she'd treated, or at least some of them.

But Rose? She remembered that wound. And that was the same size as the teeth he had and certainly the same spacing.

So she couldn't deny that he was guilty. Because he was. There were plenty of women throughout this kingdom who had offered themselves to him in exchange for money, and he'd taken them up on that. It was wrong. It was disgusting.

And he'd felt so good lying between her legs like he had.

Eventually he stirred, interrupting her distressing thoughts. First, his hand twitched, then a fine little wrinkle appeared between his eyes before he groaned.

"What?" he muttered as he tried to sit up. Then he must have realized his arms were bound behind his back because his eyes widened in shock before narrowing in distrust.

He didn't know how to roll upright in this position, obviously, because he laid at her feet, glaring up at her. "What is this, pet?"

"This is me getting your attention." Katherine leaned down, making sure he was staring into her eyes when she said her next words. "And I'm not your pet."

"Perhaps not now. But you will be."

"Big words for a man currently bound at my feet."

Those red eyes flashed. "Maybe this is where I like to be."

Katherine shrugged. "Then behave, and I'll let you stay like this for a while."

Heat sizzled between them. She'd never thought of herself as an overtly sexual person and yet here she was, tempting a demon king with what? Lies? She had no idea what she was doing.

Finally, he ground his teeth and asked, "What do you want?"

"I want you to get out of my room."

"And I want you." That was it. That was all he said. Just a period at the end of that sentence as though it explained itself enough.

What did he expect her to say to that?

"You can't have me," Katherine replied, although it felt like a lie. He could have her, she knew that. But she was going to make him work for it.

Again, those red eyes flashed. "I don't like a challenge, pet."

"Why not?"

"Because then I can think of nothing else but winning. And I will win." He trailed his tongue over those sharp teeth. "Didn't you ever learn not to taunt a predator?"

Katherine scoffed, although again she wondered how smart the sound was to make. "You are no more a predator than I am a beauty, demon king."

"Perhaps I will prove you wrong on both accounts." Those sizzling eyes trailed over her body again and she almost felt... wanted.

No, this was wrong. All of it was wrong.

But she had a feeling he wouldn't leave her alone if she didn't do something.

So she took a deep breath and said, "If you leave my room now, I will come and see you at your castle. But you must promise never to return here. No more staring in my window. No more stalking."

"I'm not stalking you."

Katherine lifted a brow.

And though he grumbled, eventually he responded, "Fine. Maybe it was a little light stalking."

"No more of it."

"Only if you come to my castle."

Oh, this was stupid. She should kick him out of this room and then scream until her lungs burned. She should let every single person in this town know that he was hunting yet another of their women.

But she looked into those strange eyes and swore she saw a wound there that needed fixing. And Katherine was nothing if she wasn't a healer first.

"I've already said I would," she replied. "Do we have a deal, demon king?"

He eyed her before sitting upright. She'd thought he was rather stuck in that position, but he wasn't. And then he broke through the ties she'd wrapped around him. Easily. He shredded through her shifts like they were nothing but cobwebs, then held one of them up in his hand. "You bound me with your underwear?"

She refused to think about her burning cheeks. "It was all I had on hand."

Gluttony grinned before standing, and then he pocketed one of her shifts. "I look forward to seeing you at my castle, pet. Enjoy your evening."

And then he disappeared. Again. Slipping out through her window like this wasn't the strangest interaction either of them had ever experienced.

Chapter 8

He'd lost his damned mind.

Going into her room like that? Grinding himself into her core like an absolute fiend? He'd taken what he wanted and then he'd pushed and pushed until she offered him more.

But it would never be enough. Never. He wanted to sink his fangs into her skin and feel her shivering underneath him while he pulsed his cock inside her body. He wanted to know what it would feel like to have her breaths puff at his neck, frantic with her passion while he feasted upon her.

Gluttony had never experienced both at the same time. The first time he'd fed, it had been a madness. The second, a treatment, in a way, for a young woman who had been so tired of living. And then it had been a necessity. A need that bloomed deep in his belly until he couldn't think of anything other than the next fix he would get.

Now? He wanted more. He wanted to experience what life would be like if he truly indulged in all his gluttonous desires. And he wasn't ashamed of it. How could he be?

She'd met him in every way, shape, and form. She'd tilted her hips to give him better access to her core. His Katherine hadn't even shivered in disgust as he played his lips up that graceful column of her throat or even winced when he sucked upon the vein there that called out to him so sweetly. He would hazard a guess that she'd even enjoyed it, as the sweet perfume of her longing filled the air.

He had wanted more from her. He'd wanted everything she would give him, and in that moment, he'd lost himself.

Her body, her pliable form. It all was so easy. Nothing in his life had ever been easy. Even his brothers pushed and pulled for dominance any time they were near each other, and Gluttony simply didn't have time for those games. What he wanted, he wanted. And when he wanted, it was very easy for people to tell.

Most of the time, they gave him anything. He was the demon king who ruled them, after all, and they all knew what his wrath looked like. But this woman was willing to tell him no. To put him in his place, even with a lamp on her nightstand, and it was... thrilling.

Sighing, he pushed his glasses back up the bridge of his nose and stared down at the solution in front of him. He'd gotten nowhere with this research ever since she'd stumbled into his life. The woman had driven him to insanity, and all his intelligence had leaked out of his ears.

He needed to figure this out, though. He had to know exactly what threat he and his brothers were facing.

If any of the other kingdoms got a hand on this substance, he did not know what would happen. Greed had already been attacked. But his kingdom was the warring one, his people ready to fight fist to skull until they fixed their issues.

What would happen if this got into the wrong hands? Like Envy's kingdom. Those dark halls and magic filled rooms were all too dangerous. They could easily knock Envy out and then drain him of his magic. His brother would make more magic, spirits always did, but they would then be given an infinite source of power to do whatever they wanted with.

Dangerous. Oh, so dangerous.

Gluttony wouldn't mind it if his people attacked him. As he'd told Greed in their time together, he was fully aware that he and his brothers were the monsters.

Staring down into the substance before him, he watched as it reacted to molten silver. Apparently, that was also not going to be the answer to all his problems. Maybe he should give up. Let this substance out into the realm and see what happened when the people got their hands on it.

His brothers would fight. They always did. Even Sloth would likely get out of his castle on the hill to fight to keep his position.

Gluttony though? He thought maybe he would just let it happen. He'd been ruling this kingdom for a thousand years, just like the rest of his brothers, and he'd seen no improvements for any of them.

"Not even Wrath," he muttered as he brought the beaker over to the trash. "Even you, brother, who considers himself so much better than the rest of us. Even your kingdom is falling apart."

They all were. Every single one of them. And no one knew how to fix what they had broken.

In his opinion, it would have been better for the mortals if they hadn't even gotten involved. He hadn't really had much of a choice.

When all the others became kings, what other option did he have? He was expected to do the same. A suddenly powerful, incredible being who had more abilities than humans could dream of.

Of course, they'd wanted him on the throne.

But they had no idea what monster they had invited into their bed.

Sighing, he tossed the beaker into the bin and then ripped his glasses off. The substance be damned. He had a raging headache, a painful hard on, and a thirst that had yet to quit since the last time he'd seen her. The woman ruled his mind, fangs, and cock. She had no right to them, but he supposed she had the control, anyway.

Wandering through his empty halls, he tried to get control over himself. At least here he was alone. No one lived here to bother him. His laboratory stretched throughout the entire castle at this point, keeping the more explosive components away from the incendiary ones had necessitated him to make some arrangements. And this was all he'd ever wanted out of his life.

To study the kingdom he'd been given, and to avoid the humans at all costs. That was all that mattered, and as such, it was all that he'd taken a thousand years ago.

Rounding a corner, he realized that dark mist was back. It thought he couldn't see it, gathered up in the corner of the ceiling as it was. Lingering. Lurking. Obviously keeping an eye on him when there was only one person who wanted to do so.

"If you were sent by Wrath, you can go back to him," he snarled. "I'm behaving myself and keeping to the rules that he put in place."

The little mist didn't move.

"You can leave," he repeated. "My brother has trust issues. I fully understand that. But I am not going on a rampage across the kingdom to prove a point to my idiot brother. Wrath thinks I want to destroy this kingdom, but I just want to be left alone. Do you understand?"

Again, nothing.

Maybe he needed to get a companion for himself. This castle was all too quiet on days like today, when a shadow stared at him from a distance and all the darkness looked a little too close.

Had Wrath sent more shadows to keep an eye on him? This kingdom only had a few sunny days a year, let alone long daylight hours. This was a kingdom made of darkness.

Wrath could monitor him all too easily here. All his brother would have to do was create these monstrous shades and tell them what he wanted to know. Was there no where private for Gluttony anymore?

Groaning, he stalked away from the shadow and tried to find a place to disappear. But now all the gloom looked back at him. Everyone and everything wanted to judge him for the things he wanted, no, needed.

"Envy," he muttered.

Envy knew better than most when Gluttony was lying. Their last conversation had likely not imbued any sense of trust. And Envy wanted the job that Gluttony had taken. Envy wanted to be the one to save their brothers, not for any altruistic reason, but simply because someone else had the job.

Perhaps that was the brother spying on him. Perhaps the shadow was his. Envy had control over his tattoos, and the man was more a sorcerer than a demon at this point.

Or it could be Sloth. Though that brother never left his castle, he knew everything that happened in other kingdoms. Far too interested in other people's drama, he knew Sloth was likely to try to find out what he could about the brother who was suddenly rumored to eat people in his kingdom.

Tunneling his fingers through his hair, he tried to still the madness that threatened at the edges of his vision.

It could be any of them. Pride had every reason to get involved if Wrath had opened his mouth. Lust was too close to Gluttony's kingdom to not have concerns, and his bride was now a sorceress of renowned abilities. Greed was the only brother he thought unlikely to be involved.

And that was only because Greed was so wrapped up in Varya that the man didn't know where he was looking most of the time.

Which meant...

He had no one to trust. Not a single person in his entire life that was trustworthy.

And should he gift that to a stranger who approached his keep? The young women who wandered to his home were thin and panic-stricken. They desired something more than they cared for their own life, and as such, they were willing to trade anything to him.

Their body. Their life force. A few of them had even offered their very souls if he would give them coin.

Gluttony knew things weren't great in his kingdom. There were so few resources he could sell in a swamp kingdom, let alone people willing to work or live here. His kingdom had the smallest population, and it would not change any time soon. Getting people to move here was almost impossible, just as leaving was equally difficult.

But for them to offer their very soul just on the off chance they might be able to leave? It was a fool's errand. They had to know his money wouldn't get them very far. He'd give them everything they asked, all for just a single drop of their blood and affection, but they never offered him either all that willingly.

He didn't want someone to sell him their soul. He just wanted someone.

That was it. That was the rub and the problem and the disease all at once. He wanted someone. To do what with? He had no idea. Gluttony had no frame of reference for what people did with each other. But he was so damned tired of being alone.

The dark mist rolled past him on the floor, already heading for the grand hall of his castle as though it had a right to be here. Frowning, he trailed along behind the little beast.

Surely it was a spirit. He had thought it was the first time he saw it, and now he was certain. It moved like a spirit. Hopping from shadow to shadow, then looking in a direction before it moved again. The little thing was quick, but it didn't move right either.

Spirits had a way about them that made it easy for him to recognize them. Spirits of happiness glowed with a little inner light and were bright green or blue. They had a bounce to their roll that belayed a certain levity in their movement. Spirits of anger were jagged edged and quick in their movements as well, though they were usually dark red.

This one was none of those things. It also had no characteristics that he recognized. So what was it? And what magic had sent it here?

"You know there is no food in my castle," he scolded as he followed the beast. "You cannot feed off of me."

It didn't respond, but considering their historical conversations so far, he hadn't expected it to.

"And if you're looking for staff, I fired them all long ago." They were too much of a temptation in the middle of the night, but he had no intention of telling the spirit that. "There is a village nearby. You could go to that place to feed if necessary."

It rolled to a stop before his front door and seemed to look through the wood before it started wriggling underneath.

"Where are you going?" he asked, watching until it was at least halfway wedged underneath the worn wood. "You know, you could just ask me to open the door."

If a dark ball of black could give him an unimpressed look, this one managed. It almost sounded like it gave him a little huff of frustration before disappearing out his front door as well.

Amused, he stared at the door for a few moments before deciding he'd follow it. Last time, the spirit had led him to her door. Surely that was a good enough reason to trust it again?

He opened his door only to find the mist had gathered so close to the edge that it had left mold in its wake. When was the last time he'd made even an effort to clean his home? This castle had once been beautiful. Though it had taken quite a bit of work to keep it that way.

All his dead gardens looked rather sad in the dim light of the morning. He hadn't even realized it was morning until this moment, and then he saw movement past the gate.

A young woman's form appeared in the mist. The white swirls clung to her waist and fingers, dragging her away from the hellish nightmare of his home. But she continued forward with a rather unique gait. And oh, she was lovely. All that red hair glowed in the morning light, framing her face in a riot of curls that exploded around her head as the mist made them even more frizzy.

His heart stuttered at the sight of her. Gluttony truly hadn't expected her to come. Why would she? He'd threatened her, lurked outside her window for days on end, even let himself into her room when she hadn't wanted him there.

He'd thought she wouldn't keep her end of the bargain, and he would survive the disappointment. If she didn't want to know he was watching her, he could be more discreet.

But here she was. Like a candle glowing in the middle of a darkened room, drawing him ever closer to her light.

He walked down the pathway through his dead garden as though in a dream. And she stood just outside his gate, waiting for him to unlock it with a disgruntled expression on her face.

"You don't have a butler?" she asked, brows furrowed in confusion. "Or did you know I was coming?"

"I don't. And I didn't." He unlocked the chain that kept his wrought-iron gate closed and wrenched it open. Gluttony winced at the ugly squeal before blowing out a long breath. "Come in."

She eyed him, still frowning, and clearly unimpressed. "Why don't you have a butler?"

"I have no staff in the castle."

"Why?"

She was the first person to ever ask him that. And he was so surprised that he blinked a few times before honestly answering, "I didn't want to harm them."

And his Katherine, brave as she was, blinked up at him before saying, "All right, then."

She walked past him without a single ounce of fear. Just strode up through the path, barely giving a glance to all the dead plants around her, and up to the front door of the castle. Stopping there, she turned around to look back at him with a lifted brow. "Are you coming?"

Yes.

No.

Maybe, he wasn't really sure how close he should get to her. He wanted her so badly that it hurt. This brave woman who had no fear in her at all.

Clearing his throat, he resolved to be the better person. Today, he could pretend he wasn't a monster, so he didn't scare her away. He could pretend that he wasn't the nightmarish creature who had destroyed her home and, likely, her life.

But then he walked up to her side and smelled blood. It didn't even reach his thoughts that it clearly wasn't her blood, it wasn't honey and wine, nor did it relax him. Instead, it sent a spike of fear right through the back of his skull, tailed only by infinite, dark rage.

Slamming a hand to the door beside her, he leaned down and breathed in deep before baring his fangs in a snarl. "You're covered in blood?"

She swallowed. "I am."

"Who do I have to kill?"

Chapter 9

Katherine had taken such a long time getting to the castle. Not because her hip was hurting. She'd made certain to stretch out the stiff joint and warm it for a few nights in a row so she could make the trek. Her slow pace was entirely due to the nerves churning in her belly.

And now here she was, pressed against Gluttony's door while he glared down at her, feral and angry and... Well, it wasn't all that bad, she supposed.

She'd never had any man get angry if he could sense that something was off. She'd been surrounded by men her entire life who ignored her injury, or if they noticed it, they just shrugged it off as something she had to deal with. They didn't want to help her, even if she was injured again.

Now, this man was supposed to be a terrifying beast who harmed women left and right. Yet, he was standing in front of her, practically foaming at the mouth the moment he thought someone might have injured her.

Perhaps he wouldn't mind injuring her himself. She couldn't forget that. But there was still the chance that he just didn't want to see her hurt or in pain. And that made something glow deep in her chest.

"You don't need to hurt anyone," she said, trying her best to sound unaffected by his anger. "Unless you want to hunt down the kelpie that attacked the traders who were coming here from the other village."

Gluttony searched her gaze, and she had the off thought that he might not believe her. Was that what his look said? Was he really pondering if she would tell him the truth?

He reached forward, wrapping one of her curls around his finger over and over until he reached her temple and gave it a slight tug. "And this wasn't your... Jackson, was it?"

He was worried another man had done this? Katherine refused to let that settle in her heart. The damned organ was already trying to beat its way out of her chest, reaching out for him like the pathetic, puppy love stricken thing it was.

She knew that her heart wanted someone to see her. Just to see her. Not as the seamstress who might stitch their wounds shut. Not as the neighbor who would show up in the middle of the night if trouble had arisen. And certainly not as the woman with the limp who had lived in their town her entire life. The one person they all looked at with pity. How many times had she heard them whisper, "Poor thing, everyone gone and only the memory of fire to replace them?"

This demon saw her, though. He was looking right at her with so much heat in his eyes, it was hard to think. She swallowed hard and his gaze tracked the movement of her throat. Perhaps the gulp was a mistake. Because even if this man looked at her like a woman—something no one had done for a very long time—he was still a bloodthirsty demon who consumed blood regularly.

Hissing out a breath, she spun toward the door and tried to open it. "I came here to talk, just as you said."

"Indeed you did." He leaned forward, and she felt him inhale at the side of her neck. "You kept your promise, pet. I will gladly reward you for that."

Oh, she didn't want a reward, but her body certainly thought she did. It wanted to melt, drift toward him, and let him take her weight. Ease the ache in her hip even as he wrapped his arms around her front and breathed onto that aching column of her neck.

Still, she couldn't do this. These feelings were madness.

Grappling with the door, she let out a little frustrated hiss again. "Did you lock this? I will not have this conversation outside."

He leaned ever closer, and she could feel the warm press of his muscles against her back. His hand slid down her arm and over the fine bones of her hand, lacing their fingers together in a weaving pattern of flesh. Then he pressed down on the handle and suddenly she was staring into darkness.

So much black. Oh, his home was so dark even though the sunlight had filtered through the mist. Just enough for her to see the first few feet into his castle, and then there was nothing she could see at all.

Was she really doing this? Was she going to walk into the home of a demon without hesitation or fear?

He didn't give her a choice. Gluttony moved her with his body, step by step, into the home and then the door closed behind her with a sudden thud. She jumped, terror streaking through her bloodstream as she frantically tried to find him as he slipped away. Then he disappeared into the shadows.

No. She wasn't this person. She wouldn't faint with fear at the very first sign of difficulty. Katherine had a plan. That was why she was here. A plan that bolstered her courage and would fix so many issues in her life. His life. And… the town's.

She straightened her shoulders and bit out, "Is this how you greet guests? A blackened home with only shadows for you to hide in?"

He snorted. "I should have expected you would be snippy."

"Snippy?" There it was. The anger that always strengthened her and gave her courage. "I'm not snippy. I cannot see, demon."

There was a long pause before he said, "Ah."

And then she could hear him move. Just the shuffling of feet on the floor, gliding until the sound suddenly stopped. She couldn't see him, hear him, couldn't even sense him until a warm gust of air trailed down her neck and disappeared between her breasts.

"I forget," he said against her throat, "that humans are so weak."

Oh, he had to be an ass about it, didn't he?

She was ready to spit fire at him, to yell and scream as she should have done the very first time he let himself into her room. This was the ravings of a man who had clearly lost his mind. And here she was, standing in his living room like all the other fools who had been tempted by his pretty face and promises of riches.

She opened her mouth to berate him, but then froze. Warm light bloomed in the darkness, illuminating his concentrated expression as he stared down at the many candles on the candelabra before him.

And she wasn't frozen because he had somehow changed her mind. He was still a monster, and she wouldn't forget that, but…

By the gods, he was so pretty.

Even with his brows furrowed in concentration, he looked like a marble statue come to life. Surely only the hands of an artist could paint a man who looked like that. He was so handsome it hurt to look at him, and she'd never experienced that in her life before.

The kind of handsome that made her want to run her fingers through that perfect hair and see if she could convince even one of the strands to curl. So she wouldn't be the only person with frizzy hair in the room and dirty shoes that tracked mud through his castle. She didn't want to be the dusty little peasant who had crawled out of the muck to make a deal with the demon king.

And yet, here she was.

Ready to make a deal with him. Because no one else could.

He finished lighting all ten of the candles and then looked up at her. His red gaze was always startling. She expected him to have deep brown eyes. Emotional, soulful eyes of an artist who had seen too much in the world and was consumed by his need to purge all the dark thoughts in his mind. But those red eyes perhaps reflected his emotion even better than the darkness she'd expected. He looked at her with his soul in his gaze, and she wasn't sure she'd ever seen another person's soul so easily.

He seemed to freeze as well. Gluttony, a demon king, stunned as he stared back at her with wide eyes.

Katherine licked her lips, watching him track the movement and she couldn't help but ask, "What do you see when you look at me?"

He shook himself at the question. "What do you mean?"

"The rumors claim you only look at a person like myself and see food. Sustenance. Someone to feed upon and that's it. But... You don't always look at me like a predator."

And maybe that was why she was here. He looked at her like a man looked at a woman, not like a monster looked at the newest thing it desired to eat. And she knew the difference. She'd been in this kingdom her entire life, and she'd been around enough dangerous creatures.

Kelpies and all the other monsters of the swamp were part of daily life. She knew what it looked like and felt like to be hunted.

That was not at all how she felt around him.

He swallowed hard, and this time she tracked his movement. Curious of the reasoning behind him feeling so uncomfortable because there was no reason for him to be.

He had all the power here. Didn't he?

Watching his movements, how uncomfortable he suddenly was, and how he turned away from her, she wondered if maybe she did have all the power after all.

He started walking away into the darkness, but then he said, "I see a very brave woman, pet. Very brave indeed."

Oh.

Oh.

He saw something in her that so few people did. No one had ever called her brave in her life, if she thought back upon it. Perhaps her father, but that had always come tacked along with a "You're foolish, girl" or something like that. She'd always taken risks for the betterment of her family or people. And yet no one had seen it.

Or if they had, they'd never told her. Never had the kindness in their hearts to realize maybe she needed to hear someone say it.

Sometimes it was all just... really hard.

A knot created itself deep in her belly and she had the sudden, insane urge to hug him. Because he cared enough to tell her how he felt, and she wanted him to know that she appreciated his words.

But he was already moving away from her. Walking with a strange stiffness to his spine that belayed how uncomfortable he was with this conversation.

So she stayed silent. Katherine followed him through the badly neglected castle. She could see it had been a very long time since anyone had even attempted to clean the place. And it was massive. If he'd really let go of all his staff, then this was too much for a single person to care for. He needed people to clean the floors, at the very least.

She couldn't even tell what color anything was. It was all ghostly with a fine layer of dust, but there was an air of beauty to it all. Neglected beauty, yes, but it was hidden in there still. Just enough for her to see past the strangeness of a home so thoroughly mistreated.

Warm wood, she thought. The floors were probably oak, stained to look like a dark brown that would be so pretty, with countless candles lighting it up. Or even the bulbs that lit the town. Why didn't he have electricity? Surely he did. Everyone in the kingdom had use of it, but he didn't have any lightbulbs.

"Why don't you have light?" she asked before she could grab the words back.

He glanced over his shoulder and took a right down yet another dark hallway. At least this one still had portraits hanging on the walls, but he was moving so quickly she couldn't get a good look at them. "That was Lust's idea for all the kingdoms. It works, but it would take a lot to install it throughout the castle."

"So you do have some lights, then?"

He nodded before taking a left.

Apparently, he didn't want to have this conversation with her. But she wanted to talk about it. At least talking made her feel less like they were walking toward a dungeon where he would lock her up and use her as a personal snack whenever he wished.

"If you have lights, then why didn't you install them in the front of the castle?"

"I just didn't."

"Ah. You're suddenly at a loss for words, I take it." She almost ran into his back. Katherine stumbled a few steps away from him, her hip screaming with pain as she twisted the wrong way to get away from him.

"Here," he said, completely changing the subject. "We can speak in my office."

"You have an office?"

Maybe she had her mouth open, staring up at him in shock, because he looked a little amused at the question before he nodded his head toward the room again. "I have an office. Most of us do."

"Why?"

"Well, I am the king of this kingdom. And though many of you villagers might think I do nothing at all for you, there is a lot of paperwork that goes into trading."

Now it was her turn to snort. Katherine strode into the room with her shoulders stiff and a bitter taste in her mouth. "Trade? For what? There's nothing coming in or out of this kingdom."

"That is where you are wrong."

The door thudded closed behind her, feeling a bit too final for her taste. But then again, she was already struck dumb by the interior of his office.

This was nice. A mahogany desk, piled high with papers in neat little stacks. There was a pretty light made of stained glass that cast rainbow colors all over the floor. And then there was a thick rug underneath her toes, warm, plush, and soft. Two red chairs sat in front of his desk, velvet covered and faintly glimmering with bronze dusted over the wood.

It was cozy. Welcoming. Easy to see how someone could spend hours in here. And it didn't require the candlelight that he still set on top of his desk as though it were necessary.

Turning toward her, Gluttony suddenly dropped the act. Or perhaps he picked up the mantle of demon. She wasn't certain which. All Katherine knew was that one moment, a warm, kind eyed man had been staring at her and the next, she was being inspected like she was his next meal.

"So," he said, leaning back against his desk and crossing his arms over his chest. "You are here to make a bargain with me."

She wasn't. Was she? That wasn't the point of her coming here.

"No, I am here because you asked me to come here." Katherine tried to remember the deal she had already thought of on her long walk to the castle. It was hard to think about anything other than the discomfort of his stare.

"That's not why anyone comes to this castle. You want something, pet, and I want to give it to you." He arched a pointed brow. "For a price, that is."

She already knew what his price was. She already knew exactly what he thought he wanted, and she was willing to give it to him. But she didn't think what she wanted to ask him would make him very pleased.

"All right," she said. "Perhaps I did come here to make a deal with you."

He nodded, although she saw the flash of disappointment on his expression before he turned to pick up something from his desk. "I have learned from my... previous deals with other that it is best if I have a taste before we go any further."

"I do not give you permission to take an ounce of my blood before you have heard me out." Katherine straightened her back, knowing she had to seem confident if she was going to get through this in one piece. "You, sir, are going to want this deal from me. Not the other way around."

Chapter 10

The absolute gall of this woman. She thought she could order him around? He couldn't have an ounce of her blood without permission, yes that was the deal he'd given his brothers. But the fact that she thought he would want her deal more than she wanted his?

How strange.

Every woman who came to this place knew what they wanted from him. Mostly it was money. Sometimes it was power. Most of the times, it was the same situation over and over again. They were poor. They wanted more out of their lives. He could give it to them and all they had to do was open a vein.

Gluttony had prepared himself after he had been so disgusted with the last woman who wandered up to his castle. First, his new rule was to taste the blood and see if it was even worth the cost. He already knew Katherine's blood would be delightful and addictive, but he wanted to make sure it wasn't some oddity of her scent. Second, he refused to drink out of their necks any longer. The intimacy of the position was enough to drive any man to madness, and he wanted to keep this as cold of a deal as possible.

But Katherine wasn't like the others. She stood there, radiating confidence and disdain as she stared him down. And for the first time in his very long life, he felt a spark of intrigue in being looked at like that.

Normally, he would bristle with anger. How dare she glare at him? He was a demon king, far superior to her in every way. She had no right to think ill of him when he could so easily rip out her throat.

Strangely enough, he enjoyed her glare. He liked it that she saw flaws in him. She poked at them, prodded them, made him realize he was being an ass.

Not that he intended to stop being an ass. In fact, he rather enjoyed the little angry blush that spread across her face.

Katherine huffed, her feet shifting on the floor as she tried to control her anger. "Well?" she asked. "Don't you have anything to say?"

Not really. He was enjoying watching her, seeing the blush spread up her chest, neck, and into her cheeks. Even the very tips of her ears turned red, like her hair.

But he supposed he should be at least some semblance of a gentleman. "I'm thinking."

"About what?" she scoffed. "I haven't told you my deal yet."

"Do you realize you're rather entitled?" Gluttony sat on top of his desk and watched her struggle to find the words to respond.

She clearly didn't think of herself as entitled. None of the humans did, but they all were in some way. They came here. They thought he couldn't turn down their offer, and that he had to give them what he wanted.

A few times, he'd accused the women of entitlement just as he had her. And they would all splutter, grow angry, threaten to take away their blood, when he could take it whenever he wished.

But this one… she surprised him. Instead of growing even more angry, Katherine stopped for a moment and actually thought about what he had said.

Finally, she tilted her head to the side and asked, "How so?"

"You walked into my home with a plan. A plan that involved offering me something that I already can have whenever I wish. You think that wandering into my castle and offering your blood is a deal I cannot turn down? But I can live without blood. It's not a necessity. I am not a vampire. I enjoy the taste, but I do not require it to live." He could feel his eyes flashing, but passion had always made them glow. "I'll admit, I long to feel it dripping down my throat, and to have my lips wrapped around the heady thud of your vein. I love to listen to your heart rate speed up, and then slow down as you realize you might actually enjoy what I'm doing to you. But more than anything else, I enjoy consuming what makes you human. It is sublime."

"Why?" she asked, her eyes narrowing on him.

"Why what?"

"Why is it sublime?" His brave little pet wandered all the way to his desk and sat down in a chair right in front of him. She eyed him as though he were a specimen underneath a jar. "I wish to understand. If you do not need blood to survive, you certainly pay an awful lot for it. And as you so willingly suggested, you could take it if you wished."

"Ah, but then I would be a murderer."

"We already think you're a murderer. Taking it when it's not freely offered does not change anyone's opinion of you. Why not just do it?"

He couldn't stop himself. Gluttony leaned forward and caught one of her curls again. It bounced against his palm, already warmed by her overheated skin. "I have accepted long ago that I am a monster for my desires. I enjoy blood and pain and everything that makes you human. Feasting upon the flesh of my subjects does not give any comfort to my brothers."

"So you hold yourself accountable for the opinions of other courts?" She arched a brow. "I'm afraid I don't believe that."

Neither did he. But he was surprised she picked up on it so quickly.

He hesitated before responding, "You may believe what you wish. I am the monster who haunts the nightmares of so many of my people. I have accepted that fate, and find there is no need to change it."

"And if you could?"

He released her curl, a bitter smile stretching across his face before he could catch it. "Ah, pet, you seek an impossible fate."

"If you knew me, then you would know I do not take any task that I will fail at." Her spine somehow straightened even more. So much determination radiated out of her body that he almost believed her. "This is why I came to you. I believe that I can be more help to you than anyone else you have ever drank from."

She would be his greatest addiction, she meant. Was this woman aware of how much he wanted her blood? Certainly she'd gotten the hint of it, considering he'd shown up at her doorstep night after night, just to watch her.

What would she ask of him if she was aware of how deeply his desire went?

Shifting on the desk, he tried to get ahold of himself and the situation. "What deal would you make, then? You clearly are aware

I want your blood, and that I am willing to pay a high price for it."

That made her restless. He watched her shoulders shift back, ever so slightly. As if the idea of giving him her blood was disgusting, but she didn't know how to tell him no.

"Right," she replied, looking down at her lap and twisting her hands together. "Perhaps you can help me understand why you are so interested in blood?"

"Make your deal, Katherine."

"If I could understand it, then it would be much easier to seek out an explanation for why you are suddenly having these cravings. Or how I intend to help you. In fact, I do believe it would be best if we considered all the options. After all, a craving for blood could be caused by many maladies."

Was she trying to diagnose him? As though his need to drink blood was somehow a strange illness that had come upon him?

Amused, he watched her try to argue herself into an explanation.

"You see, I've spent a good amount of time in the almshouse and I know how to tell when someone is ill. There are plenty of potential realities that would make you crave something like blood. Perhaps a lack of iron in your own, for example. Have you had anyone look at your gums? You can tell a considerable amount about someone based on the health of their gums."

"No one has looked at my gums."

"So you see, there could be a reasonable explanation for all of this, and you have no need to continue feasting upon anyone's flesh."

"Katherine," he stopped her and leaned over her chair. Bracing himself on either arm, he loomed over her as he stared into her eyes. "I do not have a malady that you can fix. I am not ill or unwell. I desire blood because I am a demon, and that need will never go away, no matter how much you try to fix me. Although I am flattered by your dedication to the healing arts, it is not necessary for you to diagnose me. I know what my problem is."

"And that is?"

He flashed her a dark grin. "I like the way you taste."

She immediately looked down, and he knew it was too much to say. He shouldn't have been quite so forthcoming with his desires. He shouldn't have laid it all out in front of her, admitting that he was a terrible monster who wanted nothing more than to eat and devour. And yet, that was who he was. He consumed. At first it had just been food, or adventure, then it was objects, and eventually it became people.

The ultimate delicacy.

"I see," she whispered.

"Do you?" He leaned down, dragging his nose up the long line of her neck just because he could. And because he wanted to prove a point. "If I let myself truly indulge in all my desires, I would already have my fangs deep in this lovely neck. I would drink deeply of you until you coated every inch of my body. Until I could smell nothing but your honeyed blood, tasted nothing but your courage and foolish bravery, and heard nothing but the sound of your gasps in my ears."

And there it was. The gasp, just like he'd thought he would hear. She let out a little sound along with it, not quite a moan, but closer than any other noise she might make.

He hardened so quickly that the zipper of his pants became painful. He wanted her. Oh, he wanted a thousand things with her, and he feared he would never get his fill.

But he would. He always did. Gluttony had never been this obsessed with a mortal, but he had suffered through such an obsession before. She would soon find that he was not the man she thought he was. Because someday, he wasn't certain when, another woman would walk by with a unique sent as well. Another woman who maybe smelled like wildflowers rather than honey, and it would be enough to draw his attention away.

No blood had ever satisfied him. Not for very long.

She tore her gaze away from her twisting hands to meet his gaze. And oh, that bravery would be his undoing.

"I want to make you a deal, demon king," she said. "I know you are interested in my blood, and I know it has become too tempting for you to deny. I wish for you to take my blood."

"And in return?" he growled.

"I wish for you to drink only from me." Her eyes narrowed, sharpened, that intelligence blaring through her gaze. "You will drink from no one else while you have my blood, and that is all."

"You ask the impossible." But oh, he wanted.

"It should not be impossible for me to ask you to have a little restraint."

"You are not asking for me to have restraint, you are asking to be my only blood donor." That was impossible. He'd kill her. Just the thought of having someone that was his alone, someone who would come to him whenever he wished to drink, for however long he wished?

He'd murder her the very first night. He wouldn't be able to hold himself back, and that was too dangerous to risk.

But she tilted her head back, and he saw the flexing of her jaw. "I know how to heal people. So I know the ways to keep them alive. I will not put myself at risk for your thirst, but I know where it would be safe for you to drink from me, and how much blood I can lose."

"You think you are good for this job because you are a healer?" he asked, incredulous. "That is asinine."

"It's intelligent," she corrected. "You have killed more people than you know with your careless feeding habits. At the very least, I know how to keep myself alive, even if you do not."

He'd killed more people... "Is that why you're here?" he asked, suddenly realizing what this deal really was. "You think that by offering yourself, you're saving all the other people in your village from the monster who wishes to drink from their throats?"

She swallowed hard, and Gluttony knew he'd caught her.

So that was the way of it then.

Here he had been, thinking that perhaps this brave little thing wanted him for the same reasons he wanted her. He thought she could feel the burning deep in her soul, and that she knew what it felt like to need another person so badly that it turned her inside out.

Instead, she hoped to become a hero. A martyr. Her people would see her as the woman who gave herself over to the monster who wanted to kill them all.

"So that is the real deal," he snarled, already feeling that cold numbness taking him away. "You wish for your people to finally see you, is that it?"

"Excuse me?"

"You want them to look at you as someone other than a young woman in the boarding house who will never get out. You want to be the hero of the story, the person who saves the day even though no one asked you to save them? I can promise you, pet, no one is going to believe that you are anything but who you already are. The people in that village see others as they wish. No amount of sacrifice will change that." Gluttony growled and then rounded his desk. Angrily, he tore a piece of paper out of the top drawer and wrote out a contract. Nothing too difficult, all too easy to write these days after years of it, and then thrust it out to her. "Sign your life away then, pet."

She took the paper carefully, not crumpling the edge like he had. And then she took her time, reading over everything that he'd written down. She'd find no difference than what they'd already said in their conversation, and yet she still handed it over to him and pointed at a line. "I would like that to say for an undetermined amount of time."

"Contracts are binding for only a certain amount of time."

"I would like it to say an undetermined amount of time," she repeated before flicking her eyes up to him and holding his gaze. "I don't care what contracts usually say. I will save my people for as long as I possibly can."

Gritting his teeth, he fixed the line before giving it back to her. "Satisfied?"

Once again, she took her time reading it over before nodding. "Do you have a quill?"

Again, he flashed his fangs at her. "Oh, no, pet. You're making a deal with a demon. Don't you know you have to sign in blood?"

She winced, but still held out her hand without fear. And when he took a needle from his desk, it took every ounce of his power to not fall upon her like an animal. One press and a delicate bead of blood bubbled up on her pointer finger. Gently, with shaking hands, he placed her fingerprint on the piece of paper and then let her draw her hand back.

"You're mine now, pet," he said quietly, watching the blood dry. "You have one week to return to me before I hunt you down. And the next time we see each other, I will feed."

Gluttony listened to the pattering sound of her footsteps as she raced away from him. He stood frozen beside his desk, watching her blood until the front door slammed shut.

Chapter 11

O h, she was a bigger fool than she realized. Scolding herself for being this dumb, Katherine limped back down the boardwalk toward the town. It was a long walk. Plenty of time to berate herself for all the moronic decisions she'd made back in that castle.

What came over her when she was near him? Was he magical enough to cast a spell upon her? Surely that was the only explanation for the heat that swelled whenever he was too close. Or perhaps that was the reasoning for why her mind wandered and she forgot everything she'd worked so hard to plan on the way up here.

How the hell was she going to make any money if she was at the castle all the time?

If she was sore for two full days after going there, then she wouldn't be able to work. The almshouse certainly would not provide her with a tall stool to sit on while she stitched people up. So she'd have to let them know that her hours needed to be limited.

But she didn't have the funds for that. She couldn't pay her rent if she didn't have the money, and she already stretched her pay as far as it could go.

Where would she stay?

Why hadn't she asked him for money as well as to feed only from her?

Groaning, she paused halfway back to the town. At least she couldn't see the castle anymore, which meant that terrifying demon also couldn't see that she'd stopped to rest.

Somehow, he had yet to notice that she had been previously injured. Or if he had, he made no note of it. Katherine was always hyper aware of her walk when she was near him. Some part of her didn't want him to realize that she was... broken.

Sighing, she used the dilapidated railing to lower herself down onto the worn boards. Here, they were a little better structurally than the ones she was most used to. Because of course, the pathway to their king needed to be well taken care of.

She snorted. Far be it from anyone to let the path crumble and then make sure no one else could bother him. And that he couldn't bother them.

But... Looking into the water at the souls who slowly rose to the surface, eyeing her feet as though they could yank her into the water with them, she wondered if Gluttony could still make it to their town even if there were no floating boardwalks.

Tilting her head, she stared into the water with a frown. "Would you drag him down with you? Or let him pass?"

The spirits hesitated. Perhaps no one had ever spoken with them before. Katherine's mother was the only one she'd ever heard of who even tried to speak with them at all. She'd been crazy though. Everyone in the town said it.

Poor Katherine with her mad mother who had wandered off into the moors because she truly believed the monsters were her friends. And poor Katherine's father, who'd gone off after her only to be eaten along with her.

The story was always the same. Monsters like the spirits below her gently swaying feet would never be kind or converse with any human. Not if they had the opportunity to kill them instead.

Still, she wanted to know.

"Would you let your king wander through these waters without a scratch?" She glanced up at the moors, the pale green light glowing from within them while the wisps danced upon the mist. Then she snorted. "I bet you would. I can already see him, emerging out of the mist like some forgotten god while you all parted for him. Are you afraid of the demon king as well?"

They probably were. Although she still couldn't understand it.

She kicked her good foot back and forth, watching the spirits track the movement with greedy eyes. The one directly underneath her had once been a warrior. He still had his armor on, although it had gone mottled green with age. His cheeks were rotten clear through, only his jaw and teeth visible as he gnashed his mouth.

"I don't understand why you're so interested in dragging people down with you," she muttered, before sighing and shaking her head. "I bet you're afraid of him. But he's always been so kind to me, or at least, his version of kind. It's hard to imagine him as the monster everyone claims him to be, when he's more interested in telling me that I'm beautiful or sweet."

She knew the sweet comment was entirely about the scent of her blood. He'd sink his teeth into her neck without a single thought and probably drink her dry if she let him.

He'd done it before.

Not lately, of course. She was the one who got all the young women he'd fed off of, and though they weren't in great condition, he hadn't killed one in a very long time.

But she remembered the one he had killed. She was a lovely little thing, the daughter of the previous mayor. Though she couldn't remember her name, or really much about her other than she'd been beautiful, Katherine had always wanted to be her.

Everyone in town did. The woman had been stunning, and walked through the town with a confidence only the rich could have. She'd traveled back and forth to Gluttony's castle so many times, people had started to whisper that maybe she'd become their queen. Maybe, for the first time in the kingdom's history, someone had tamed the demon in the castle.

And then she'd died. Returned with wounds on her neck and so pale her body had looked deflated.

Katherine could still remember the mayor's screams. He'd been so distraught he'd left the next day. Just up and left an entire town who had relied on him for years because he refused to be so close to the monster who had taken his daughter's life.

Biting her lip, she looked back into the water. "Why do you think he did it?"

The spirit below her froze, and she met his wide-eyed stare. How had his cheeks rotted clear through when his eyes were still there? Maybe it was part of their curse. They'd be able to see, no matter how much they didn't want to see any longer.

"Killing her, I mean." She cleared her throat as though the question was a little too awkward to ask. "Everyone thinks he did it because he couldn't help himself. They paint him as the picture of a villain, or perhaps as some bloodthirsty animal who can only devour everything that comes in his path. But he hasn't done that with me. In fact, I'd argue he's been nothing but a perfect gentleman in my presence and I suppose that's rather unsettling. You see, I wanted him to be the monster as well. It's so much easier to deal with someone like him if they're a terrible person. And not just... human."

A soft snort interrupted her musing. "He's not human."

That raspy voice was rather surprising. She hadn't expected anyone to be listening to her, let alone respond. It definitely wasn't the spirit in the water. For all that her mother had been certain the spirits retained some memories, they absolutely could not speak.

Freezing, Katherine looked around herself for someone who might have been listening to her musing. But she was well and truly alone in the mist. Even the comforting blanket of fog parted a bit for her to look up and down the boardwalk. Nothing. No one. Just herself and her thoughts.

Frowning, she muttered, "How would you know that?"

"It's easy enough to see. Just look at him." Again, the voice seemed to come without a body at all. But she could definitely hear it, and maybe if she kept it talking, she might be able to pinpoint where it was coming from.

"I see a human when I look at him. Isn't that the point of his figure?"

"You're an idiot if you think red glowing eyes and fangs are as human as they come." A snort accompanied the angry words. "You should leave him up there in the castle to rot on his own. It would serve him right."

Were the words coming from... underneath the boardwalk?

Oh, that wasn't good. She was likely talking to some creature she was completely unaware of. Suddenly frozen with fear, she looked down at her feet and swore she saw a shadow reaching for her from underneath the planks.

She'd never moved so fast in her life. Katherine ignored the twinge of pain and stiffness in her hips as she drew her legs out of the creature's reach. She nearly pitched off the opposite end of the walkway. Breath wheezed from her lungs, ragged and horrified as she contemplated how close she had just been to being pulled into the water.

Whatever creature spoke with her wheezed in laughter. "Oh, that was hilarious!"

It took a while to get her breathing under control, but once she did, anger took the place of fear. "What a cruel thing to do!"

"How many young women dangle their feet over the dangerous muck of this kingdom? I taught you a lesson."

"You were needlessly mean. If you aren't going to yank me into the water, then why threaten me?" Katherine wrapped her arms around her waist, sitting uncomfortably on the hard planks and waiting for whatever it was to rise out of the water.

And yet, nothing did. Nothing even moved at all.

She listened to the faint hum of zipping dragonfly wings and the burbles of popping bubbles before she cleared her throat. "Are you going to answer me?"

"I'm waiting to see what you'll do next."

"Why?"

"Because I have never met a human who could speak with me before. Your kind are... well, notoriously unaware of their surroundings."

She wondered why it had struggled to find such cutting words. When it paused, she'd already assumed it was thinking less than savory thoughts. But then it seemed to pick the worst words to say to her, as though it was searching for what would insult her the most.

A fluttering memory cut through her thoughts. Gluttony, his back turned to her but golden candlelight illuminating his handsome features. He had called her brave.

So she supposed she would continue to be brave.

Katherine rolled onto her belly and crawled to the edge of the walkway. Curling her fingers over the edge, she took a deep, steadying breath before slowly pulling herself over the edge and peering underneath.

At first, all she saw were shadows. Just the green glow of the same spirit beneath her, his grin a little too toothy for her comfort. And then there was nothing at all. She'd thought to see some giant, frog-like creature with a mouth full of sharp teeth. Instead, she looked into nothing. Just boards that were covered with algae and moss, as expected, and the bubbling surface of the water.

And yet... Narrowing her eyes, she turned her attention to a strange mass of shadows that coagulated in the very corner where there was a post holding up the walkway. There it was. A strange mass of shadows that shifted when it realized it was the object of her attention.

"So it's you," she muttered.

"You can see me?"

"I can see spirits, yes. My mother could as well. It's why she was so obsessed with your kind." And perhaps her mother hadn't been crazy after all. Katherine remembered her prattling on about spirits that looked like colored mist.

People in the town had always assumed she'd meant the ones in the water. The dead bodies that stared up through the bog, with no memories or feelings at all. Just rage.

But this was a real spirit. Like the ones her mother had spoken of.

"My mother used to tell me about balls of light that followed people around," she murmured, still upside down and staring. "She told me they were always here, no matter how many times we tried to escape them. She said it was a gift for us to be able to see you all, and to know who you were. To speak with you as though you were like us."

The undulating darkness paused a bit, and then shuddered. "Humans aren't meant to know we exist."

Perhaps not. But her mother had been deemed mad for knowing it, so really, there weren't a lot of people like her.

Fingers carded through her hair, and she realized her horrible mistake. Her red locks had gotten too long lately, and leaning over like this only caused them to dangle just above the water. And one stray coil had touched the surface. Just enough for the spirit to reach up and run his fingers through her hair.

"Ugh!" Disgusted, she wrenched away from him before he could grab a handful and tug her into the bog. She'd never get away from him then!

Drowning would be a terrible way to die.

Landing hard on her rump yet again, Katherine stared at the water as the little black spirit burst into laughter. It seemed to enjoy her fear and her reaction to the horrible sensation of that dead man's fingers. She would never forget that moment. Even now, her skin crawled as though he had touched her all over.

The black mass rolled up onto the boardwalk, shuddering with its own mirth. "Oh, that was hilarious! I enjoyed that very much. Do it again."

"No," she hissed, wringing out the stray drops of water in her curls. "Who are you, anyway?"

It gathered itself up, almost as though it was trying very hard to look larger. "Do you not recognize a dangerous spirit when you see one?"

She pointed toward the water. "Of course I do. That one is very dangerous. I don't think you hold much danger to you at all."

It deflated before muttering something so quiet she couldn't hear. "Fine. You may call me Spite."

"Spite?"

"Yes. It's an emotion. I know you have felt it before. It's a rather common one with your kind."

She wasn't so certain of that. Her mother had said something about spirits feasting upon human emotions, and some of them were as tall as her father. Walking along behind people, feeding off them, like leeches.

This one was very small.

"Ah, yes." She nodded as though she agreed with what it was saying. "Terrifying indeed. Perhaps you wish to return to Gluttony's castle?"

"I have no interest in that."

"But you know quite a bit about him, I assume?"

Were those... eyes in the darkness? It seemed to blink, two orbs of dark grey, rather than black, moving underneath the mass of its shadows. And she swore those must be eyes.

"I know everything about Gluttony," it replied.

"Hmm." Without thinking, Katherine bent down and scooped it up. The spirit was very cold, rather like holding icy frog eggs in her hands, but it remained in her arms as she started back toward the town. "I think you and I need to have a little chat, then. Do you think you could tell me everything you know about Gluttony?"

"Will you use it against him?"

"Most likely."

It shuddered in her arms. "Then I will tell you everything."

Chapter 12

Gluttony had spent far too long getting everything ready. But he didn't need to sleep like the mortals did, and he'd forgotten how long a few days actually were. He had spent the first entire day picking out her bedroom. There were plenty in his castle, but very few that were good enough.

In fact, he would still argue that none of them were good enough for her, and that was entirely why it had taken him so long to choose. Some of them had views of the garden, and in its day, those would have been the best. After all, that garden had once flourished and been the only color for miles on end that wasn't some shade of green.

Except, now the garden was dead, and it was a rather morbid sight indeed.

So he obviously couldn't put her there.

The opposite side of the castle had a beautiful view of the moors, but it was infinitely closer to him. Which he worried about because... well. It was rather obvious. If she was so close to him, how long would it take for him to succumb to the desires that still raged through his chest? He wanted her, and no one else, and he would have her if he could.

So he couldn't give her the best view, in his opinion. But every other room he looked at was wrong. All of it. The colors, the floor, the age of the items within it. The view. Nothing pleased him so much as the room with the best view of the kingdom.

Somehow, he'd ended up back in that room. Standing in the center of it, feeling the rightness in his chest.

And he'd known there was no other option. He had to make this room the one she stayed in. And though his mind didn't know why, his soul did. The rest of the evening, and well into the next day, he'd spent cleaning. Making sure everything was absolutely perfect for her.

The room had once been opulent, but everything in his castle had been. Now, he feared it wasn't up to her standards. He'd had to remove the lovely curtains that hung around the bed. They'd once been a shade of pale pink, gold leaf woven through it as though the gold itself was thread. Unfortunately, age had made the actual fabric threads hang limp and moth-eaten, while the gold had chipped away.

And the fireplace had once worked, but he had to spend hours clearing out multiple birds' nests within the chimney so she didn't set herself on fire while she was staying with him.

He'd been covered in soot and grime, and tracked it all across the warm carpets by the time he'd finished. Lighting a fire for himself, he had then carried all the rugs out of the room and threw them into another bedroom he wasn't using. Then the canopy for the bed. Then the chair that was broken in the corner.

When he returned, the room suddenly appeared very barren. There was only the bed, still covered in dust and mold. A single dresser with a broken leg that leaned to the side, and none of that would do.

So he then spent the next day dragging all the furniture out and replacing it with his own.

Was it a waste of time? Probably. He didn't even know if she was even going to stay. She might want to return to her town and her own bed. He'd likely follow her there, and she had no way of knowing that, but he would. Gluttony could already feel the obsession getting worse, and he had only scented her blood on that contract.

A contract he'd placed within reach, so whenever the madness clung a little too tightly, he could inhale the scent and ease the torment in his soul.

He was a mad villain, but he was quickly becoming hers.

And when the room was finished, he started on the front hall. All the while, logic battered in his skull. He had a job. Figure out what the substance was that threatened him and his brothers. If he didn't think he could do that, then he needed to let Envy know.

But his brother would win then, and Gluttony didn't want his brother to win. He wanted to be the one to figure it out after he had this young woman in his grasp.

Some other voice told him that once he drank from her, he'd be able to think again. He just needed a taste. Then he'd be back to himself and he could start to work again.

But right now? He could think of nothing else but that lovely swan-like neck, the way his heart throbbed when she wasn't here, and how much he wanted to be by her side.

All the time. It was madness. He knew this obsession could only end in heartbreak. She'd either leave, or she would die. And he would be stuck here, yet again, alone.

But she'd come to him of her own volition and for the first time, he'd not felt like the monster he had certainly become in the past few hundred years. Gluttony had given himself permission to enjoy that feeling, even if he knew it would only end in destruction.

Finally, he had everything ready for her. The castle, the room, and food because he had remembered at the last moment that humans ate food much more often than he did. And that was enough.

He settled himself down in front of the door, just on the inside so she wouldn't think he was such a sad sap, and waited. He had no idea how long it took. There were no windows in the great hall. They'd all broken years ago so he'd boarded them shut in case anyone tried to sneak inside without his knowledge. So he sat in the darkness until he heard a soft knock.

Standing quickly, his body creaking with the effort, he ran his hand down his vest and clean cut clothing. He made sure everything was in place before he strode up to the door and threw it open.

The light blasted his eyes, and he almost couldn't see at all for a few moments until he finally focused on her.

"Katherine," he said, his voice a little breathy.

But how could he not let emotion get the better of him? She stood there, her wild red curls framing her face that was covered with so many freckles he just knew they were a challenge to count. She'd pulled it back with a tie, but those curls had a mind of their own. A soft, cream-colored dress covered her body, tied around the waist with a small brown corset. With a basket held in her hands, she was a dream he had when he first took this mortal form.

He'd always wanted a soft afternoon with a woman who looked at him with a quiet gaze that said she recognized him. Knew him for who he was and not who everyone thought he might be.

Her gaze flicked to the side, clearly looking around him before she frowned.

Frowned? Why? Why did she wear that expression when she was the one who had come here? He must have done something wrong. Obviously, he had cleaned something in a way she did not like and he was the foolish one who was standing here thinking she would actually appreciate or like what he had done.

But he froze as she leaned forward and plucked a rather impressive cobweb out of his hair.

"What have you been up to?" she asked, shaking the cobweb off her fingers. "Obviously, you've been quite busy."

"I have." And already he was shaking with the need to taste her. What would it be like? The first time he drank out of her neck would be rather intimate. He told himself he would drink from her wrist this time, but even that made him shift on his feet. His pants were rather tight, weren't they? He should do something about that.

"Gluttony." She arched a brow, and for a moment he thought he'd been caught. But all she said after that was, "Are you going to invite me in?"

"I have no need to do so." He immediately stepped aside, gesturing for her to enter. "What is mine is yours."

She gave him another odd look before walking through the door. "It seems... cleaner in here than before."

"It is."

Why did she keep twisting her face up like that? She had rather beautiful features, but they were less so when she made that expression.

"What?" he finally asked. "Do you not like it?"

"I—" Katherine paused in the middle of his entrance hall, that frown on her face as she glanced around. "Did you do this for me?"

Yes. Of course he had. Because he'd suffered for days without her, incapable of thinking about anything other than her. He'd had to entertain himself somehow.

Instead of saying all that, he tucked his hands behind his back and lied. "It hadn't been done in quite a while. I wouldn't say it was entirely for you, but merely the recognition that frequent visitors often requires more cleanliness than I am used to."

"Huh."

Now what was that noise supposed to mean?

He glanced around, uncertain that he'd done it right. And he knew it wasn't much. The meager light flowing in from the outside revealed a building that hadn't been a home in a very long time.

There were boards over the windows. His floor had once gleamed with polish and now it looked more like a regular, scuffed oak floor. He'd swept up all the shattered pottery, but that left no decorations at all. He didn't know where to find more, and hadn't spent enough time in this area to get them all set up for her.

It wasn't very welcoming. That much he could see.

And now he had a guest who was looking at everything with a rather critical eye, and he didn't know what to do with her. Did he make excuses for why his house looked like this? Was he supposed to bring her a refreshment?

But oh, his fangs ached because she was supposed to be the refreshment. He'd mistaken her reasoning for being here. They weren't friends. She wasn't some young woman coming to his home for a date where they would talk and find out more about the other before she wilted into his arms.

This was a transaction. He could pretend it was all the other things in the world, but she wasn't here for him. Not really.

He stepped closer to her, perhaps a little too quickly, because she took an answering step back before nervously thrusting her basket out to him. "Here."

"What is it?" Gluttony had no option other than to grab what she threw at him, although he had no idea what was in the basket. Food? She had to know he wasn't all that interested in eating.

He had eaten when he'd first taken this body. Enjoyed all the food as well, because there was so much of it for him to eat. But none of it really satisfied him after the first bite. Tasting something new was always enjoyable, but it never lasted. Nothing ever did.

"A gift." She tilted her chin up, looking back at him defiantly.

Her expression made him nervous. He might not know her very well, but he had seen enough to be wary around her. She was a wily one, this mortal, and the last thing he needed was for her to trick him.

It wouldn't kill him, of course, but he'd seen what other mortals were doing in the other kingdoms.

Hesitantly, he opened the wicker basket, only to jerk back as a shrieking spirit erupted in a mass of darkness. It spilled out of the basket, icy cold on his hands, as it burst into hysterical laughter.

"You," he hissed at it.

"You should have seen your face! The great demon king, all wide-eyed and terrified." The spirit snickered again before looking at Katherine. "Told you it would be worth it."

"Not really," Katherine muttered in reply, her voice shaking.

He narrowed his eyes upon them both, but focused on Katherine, who gripped her skirts a little too tightly. He inhaled deeply, scenting her fear in the air and the sweat on her palms. She was nervous.

She'd known this would perhaps enrage him, and she'd still taken the risk. Why?

With another step closer to her, he inhaled again. Those large eyes watched him, a little too wary of him for all that he'd done. And still, he found this a rather curious situation.

"Why take the risk?" he muttered, reaching out a hand to coil one of her curls through his fingers. "You clearly were afraid that I would be angry."

"I'm not afraid you'll be angry about the spirit." She tilted her chin up, eyeing him up and down. "But I am very wary of what you'll think when it all hits you what that situation was."

"What do you mean?" He could smell her now. That honey coated his throat and spun through his mind like a spell. He could think so little other than what she would taste like.

"It talked to me and I responded."

And then he froze, because she was right. The spirit had spoken to her, and she to it. Like they'd had a conversation before arriving here, and they must have. There was a plan they both followed. Which meant...

He looked at the black mass before searching her gaze. "You can see it."

Katherine nodded, biting that lip in such a way that made him want to do it as well. "And I can see you."

Oh, but those words froze him to the bone. Bitter, icy, he remained locked in place as her words played across the ends of his nerves. "What do you mean, pet?"

"My mother could see spirits. The townspeople thought she was mad, and when she wandered off into the moors, it only made them more certain they were right. But I can see that spirit just fine." She paused, licking her lips before continuing. "And I can see you."

Gluttony wasn't proud of the snarl that ripped out of his throat. "See me?"

"I thought there was something underneath your skin. Ever since I first saw you, there were flickers of something else. Something I didn't understand until I spoke with this one, and now I realize why I have always been able to set you apart from that monstrous side other people see. You're a spirit as well, Gluttony. And I can see it."

This changed everything.

His brothers were going to murder him. Not only was he taking his sweet time in deciphering what the substance was that waited for him in his laboratory, but now he had a young woman who could identify that they weren't demons at all.

He tried to fix this. "I'm a demon."

"No, you aren't." She lifted a hand and placed it on his chest. Right over the spot where his heart thundered against his ribs. "You have a mortal body that your spirit has given powers, yes. But you are not a demon. You're a spirit who has taken flesh."

Staggering away from her, he waved the words away with a coarse laugh. "You have no idea how dangerous those words are, you foolish girl."

"Why?"

He shook his head, denying this conversation had ever happened. He needed to think. This lovely, perfect woman who smelled like honey couldn't know the danger she put herself in.

His brothers would kill her if they realized she existed. They'd come right out to his kingdom and slit her throat in her sleep. No one could know what they were. Where they came from. There were so many vulnerabilities that would be revealed if everyone knew the truth about the demon kings.

"Fuck," he muttered, running a hand down his mouth. "Fuck. I need..."

She took a step away from him again, her eyes going even wider. "Did I do something wrong?"

"Yes," he hissed before shaking his head and pointing down the hall. "There is a room I made ready for you. Go there while I... I have to figure this out."

And he knew he was scaring her, but he needed time. Time to think. Time to plan how to keep her alive.

Chapter 13

Katherine wasn't exactly sure what she'd done to make him so angry. He'd stomped away from her like she'd insulted his very existence. Though, at the very least, he hadn't fed from her yet. Small reassurances, but… it was something.

What would it be like? To have someone pierce her flesh with their teeth and then drink her blood? It seemed wrong. Abhorrent. Something that only the worst sort of monsters did.

And yet, she was the fool who had offered this. And truthfully, she wasn't sure why she'd offered it. Katherine wasn't all that special as she pretended to be.

Maybe he was right. Maybe she just wanted to be a hero.

She meandered through the hallways, comfortable by herself. She probably should have run after seeing those red eyes flash with so much anger, but she hadn't. Instead, she took her time. Peering through the shadows and trailing her hands along the walls so she could find her way. He'd made it seem like the room would be easy to find, but it wasn't. Not really.

She looked into six other rooms before she found one with a fire cheerily crackling in a hearth that had recently been cleaned. The bed was too large for her, and could have fit five people in it. Black sheets slid down the sides, and there were no posts around the edges like she'd expected in a place like this.

The mayor's wife had once had a meeting with all the women in the town. She'd informed them that they were living like paupers, and not a single person would dare to have a bed without posts. In fact, every woman with any means should have one. Not to mention a vanity table with a mirror that wasn't cracked or warped, at least three different kinds of face powders, and ten different pairs of underwear.

Even the memory made Katherine snort as she strode into the room. No posts on the bed, but at least there was a vanity table in the corner with a mirror.

Then she sat on the edge of the bed and it felt like she was sinking into a cloud.

"Oh," she murmured as she flopped onto her back. "This is the difference."

Her own bed was only filled with straw. There were many nights she'd woken with one poking into her side and she'd had to get up and pound the mattress with her fist until everything settled. And it had been filling her room with a very strong scent of mold, so she knew she'd have to empty it soon.

She had no idea what stuffing filled this heavenly bed, but she could only assume it was angel wings and fairy dust.

Even her hip didn't hurt so badly when she was lying on this. Like the mattress was cushioning her wounded body, easing it into a state of relaxation that she hadn't felt since before her injury.

The sound of sinister snickering moved up from underneath her bed. A dark shadow pooled beside her injured hip, still shuddering with glee as it watched her. "That was well worth it."

"You tricked me," she murmured, although she wasn't all that angry. "You said he would be intrigued by a woman who could see spirits."

"And he was, wasn't he?"

"I think you and I have very different opinions on what intrigued means." Katherine rolled onto her side so she could look at the little spirit, her head cushioned on her bicep. "He looked more horrified, shocked, and then angry with me."

Spite snickered again, this time rolling onto what she assumed was its side before righting itself. "He did! Ah, it was perfect. He was so mad at you and the entire world for putting you in his path. Beautiful, that's what that was."

And she was understanding that trusting this spirit would be difficult. Her mother had always said spirits fed off of the emotion, but this one seemed a little different. Almost as though Spite had to feed off the actions of humans, rather than just the emotion within them. Because Katherine certainly didn't want to see Gluttony get angry with her, nor did she want to make his life more difficult.

This was a transaction that served her as well. And her people. If he stopped feeding off everyone else, she had less work, and more people could figure out how to fix this mess of a kingdom they all lived in.

And yet, none of this seemed to be helped by the little spirit still laughing on her bed. Without hesitation, she shoved it back onto the floor. "You're no help."

"He deserves it!" Spite shouted from the floor. "He's a terrible king, and not even remotely a good man. Don't let him fool you, little human. He's a monster through and through."

"That I am," Gluttony's voice cut through their conversation.

Katherine should have known he would come to find her. She just thought she'd have a little more time. Wincing, she sat straight up on the bed and tried to look somewhat put together.

He loomed in the doorway, rivaling the Spite spirit's darkness as he stayed away from the firelight. Almost as though he didn't want the light to touch him.

She had no idea why. He was a stunning vision of a man, and he must know that. So many women had come here, and clearly they hadn't run screaming when they saw him. Hundreds of years worth of women, and she knew many of them were good years. Years that were still in the history books as the best time in this kingdom.

That only brought up more questions. Questions she shouldn't have or care about the answers to. But sitting in a bedroom that he'd clearly cleaned for her, her hands fisted in her lap, his eyes on her, Katherine couldn't help but feel a strange surge of jealousy in her stomach.

"Is it—" Don't ask, don't ask, don't even think about asking. "Is it customary for you to expect the women who give you blood to stay the night?"

It was a stupid question. She knew the answer. The women didn't stay, ever. They returned to the village, broken and bleeding, so that Katherine or one of her coworkers could stitch them back together.

Somehow, the outline of his body stiffened even further. Board straight, he answered her through what sounded like gritted teeth. "They rarely stay long enough for me to offer."

She shouldn't feel any pity about that. She shouldn't care that women ran screaming from him after he almost tore out their throats. The women were right to run from him.

But as he took one step into the room, the light fracturing around the high peaks of his face, she caught his expression of devastation before he hid it. Maybe he wasn't ashamed of feasting upon mortal flesh. Maybe he knew that it was wrong and did it anyway. But the fact that he had been alone for so long, and people ran from him? That ate at his soul.

It wasn't pity that burned in her chest for him. But it was something akin to that.

She knew what it was like to be viewed as different. She knew how it felt to have people look at her as someone that was only good for one thing.

And if her sacrifice could help her people, then she would stay here with him. She'd have to find some common ground, or she'd go mad.

But this feeling had to stop. She had to do something to remind herself that he wasn't just a man who had been cast aside by so many. He was a monster, and monsters deserved to be punished.

Spine still straight, lip curling in disgust that she couldn't help, she asked, "So? Do you wish to feed?"

His hands flexed at his sides before he caught ahold of the reaction. Gluttony gave her a little bow instead and retreated that single step back to the door. "The unique circumstance of your abilities have made me question this entire situation. I need a night to consider what has happened, and the implications of your words."

"That I know you're a spirit, you mean."

He visibly flinched back at the word. "Indeed. No one is supposed to know what we are."

"You can't really believe no one else knows."

"Only the wives of two of my brothers. They are aware of our circumstances, though I highly doubt those conversations were taken lightly. They would never betray the men they love." He cleared his throat, as though the word had stuck in his throat. Love. Did he not believe in the emotion? "This is a different situation. Their partners wished to be with them, and that is why they know what they know. You know nothing about me, nor I you. You could tell anyone, and that is a significant issue to be addressed."

Oh, Spite had done more damage than she'd realized. Folding her hands in her lap so they didn't shake, she nodded. "Ah. So you're going to tell your brothers about me."

His right eye twitched, and he hesitated before responding. "I have not yet made a decision regarding that."

They stared at each other, surveying the situation, before Katherine nodded again. "I will wait until you make your decision, then."

"Good. That is good." He paused in the hallway, looking down into the shadows like he'd rather be anywhere but here. Finally, he said, "Do you require anything else?"

What kind of question was that?

Furrowing her brows in confusion, she replied, "No. This room to wait in will suffice."

He nodded once, twice, three times before awkwardly reaching into the room and closing the door.

"How strange," she muttered, still staring at the ancient wood as she tried to puzzle this man out. Why was he being so kind to her when she was so clearly a risk? His brothers wouldn't enjoy knowing she existed. They'd kill her, maybe. She wouldn't put it past the ruthless lot of them to remove the issue on their own. Maybe they would even send assassins to kill her.

Was that why her mother had run into the moors? Had she realized that someone knew about her existence and known it would be easier to take her own life than wait to see what a demon king chose to do?

The door to her bedroom opened again. Gluttony held a hand over his eyes, as though he'd already expected her to begin undressing in his absence.

"Yes?" she asked, again more confused than she'd ever been in her life.

"Spite," he said, a command in his tone. "You're coming with me."

The little spirit rolled across the floor, grumbling the entire way about evil men and villains who thought they had a right to any maiden in their lives. She watched the entire situation with an amused, soft smile on her face.

But then Gluttony parted his fingers, peering between his middle and pointer. He gave her a soft smile of his own. "Good night, Katherine."

"Good night."

It was altogether strange, wasn't it? He admitted to being the monster everyone thought he was. He didn't hide away from the fact that he was a terrible person doing terrible things. But then he wanted her to have her privacy, and even made certain that the dark spirit who had certainly gotten her in trouble, was gone.

He'd given her this comfortable room and made certain that she needed nothing else. It was...

She would not think about it.

Katherine was going to go to bed, and then she would wake in the morning with a clear head. That's all it would take.

Undressing down to her shift—what else would she sleep in?—Katherine stood in front of the windows and looked out over the moors as the sun sank and the moon rose. She'd always thought this time of the night was magic. When the moon turned everything to gilded silver and sharp-edged gleaming.

She slipped into bed, massaging her hip as well as she could on her own, and then drifted off into a dreamless sleep. So comfortable, even her usual nightmares didn't dare return until she woke in the dead of night, certain something was watching her.

There was a chair in the corner, she realized, with an outline of a man seated in it. He shifted, perhaps realizing she was awake. And he slowly moved the curtain of her window so a slash of moonlight turned his pale skin to a lovely shade of marble grey.

Gluttony sat there, clutching a metal goblet so tightly she could see the dents in the metal. His red eyes weren't glowing, though, and she considered that to be a good sign.

"Hello," she whispered, tilting her head on the bed to look at him. "Why are you here?"

"I shouldn't have put you so close to my own bedroom," he murmured. "I can smell you."

"I can bathe if you need me to." She hadn't thought to bathe before coming up here, obviously. But she'd rather thought it would work in her favor to smell like the almshouse. It was a terrible scent.

The goblet in his hand creaked. The sound was ominous in the dark room. "That's not what I'm talking about."

"Oh." She swallowed hard. Because of course it wasn't. His eyes were locked on the thundering pulse in her neck, and he clearly

146

couldn't think straight.

Maybe she had underestimated the situation. He wasn't acting like a man who wanted what he wanted and would stop at nothing to take it. These were the actions of a man obsessed, of an addiction controlling his body more than it was anything else. He needed, and she had the ability to give it to him.

Nothing had prepared her for this. But she was exhausted and her consciousness was still in that somewhat liminal space between the realm of the waking and the realm of sleep. So she rolled up and then her feet were touching the cold ground. Bare toes already curling, she padded over to him, her limp somehow under control until she paused right before him.

Katherine feared what he could see through her shift. The moonlight glimmered through the thin gray fabric, and she was certain it covered very little. And yet, she still held out her bare wrist for him to take.

He eyed her, gaze wide with some emotion she couldn't name. But then she nodded toward his goblet. "Take what you need, Gluttony. Then I will go back to sleep."

She recognized his expression. Disappointment. But he still cleared his throat, nodded, and then lifted a hand that suddenly had long, thin claws. He almost tapped a rather dangerous part of her wrist before she grabbed him. Gently, she shifted that glinting claw to a safer part.

"Here," she murmured. "Otherwise I'll bleed out in my sleep."

She heard an audible click as he swallowed, but then he made a delicate slice and they both watched in silence as her blood slowly dripped into the goblet. There were only a few clinking noises before he stood.

He was so tall compared to her. She had to stare straight up to even look at him, and she could see him swallow before he gave her a hard nod and then fled her room.

"Strange," she muttered as she turned to find a cloth to bind her wrist with. "Such a strange man."

It didn't escape her notice that his hands had been shaking when he'd cut her wrist. Nor did it escape her notice that the cut had been so shallow it barely bled.

And that he'd only taken a few drops of her blood. As though he was afraid to hurt her.

Chapter 14

He'd never scrub the vision of her like that out of his mind. Silver light touching every part of her body, turning her red hair dark as the blood that drained from her wrist into his goblet.

And oh, she'd been so lovely standing there. Her shift hadn't hidden her form from his eyes in the slightest. He'd seen the soft curve between her ribs and her hip, where his hand would fit so perfectly. Her soft breasts with those dusky rose tips. She'd been cold. He knew the reaction wasn't for him and still seeing those stiff peaks made him want to pull her into his lap. Just a taste. That's all he needed.

Still, she'd given him a taste. He held it in his shaking hand after he'd fled from her like he was terrified of what he would do if he stayed much longer.

He was.

But he'd been terrified for reasons she likely never imagined. Because he had wanted to wrap his hand around those curves at the top of her full hips, to draw her down onto him and let her feel the hard bar of his passion between his legs. He wanted to grind her down onto him, just as he'd done when he'd had her pinned to her bed.

Then he'd thought about how his bed was right behind her. Soft and plush and comfortable enough for him to stretch her out on.

But no. She was here as a deal between him and the rest of her town. Katherine wanted him to feed upon her in trade, nothing more, nothing less. She didn't see him as a man, but an animal that needed to be appeased.

He rounded a corner to the kitchen. It was the warmest room in the castle when the fires were going, and he didn't want to feel so cold right now. Besides, he had to heat her blood before he drank it. Cold blood was terrible, and he wanted...

Ah, he could admit it to himself in the dark room, lit only by firelight. He wanted to pretend he was drinking it from her neck. He wanted to close his eyes and dream up a story that she willingly allowed him to latch onto her throat. That he listened to the beat of her heart and the little gasps that he'd only heard that one time, but had somehow branded itself on his mind.

Gluttony realized he was turning more and more into the monster that he feared he already was. Her presence was making everything worse and yet...

He would survive this. He'd be happy with whatever she gave him, even if her blood was in a goblet. She didn't have to fear what he would do, because he would take the utmost caution with her.

This one would last.

Nothing would happen to his little pet, not while he was here to watch over her.

Gluttony took his time heating her blood, making sure everything was perfect even as he placed the metal goblet into a pot of boiling water. It took a while, but that was all right. He had learned patience in his ancient years. Patience and how to remember to be human.

If he leaned against the counter with spots dancing in his vision, it was only because he was tired. Not because his gaze was locked on that goblet of dark liquid, staring into it like he had lost all sense entirely. He didn't need the blood. He didn't have to drink it. It was a compulsion, nothing more. He was the master of his own body and his own mind and...

The moment it was warm enough, he lunged for it. Gluttony had no self control at all, it seemed, because he tilted the goblet and poured the single mouthful of warm blood down this throat.

He tried to savor it. Tried to keep the blood on his tongue and swirl it around in his mouth so there would be the lingering taste for hours. But the moment her taste hit him, it was enough to send him to his knees.

Honey was right. Honey and everything sweet that he'd ever had in his life. He was suddenly a child who had gotten the best candy, so sweet it made the glands in his throat contract, but he wanted more. So much more that soon he would be sticky and coated with it, and still it would never be enough.

Just as he feared, a single taste made him realize what he'd been missing. If she had been a candy jar, he would have eaten and eaten until he threw up and then still he would have eaten more. She was impossible to resist. A single drop of that blood would have sent him into a frenzy and he was so glad he'd come all the way into the depths of the kitchen because it was that much harder to turn around and race back to her room.

He might have, if he had less control over himself. Gluttony had no question that he would have turned upon her if he'd had a sip in that room. If he'd touched his tongue to her wrist like he'd wanted to, and it all would have been over. He'd have drank her dry and mourned her for the rest of his existence.

This wasn't blood. It was ichor. Dripping in gold and giving him more power than any blood ever had before.

He could feel it. It hit his stomach and traveled throughout his body. Stretching through his arms, through his legs. Making him bigger, stronger, harder than he'd ever been before.

And, oh, the ache in his body was infinitely worse. He couldn't think past the sudden throb in his cock and the images that flashed through his mind as her taste swirled throughout his mouth.

He remembered the little gasp she'd made when he'd laid upon her in that bed. The fire in her eyes had burned so hot he'd wondered what she would do if he'd let her up. And then she'd tilted, just slightly, just enough for him to settle a little more firmly between those legs and he'd felt her heat through her dress.

His hand skidded down his stomach, struggling with the ties of his pants. He'd rocked against her then, just as he now did into his own palm. The little gasp she'd made had been hot and wet in his ear, and even then he'd known it was the same sound she'd make if he indulged himself with her. If he'd smoothed his hand down her swan-like neck to cup her breasts in his hands.

They weren't massive, but they would fill his palms nicely.

Gluttony bucked into his palm, breathing hard as he thought about biting those pale globes. He'd leave teeth marks, signs for any man who ever came again. Scars that would never leave her flesh so that everyone and anyone would know she was his. She'd enjoy it, because he'd make it enjoyable. He'd bite her all over her body if he wished, little trickling trails of blood, just as the one that had leaked down her wrist.

Her flavor would explode on his tongue. Sweet and rich, like honey dripping down every inch of her body until he could feast between her legs. He'd gorge himself on every ounce of her taste, every inch of her form, every drop of her blood until there was nothing left of him at all. Only her, only the essence of her that blasted out any part of him that remained.

Breathing hard, he worked his cock with his hand and lifted the goblet to his nose. He inhaled, drawing her scent deep into his lungs as his passion turned into a frenzy.

Bending over the kitchen table, one forearm braced against the cold tile, he stared unseeing at the condensation of his own breath on the tabletop. His cock ached, his balls drew up tight as he imagined going back to her room.

She'd turn over like she had before, all sleepy and bleary-eyed. Not scared at all, just accepting that he was there and that he needed her. Maybe she'd stand again, or maybe he would draw back the covers and reveal the long limbs of her body. Inch by mouth watering inch. Maybe she would grab the hem of that ugly shift, slide it higher and higher up her thighs until he could finally see all that pretty, pretty pink flesh...

Groaning, he bared his teeth in an ugly snarl as ropes of his cum splattered onto the floor. His heart thundered in his chest and his legs grew weak with the force of it. He hadn't come like that in ages. In centuries. Not since the first time he'd tried it out and realized this human form was worth more than just food.

He'd forgotten what it felt like to have a piece of his soul ripped out in ecstasy, all by the thought of a single woman. He forgot how to breathe. How to think. He could only focus on the sensation and the sudden relaxation that made him sag against the table.

For the first time in years, he thought maybe he actually wanted to sleep. He wanted to curl up on a comfortable bed, with a warm fire crackling in his ears, and a soft woman resting against his chest.

Wincing, he forced himself to stand and tucked himself back into his pants. Reality quickly crashed down upon his ears.

He wouldn't have a pliant woman in his arms. This wasn't a relationship that he'd fostered for years while he wooed her into a lulled sense of safety.

The woman upstairs had traded her life for him to leave her people alone. She hadn't come here because she wanted him, but because she'd seen him as a problem that needed to be fixed. And she was the only one willing to do so, apparently, or the only one that he'd obsessed over for weeks on end.

The mayor of that town might have sent her to him. She might have come here under duress, or without any other options. He'd never asked.

But the truth of the matter was that she didn't want him at all. She was a sweet minded young woman who tasted like candy and he couldn't ever have her, because she didn't want him like that.

Instead, he was the monster in the basement. Masturbating to the thought of her touch when she was likely terrified of him.

Staring down at the puddle between his feet, he resolved himself to this fate. At least if he was the asshole in the basement, he wasn't touching her. And he knew, without a doubt, she wouldn't welcome his touch. She was so beautiful, she could get anyone. All the men in the village must be trailing after her like fools. She didn't need him to be added to that nonsense.

Someday, when all of this was said and done, she'd make herself a family. A handsome, strapping man would find her and they'd make a home on the edge of the moors. He'd give her fine children, tall and lean, with red hair that turned into a bird's nest at the slightest hint of humidity in the air.

And he'd make sure she got to that point. He wouldn't kill this one. He wouldn't even harm her, not in the slightest.

Even if the thought of her leaving someday, the thought of her with another man, made his claws come out and dig long grooves through the tile of his kitchen table.

He didn't have time to think about this. Gluttony needed to clean up. He needed to stagger past her door without knocking, and crawl into his own bed. Maybe he would sleep for a day on end like the last time. Maybe he wouldn't wake up at all, and all her problems would disappear with him.

"She's not happy here," a dark voice split through his thoughts. "You really are a monster to take her away from her friends."

"I know."

"She had a job. An important job in the village, piecing together all the wounds that you yourself have wrought. Did you know she saved a young woman you almost murdered mere nights before you were stalking outside her window?"

He flinched. The dark spirit knew exactly where to prod. It somehow looked deep into his fears and yanked them out, one by one.

"I know she has seen the worst of me," he snarled, still bracing himself against the table. "I know she is aware of the monster inside of me."

"Is it inside you?" Spite asked, slithering onto the opposite end of the table. It crouched there, like an animal that had gotten into his home. "Or are you the monster, Gluttony? How long have you fought against this side of yourself? How long have you realized that there is no hiding from it?"

"I am in control." He ground his teeth so hard he heard the fine bones creaking in his ears. "I will not harm this one."

"But she's already seen all the harm you can do. She's already patched them up. Held their hands while they cried and whimpered, asking her to end their suffering. You have done that. Time and time again." It seemed to grow larger with every word, spreading across his table like black ink until its icy touch reached his hands. "You could end it all now. Show her the real you and indulge in all that you desire."

He shuddered at the mere thought. "You came here with her. Surely you wouldn't want me to barge into her room and drain her dry?"

"It's in my nature to hurt." The dark shadows gathered up into sharp points, thorns that dug into his hands as it anchored him to the table. "And it's in your nature to consume."

Gluttony ripped his hands away from the little beast. He refused to do that to her. He would not harm Katherine, not with her pretty freckles that dusted her nose and the soft, sleepy way she'd approached him.

Like she'd been in a dream.

As if she dreamt of him coming to her in the middle of the night while she allowed him every dark desire. She was more than just food. She was an indulgence to his worst and best memories.

Times when he had thought he could be human.

She was the sacrifice. The moment in time when he would remember exactly how much he had once wanted to love and be loved. She was the proof that though he was a monster, though he had sunk to his lowest in years, that he was still capable of control.

He could still consume without murdering. He could still be a person around others, even though he had known for a very long time that he was nothing but a beast. An animal.

A lost cause.

"No," he hissed. And perhaps there was power in his words, because even Spite recoiled from him. "I will not be the monster to her. She is welcome here. Do you understand? Welcome and alive for the rest of her time in this castle and for all times after this. You, however, are not welcome. If I see you again, I will crush you beneath my heel. Do you understand me?"

"One cannot kill a spirit."

"Perhaps not." He leaned over the little creature, seething and desiring to tear into it for all the harm it had caused. "But you forget that I am Gluttony. There are many things I have yet to try to consume, little spirit. But your kind is not one of those. I have eaten many spirits in my time, and devoured many souls in my attempt to become something other than what I am. Do not tempt me to try again, Spite. And oh yes, I remember now who you are. You'll find it is very easy for a demon king to end your suffering."

The spirit rolled off the table and disappeared into the shadows. And though it should have felt like a victory, he remained alone and defeated.

Gluttony once again braced himself against the table, head dangling between his shoulders as he tried to get a hold of himself.

"I am not always a monster," he whispered. "I am in control."

Chapter 15

Although the castle was as beautiful as it was terrifying, Katherine quickly realized she wasn't needed here. There wasn't anything for her to do. He asked her to stay for a few more nights, and every night was the same.

She would cuddle into the bed after a boring day of doing nothing and poking around the castle, hoping to find something entertaining, and then he would wake her when the moon was at its peak.

Every night she staggered out of bed, a little more tired than the evening before, and allowed him to cut through the same scab on her wrist. He never took too much blood. In fact, she thought he was rather careful to make sure that he didn't drain her. Or even really take enough to affect her all that much.

But she was already tired of it. Just last night, she hadn't even been able to fall asleep by the time he'd come to her room. Not because she was anticipating his arrival, but because she wasn't tired.

Katherine was used to doing things. Anything. Sometimes when the clinic was quiet, she would be the person to wander out to people's homes. Just to talk with them, make sure they were healing well enough or that their stitches weren't infected.

She had never had such a long amount of time where she did nothing. Katherine was dying from it. She was certain. And though she would have told any patient that no one could die from boredom, she was quite certain that she was wrong. Because she was going to die.

Today, she would not stand for it anymore. She had dresses to wash, shifts that had turned into sweat stained messes, and she had enough energy to burn. If there wasn't a laundry room in this place— which she was certain there had to be—then she would make do in the kitchens. It wouldn't be the first or the last time that she'd washed her clothes in a sink.

Wandering out into the hall, she paused to listen as she always did.

There were no sounds here. None. Every house she'd ever lived in had the normal sounds of life. People shuffling around, creaking floorboards, the soft scrape of mice chewing in the walls. All signs that another person was around her and that she wasn't alone.

Here? It was only silence.

Unnerving, unnatural silence, as though the entire world held its breath because it didn't know who or what would arrive next. Would yet another victim present themselves to the demon king? Would he rip out their throat this time or would he let them live?

They were morbid thoughts, but what else was she supposed to think? Wandering through the dark halls, usually with a candle in her hands because light never penetrated through the dusty windows, she had come to think of herself as living in a tomb.

Maybe she was already dead, she mused as she rounded a corner and picked up the candelabra she left just for this purpose. The small matchbox next to it was already running low on matches, but she kept forgetting to ask Gluttony about getting more.

Perhaps because their interactions every night always felt like a dream. He was there right at the edge of sleep, every time she thought maybe it was a nightmare, but he was always so kind about it. Gluttony looked over her wrist, watching her movement, perhaps to see if she walked funny from lack of blood.

Katherine always had the thought that perhaps this man did not understand humans very well. He only took a few thimbles full of blood every night, and then food always appeared in front of her door. Piles and piles of food, as though he thought she ate as much as a village.

But she knew enough about humans and loss of blood, so she ate. Just as much as she wanted.

"I'll get fat if I stay here too long," she mused as she wandered down the hall. "Now, if I were a laundry room, where would I be?"

Her village had one that they all shared. It was very close to the water, and had a wall built between the swamp and it, so a tiny stream of liquid could trickle through without risking anyone's lives if a creature fell through.

They'd all heard stories about towns who didn't have that. Washing their clothing in the water was a risk that so few of them could afford to take. Unfortunately, that meant most of those towns had a lot of illness.

This castle definitely had a laundry room. It had to.

Squaring her shoulders, she marched through the eastern wing of the castle. She hadn't been in this part very much, considering her own was in the western wing, and she chose to work in a clockwise search. Although she wasn't nearly finished with any of the wings. This castle was so large it would take her more than a few days of exploration to see even one.

But she knew the kitchen was in the east wing. Which meant maybe that wing was meant more for servants than for visitors.

"This is the right way to go," she muttered to herself.

And that was the other part of her problem. She was so lonely.

Gluttony didn't speak to her in the middle of the night. He was just there when she woke and then gestured for her to move with a single flick of his fingers. She could see the hunger in his eyes, but that was for her blood. Not for her.

Then he left. With no thank you or how are you feeling, nothing at all. He just disappeared into the shadows of his castle and she was always so tired she never thought to follow him.

Strangely, it had left her feeling rather achy with a spot on her chest that refused to stop hurting, no matter how many times she rubbed at it.

The eastern wing was not as quiet as her own. She picked up on the crackling sound of a furnace hidden somewhere, likely the reason why the entire castle wasn't as cold as a tomb. And there were a few scratching noises that she assumed were rats. Perhaps there was a room full of food, where Gluttony collected her meals only to place them in front of her door and race away before she could see him.

Rolling her eyes, Katherine adjusted the weight on her shoulders and continued forward until she heard the faint sound of bubbling.

She'd know that sound anywhere. Perhaps she was mistaken, but those sounded like burners and bubbling concoctions that she'd worked with in the almshouse. At least, a little. And there, that was absolutely the sound of glass clinking against glass.

Why would those sounds exist here? She couldn't imagine he had a place for healing in this house of blood sacrifices, so...

Katherine changed her searching direction and went instead to the sounds. It took her a few times of pressing her ear against a door before she was relatively certain she had found the correct one. And then, gently, she eased the door open so no one would hear her.

It wasn't an almshouse. It was a laboratory.

Jaw falling open, she stared into the room full of glass jars, beakers, winding glass tubes that rose and twisted through each other in intricate knots of bubbling, colored liquids that funneled and wove around each other.

The room was lit by electricity, much like Gluttony's office. Naked bulbs hung from the ceiling and illuminated the entire room with very clear precision. It glinted off the glass of the tubing, and she wondered why there was so much of it.

She supposed he might have an alchemist working for him. Though she couldn't imagine a reason for an alchemist to even be here. Gluttony had made it very clear that he didn't think he could be cured. So there was no reason to have an alchemist on the premises.

Decorum entirely forgotten, she strode into the room with curiosity burning through her veins.

Katherine set her laundry on the floor so she didn't knock into any important glass pieces, and then strode over to one of the nearby tables. There was more glass on this one, she thought, perhaps rejects of the research going on here.

At least, she could only assume. She had watched over the shoulder of the two alchemists who came into their almshouse to replace all the potions necessary to heal their patients. She had watched them avidly, wanting nothing more than to become like them.

The beakers on this table were full of a tar-like black substance that clearly was an experiment gone wrong. Those were usually thrown into the moors or the muck in the almshouse, so she was rather surprised to see them preserved here. In a jar, of all things.

Humming underneath her breath, she made her way from table to table, in the room that easily could have fit an entire crowd of people. Had he converted a ballroom into this space? But why?

And then, as she got closer to the back, she saw him.

Not an alchemist at all. But Gluttony himself.

He'd taken off his vest and dropped it on the floor as though the hand embroidered piece wasn't worth the cost of an entire town here. He'd rolled his sleeves up, revealing long, pale forearms that flexed with each of his movements. Graceful fingers danced between the beakers, lifting one, letting a drop of liquid roll out before carefully placing it back where it had come from.

She could only stare at his broad back and tapered waist where he sat on a small, uncomfortable looking stool as he worked. Even now, the black waterfall of his hair had not a strand out of place.

But at least she'd seen it with dust covering that darkness. It made him seem a little more... real.

Swallowing hard, she told herself not to look at the veins on his forearms or the way their dark color seemed to ripple underneath his skin.

Katherine didn't try to hide her presence. She didn't have to. Her booted feet were loud, and the tell-tale thud, slide of her bad leg announced her presence even when she wanted to hide herself.

So instead, she walked up to his table and looked down at what he was working on. He had multiple beakers, two of which appeared to only have a colored mist in them, two with black liquid, and another with a strange dark smoke that swirled around as though it were fighting to get out of the beaker.

A single glass orb was in front of him. More of that swirling mist inside it as he had dropped a single speck of liquid upon it. And as she watched, he looked more at the other smoke than the orb in front of him.

The black mass swirled, stilled, and then seemed to go back.

"Shouldn't you pay more attention to that?" she asked.

Gluttony let out a sound that she had never heard a man make before. With a shriek somewhere between a growl and the haunting call of a banshee, he moved so quickly that she didn't even see the claws erupt from his hand. She only felt the wind of them, as he froze with those long, dagger-like nails so close to her throat that she didn't dare swallow.

He was wearing glasses, she realized. Circular glasses with thin wire frames that perched on top of his nose and, damn it, that shouldn't be so attractive, but it really was.

His eyes widened as he realized who she was. "Katherine?" he asked, as though he didn't believe she was standing right in front of him.

"I didn't mean to startle you." She risked swallowing, his nails brushing the long column of her throat and leaving what felt like welts behind.

He grunted, dropping his hand immediately. "I am unused to anyone else being in this home, pet. I should be the one apologizing."

"I didn't realize there were places in the castle I wasn't supposed to go."

"There is not a single room that you are barred from in this place."

Gluttony stood, knocking over his stool in the process. He winced and bent to pick it up. "Is it lunch time already? I have been very busy and I'm afraid time must have gotten away from me."

"It's not lunchtime."

"Oh." His usually smooth brow furrowed in confusion at that. "Why are you out of your room, then?"

She was going to hit him. She was going to smack that confusion right off of his face because surely he wasn't so dull that he couldn't see the problem?

"I..." Katherine blinked, trying to get her words right so he wouldn't kick her out of the castle outright. "I'm bored."

He had yet to stop staring at her like she'd grown an extra head. "Why?"

"Because it's been days and all I've done is sit in that room or perhaps look around a little in the castle, but there's not really a lot here for me to do."

"No, I suppose there isn't. But is that not what you want?"

"To do nothing?" There was her temper again. Perhaps she spoke a little too curtly, but she couldn't stop herself from adding, "What woman doesn't want to waste away in a corner until she grows mold?"

"Excuse me?"

Katherine jabbed a finger at him, poking him so hard in the chest he flinched. "I don't want to sit around and just be some mindless blood donor for you! If you wanted me to do this, then at least let me go home! I have use there. I work in the almshouse, and there are people who could use my stitching right now. I'm certain of it."

Gluttony took a step away from her, his eyes somehow going even wider as he lifted his hands in peace. "I'm not requiring you to stay. I just thought you'd be more comfortable here. My home has down feathers and silk sheets and all the food you could want."

"And I refuse to be some rolling ball of food for you!" Katherine jabbed him again, her hand quickly slipping between the defense of his own to hit him hard in the ribs. "I'm going back to the almshouse and you can't stop me."

"You'll reek."

"I don't care what I smell like to you," she hissed. "I'm not your pet!"

He tilted his head to the side as though disagreeing with her. "Well, if you want to get technical—"

"Finish that sentence." Katherine curled her lip in threat. "I dare you."

He almost looked... frightened of her until he shook the emotion off with a visible movement. "Ridiculous. You cannot threaten me."

Katherine was apparently feeling rather reckless. She should have backed down, she knew. This was a demon, and she could still feel his marks on her neck where he'd just barely grazed her with his claws.

If he wanted, Gluttony could remove her head from her shoulders and he wouldn't even feel all that bad about it. He was as dangerous as holding a knife to her jugular. But she wasn't afraid of him right now.

And frankly, she was a little thrilled to finally be doing something other than sitting and staring at a wall.

She took a single step back and grabbed a beaker full of yellow mist. "I can threaten you all I want. I will pour this entire bottle into that one if you don't give me something to do."

The other bottle was the one with the black mist, and the one she was quite certain was more important.

Considering the flash in his red eyes, she'd guessed correctly. "You don't know what you're doing."

"Maybe I don't. Or, maybe I do." She tilted the yellow mist in her hands. "I think you already tried this combination, and that's why you were staring at it. You know this yellow stuff will destroy what you're testing."

"Easy there, pet."

"I have steady hands," she assured him, but those steady hands were still tilting the bottle. "I'd like to help you in your lab."

"It's far too dangerous for a human." His nose wrinkled and then smoothed out. Perhaps a desperate attempt to keep his glasses on his nose where they were already sliding a bit. "I will not risk you."

"You don't want to risk my blood, you mean. Truly, I have no intention of murdering myself in this room full of what I can only assume are explosive substances."

Mouth off one more time, she thought to herself. Just do it. She wanted to see what would happen if he thought she wasn't serious.

Gluttony crossed his arms over his chest and frowned at her. "Your skirts will get in the way."

"I doubt that."

"They will." But then he waved his hand at her, as though he were the king submitting to all her desires. "But if you think you will be of use, little human, let's see what you are capable of."

Chapter 16

Gods forbid his little pet was bored.

Gluttony was a fool. He absolutely should not have given in to her request. Namely, because having her this close to him, in his space, did things to his head that he wasn't proud of.

Like how a voice whispered that he could still smell other people on her skin. That maybe if he just rubbed his face against the crook of her neck, where most women would put perfume, then he could make her smell like him. And then he could run his tongue up that lovely column, feeling her heart beat against his lips when he sank his teeth into her throat. Drinking from her? He knew that would be as close to holy as he would ever experience.

And yet, another part of him realized these thoughts were foolish. He would never be anyone to her other than a monster. This was why he'd been treating her like royalty. She had food, time to herself, space away from the beast that demanded so much from her.

But if she wanted to sacrifice her time to him as well... He was too weak to resist.

Giving her new clothing had been, in part, a distraction. He needed time to get his head on straight and prepare himself for her nearness. The longer he was in her presence, the more it was likely he would beg for more than a taste of her blood.

His fangs already ached. His claws wouldn't go back into his fingers because they wanted to touch her one more time. The desire to drag the tips along her freckled skin consumed him. What would she do if he touched her like that?

Would that lovely, lily white skin pebble with bumps? Would she shiver in anticipation at what he would do next?

Of course she wouldn't, he reminded himself as he put the beakers back in their places. She would shudder in disgust because a monster dared to touch her. That was what she would do. He had no reason to think she would do anything otherwise.

Sighing, he shook his head to clear it of all those terrible thoughts. She only wanted to feel useful. As anyone else would wish to do.

The door to his laboratory opened—this time he heard it just fine—and she approached him, already muttering. "The man thinks my clothes would get in the way? What does he think this will do?"

He'd given her some of his own clothing to wear. Just a plain white peasant shirt and some pants that would cover her legs. Her skirts would have gotten in the way. She could so easily trip over them, or knock into a table. It was easier to wear pants here, and much easier to be able to roll her sleeves up. They were in a lab, not some silly human house, where they tried their best to heal people.

This was real work. Not just stitching.

But then he turned around, and all thoughts fled from his mind. His clothing swallowed her up. Entirely. She could have just worn his shirt and belted it around the waist, and it would have been perfectly fine to wear. The sleeves came down so far over her hands that he couldn't guess even where they were. The pants fared better, or at least he assumed so. They weren't down around her ankles, although they were bunched up at the bottoms since they were so long.

A soft smile crossed his face before he could catch himself. "Ah," he breathed, then gestured for her to come closer. "Those are much too large for you."

"And you think they would be better in a laboratory? You realize I'm going to set this on fire if I lean forward at all?"

That smile refused to leave his face. Even though that was a terrifying situation to imagine, she was just so... adorable. All flustered and angry with him, with clothing that was far too big for her.

"Come here," he said, gesturing for her to approach him where he sat on his stool.

And when she stood between his legs, he was shocked to realize she was only barely taller than him while he was seated. How was he only now realizing how short she was? How small?

It made him want to wrap her up in his arms and tuck her away for good, but he could already see the fire in her gaze, like she knew what he was thinking. Like she dared him to say that she was small or needed to be taken care of.

So instead, he reached for her sleeve and tugged her a step closer. "We don't wear these down," he said, gently rolling them a few times before he discovered her hand. "Roll them up until they're above your elbow, pet, then you won't have to worry about the fire."

He settled into the pattern of rolling fabric and making sure she was all right. And in doing so, he realized how easy it was to just... be with her. There was no difficulty, no nervousness, no awkward feelings of whether or not he was messing this up or doing it in a way that made her uncomfortable. None of that.

She just stood there, watching him roll her sleeves with a soft expression on her face. And when he looked at her, his red eyes flicking up to her green, he wondered what she was thinking. Why she was looking at him as though she wanted to touch him, to lean in and press her lips to his own so he could feel how sweet it was to be thanked by her.

Katherine cleared her throat and took a step back. "Right. Well, thank you."

"You're welcome."

He sat there, just looking at her. He wasn't afraid to do so, obviously, considering he'd stalked her for weeks before this moment. But he'd never noticed how the light could sparkle in her eyes, or how she stood with most of her weight on one hip. It tilted her body in a lovely curve, on display for his eyes if he so wished to let them linger on her curves.

"Why are you looking at me like that?" she asked.

"Like what?"

"Like you do when you wake me up in the middle of the night." She brushed a stray curl behind her ear. "I could... If you wanted to..."

The poor dear really thought he was hungry all the time, didn't she? He was, he was ashamed to admit. Gluttony would feast upon her if she offered it, but he knew she didn't want him to. She only offered because she didn't know what to do with his eyes on her like this, and he was ruining it.

He turned his back to her and put his attention back on the table.

"Ah, pet, there's no need for that. My nightly visits are more than enough."

"Are they really?"

Her words seared through him.

No.

They weren't.

They would never be enough because what he wanted was to be buried so deep between her thighs that he couldn't tell where he ended and where she began. He wanted to hear her whimpers in his ears, echoing with every one of his thrusts as he drank deeply from her neck, her breast, between her thighs. He wanted to be so covered in her that his sensitive nose would know where she was everywhere in his kingdom. No matter how far she ran.

But he couldn't tell her any of that. He'd terrify her. She would run off to one of his brothers and only reiterate that he'd lost his mind. That he wasn't safe for any of his people to be around.

So he reached for a beaker and he did not respond to that question. Instead, he blindly held it out for her to take. "Hold this."

A pale hand reached past his shoulder and he could almost feel her against his back. A sudden desire flushed through him, turning his cheeks bright red. It wasn't even that he wanted her blood, but he wanted to know what it would feel like to wake with her pressed against his back like that.

Would she be limp and quiet, like she was in the middle of the night? He'd wake, the sunlight playing across his face in a rare moment when they could actually see the sun. Her warmth spread across his back, her face pressed right between his shoulder blades as though she fit against him like a puzzle piece.

Warmth. When was the last time he'd woken and been warm?

She held onto the beaker and gave the liquid inside a little swish. "What is this?"

Breaking himself out of this strange melancholy, he looked over at what he'd handed her. "Sweet vitriol, it's, uh—"

"Sulfuric acid and wine," she supplied, swishing it again. "Why am I holding it?"

"So you have something to do."

To his complete and utter shock, she gave him a gentle smack to the back of his head. "Don't be sassy. Answer the question."

"That is the real reason," he replied with a soft chuckle. He ran a hand over the back of his head as if she could ever really hurt him, before turning back to his table. "I am uncertain what this substance is, and it's been fighting with me every step of the way."

"The black smoke?"

He nodded, trying to get his head back into the same place it usually was. Clear-headed. Capable of seeing straight through any material and knowing what was in it. But this smoke continued to evade him.

"Have you considered it may be magical in origin?"

"I've tried all the spells that I know of, and my brothers are also researching it." Too much information, he reminded himself. She didn't need to know what it was. She only needed to have something to do.

With that in mind, he picked up a pair of metal tongs and handed them to her as well.

"So it's definitely not magical, then?" She moved, leaning past him to pick up another beaker and organizing them next to each other. To his surprise, she had organized them correctly. Both of them were magical in origin, spells that he'd funneled into beakers before they overheated the glass. "You aren't lacking in knowledge that's holding this endeavor back, I assume?"

"You truly enjoy thinking the worst of me."

"I'm merely asking if you missed something, that's all." She smiled at him and he felt like the entire ceiling had ripped open and let the sun pour in. "I often watched the alchemists when they came into the almshouse. They were quite certain they always knew the correct answer to every question they had, but I often thought perhaps they were missing things."

"Such as?"

"How human bodies work. How people think. What they should consider when they were trying to cure a person's sickness. Most of the times they thought they knew what was wrong long before they even spoke to a patient. It was frustrating for the sick person, who often had an idea of what might be wrong. And instead, they were told they were wrong without the alchemist or healer even asking how they felt. It often delayed the healing process considerably." A tiny wrinkle appeared on her brow.

He paused again, curiosity peaking from her expression. "And you thought you knew better?"

"I was certain I did." Then she bit her lip and shrugged. "In most cases, at least. Sometimes they were right. But when they were wrong, it was always to the detriment of the patient."

"Interesting."

And it really was. She had become an object in his mind, an obsession. And honestly, he would have seen none of her flaws even if she waved them in front of his face. He would take them all. Beat him, try to murder him in his sleep, shove a knife in his throat. He didn't care what she did to him as long as he could drink from her veins.

But now, he was faced with the reality of an actual person. A thinking, breathing, intelligent woman who tempted him more than he'd realized possible.

Katherine's brows drew down again, and her glare seared right through him. "You're looking at me like that again."

"I..." He cleared his throat and turned his attention back to the table. "You are surprising, pet."

"Am I?"

"Most women who come here have no interest in learning anything about the castle or myself. They had their desires. I gave them what they wanted in exchange for my own desires. I am... I find it difficult to know what to say or do with you." Speaking of which, he handed her a small glass vial that was empty but didn't need to be on his table.

She took that as well and then rearranged it on a table nearby. It was so easy for her to see where to put things, and even the tongs had gone to the waistband of her pants as though she was well aware that he'd need them again soon enough.

"I see," she replied, when she reached his side again. "It's rather difficult to speak with people and have them in your space when you've never had that before. Is that it?"

"That is part of it." The other part was how badly he had to focus to not stare at the throbbing pulse at her neck, but he supposed she didn't need to hear that.

"Then I don't wish to distract you any further from your work. I can find something else to do in this giant castle."

She moved to take the tongs out of her waistband, but he stopped her with a hand around her wrist. Holding her in place so she didn't... Just didn't.

He swallowed hard. "You don't need to do that. It's rather nice to have someone else around. I don't mind it."

"But it makes you uncomfortable."

He stared up into those bright eyes and felt himself shatter a little. He didn't want to be alone anymore. Couldn't she see that? Even though he knew he and his brothers were monsters, and they had single-handedly ruined this entire realm, and torn apart the kingdoms, so they would never come back together again... He only wished he deserved an ounce of her attention.

"You make me nervous." He shook his head and started again. "Stay. Please."

Could she see inside his head? She stared at him as though she could, peering through the very vestiges of his soul before she nodded. "If you'd like the company, I can stay."

Relief made him a little light-headed. With a clawed finger— when had those come out again?—he pointed to another table that was mostly empty of dangerous substances. "You can start there. I can already see you're much better at organizing than I am."

"I'd rather see if I can make something blow up."

The strange spell she'd weaved around him shattered. Chuckling, he shook his head and turned back to his own project. "I imagine you would, pet. I imagine you would."

And so they spent the rest of the afternoon in relative silence. But he could hear her. Humming underneath her breath as she tackled the arduous and rather impossible task of organizing his laboratory.

For an afternoon, he didn't feel quite so alone. Gluttony feared he could get used to this.

Chapter 17

The first day she came to him and said she was going back to the clinic, Gluttony had no issues with it. He knew there wasn't enough to do here, and they had made no progress in his laboratory. Of course, she wanted to do something with herself.

He'd paced beside the front door for hours at a time, waiting for that knock that made his soul ease, but he had not argued. He'd let her go, and then she'd returned. Just as she promised.

The relief he'd felt when she walked through those doors again? Ah, it was better than anything he'd ever imagined.

And yet, the more she did it, the worse he felt. He didn't want her leaving the castle. He didn't want her returning with the scents of so many people on her. He wanted her to stay here, and he wanted to rub himself over her entire body so he could forget that she'd spent hours with others.

Gluttony knew those thoughts made him almost like Greed. But he wanted every part of her, every ounce of her time and attention as well. He wanted to swallow up all those hours with her and consume them until there was nothing but him and her and the rest of the world was gone.

And then the madness set in.

He could feel it even now, crawling up his throat and gripping him by the neck. She didn't know that when she left, he could do nothing but sit on the floor beside the door. At first, he'd tried to busy himself with work or with cleaning. Katherine deserved a castle that was built for a queen and he wanted to be the one who gave that to her.

But he couldn't. He'd tried to force his limp body up, but all he could do was sit in the shadows, waiting until she knocked on the door.

Tonight, she was late. So late that it made his heart thud harder in his chest. Should he go and get her? No, that was an overreaction. No one in the town wanted to see him, anyway. They'd run from him screaming if they realized their demon king was in their town. She was a capable woman. She'd lived there her entire life and hadn't fallen into the swamps yet.

But what if she had? What if she had fallen, and some creature had snatched her up? He could help her. He could save her from that situation like no other mortal could.

A black mass coalesced beside his hip and he knew the little spirit was only going to make this worse. It did every single day, and yet he couldn't care less.

Gluttony almost wanted to feel its words digging into him like sharp knives. He was not and never would be, what she needed.

Spite sat down beside him and hissed out a long breath. "She's not coming back this time."

"She'll be back," he replied, although there was no certainty in his words. "She promised."

"Promises mean nothing to her kind."

"She has come back every day. She won't leave us here alone."

"Why wouldn't she?" The dark spirit rolled in front of him, rising a little taller. It hadn't been feeding off Katherine, Gluttony was relieved to see. The spirit was still rather small. "She has nothing here, and no reason to return. You haven't convinced yourself that she feels something for you, have you? That girl has a life outside of you."

"I have given her so much here." Gluttony had to believe that. He had to believe that she would return, because otherwise he was just the monster in the castle who hadn't changed. Who hadn't proven to anyone that he could change.

"What? A comfortable bed and food?" Spite snorted. "You do not know humans if you believe that will satisfy her for very long. She does not care if you are a king, Gluttony. She wants a life and people to be in it. You've asked her to rot here in this castle with you."

Had he?

Gluttony had thought they'd started a rather decent life together. She worked with him in the laboratory most days, cleaning up everything that he'd made a mess of. And then she'd head off to the clinic, after which he would unfortunately sit frozen in this same spot. Once she returned, he made sure she had dinner and then popped her off to bed.

Then, once he returned to his lab and realized he needed to feed, he would...

Spite hissed. "Do you really think she wanted to be your blood donor forever? Gluttony, you fool. She doesn't care for you, or me, or this place at all. This is a transaction and you haven't given her any reason to stay. She's going to remain in that village just like the rest of them. She's no different from any other woman who came here and asked for something."

A stuttering breath escaped him. He couldn't... He couldn't believe that. She would return. She always had, and there was no reason for him to question her integrity.

Until she didn't come back.

He sat there, frozen as the night came. The sound of crickets erupted into a symphony that then died down yet again. Until there was nothing. No one. Just him in the darkness.

The next day came and went. The sun rose and the moors burst into life. He could hear the dragonflies flitter past his door and the burbling sounds of kelpies and their kin. He could hear it all, and yet, no human came to his castle.

Even Spite said nothing. And in his mind, even though he knew the spirit was enjoying this terrible thing that had happened to Gluttony, he liked to imagine that the spirit had some sense of guilt.

He had been left alone, yet again. And never in his life would he find another like her, because he didn't think he had it in him to do this with another.

Katherine would be the last, he decided. He would lie down in one of the comfy beds upstairs, perhaps hers, and then he would waste away into nothing.

It was long pastime. Maybe someone would eventually come to the castle again, and then they would spread the rumor that Gluttony had left. He would disappear into the storybooks and nightmarish stories that people told. Not even his brothers would look for him.

No one cared about the monster in the castle. Their lives would be better without him, and they certainly had no pity in their hearts if he simply disappeared. They'd rejoice, and the world would be a better place for it.

"Get angry at her," Spite hissed. "She made you a deal."

"And she went back on it." What was the spirit's point? "They all do, in the end."

"No, they don't. They all get what they want. They give you something in return. You should be furious! So angry that you could tear out her throat and take all that you want in one swallow." Spite rolled in front of the door, staring up at the wood before turning to look at him. "If she ever walks through this door again, you should feast upon her."

The need was there. Oh, it burned inside him. He hadn't gotten a taste of her last night, and he had been so certain that those little tastes were holding the hunger at bay. Now he wanted more. He wanted everything she could give him, and he knew it was wrong.

He sat in that hunger, in that terrible feeling until suddenly, a knock at the door.

Gluttony surged to his feet, ignoring the creaking sound of his knees and hips. He stumbled, catching himself on the wall before he staggered over to the door.

Wrenching it open, he braced himself on the door frame and stared down at her.

She had dark circles underneath her eyes. She looked as exhausted as he felt, and Gluttony rarely slept at all. The same clothes she'd left in hung from her body, limp and wet at the hem from her journey to his castle. Those green eyes stared up at him, and he could feel something unspoken pass between them. His Katherine was home. He was too addicted to her, too reliant on having someone in this cold house with him.

And yet, on the tail end of that thought, came the anger that she'd left at all. She hadn't needed to go to the almshouse. And she hadn't even asked if he was all right with her going. She'd done this to him, leaving him here on his own and with all these emotions festering deep in his core.

The anger was swift. It scorched through his chest until he could hardly think of anything else. But he pushed it aside for a few seconds.

He quietly asked, "Are you well?"

"Tired," she replied, but her shoulders squared like she already knew what was going to happen. "But well enough."

"Good." He moved only slightly to the side, one arm still braced over her head. "Get in."

She had to skirt past him, her body brushing against his as she moved underneath his arm and into the house. He told himself to have better control, to not give in to this anger and temptation and... fuck, he just wanted to hold her, but he wasn't capable of doing that.

He wasn't a man. He was a monster. And now he would prove that to her.

Hissing out an angry breath, he spun and let the door slam shut behind him. To her credit, Katherine didn't even flinch at the sound. She froze in the center of his hall, waiting for his next move.

"You've been gone for such a long time," he snarled, moving closer until he was right behind her. She must be able to feel the heat pouring off his body in waves of rage. "Where were you?"

"There was an accident. The almshouse needed assistance, and I stayed overnight to help."

"What kind of accident?"

"The kind only a demon can cause."

He had done nothing, but if she wanted to think of him as the monster, then that suited him. Gluttony didn't care what she thought of him tonight. He only cared that she was here, and he was hungry.

So hungry.

Brushing her hair off the column of her throat, he licked the pointed tips of his fangs. "You did not warn me that you would be gone for so long."

Her bravery was admirable, but it was not limitless. Katherine swallowed hard, then took a step away from him. She turned, her eyes narrowing upon him. "I wasn't under the impression that I needed to tell you where I was going, as long as I was here for your food at the end of the day."

"And were you?"

Her eyes flashed with anger. "No."

He could see her highlighted with a red glow. It played across her features and set her hair on fire, blazing with all the anger that she likely felt as well. And oh, he was nothing but a moth to her flame.

"I have waited a very long time, Kat." He backed her down the hall toward one of the receiving rooms. It was covered in dust, white sheets over the furniture and every mirror in it covered. The only decorations were the spiderwebs above their heads that hung from the chandelier like strings of pearls.

Once inside, he slowly sat down on what he remembered was a couch. Spreading his legs wide, he placed one hand on his knee and the other gestured for her. "Come here."

His little pet took one step and then stopped.

Did she really think it was a good idea for her to toy with him? Now?

"Closer," he snarled.

"I can find the goblet, if you desire—"

"I don't." Gluttony shouldn't interrupt her. He shouldn't be this demon that turned the room red with the power of his desire, but he... wanted. "I have waited long enough, don't you think? We've played this game for quite some time."

"And I have yet to lose the game."

"Checkmate." He curled a single, taloned finger. "It is time, Katherine."

"Because I left?"

"Because I stayed in front of that door for hours waiting for you to return! And you didn't. Do you know what that does to a man?" He was saying too much, damn it. He was supposed to be the monster, not the pathetic sap who waited for her. "Now, come here."

She was so beautiful walking toward him. It took everything in him to not reach out and slam her down onto his lap. But she did that on her own.

Delicately. Gracefully. Katherine strode between his open legs and then set herself down on his thigh. With a practiced move, she brushed the hair from her throat and looked at him defiantly. "Shall we, then?"

The deep groan in his throat proved just how much of an animal he was. Gluttony lunged, his arms locking around her and tilting her entire body. He dragged her where he wanted her, spreading her thighs over his hips as he positioned her. He wasn't sure Katherine was even aware of how she draped her arms delicately over his shoulders, or how she'd pressed her core to his.

Blood, life, the smell and taste of her surrounding him. That's what he wanted. Needed. Desired.

Until her fingers ghosted over his lips as he descended toward her throat. And he paused. Somehow, he held himself back as her fingers traced the outline of his lips.

"Not there," she whispered, gently moving his face to a higher portion of her neck. "You'll hurt me."

And he didn't want that. No, he didn't want this to hurt her. He wanted her writhing on his lap, moaning in his ear, enjoying this as much as he would. And yet, he realized he was too far gone for that. Too far gone for any of it.

Fangs flashing, he sank his teeth into her throat. The long points did the job so quickly she only had a chance to stiffen before he drew them out of her flesh. It was a simple puncture, enough for him to draw deeply from her throat.

Her blood splashed out on his tongue and oh, honey. Pure honey straight from the hive poured down his throat, and it was divine. It was everything. It was life, warm and glowing as it spread through his body.

He was vaguely aware of his hands flexing against her waist. How he dragged her even closer, setting her down hard upon his stiffening cock so that he could grind up into her.

And Katherine... Oh, his pet pressed back.

Her long fingers carded through his hair, rasping her nails down his scalp as he bent over her like the monster he was. She held him closer, her legs clamping down around his hips. She even moved. Shifting against him. Rocking back and forth like she couldn't help herself.

The gods looked down upon them and wept.

His pet in the arms of a devil, giving away her very soul so that she could save countless others. Ah, he was the monster he always feared.

But he couldn't stop. He clutched her harder, drawing her further into his embrace and drinking so deeply he felt her shudder. Yes, this was what he wanted. He wanted her shivering and shaking and needing him for all eternity.

She would never leave this place. He would keep her safe and sound for the rest of her life because he couldn't ever let her go. Not after this. Not after knowing what her blood tasted like pouring down his throat and into his very being.

He would smell like her. Taste like her. He would consume her until there was nothing left.

Katherine tapped his shoulder once, twice, but he couldn't let her go. His hands curved into claws, sinking into the fabric of her dress and through the soft skin beneath. He snarled at the scent of more blood. Would it taste better from her back? Her breast? That pretty little dip where her hips and waist met?

She sagged and clarity hit him as hard as a gong being struck.

His Katherine, limp in his arms because he hadn't been able to control himself.

Gluttony wiped at his lips, licking the blood off the back of his hand, and he stood with her in his arms. Though fear made him sick to his stomach, he also felt stronger than he had in centuries. She was his elixir, and now he would keep her.

Chapter 18

Her dreams were full of him. And strangely enough, she knew they were dreams.

Katherine was very much aware that she was walking through a dreamscape as she strode through misty halls. A pale white gown swirled around her knees, so sheer she could see straight through it. And at the end of the hall, a monster waited for her.

Red, glowing eyes illuminated the mist that surrounded him. The light left him in a swirling, blood-red massacre and yet she wanted him. Oh, she wanted him so much it hurt. Her heart thundered, her neck throbbed and pulsed, and she could feel herself growing wet and slick.

She wanted him to hold her again. She wanted to feel his heat pressing between her legs, urging her forward. To rock. To move in ways that she had never before. She wanted to feel him between her legs and in her neck. At the same time. Devouring her whole as only a creature like him could.

She'd never thought she would be like this. Katherine was scared of the creatures that surrounded her town and had a healthy respect for them as she walked by. But she'd never wanted to touch one of them. She'd never wanted them to do what he had done to her.

What kind of person enjoyed that?

But she supposed it didn't matter because this was her dream, and in dreams, there were no consequences. She could race toward him, arms outstretched as she cupped the back of his neck and drew him down to her shoulder.

His fangs pierced through her skin so easily, sliding into her as she wished another part of him would. And then those big hands... She could feel the ghost of his touch, not quite where she wanted him, as though even her dreaming mind couldn't conjure what it would feel like for him to touch her.

But she wanted to know. Katherine wanted him to palm her breasts, to squeeze them a little too hard until he trailed his hands between her legs. Would he be good at that? She'd heard the women in the village talking about it, but Katherine had never been the person they wanted to speak with.

She'd never... No one wanted to fuck a woman with a bad hip. She was the villager on the outskirts. No one even knew if she could have children, or if the pregnancy would kill her because she couldn't move her leg out of the way. She had to keep it down. Had no mobility to move it to the side.

Even Gluttony must have noticed the way she sat on his lap and had to lean to the side. It left her neck bared for him, and gave him easier access, but her weight had to move almost entirely onto her bad leg. It could take the weight. It was just so stiff that she couldn't actually open that leg wide enough, and...

Now the thoughts changed the dream. He looked down at her with disgust, his hand moving to her hip and flicking it with a claw. "This is a problem," she heard him say. "I cannot have a broken woman in my castle."

"I'm not broken," she whispered, but the hurt seared right into her bones. Almost as though she could feel his disdain inside the marrow of her hip.

"You are broken, Katherine. Not even I can help you."

Kat. He'd called her Kat when she returned, or pet. Not Katherine. And this wasn't... this wasn't real. It was just a dream and she could control her dream.

"Come back to me," she said, opening her arms and struggling to control her own dreamscape. "I want to feel you against me."

She knew what that felt like. Surely he would give her this. He would let her press herself against his body, because her mind knew how to conjure that. Maybe if he held her, then it would all... all...

But his smile was so cruel. "No, I'm not going to do that, Katherine. You're so broken. Why would I ever want to touch you again?"

She could feel her heart shattering. It hurt so much to hear him say that. Like everyone else. Like everyone who thought she was too broken, too weak. She couldn't do anything with her leg like that and poor, poor Katherine. Someone should help her. Someone should send her food, because clearly she couldn't take care of herself. Why would she even try?

A loud rumble of thunder speared through her dream. And for a moment, she saw someone else in Gluttony's eyes. A black shadow that had never been there when she'd seen him before.

Then she blinked her eyes open.

The darkness of her room was startling as she coughed and yanked at something sinister that covered her eyes. It was sticky, clinging to her fingers with an icy cold. And then a sharp snap of lightning illuminated the room, and she saw her fingers were coated with a dark mist. A mist that gathered together with a laugh as it rolled off her bed toward the floor.

"Cursed spirit," she hissed, flinging Spite away from her. "Stay out of my dreams."

It didn't reply, which was likely good. She would have argued with the damned thing long before she let it touch her again. She'd need to talk with Gluttony about a way to give her better privacy in the room he'd gifted her.

Her room...

Peering around, Katherine realized she was in her bed. Hadn't she been downstairs with Gluttony the last time she remembered? Yes, she'd been on his lap and been thoroughly enjoying herself when she'd felt a little woozy. Realizing that she was very quickly getting a little too lightheaded, she'd tapped on his shoulder and then... nothing. Just the dream.

Oh, she'd passed out.

She shouldn't be so embarrassed by that. Gluttony had nearly killed countless of his own subjects with his feeding, but she had wanted to be different. Maybe she had wanted to be the one who could take him.

Ridiculous thoughts. Foolish thoughts of a little girl who didn't realize what she wanted. That's all.

Lightning illuminated the room again, falling upon the tall, broad form of a man next to the window.

Katherine screamed before smacking her hands over her mouth so hard it hurt. "Sorry!" she gasped when her heart finally stopped racing. "I should know it's you by now."

"Most people scream when they see me," Gluttony replied, though he stayed where they were. "I'm used to it."

"That doesn't make it right." Clearing her throat, she sat up in her bed and curled her arms around her middle. "What are you doing here?"

A match struck in the darkness. He lit a few candles beside her bed, and a soft, warm glow surrounded them. He looked better than he had when she'd returned, Katherine realized. Those dark circles that were always under his eyes had disappeared. Even his cheeks had a merry, rosy glow that he'd never had before.

"You look well," she said as he set something down on the side of her bed.

"I feel well."

"Better than me." She looked down at her hands clutching the bed sheets and frowned. "Why is that?"

"I believe feeding upon blood does more for me than regular food." He hesitated at the side of her bed, looking down at it and then back at her. "May I?"

"Of course." She smiled at him, suddenly realizing that she was rather shaky. "I'm sorry you have to see me like this. I'm not really sure why I feel so strange."

He snorted. "Probably because I drank too much blood."

"Ah. That would explain it." Right. She remembered that. But she was just a little confused right now and very foggy.

Instead of asking more questions, Katherine watched as he gathered the things he'd set on the side of her bed. She recognized them. Clean bandages, a small bottle of salve, and a spiced drink that he handed to her. Without thinking, she automatically held it.

Just like she'd done in his laboratory.

Inhaling the scent of ginger and honey, she took a small sip while he measured out the roll of bandages and started cutting it with his claws. "This is quite nice."

"What is?"

"The tea." She watched his brows furrow in concentration before pointing to an edge of the bandage. "You can just rip it from there. No need to use your claws."

He sighed heavily before letting the bandage fall into his lap, hands limp. "I'm not very good at this."

"What? Talking with someone after you've fed? You've talked to me before."

"No, um. Taking care of them afterward."

And he looked so sad to admit it. His eyes remained on his lap, as he refused to look at her. The bandages were limp in his grip, so clearly he intended to try to heal her after what he'd done. And sure, she didn't feel very good. But she wasn't dead, and that was good news.

"Oh." She sipped at her tea, waiting until he flicked his gaze to hers. "You are quite rubbish at this, yes."

A bark of startled laughter erupted from his mouth before he got control of himself. But some of the shadows in his eyes had fled. "You, however, are very good at that."

"What?"

"Making me feel comfortable around you."

"Well, it's not hard." When he gave her a skeptical look, she shrugged. "You have very low standards."

Again, he laughed, and she saw something in him ease. Gluttony leaned forward and worked the bandage around her neck, gentle as he left it loose so he could swipe that balm over the wounds. Considering she felt very little pain at the action, she had to assume that the puncture wounds were already closed.

He was so careful the entire time. This massive man with claws that ripped and tore anyone who stood in his way, worked with her like she was as fragile as the thinnest of glass.

She watched his eyes as he moved. Dark and hiding so many secrets, it was hard for her to guess what he was feeling. She only knew that he felt a considerable amount of shame, and she wondered if that was partly because he thought she was in pain.

"It's all right, you know," she whispered. "I'm fine."

"You aren't fine."

"I'm just a little groggy. I'll feel better in the morning after I get something to eat. Blood can be remade."

He shook his head and his throat bobbed in a swallow. "But you cannot be."

And what was she supposed to say to that? She'd never had anyone care about her well being or whether or not she was in pain. Katherine was always in pain. This was nothing compared to the dull ache in her hip where she had spread her legs too wide to straddle him. Nor was it anything like the ache that happened in her skin, the tightness in her side when she thought about the fire. And he'd never even mentioned her scars.

Maybe he hadn't seen them.

Maybe, after all this time with her, he still didn't realize that she was broken.

Licking her lips, she watched him track the movement before asking, "Why me?"

"Because you taste like honey." Gluttony traced his thumb over her bottom lip. "Because you look at me like I'm a man, and no one has done that in a very long time."

"But you are a man."

"No, I'm a demon." He tucked in the ends of the bandage, making sure it was perfectly situated around her neck so she could breathe and swallow. "You said when you came here that you've treated women who have been in my thrall before?"

"In your thrall? What a presumptuous thing to say when it was clearly a business transaction. They came home with money, did they not?"

He shook his head. "The entire time you've been here, pet, you've asked me 'why you'? But have you paused to think for even a moment that I might ask the same of you?"

She blinked owlishly. "Whatever do you mean?"

"You could have anyone you wish." His gaze softened, and he reached for a lock of her hair. Gluttony coiled it around his finger, as he always seemed to do whenever he could touch it. "Surely you are not blind to your own beauty? Any man in your town would be lucky to have you, and yet here you are, standing in front of my castle, no matter what I do to chase you off."

Every part of her froze as he brushed the back of his fingers against her cheek. He looked at her like a starving man, and not for food. He looked quite content, in fact. He was not hungry for her blood, but just for her attention.

And she didn't know what to say to that.

Did she tell him that she was wounded and that no one in her town had ever been able to see past that? It was a lie for her to not tell him. She could so easily let the words slip past her tongue.

When I was a child, a fire took my ability to walk normally, and no one had been able to see past that. Just say it, she told herself. Rip the horrible feeling off and let him know the truth. Why couldn't she just say the words?

Instead, she shook her head. "I don't know how you haven't guessed yet."

It was the wrong thing to say. His eyes shuttered, and that darkness that she saw sometimes reared its ugly head. "Ah, I see."

"What do you see?" She felt as if she'd lost control over the conversation all of a sudden. He'd jumped to conclusions, and that wasn't right. It wasn't that she didn't like him.

Katherine had seen a different side of the monster, but she couldn't forget all the wounds she'd healed and all the terrible things he'd done to so many people. She'd pieced them together. Stitching that skin as though it were a quilt for her to fix, and into those stitches, she had poured her anger and her rage.

At him. Everyone in this kingdom was always so mad at him.

Her heart broke for the man she had seen so many times, and the monster reflected in his eyes. Maybe that was why she stayed. Less because she wanted to be a martyr, and more because she'd been so tired of it all.

Katherine had really expected to stomp up here, tell him to go shove it, and then likely die for it. But what kind of life had she lived before this? What adventure had ever come into her world?

Reaching out, she cupped his jaw in her hand and felt him stiffen, freeze, and then slowly turn into her touch. "You have a bigger heart than I expected, Gluttony."

"Ah, but you have seen the monster as well." He ghosted his lips over her palm and then stood. "You, more than anyone else, are aware of what I am, Kat."

And as he walked out of her room, his shoulders curved in and with the bandages clutched in his fists, she whispered, "I'm not so sure I know who you are at all, Gluttony."

Chapter 19

Gluttony kept himself away from her after that. He refused to be the person who used her, nor did he have any desire to feed off her again for a while.

Which, in itself, was strange. He'd never felt the hunger ease. Not once. There was always some lingering darkness that bubbled up inside him, whispering that he needed more blood. Needed to feed.

The only time that had even remotely quieted down was after... Well, Larissa. And he didn't think about her because it was a terrible thing in his past and Gluttony was trying very hard to not believe he was a monster. Right now, he just wanted to be a man. For Katherine.

Kat.

A soft smile crossed his face even as he peered down at the substance that had thus far bested him. Just the thought of her made him feel a little better. He could sense the blush that burned in his cheeks, and when was the last time he'd blushed? He hadn't ever felt like he could do so, physically that was. And now, he blushed all the time.

It had nearly been a week since he'd fed from her, and he still felt more like a person than he had in years.

Lifting a beaker, he gave it a swirl while watching the smoke slowly turn white. It was a start. Not a fix, per say, but a start toward figuring out what it was.

She had given him not only a few wonderful days of freedom from his own vices, but she'd given him the space to actually work on this. And she'd cleaned his lab from top to bottom, making everything so much easier to find and access. Truly, she was a gift.

And he was the monster who had to keep her. But he would make sure she lived the best life she could.

If he got stuck thinking about her smile or the way she tilted her neck just so, then that was all right. He'd gotten somewhere already with his alchemical investigation, and that was enough, wasn't it?

Until his door busted open so hard he heard the beakers rattle.

"What are you doing?" he scolded, spinning on his chair and whipping off his glasses in anger. "You know better than to... to..."

Ah, shit.

It wasn't his lovely Katherine with all her wild hair and sparking green eyes. Instead, he had another monster now inside his castle, which he had most certainly not agreed to.

His brother was far more massive than the illusion let on. Envy stood a full head taller than him, broad and wide across the chest, with thick tree trunk legs. He might even be larger than Greed, now that he was taking up all the space in the laboratory. His full head of wavy dark hair was cropped short, unlike Gluttony's very long locks, and there was the faint shadow of a beard that suggested Envy hadn't shaved this morning. Unusual for him. He usually was more aware of his looks.

Envy stood with his arms crossed over his chest, a critical look in his eyes as he surveyed his surroundings. "This looks different from how it used to."

"Yes, it does. It's clean." Gluttony placed his glasses on the table so he didn't break them when he clenched his fists. "What are you doing here?"

"The brothers and I have decided you need a babysitter. You aren't working hard enough or fast enough, Gluttony. We're concerned about this new weapon, and so far, you've been unimpressive." He grinned, sharp toothed and a little too aggressive for Gluttony's liking. "If I don't find something I like, then I will take this project from you."

As if Gluttony would ever let him. This was his chance to be something more than what he already was, and Gluttony refused to let it slip through his fingers because Envy didn't know how to leave things alone.

"Everything is going well. It's been fighting me a bit, but I've already made progress."

"Have you?" Envy leaned in, trying to peer over Gluttony's shoulder. "I don't see any progress. I just see a mess of beakers."

"Magic won't fix this."

"So you say." Envy lifted his hand and a green flame burst to life around his fingers. A new trick, but Gluttony remembered parlor magic when he saw it. "Perhaps you should admit your defeat, brother. There are many others who know how to manage alchemical solutions."

"You?" He snorted. "You know nothing beyond magic. Everything has been given to you, Envy, or you took it when you wanted it. Of all our brothers, you are the least likely to figure out this puzzle."

There it was. The flare of dark green in Envy's eyes, the bubbling of his skin as creatures writhed beneath his flesh. "Really? That is only how you see it, brother. Perhaps I should take something of yours to prove myself, then."

"Now you sound like Greed."

"We are very similar." A snake poked its head out of Envy's collar, black and iridescent in the overhead lights. It coiled around his throat, lifting its head and flicking the air with its tongue. "That is why we're not allowed anywhere near each other. Or had you forgotten that?"

No, he hadn't. Gluttony remembered the last time Greed and Envy had been in the same room. The two of them nearly destroyed each other, ripping and tearing at the very fabric of the world until the mortals around them had all fallen to their knees in anguish.

It was a hard memory to suppress. It was one of the first times he'd realized just how much pain they were causing their people. They were gods playing at a game, not realizing that there were humans in the middle who were getting hurt.

He hadn't wanted to be a god like that. Not then, and not now.

"It's hard to forget that night," he muttered, turning back to what he knew. Beakers and solutions and alchemical messes that might explode in his face. At least it wasn't his brother looking at him with disappointment in his eyes. So certain that he would find Gluttony lacking, yet again.

"And your... problem?" Envy asked, though his voice betrayed what he meant. "I suppose you've taken care of that as well?"

"I have."

"How did you take care of it?" Apparently, Envy had no plans to let this go. And when Gluttony didn't respond, Envy prodded more. "You took care of it, didn't you? You said you were going to get it out of your system or ignore it. You know you cannot afford any distractions while you are working so hard."

Working so hard. The thought was laughable. Gluttony wasn't working any harder on this than he had any other project. All he wanted was a few quiet nights with the lovely little thing who had captured his attention. He didn't want to be here, in front of Envy, trying to justify his choices to a brother who had never truly been there for him.

"I took care of it." Setting his hands on the table, he stared down at his fingers and willed his claws to go away. "I have no reason to lie to you, Envy."

"You have no reason to tell the truth, either."

That was it.

Gluttony stood, whirling on his brother, ready for the fight that Envy apparently wanted. His claws sliced out of his fingers, and his eyes cast a red glow throughout the beakers. His brother, to his credit, was ready to fight as well. That snake hissed next to Envy's ear, and more of those black tattoos rippled underneath his shirt.

If they weren't careful, they would set this entire room ablaze with their fight. And maybe that would be for the best. They'd destroy the substance that had been used against them. The demons would have to fight the mortals, as so many clearly wished for them to do.

It would be over. All of this could end and then Gluttony would return to his quiet existence, with only Katherine to keep him company.

Such a future would truly be divine.

The door opened again. This time both of them froze as they stared at Katherine. She walked backward through the door, her hair twisted up on top of her head, with a riotous mass of curls tumbling down her back. In the week since he'd fed, she'd gained much of her health back. And so it was with rosy cheeks and a bright smile that she turned around.

He watched it all unfold before him in slow motion. Katherine startled seeing his brother. The tray in her hands swayed and then fell, twisting toward the ground with the glass vase she used to carry water back and forth between the rooms. The two glass cups fell with it.

She gasped, Envy reacted. They both moved toward the water that cracked against the ground long before either of them could grab it. But then he saw some twinge in her face, a reaction that had her shuddering, stuck in a single position when Envy ran right into her.

His behemoth of a brother didn't even try to pull his weight. He just plowed into Katherine with all the force of a bull, and she was thrust backward.

He watched her arms pinwheel as she tried to catch her balance, but she was going to fall. She was going to fall right onto that floor, now littered with sharp glass shards and water that would only make her slip more.

Gluttony had never moved so quickly. He lunged forward, uncaring of the glass shards between him and her. He just had to make sure she didn't get hurt.

It was only a few brief moments when he didn't have her in his arms, but he caught her. And then she was right there, looking up at him with those bright green eyes, shock radiating from every pore of her body.

His arm was banded around her back, but he had forgotten to put his claws in. To his horror, he could smell her blood. Somehow, when he'd grabbed her around the waist, he had sliced through her clothing and into her back. Though she didn't react like she'd been injured, he had failed to prevent her from being harmed.

She didn't deserve to bleed in front of his brother. And he hated knowing that she was.

A few drops of bright red fell from the tips of his claws, the soft sound of them striking the pool of water hitting his ears. Carefully this time, he gathered her a little closer to his chest and stood them both upright.

Her mouth was still slightly open, and her breathing a little ragged. "Gluttony," she said, as though she didn't know what else to say. "I'm... I..."

Envy interrupted them. "So this is how you fixed your problem? I told you to get rid of her!"

Of course, that made Katherine look at him with wide, stunned eyes. "What?"

"I'm not getting rid of you," he replied before glaring at his brother. "You almost hurt her."

"You are getting rid of her, now," Envy said with a menacing step forward. "She cannot and will not stay here. She's a distraction from what you're supposed to be doing. Did you really believe any of us would let you keep her?"

"No one is keeping her," Gluttony growled. Then he ignored his brother, gently running the back of his finger down her cheek because he couldn't seem to get his claws back in. "Are you all right, pet?"

"Pet?" Envy repeated with an aggressive snort.

But even Katherine ignored his brother, having eyes only for Gluttony. Her tiny hands pressed against his chest and he felt like the world was only the two of them. "I'm fine."

"I cut you."

"It's not the first time."

Envy tossed his hands up behind her and groaned. "Not the first time? Gluttony, what have you gotten yourself into?"

Ignoring his brother—although it was starting to get a little harder now—he brushed his fingers down her back. Katherine's dress was cut in three places. He'd been too careless with her.

There were bandages up in her room, and that would be enough to get her through the next couple of hours for him to deal with his brother. Then he could at the very least put the balm on her. Or stitch her if she needed it, but he could not do that when his damn claws wouldn't go down because his brother was far too close.

Grinding his teeth, he forced himself to let her go. "Return to your bedroom, pet. I'll come up in a while. I just need to get rid of our unwelcome visitor."

But his Katherine was far too brave. She patted his chest and turned to Envy with a soft smile on her face. "Nonsense. I'd have to be blind not to see this is one of your brothers. Which one are you?"

Envy eyed him over her head, one of his brows raised in surprise. "Envy."

"It's lovely to meet you, Envy. I'm sorry I ran into you. If you'd like something other than water to drink, I can bring it?"

"Wine."

Over his dead body. "You don't have to bring him anything, Kat. You are not a maid."

"I'm going to bring him wine, and I'm going to bring the bandages back with me." Her gaze watched him as he winced, but then she surprised him again. Katherine reached out and put her hand on his chest again, gently nudging him back. "You're not wearing any shoes, Gluttony. You've got glass all through your feet."

He looked down and realized he did. There were shards sticking straight out through the top of his foot where he'd rushed to get to her.

He hadn't even felt it in the moment, but now he was standing in a puddle of his own blood.

"Damn," he muttered. "That's going to take a while to get out."

"I'll do it. I work at the almshouse, remember?" She smiled at him, all confidence and poise, even though he knew she must be shaking at the realization that she was surrounded by demons.

Sighing, he waved her off. As if he needed to give her permission to slip out of the room as he hobbled back toward his table. The damned glass did hurt, surprisingly more than he'd expected.

"Really?" Envy broke the silence first. "You not only kept her around, but you brought her to the castle? What were you thinking?"

"That I didn't wish to be alone any longer." He reached for a pair of tongs and rested his ankle on his knee. Picking out the glass would take time, but at least the pain would prevent him from trying to attack his brother. "And that she smelled divine."

"You're an idiot."

"I'm tired of being so lonely." He looked Envy in the eye. "Aren't you?"

And there was the slightest flicker in his brother's gaze. Almost as though Envy felt the same way, or perhaps that he was upset Gluttony had found someone who would stay.

It was rare to find a human who could stand them. And Gluttony knew how short her life would be in comparison to all that he would survive.

Still. He wanted his brother to understand why he was doing this.

Envy gave him a little nod. "I hope you know what you're doing, brother."

So did he.

215

Chapter 20

There isn't enough balm for the both of us," Katherine said, sitting between his legs and staring up at Gluttony's angry expression. "I'm putting it on your feet, or we're saving it for the next time you wish to feed."

He made a sound halfway between a snarl and a hiss. "No, we will not. You will let me put it on your back so my claw marks don't get infected, and I will heal fine on my own."

"You won't."

"I am a demon, woman. I'll be fine."

She arched a brow. "You have no idea how mortal bodies work, nor do you take care of yourself. I've seen how little you eat and sleep. You cannot exist on blood forever, and I highly doubt that you'll allow these feet any rest. I'm putting the balm on you."

"You need it more than I do."

"They're barely scratches, but if you insist." Katherine patted his knees and then stood. Her hip ached from Envy bumping into her, but she thought it was possible for her to get to the village and back. "I might need to stay the night there, but I can get more balm at the almshouse. Then both of us will be healing."

"You know I don't like it when you spend the night away from me."

He really didn't. She'd learned that the hard way, and strangely, found the same reaction in herself. Katherine hated staying in her old bedroom. She hated how many questions everyone had for her.

Of course, she'd been very vague about where she had gone. She'd lied and said her mother had property elsewhere that she was trying to fix up. But she hadn't been able to keep the secret from Grace. Now her friend knew Katherine was staying in the castle, and she didn't know if that was a good or a bad thing that Grace knew.

Regardless, her hours were much less than they had been before. And apparently her boss didn't mind. He'd even gone so far as to say that it was probably better in the long run.

Considering her leg and all.

Katherine tried very hard not to let her limp show as she started out of the lab, but she didn't manage very well. Once she made it to the door, Gluttony called out, "Did Envy hurt you?"

"No."

"It's just that you're limping."

The laugh she forced out was definitely not something she was proud of. "Oh, he must have jostled me when we collided. I'm fine, though."

Gluttony stood. He winced the moment his feet touched the ground, but he wasn't limping as he approached her. He looked fine, honestly, but she didn't want to risk an infection.

She'd become rather... fond of the strange man. And even worse, he made her heart do funny things in her chest whenever she thought about the way he'd touched her.

"You're not going to the town if you're limping," he grumbled. "I'll go. I'm certain the almshouse won't turn me away."

She was almost certain they would. "You're going to sit right there. If I was in so much pain that I couldn't walk, I would tell you. I'm fine, Gluttony. You are not."

He grumbled again, making little blustering sounds of discontent before he sat back down. And she knew how much pain he must be in if he argued no more than that.

"I'll be back," she said, then narrowed her eyes at him. "I mean it, Gluttony."

He waved a hand, but he wouldn't look at her. She wondered if he thought she was lying.

Dark thoughts clouding her mind, Katherine left the castle with a shawl over her shoulders and a mission to complete. Gluttony wouldn't let himself be taken care of. Why? She had no idea. He clearly hadn't experienced someone taking care of him before, and that wasn't something she could teach him.

He needed to learn that taking help from others wasn't a bad thing. She wasn't trying to take advantage of him or get some gift out of him. All she wanted was for him to be happy and well. Surely that wasn't such a terrible thing?

The moors were quiet today. Dragonflies buzzed around her head, zipping past on their way to get food. Even the wisps were a little dimmer, less threatening as they watched her move by.

In fact, most of the swamp creatures had left her alone lately.

Gluttony hadn't minded if she worked in the almshouse on days when she was bored, and she found herself making this trek more and more.

Just a few days ago, she'd realized there were new planks in place. Painted a bright, new yellow to show where it was safe for her to walk. She had a sneaking suspicion that a particular demon hadn't wanted her to fall into the water without him there.

He did things like that all the time. Insignificant actions to help her. And he didn't even realize her bad hip made this trek even harder. He did these things just to make her life easier and, as such, it was.

She hadn't expected him to be quite so... kind.

The thoughts filled her with a sense of levity. She would make it to the almshouse. She'd do something for him, after all this time that he'd been taking care of her. For once, she could do the same for him.

Once she was close to town, Katherine noticed there was a shadow behind her. Not much of one, really. Perhaps a person on their way back home after a particularly long day working in the mines or in the swamps gathering peat. Until she saw a second shadow join that one as well.

Nerves churned in her belly. There was no reason for her to be so nervous, but she was. And then a third shadow, this one much closer than the others and therefore infinitely taller.

She shouldn't have been so nervous. This was her town. Katherine had grown up on these planks and boardwalks her entire life. No one questioned where she came from, how she'd gotten here, or what she might be doing.

They knew her, just as she knew all of them.

But something deep inside her soul told her to be afraid. That those three shadows were a direct threat to her wellbeing.

She could only shrug it off for so long. Katherine told herself that Gluttony had gotten into her head. She was in no danger in her own home, and no one would dare harm her. Goodness, she'd stitched almost the entire town back together at some point, and many of them she'd stitched multiple times.

They wouldn't want to get rid of her. Nor would they attack her for any reason whatsoever.

Unless they heard she was staying with Gluttony.

Unless someone had told them that she was with him, and then maybe someone might... might...

Finally, she couldn't take it anymore. Katherine turned around and met the stares of three men who watched her with hungry eyes. They didn't seem surprised that she'd turned, as someone might if they weren't following her. Instead, they crossed their arms over their thick chests and just stood there. Blocking her way back to the castle.

"Do I know you?" she asked.

"You don't, miss," the one on the right said. He was larger than the other three, a bit heavy around the middle, and significantly taller. She had to crane her neck to look at him. "You Katherine?"

"I am."

"What are you doing back here?"

She didn't need to justify herself! How dare he? She drew herself up a little taller, squaring her shoulders so she looked a little more impressive. "I'm going to the almshouse. I work there."

"Do you now?"

"I have for years." And then she realized she didn't know any of these three men. Not a single one of them.

Katherine knew everyone in her town by name. She'd been there for many of the children's births. She had played with every towns person and even walked by them a hundred times. She knew the people in this town.

These were strangers.

Swallowing, she took a step away from the three. "You're not from around these parts."

"No, miss." The one on the left took a step toward her, closing the gap she'd just made. "We're here to make sure everything runs smooth, you understand? There's been a lot of people getting hurt in these parts, and we just want to make sure that won't happen anymore."

What were they talking about? She took another step back, wondering if maybe one of her friends would be out and about this time of the day. Maybe, if she was lucky, Grace might be heading to the almshouse.

"I'm afraid I don't know what you're talking about," she said, craning her neck to look behind her very quickly before turning her attention back to them. "I have a bad hip, so I really need to get to the almshouse before there's too much of a line. If you'll excuse me."

"Oh, I don't think we'll be doing that." The man in the middle didn't move, but his thin features and beady eyes made her freeze all the same. "Word on the street is that you've got yourself a demon friend. Now, I find it curious that any self-respecting young woman would stay around a monster like that for very long."

"I've been visiting my mother's property in a neighboring town. I don't know what you're talking about."

"We both know you're lying." He tapped his nose. "Easy enough to smell the stench of fear, lovely. I don't have to be a demon to sniff that out of you."

Her heart raced. Her palms grew sweaty, and she grabbed her skirts to keep them at least a little dry.

Who were these men? And why were they following her?

"I still don't know what you're talking about." Katherine licked her lip, trying to get her dry mouth to work. "I really need to be going, though."

She didn't give them a chance to say anything else. The last thing she wanted was to show them her back, but she couldn't run no matter what. Her hip wouldn't let her move that fast, so she was forced to keep her back straight and her breathing even as she trusted them not to attack her from behind.

They didn't, thank goodness. But she felt the weight of their gazes all the way through the town.

It took her far too long to get through the familiar boardwalks and onto the path that lead to the almshouse. She would have liked to stop at her old apartment—the one that her landlord now said she didn't need to worry about payment for—but she was afraid they'd break in and go through her things.

So she kept her head down, her attention on her feet, and made her way all the way to the almshouse without anyone trying to hurt her. But she could feel the sizzling intensity of their regard as she moved, and it made her skin crawl.

They wanted her to be uncomfortable. They wanted her to know they were there. What she didn't understand was why?

No one had any reason to threaten her. Other than Gluttony himself, and even then, wasn't she doing the right thing? She was keeping his attention away from everyone else. She had made certain that he wouldn't attack anyone at all. She'd given herself, freely and without question.

The almshouse door opened at her knock and Grace stuck her head out. Her lovely friend looked exhausted, so pale she rivaled paper as she looked Katherine up and down.

"Oh, thank goodness it's you." Grace grabbed her arm and yanked her inside. "We need all the help we can get today. I'm sure you've heard, but it's so much worse than you imagined."

"I haven't heard anything. I've been..." She didn't need to finish the sentence. Not with Grace looking at her with all that pity. "What?"

"It's Gluttony," Grace said.

"What about him?"

"He went on a rampage last night. There's easily ten of them, Katherine. More coming in every hour and their necks..." Grace went even paler somehow, pressing a shaking hand to her own neck. "We've lost six already. Maybe you can... Maybe you can help?"

Katherine felt like the world tilted underneath her feet. It all hit her at the same moment. The sound of groaning from the other room. The metallic scent of blood in the air and the exhaustion of her friend, who must have not slept at all last night. And then there was the betrayal, the sudden, strange feeling of jealousy burning in her stomach.

Grabbing Grace's arm, she tugged her to the side so no one would overhear them. "Are you sure it was Gluttony? He's been with me, you see, and after our deal, I was certain that he wouldn't... He wouldn't..."

Oh, that pity on Grace's face made her want to throw things. "When was the last time he fed from you?"

She could feel her friend's eyes on her neck. The mark he'd left on her had almost healed entirely. It was hard for even Katherine to see, and she'd been staring at it for days now.

It had been such a long time since he'd fed. A week? Maybe more?

"Not that long," she replied, suddenly feeling as though she needed to defend her demon. Her... friend.

Grace shook her head. "Does it matter? He's killing people,

Katherine. Again. Maybe it was a good idea you had, and it sounds like he doesn't want to break you, and that's a good thing. But he's got to be getting his food from somewhere if he's not getting it from you. So, can you help or not?"

Nodding, not quite realizing she was doing it, Katherine looked back to the room where all the moans were coming from. "I can help. Just for a little while, though. He's expecting me back."

"Of course he is." Grace's face twisted into an expression that was truly ugly. "Why would he want to give up his favorite meal?"

That wasn't anything Katherine had ever said. Gluttony hadn't said that to her either.

Confusion set in. Why was her friend so adamant that this was Gluttony's doing? And why did it seem like Grace resented that Katherine was in the castle?

She'd done what no one else wanted to do. She'd thrown herself at him for keeps and she had let him keep her. Not for money, not for anything other than their safety.

There would be time to think about this, but right now, she needed to put her attention on the poor souls moaning behind the curtains. But when Katherine made her way back, wrapping herself in a thick apron that would hopefully keep all the blood off her clothing, she couldn't help but look closer at the wounds.

When Gluttony had fed from her, he'd left two perfect puncture wounds on her neck. They were thin and narrow, easy enough for him to feed from, but certainly not as wide as these.

She bent, gently tracing her fingers over the wound of the nearest body. The person had unfortunately passed, but even she could see these gash wounds weren't like what Rose or herself had experienced. Her former neighbor had twin lines down the back of her neck, like she had ripped herself out of Gluttony's arms.

These were rips of the flesh. They looked like knife wounds. Long and gashing, like someone had been very determined to kill this person.

"Katherine!" Grace called out. "Don't waste your time looking, just get to sewing. There's two more on the front doorstep. Someone just dropped them off."

With a pit in her stomach, she went to gather her tools. But she couldn't stop thinking that this wasn't right.

She didn't think Gluttony had done this. But someone else certainly had.

Chapter 21

"So you're not even going out and talking with the people in your kingdom?" Envy asked, sitting down in the chair across from Gluttony's desk and splaying his legs wide. "Why are you not doing that?"

"Why are you still here?" Gluttony groaned.

He tilted his chair onto its back legs, dangling between falling and hovering, but he didn't want to look at Envy right now. What he wanted was his space back. His privacy. He wanted everyone to leave his castle and by everyone, he meant his brother. He wanted Katherine to come back, which she hadn't last night.

Logically, he knew that was probably the best circumstance for all of them. The longer Envy was here, the more likely he would be to take the young woman who had captured Gluttony's attention. Not because Envy enjoyed her, of course, but because Envy kidnapped everyone he wanted. Any time he wanted.

And Gluttony would start a war over that. He'd do whatever it took to get his pet back, even if that meant tearing into his brother, who had never once lost a battle in his kingdom.

"I'm here because everyone wants results that you aren't providing. Yet." Envy leaned forward, bracing his forearms on his knees. "I still believe you can do this, brother. But I will not take the fall for you if you cannot do this because a woman distracted you."

"You have yet to understand what this feels like."

"You believe you are in love." Envy's eyes flashed bright green. "I know what it is to covet someone so thoroughly that you would do anything to keep them. And isn't that what you're feeling?"

He wasn't in love with her, that much he knew. Gluttony pinched the bridge of his nose and sighed. "Of all our brothers, don't you think I'm the least capable of love?"

"Look at Greed and Lust."

"They were forged under extreme pressures. Diamonds of relationships that were thrust upon them without choice or reason." Gluttony pointed at his door, as though he were pointing to Katherine herself. "I found her in the squalor of my own kingdom. I was the one who chose her, not for any reason other than that fate thrust us together. I found her, I took her, and then I did what I wished with her."

"And now you are falling for her."

Gluttony rolled his eyes. "It is an obsession, and you know more than anyone else that it will end. My thirst for blood will eventually be satiated, and then I will need to search for the next person to capture my attention. It is an exhausting existence and one that I will likely end after her. But for now, I am merely enjoying myself."

Envy's brows furrowed. "Yet here you are, quite certain that you would do anything to keep her."

"I agree that it's a strange combination of feelings, but I assure you, what I feel for her is nothing out of the ordinary. I've felt like this for countless blood donors before."

It was a lie.

He'd never felt like this before. In fact, every blood donor before her had made him feel dirty. Used. Like he was only good for one thing, and that was money. Like he was hiring whores to come to his home and bare themselves before him just so he could get off.

He'd never gotten off with any of the others. He'd never felt this full body experience when he drank from them.

Envy leaned back, his lips pursed and his brows drawn down. "Oh, you are in so much deeper than you're willing to admit."

"I'm not."

"I can see that expression, Gluttony. You want to keep her, not for a little while, but forever. And there's something about her that's wriggled its way underneath your skin."

"Shut up." He stood from his desk. The last thing he wanted to do was sit here and be berated about his own feelings. "You can leave whenever you wish. Clearly, I am making progress on the substance and soon enough, we'll know what it is."

"Not soon enough for any of our brothers." Envy didn't stand. He didn't even move. He just kept talking as Gluttony approached the door. "Did you hear that Sloth was attacked a few days ago?"

Gluttony froze with his hand on the door. "I had not."

"I suppose news doesn't travel as fast here, and that's quite all right. But he was attacked, brother. A group of people broke into his castle. Thankfully he has loyal guards, but if he hadn't? Sloth would be gone, and we'd all have a much larger problem on our hands."

He hated this. He hated that his brothers' wellbeing rested on his shoulders, and there was nothing he could do about it.

"Alchemical solutions take time," he said quietly.

"Time that you are not giving it." Envy's eyes were still trained on the wall behind Gluttony's vacant desk. "That is why I am here. To ensure that you are focused, Gluttony."

"Even without knowing she was here, you were already coming." Gluttony sighed. "So they do not believe that I am capable of doing this."

"They believe in you, but your attention? They do not. Pride was very quick to tell me to come here."

A flash of anger had him whirling, claws already drawn out for battle. "What does Pride know of me?"

"Pride has eyes in every kingdom. You know this."

"Because he wants to control everything within reach, but he is not welcome in my kingdom!" Gluttony slashed his claws through the air as though a spell was woven before him. "He knows that I see the truth. That our kingdoms would be infinitely better if we were not involved."

"Would they?" Envy finally rose to his massive height, turning on Gluttony with anger bunching through his muscles. "Look at your kingdom, brother! It is falling apart."

"It survives fine without me."

"There are starving people on every street! Injuries that never seem to stop happening, no matter how many measures they take to prevent them. Even your little mortal worked at the almshouse, stitching people together. You think that's normal, Gluttony?"

He slashed at the air directly in front of Envy's face, provoking him to battle even though he knew it was one he could not win. "I took the worst kingdom. All the others were so clearly matched to all of you, so what was I to do? I took the swamps. I took the moors and the madness and the poison that comes with it. You should all thank me for it!"

"Thank you?" Envy burst out, the words releasing in a roar of rage. "You've never lived up to the potential of this kingdom nor the throne we gave you!"

The words settled between them, dust clearing enough for Envy to realize what he had said.

"So that is what you all believe," Gluttony breathed, shaking his head in disgust. "That you handed me a kingdom I've never taken care of. That I squandered what was given to me."

Of course they did. His prideful, boastful, arrogant brothers had thought that because he hadn't had to battle to keep this kingdom, that it had been given to him. Like a gift.

He staggered away from Envy, shaking his head still as if he might dislodge the reality from his mind. "No one wanted this kingdom. No one wanted the mud and the muck and the centuries of work that were thrown upon me when I took this place. The humans were living in the roots of trees when I got here. I built their homes by hand and then fled when I realized they wouldn't even build a fire if I was near them. I tamed the creatures here, taught them how to hunt only if the humans were in the water. I was the whisper in the ear of every mortal and creature who lived here."

"We all know that. I did not mean—"

"You meant exactly what you said." Gluttony lifted his hand for silence. "You cannot save this, brother. You have revealed much, and for that truth, I thank you."

"It's not the truth, Gluttony." His brother even stepped forward, eyes wide, as though he realized he might have broken something important. "We do not believe you are weaker than us, only that... that..."

"You cannot even come up with a lie," Gluttony finished for him. "Whichever brother spread these rumors likely knows that I'm aware of something you all aren't. That we are the monsters in this story, and if we wish to fix that, then we must tear apart what we are."

"You don't believe that." And it looked like Envy had gone mad. His eyes were so wide that the whites showed around those dark rings of color, and he held out his hand for Gluttony to take. Why? Gluttony had no idea.

"I know this to be true." Gluttony placed a clawed hand against his heart. "And you know it as well. What future did we steal from the humans? What kingdoms would have existed if we had not walked out of the mist and named ourselves gods?"

With that, he turned from his office. He left the room and his brother behind, walking blindly until he heard the knock at the front door. The knock that solved all his issues and turned his attention toward a darker one indeed.

The hunger flared bright and hot. More than it ever had before. His fangs ached, and his forehead suddenly spiked with a sharp pain. His nails were already out, but they were darker as he looked. Turning black with need as he descended the stairs toward the front door.

He needed her.

Oh, he needed her in his arms and his fangs in her neck. He needed to feel those strong hands holding onto his waist, or maybe smoothing down his back. She would know he was upset. She always did.

He threw open the door only to freeze when he saw her red ringed eyes, rounded shoulders, and an air of defeat.

This wasn't his pet. This wasn't his angry little healer who had always peered up at him with fire in her eyes and a challenge squaring her jaw. This wasn't... her.

"Katherine?" he asked, stepping aside to let her walk past him.

It didn't escape his notice that she wrapped her arms around her waist rather than touch him at all. She didn't even look up at him again until she was well inside the room and could then turn.

He tilted his head to the side, watching her as he sealed them into the darkness. He flicked his wrist, lighting the candles that he'd forgotten to light before her arrival. "Tell me."

"I was stopped on my way to the town." She swallowed hard. "There are new men there. They wanted to ask me about you, and why I was still with you when you were slowly killing this kingdom."

"Did they touch you?" Anger swelled. He would hunt them as Greed did, if he had to. No one would touch Katherine. No one but him.

"No." She shuddered. "But they wanted to."

"They would not be wrong in claiming I've destroyed this kingdom." He took a step closer to her, watching her for any flinch or recoil. But she didn't. She just stayed there, her arms firmly hugging herself, watching him. "But I will not stand by and see you harmed. I will take care of them for you and make sure they no longer bother you on your walks."

He couldn't stop himself. Gluttony brushed the backs of his fingers down her cheeks, his wicked claws turned in toward himself. And his heart stuttered in his chest as she tilted her face into his touch.

"There's more," she whispered.

"There always is."

"A group of bodies were delivered to the almshouse today. Twelve people total, all of them injured beyond recognition. We could only save two of them." Her troubled gaze met his. "Their throats were ripped out."

He winced. "A sad way to die, indeed."

"They're blaming you." And he saw the thought in her eyes before she took another big breath and asked, "Have you broken our deal, Gluttony?"

He dropped his hand and took a large step away from her. How could she even ask that? How could she wonder such a thing when he had practically prostrated himself before her and begged her to never leave?

Or had he?

Gluttony wracked his mind, trying to see if he'd ever really made it clear that he valued her. Perhaps he had in his actions, but never in words. What a fool he had been. She wouldn't stay if he didn't let her know she had become someone more than just a villager to him. So much more than any peasant who lived in that town.

Pressing the hand that had been touching her lovely face to his chest, he stared straight into her eyes as he replied. "I have not broken our vow, Kat. I never would. You offered yourself to me, and I would never, ever break that trust. You've come to be like a... friend. I suppose. I'd hoped that you felt the same."

A soft, but sad, smile crossed her features. "I'd like that quite a bit. You are not what I expected, Gluttony. Not at all."

With her words, the hunger flared bright hot again. He wanted to grab her in his arms. He wanted to taste her and wrap her up and never let her go. He wanted to hold on to her until the very world ended.

What if he never let her go? Would she complain, or would she not mind?

Katherine licked her lips, and he watched the movement with avid attention. "The people in the village believe you are a monster. The only friend I told about my time here, she said I should try to kill you in your sleep. That because I was so close to you, I should take this as the advantage the entire town has been seeking."

"You should," he replied, his voice guttural and low. "You really should."

She took a step closer to him, lowering her voice as well, as though talking to a wounded animal. "Gluttony, I'm going to say this now as a friend. Are you listening to me?"

"Yes."

"Are you sure?"

His heart raced in his chest as she came closer and closer. She was right in front of him, a temptation unlike any he'd ever suffered through. Every muscle in his body was locked tight to keep himself under control.

He wanted her.

More than he'd ever wanted anything in his life.

"I'm listening," he said.

"Sometimes you frustrate me to no end with this self hatred." Katherine stopped in front of him, then shifted the hair off her shoulder to bare her neck to him. "So would you tell that part of you to fuck off, sad boy? You're a little busy with me."

Chapter 22

Where she had gotten all this confidence, Katherine had no idea.

All she knew was that her entire body hurt. The walk back had been arduous and long. The voices of her friend and patients had rung in her ears the entire way.

"The monster has done this."

"Will we never be free of him?"

"It's your duty, Katherine, to take care of this for all of us. If he won't stop because he has a specific blood donor, then he's never going to stop. Your heart was true, but it's in the wrong place."

And none of it felt... right. None of it. No matter how many times she'd stitched those patients or held their hands while they died, she knew that this wasn't Gluttony.

He hadn't left the castle. Sure, she slept through the night and he might have gone then, but why would he attack so many? He'd existed on just a few drops of her blood long before he'd taken her neck. And even then, drinking that much from her had satisfied him for a week! More, maybe, if she'd stayed without antagonizing him.

And those wounds... They hadn't looked right. She knew what wounds Gluttony would make. She'd treated women like herself multiple times. Even when he tore their flesh, it didn't look like the wounds in the almshouse.

None of this was right. None of it. And everyone was so quick to jump upon the idea of the monster in the castle who clearly was their problem rather than looking around themselves.

It had made her angry. So angry that the emotion itself had carried her all the way to the castle and then even to this moment.

But she wasn't angry at him. How could she be angry at the man staring down at her like she was a gift from the gods themselves? He had never been unkind to her and had gone out of his way to take care of every one of her needs. He was a good man, and she refused to believe otherwise.

Not, at least, until he proved himself unworthy of those thoughts.

"Katherine," he said, and the tone of his voice sent a shiver down her spine.

That shudder made her entire body weak. Oh, she wanted him. And she was tired of denying the sparks between them. Did a demon taste different from a man?

His breath puffed over her pulse. "Are you sure?"

"I'm very sure," she replied. More confidence than she really felt melted into her words. "You are not the monster they say you are, Gluttony. And I am not afraid of you."

The deep groan that echoed through his chest rocked into her a moment before he latched onto her throat. The sharp prick of his fangs punctured through her neck, a little painful like the last time, but no worse than a paper cut. And then there it was. Again.

The long, slow draw of his tongue against her skin as he drew her blood into him.

And, just like last time, it felt a little religious. As though she had given herself to a god of this kingdom, allowing him to draw her soul out through her throat as he dragged upon the very essence that kept her alive.

She curled her fingers into his jacket, holding onto him as she swayed against his chest. It was wrong. This was a demon feasting upon her flesh and yet white hot heat flooded through her entire body.

Slickness rushed between her thighs, so much that she could feel it as she tried to press them together. Nothing eased this torment, though. She remembered it from the last time. How she'd gone back to her room and spread the softness between her thighs, seeking a release from the pressure that only he could inspire.

A breathy moan escaped her lips and, for a split second, she wanted to snatch the sound back. Heat flooded her cheeks, embarrassment turning her bright red. How could she make that noise?

It was wrong.

It was right.

Because his answering groan rocked right into her core and she clenched her hands in his shirt. Drawing him closer as his hands spasmed against her back, crushing her against him.

She didn't know which one of them started walking backward. Perhaps she dragged him with her, but it felt like he led her in a dance until her back hit the wall. Something rattled beside her, a vase he'd set out maybe, and then a candelabra fell onto the ground.

"The fire," she whispered with a soft laugh as he ripped away from her neck to yank his shirt off.

And oh.

Oh.

She'd seen him shirtless before, but only in darkness. The liquid warmth of the candles illuminated the impressive planes of his chest. The rigid bumps of his abs, the "v" of muscle dipping into the low hanging pants that barely clung to those narrow hips. She could have counted the bumps of his ribs if she wished, and the tiny mounds of muscle that framed them before he dropped the shirt on top of the flames and stomped them out.

Then he was on her again. His chilled hand sliding around her waist. The other, he braced above her head, his forearm pressed against the wooden paneling as he slowly dipped his head back to her neck.

She moaned again, not trying to hide the sound this time as he licked his way up her collarbone to the twin punctures over her throbbing vein. He chased the tiny drops of blood that had leaked out and then closed his mouth around her again.

Katherine arched her back, pressing against him and her hands came down on his smooth skin.

It was vaguely like touching marble. A statue come to life. So smooth that nothing stopped her hands from gliding along his skin, seeking out her fill when she knew there would be no fill from this.

She wanted him with a ferocity that startled her. And there weren't words to describe the way she wanted to claw her way out of her own skin to get to him. Or maybe she just wanted him to claw his way inside of her.

Her hands flexed against his back, drawing him closer, needing more. More than what he was giving her, and more than either of them had desired.

But he didn't move, and she was impatient.

Katherine reached for his hand at her waist, twining their fingers together as she drew his hand up to her breast. They both groaned at the same time. Her into the air, him into her throat, and his fingers gently cupped the soft flesh there. He squeezed, then shifted ever closer to press his hips to hers.

The hard bar of his cock rubbed against her hip. She wanted to touch it, to grasp his heat in her hands, but then he used her own thumb to slide over her nipple and an electric bolt made her buck against him.

He chuckled, that tongue working its magic against her neck. He used her own hand to pleasure her, plumping her breast, pinching her nipples, all of it done by her own hand with his on top of her fingers. It was unlike anything she'd ever experienced.

Gluttony used her own body against her in so many ways. He played her like an instrument and made her sing with moans that she couldn't stop making.

"Katherine," he whispered against her neck.

And suddenly, he wasn't there anymore. He was right in front of her, his lips pressed against her own.

His warm lips spread over hers, sweet and metallic with her blood, but the taste of him as well. And it speared right through her entire body.

She threw her arms around his neck, pressing herself to every inch of him that she could. It was perfect. It was wicked, and mad, and wrong, but she wanted him more than she'd ever wanted anything else.

He growled, and she swallowed the sound deep inside herself. She didn't care anymore if he had been the one to attack those people. She didn't care if everyone else thought she'd lost her mind.

Katherine wanted this man who held onto her with a grip like iron, but whose lips remained soft and plush as velvet.

He devoured her lips far rougher than he had her neck. His tongue coiled around hers, his teeth clashing against her own, devouring her whole and coating her entire mouth with the taste of her own blood.

"You are so sweet, Kat," he muttered, pressing harder into her until she wondered if he was trying to crush her. "So sweet."

She couldn't think. Couldn't do anything but nod and drag him down for another mind numbing kiss that turned her inside out. "More," she finally bit out, and his answering growl did things to her that she hadn't expected.

"Oh, for fuck's sake." The voice sliced through her conscious.

Immediately, Katherine tore her mouth away from Gluttony's and stared up at him in horror. They both looked at each other, and she could see the blood smeared across his lips.

Hers must look like that, too.

Oh, by the gods, what had she done? What had possessed her to think this was a good idea to kiss a demon and then stand here with her blood all over her own mouth like this was normal?

"Is that why you're keeping her around, then?" Gluttony's brother laughed, but the sound wasn't kind in the slightest. "Oh, well just keep her, brother. If you just wanted to fuck, you should have told me."

"Envy," Gluttony snarled, his lips curling up like the animal so many people claimed him to be.

And those fangs. Ah, they reminded her so much of why she shouldn't be doing this.

"What?" Envy said, and she could hear his footsteps coming closer. "If I had known all this, then it wouldn't have mattered. I appreciate you trying to save her delicate sensibilities, but what man could deny you a sweet haven for release?"

Nope. She was done.

Before she smacked him or he said something else stupid, like wondering if Gluttony would share, Katherine slipped out from underneath Gluttony's arm.

She fled down the hall, not even pausing when she heard Gluttony's heartbreaking voice say, "Katherine, wait—"

She couldn't wait.

Her cheeks and ears burned so hot with embarrassment she wasn't sure if they would ever turn back to the same color they had been before. What had she been thinking? What was she doing?

This was a deal. Nothing more. She was supposed to come here, offer him her blood, and then go back home to her tiny little room in that boarding house where no one cared what she was doing.

Katherine wasn't the kind of person who got to have the attention of a demon king. She was born to poor parents and knew her place in this realm. No one crawled out of poverty by handing themselves over to a king like him.

What they did was become a whore. And clearly, he'd expected that from her.

Not that it was a problem. She wouldn't have begrudged any woman who had offered herself to him. Katherine would have probably cheered for them, done her job to thank them and look after them once they returned to the almshouse for her stitches but... but...

Slamming her bedroom door shut, she slid down it until her butt hit the ground. Her bad hip screamed with the effort of it, stretched straight out on the ground and slightly at the wrong angle.

She cared for him, she realized. A lot. Enough so that the idea of him wanting to buy her body along with her blood? It hurt. So much more than she'd expected it to because she wanted him to see her as the woman she was.

No one else had ever seen her like he did. They looked at her limp and knew her story. They knew who she was, where she'd come from, and everything that had happened to her.

And then they would look at her with pity. Gods, she hated that expression on people's faces. She hated how they offered to help her, like they didn't think she could take care of herself. Like the injury that slowed her down had ruined her life.

He didn't look at her like that.

Maybe Gluttony was blind to it. She'd gotten better at hiding the limp, but it didn't mean she... ah. This was all so jumbled and she was such an idiot.

Now she'd kissed the man. Maybe he would expect more from her, and she hadn't been so certain that she wanted to give him more. At least, not now. In the moment? Oh, she would have spread her legs, pain be damned, just to find out what that massive cock would feel like as he slid inside her. All the way in.

Deep.

Hard.

She thudded her head against the door and sighed. Now was not the time for such thoughts. She needed to get her head back on straight. She needed to remember that this was a job. Sacrifice herself for the greater good. Do something other than be the cripple the town thought they owed.

She just wanted... wanted...

The door shuddered with a forceful knock. Her first instinct was to press herself firmly against the door and shout, "Go away, Gluttony!

I don't want to talk right now!"

No other sound came from the opposite side of the door. Just silence. It took her a long time before she finally got the courage to roll onto her hands and knees, then push herself upright.

She could do this. She could face him and not turn into a puddle of goo. Or yank him into her bedroom and insist that he finish what he had started.

But when she opened the door, there wasn't anyone there. Just a small golden tray with plenty of bandages and a new jar of balm. One she had forgotten to bring back from the almshouse.

A dark mist emerged from underneath the tray, although she had to admit that Spite looked a little gray right now.

"Oh, it's you," she said quietly, gathering both the tray and the spirit up. "What are you doing here?"

"I never left."

"I haven't seen you in a week, though." She closed the door behind her with the good side of her hip and then limped over to the bed. She put everything down and then unwound the bandages. "Are you well?"

"Am I what?" It stared at her, and she wondered if anyone had ever asked if it was well. "Why do you want to know?"

"Well, I'm making friends with spirits now." She patted the little spirit on top of its head before handing it the mirror that had been hidden underneath the bandages. "Hold this, would you?"

The spirit was quiet as it propped up the mirror. Katherine took her time winding it around her neck, making sure she applied a thick layer of the healing balm before tying it off. It looked like a macabre necklace, especially with the blood still smeared around her mouth.

Sighing, she tried not to look at herself for too long.

Spite peered around the mirror, a little dark face appearing in the mist. "Did you mean that?"

"What?"

"That we're friends?"

Oh, her heart broke. "Yes. Of course I meant it."

The mirror wobbled. "Even though I haven't been very kind to you?"

This Katherine could deal with. And it was the perfect distraction from her own emotions that were rioting inside of her. She scooped the little spirit up and hugged it close. "Even though you haven't been very kind lately. Everyone deserves a friend, don't you think?"

It didn't say much after that, but she swore it was a little lighter as the day turned to night.

the demon prince

Chapter 23

Katherine wished she could say she was a braver woman. She wanted to live up to what Gluttony had called her all those months ago. Brave, kind, and confident. That was the person she wanted to be.

But for the next couple of days after their kiss, she was not that person at all.

She hid in her room. She remained avoidant and, frankly, upset about all of it. Not at him, never at him. But at herself for falling so deeply head first into a complicated situation.

Everything had been so easy in the boarding house. She had her room and her friends, or at least the people who could tolerate her. She had her job and all the people who needed her there.

Sure, she'd been lonely. Even surrounded by people, she had been more alone than she was here. And she'd recognized that.

Some nights she'd laid in bed, staring up at the ceiling, wondering if this was all she was going to have. Just her own little room, until she couldn't afford to pay for it anymore, and then what?

No one to hold her at night. No one to care if she was even gone.

But she hadn't thought the solution to that problem would be the most dangerous man in the kingdom, kissing her and touching her in such a way that the mere memory still sent flames throughout her entire body.

She wanted him.

Oh, by the gods, she was an idiot who wanted a demon king.

And so she'd spent a large amount of her time just sitting and staring out the window. Trying her best to muddle through her thoughts that were rather complicated and certainly weren't productive. She wanted to smack herself across the cheek and say that this was foolish.

But she couldn't. Because every time Katherine had settled that she would just thrust these emotions aside and forget about it, she saw his face in her mind's eye. Or she would hear a quiet knock at the door and open it to find food on the other side.

He never pushed her. Never rushed her. Gluttony was the perfect gentleman who gave her all the space and time she needed to make her own decisions. Almost as though he was well aware that she was uncomfortable about the entire situation and that he couldn't fix it.

A gray mist rolled from underneath the door, sliding through the cracks and then gathering back up in a familiar shape.

"Spite," she said quietly, returning her attention to the stunning view of the moors. "What are you doing here?"

"I should ask the same of you," the spirit grumbled. It climbed up to the windowsill to sit beside her. "You're wallowing."

"I'm not."

"You haven't left this room in days. Not even to go to that job you're so ridiculously proud of." It sounded rather disgusted that she was proud of it, though. "You should at least go into the kitchens. Get something to eat. Walk, maybe. You'll turn into soup on the floor if you stay here much longer."

She chuckled at its dramatics. "I won't turn into soup on the floor, you silly spirit."

"Silly," it muttered. "When was the last time someone called me silly?"

Katherine leaned back, more grateful for the distraction than the spirit would want to know. "Well, I don't know. I know nothing about you, really."

"Didn't your spirit seeing mother teach you anything about us?"

"If she did, I didn't listen. Everyone told me she was stark raving mad, so what little girl would listen to her mother when everyone else said spirits were made up stories?" She leaned back in her chair, letting the moors disappear from sight as she focused on the spirit. "So, go on then. What's your story?"

"Not much of one. I've been in this kingdom my entire life."

"Are spirits born?"

Spite turned slightly, the long wisps of its body falling over the windowsill like trailing water. "No. We can be created if there is a sizeable amount of one emotion in one area. Like a blast of feeling. It takes a lot of human emotion to create one of us. But it happens."

"And you were created as Spite? That's hard for me to imagine a large group of people who all felt that at the same time." What would have caused that? She knew little about the kingdom's history. So few people had any chance of schooling in Gluttony's kingdom, let alone the time to study history or art. Katherine had been thrown into working at the almshouse when she was very little. And that's where she had stayed.

Spite curled in on itself a little tighter. "I wasn't born as Spite," it muttered. "But I turned into this all the same."

Her mother had spoken of that before. That spirits, if compressed, could turn into something else.

"Do you remember what you once were?" she asked.

"No."

"Do you think you could ever go back to it?"

"Not if I don't remember what it was," Spite hissed. "What are you trying to do, human? I'm not interested in changing and you don't really want to see me change. I am what I am, and that's not going to change any time soon. So stop trying to manipulate me."

"I was just trying to help." And Katherine had gotten quite used to Spite's little outbursts lately. For all that the spirit blustered, it was turning lighter and lighter gray. The longer she was around it, actually.

"I don't want your help." It rolled off the windowsill and made a frustrated little noise. "Now get out of this damned room! Go do something."

"Like what?"

"I don't know! Help Gluttony. He's been throwing things in the lab for hours now, and I don't know what's going wrong with that stupid alchemical bullshit that he's working on." Spite hesitated at the door and then added, "But it might have something to do with the fact that his brother is still here."

Katherine's hands were on the chair arms before she noticed she'd moved. "Envy hasn't left yet?"

"No, and he's making your demon king all kinds of angry. Best get on with it. You seem to be the only person who can calm him down."

And with that, the spirit left. It left her feeling horrible for hiding. Horrible that Gluttony had to face his brother on his own and that she'd fed him to the wolves.

Sighing, she stared up at the ceiling before she nodded firmly. "All right, Katherine. You need to get yourself together."

So she did. She took a bath, washed her hair, dried it in the best way the curls would let her, and then got dressed in real clothing for the first time in a few days.

Spite had said Gluttony was in his laboratory, so that was where she'd head first. At least she could apologize for her behavior and then ask him about Envy. Together, they might be able to figure out the best steps to get his brother out of the castle.

If Gluttony even wanted to talk with her. She'd handled all of this like a child rather than the grown woman she was.

Tsking, she made quick work of eating up the distance between them. A few nights in that comfortable bed had done wonders for the ache in her hip, although she still had a bit of a limp as she rounded the corner and walked into the lab.

"Gluttony?" she called out as she strode in. Her skirts tangled between her legs, hanging her up for a second as she paused a few steps inside. "Are you in here?"

"He's not."

The door shut behind her. And she had the horrible feeling that she'd just walked into a trap.

Frowning, Katherine turned to see Envy leaning against the wall on the other side of the door.

"What are you still doing here?" she asked.

He looked far too comfortable leaning against that wall, and far too large. Katherine had never once looked at another person and been concerned for her own well being as much as she was when she stood in front of Envy. He was massive, tall and broad, and a little too watchful. His eyes trailed over her, seeing far too much.

And after his perusal, she felt lacking.

He leveraged himself off the wall and walked toward her, arms still crossed over his chest. "What am I doing here? I'm his brother. I can come and visit whenever I wish."

"I don't think he really wants you here."

Envy walked around her, leaning down to breathe into her ear, "The real question is, what are you doing here?"

She stiffened. "I'm here to help my people and to help Gluttony at the same time."

"Is that so?"

It was the truth, in a way. She was here for both of those people, even though it didn't feel like it sometimes. She wanted both her town and her king to be... happy. In whatever way that took.

Gluttony deserved happiness. She firmly believed that, and she believed that the townsfolk saw him as something other than what he truly was. How to convince them otherwise? She had no idea. Katherine wasn't the person that came up with all the plans. But she would help. She was good at that.

Envy circled her and then paused in front of her. She had to crane her neck so far back to even look up at him. She hadn't expected him to be quite so tall. Gluttony was massive, after all. And yet, this brother was even bigger.

He had tired eyes, though. And that softened her. "What do you want from me?" she asked. "I'm here for the right reasons, even if you don't believe that."

"I'm not sure you understand what the right reasons are." Envy reached out for a lock of her hair and the greasy feeling that his touch left behind made her shiver.

Only Gluttony touched her like that. He was the one who curled her hair around his fingers like it was the finest of rubies, and that made her feel good. She liked it when Gluttony touched her.

Not this man she did not know.

Katherine shook off his grip, taking a shuddering step backward. "Please don't touch me."

"Why not?"

"I don't like to be touched."

"You like it enough when my brother touches you." Envy trailed along in her footsteps, his eyes narrowing. "You seem to think that there is a connection between the two of you, but I am here to warn you, little human. Gluttony does not make attachments. He does not stay with any of his playthings for very long. You would be wise to run."

Frozen in fear, she stayed where she was, shuddering as he brushed her hair to the side and skated his fingers over the faint scars on the side of her face. "These are almost impossible to see, you know."

She did know. But that didn't mean the others, the more permanent injuries, were as hidden. She swallowed hard, trying to jerk away from him again only to find herself pressed against a table. "I said, don't touch me."

"Envy," Gluttony's voice lashed out from the doorway. Barely contained rage had him standing there, and his gaze locked on hers. "Let her go."

"Oh, hush, brother. I'm just showing you that your pet is already broken. You were unaware." Envy's eyes flashed green for a moment before he took a step back. With a satisfied expression, he gestured at her. "Haven't you noticed her limp? She's good at hiding it. And with those faint scars on her face, I'd guess she's a lot more broken than she's letting on."

This was all falling apart. Everything. Right in front of her while her heart tried to beat its way out of her chest.

She wasn't broken.

She had gotten away from all that here. Katherine had fought tooth and nail to be someone, and here she was. Sacrificing herself to save her village, with the only man who had ever seen her as a person. And he stood in that doorway, shocked, with an open mouth as he stared at her.

"Kat?" he asked.

And oh, it tore her into pieces.

He wanted to know the truth. He wanted to hear how she'd been lying to him all this time. Who was she to deny him that? Everyone deserved the truth.

Tears stung in her eyes, and she had to look at the floor for the words to come pouring out of her mouth.

"My father was lost after mother disappeared. He thought that maybe she would come back, so we stayed in the same house. Then she didn't. He went out after her and I was far too young to be alone. I was only eight years old, and I was cold. So I lit a fire in the hearth, but I didn't realize that the rug was too close after I'd been playing. I fell asleep and woke to the whole house in flames."

Katherine twisted her fingers together, beating back the memories that threatened to overwhelm her. She didn't want to think about this. It was hard enough to live it, let alone to tell him that his brother was right. She was broken. And she was a fool.

"Our house had two stories, and I tried to run down the stairs to get away from the flames. I fell down them and twisted my hip out of place, then broke my pelvic bone on the way down." She took a deep breath, steeling herself for the worst part of it. "But there was no one else in the house, and we were on the outskirts of town. It took a long time for anyone to realize the house was on fire, and I was not awake after the injury. I don't remember much, but apparently someone came and saved me. I had horrible burns all down the right side of my body along with the broken bone."

Gluttony took a staggering step into the room. "Katherine."

Even Envy looked shocked at her words.

But she couldn't stop now. So she lifted her hand, holding her palm up for silence. "They couldn't heal the bone right away because of the burns. Apparently, every time they touched me, more skin came off. So I have a permanent limp. And I have scars. It hurts every time it rains and even worse if there's a storm or a long day of walking. But I walk."

Fierce now, she looked up and met Envy's wide-eyed gaze. "I walk from here to the village. It took me two years to learn how to do that again, and I am proud of it. I stand for hours at the almshouse on my own, without sitting down. I manage the pain as best I can. I am not broken."

He pressed a hand to his chest and opened his mouth, but she wasn't ready to hear his apologies. He didn't get to apologize for something like that.

So she interrupted a king. "I am not broken," she repeated. "I was cracked and now I have been remade. Shame on you for revealing that without my permission, and for using such nasty terms."

"I didn't—"

"I don't want to hear your apologies. I don't have to forgive you."

Katherine dropped into a low curtsey before she started crying. Before the panic and anxiety of what Gluttony would think could swell and drown her. "Goodbye, gentlemen."

And with that, Katherine left the room.

Chapter 24

"Y̶ou idiot," Gluttony hissed.

"Me?" his brother growled in response. "You're the one who's had her living here this entire time and didn't know she was injured?"

"She's not injured!" Don't kill your brother, Gluttony told himself. Repeating the words in his head until he got his breathing under control. "She was injured. Just like the rest of us. We've all been injured at some point in our lives. It doesn't mean you get to point out her history!"

"I didn't! I merely noticed that she has a limp, and that she is rather covered in scars. Both details that you obviously ignored!" Envy slammed his hand down on the table and it cracked right down the middle. "I understand that I was out of line. But you cannot keep someone so fragile, Gluttony. She's already been through enough. Is this not proof that you need to let her go?"

Gluttony lunged forward. He grabbed his brother by the shirt and jerked him close. "Listen to me right now, Envy. That woman is braver and stronger than any of us. She has been through a lot. Yes, I understand that. But I will do everything in my power to ensure she is never harmed again. And right now? You're the closest thing that might harm her. So I suggest you leave."

"Or what?"

"Or I will find out just how powerful of a spirit I can consume." He snapped the words through ground teeth. "You are no brother of mine. Get out."

He tossed Envy back a few steps and then whirled to leave. He had no idea where Katherine had run off to, but there was so much for him to fix. So much that made his heart ache.

He hated she even had memories like that. Burning alive when she was so young? The pain of a twisted and broken hip that had lingered with her for the rest of her life? None of it should have been part of her memories. And wouldn't have been, if he had been with her since the beginning.

Mad thoughts danced through his mind. He wanted to break something. He wanted to hit someone for daring to hurt her, but there was nothing for him to hit. The only person he could yell at was her, for daring to put herself in danger long before he met her. Even then, he knew the thoughts were a lingering madness. He couldn't yell at her for taking risks in her life. He couldn't scold her for what she didn't know as a child.

But what he could do was be here for her. And she needed him. Because the look in her eyes when she realized she had to tell him all that? He knew what that emotion was.

Shame.

He'd seen it in his own eyes more times than he could count, and it struck him like a knife between the ribs to see it in hers. She didn't deserve to ever feel like that.

Not in front of him. He didn't care what she had been through or where she came from.

Katherine was his. And those memories were his because they were hers.

Setting his jaw, he followed her scent through his home and all the individual rooms she'd tried to hide in. He paused in one she'd only explored a few moments. She'd wandered into this abandoned study, seen all the sheets over every single piece of furniture, and then turned around.

Where was she?

It took him a little while to follow the trail outside, and then he found her. Limping down the boardwalk. She kept dashing the palms of her hands over her cheeks, and he hated to see that she was crying. For him. He'd never wanted her to cry for him.

"Katherine," he called out, making his way down the wooden planks.

"Go away, Gluttony! I don't want to talk."

"Well, I want to talk."

"And we do everything you want, is that it?"

Oh, this stubborn woman would be the death of him. Grumbling, he sped up his pace. "No, we don't. I listen to what you want, and I ask what you want. Why are you running from me?"

She tried to speed up, but then the worst happened. Her leg, oh gods, her leg. He should have noticed that limp a lot sooner than he had. But it twisted underneath her, moving a little too fast and getting caught underneath the other one. She tripped, her hands outstretched to cushion her fall, but he could already hear the snapping of her wrist bones if she fell like that.

So he sprinted forward. And he knew she didn't want him to touch her, but he had to touch her.

He had to know she was all right.

Gluttony lunged, wrapping her in his arms long before she hit the ground. Her breath stuttered, her eyes finding his arm around her waist as he drew her upright. Carefully, always so carefully.

He put her back onto her feet, holding onto her only until she was stable before he released her and held up his hands for peace. "I just want to talk," he said. "Will you let me talk?"

"I don't want to talk to you right now."

"That's fine. You don't have to say anything back. Just listen to me." He dipped slightly, forcing her to look at his face. "Yes? Will you listen at least?"

His heart wouldn't stop its rapid beat until she finally nodded. And though that made him sweat, it was permission for him to at least try to save this.

"My brother is an idiot."

She curled her lips in and he knew that she was trying to hide a disbelieving laugh. Maybe that wasn't what she'd thought he would lead with.

He smiled, relieved she could at least find some humor in all this. "I don't care what he thinks or what he says. I'm sorry you went through that. I'm sorry your life has not been as easy as I wish it had been for you, but that changes nothing. You're still Katherine."

He saw her melt, just a little. She looked at him, at least, and that soft expression returned to her gaze. "You don't agree with him?"

"That you're broken? No." Desperately, Gluttony moved a little closer and then wrapped one of her curls around his finger. He moved her hair and gently revealed the faintest of scars on the side of her face. Scars he'd never noticed at all. "Like mended bone, you are stronger now than you were then. And that is admirable."

She swallowed, and he tracked the movement with a desperation he wasn't used to.

He wanted... No, he needed her to stay. He couldn't survive without her. Didn't she see that? And he was willing to do anything, say anything...

"I don't want to say goodbye to you," he said abruptly. "I don't have a lot of friends, Katherine."

"That's rather obvious."

"You could have at least pretended to be surprised," he grumped, pleased when she finally smiled at him.

"I'm not surprised, though, and I have no wish to lie to you." Katherine swallowed, and that shadow passed in front of her face again. "Or at least, anymore."

"You never lied." Gluttony reached for her hip and then tugged her into his arms. He wrapped her firmly in his grip, needing her to understand that his words were true. "You had no reason to tell me about your history or how you were hurt. I never asked. You never offered. Neither of those are lies."

"I don't think we've been very good friends to each other," she murmured against his collarbone. "Friends know about the things that happened in each other's pasts. They know everything about the person, as though they are an extension of another."

"Is that true?" He rocked her side to side. "I've never had a friend. I'm afraid you'll have to teach me how to be a good one."

"Well, I suppose we could start over..." Katherine pulled out of his arms and held out her hand. "Hello. My name is Katherine. I was injured in a fire when I was very little, and I have a permanent limp and a very painful leg."

He took her hand without hesitation. "Hello, Katherine. My name is Gluttony. I am a spirit who has taken flesh and then named myself a god. Most people in this kingdom are terrified of me. You probably should be too."

"Why's that?"

"Because I wish to drink your blood, and the smell of it makes me forget that anything else exists."

She bit her lip. "That sounds like an obsession."

"Oh it is." With a solemn nod, he tugged her a little closer, leaning in for dramatics. "I would burn this whole kingdom to the ground for a drop of your blood."

"How terrifying."

"Indeed. You should be very frightened."

She stared up into his eyes, so joyful and pleased, when moments ago she'd been running in fear. "Why would I ever be frightened of you?"

Gluttony bared his teeth in a snarl, knowing his fangs were on full display. "You're right. I can't imagine a single reason at all."

They stared at each other for a few moments. He didn't know what was going on in her mind, but he knew that in his, he was just happy to be here with her. That she hadn't left. He'd successfully convinced her that he wasn't a monster, yet again, and she wasn't running any more.

That was enough.

It was enough to know that she looked at him and saw a man. Still. After everything she had seen and experienced.

"Well?" he finally said, interrupting the moment and releasing her hand. "Are you going to come back with me?"

"Is Envy there?"

"My brother goes where he wants," Gluttony replied with a heavy sigh. "I asked him to leave, and I believe it was very obvious I have no interest in taking no for an answer this time. But whether or not he does leave... That is the question."

"You cannot make him?" Katherine started back up the boardwalk, toward the castle that was a surprising distance from them.

"None of us can make any of our kind do anything. Though we are all powerful in our own way, we are all equally yoked." He shrugged at her strange expression. "Similar power levels. He has illusions and nasty tattoos that can take any form he wishes. Although I am quicker and stronger, with claws that certainly could rend his flesh, it would be hard to reach him through the guards he keeps quite literally in his skin."

"And if he were to attack you?"

"I would put up a fight that would destroy most, if not all, of his magical guards."

She hummed low under her breath, the strange gait of her limp no longer hidden as she stepped across the boards. "Is that the same with the rest of your brothers?"

"In a way." It felt rather freeing to talk about his family with someone who didn't know them. Someone who would side with him no matter what he said. "There are two of my brothers who are significantly stronger, one in particular that none of us would wish to fight. Wrath is the dangerous one. But Pride is the brains behind everything, and he plays Wrath like a puppet. So it is... dangerous for any of us to go up against those two."

"Theoretically, you could team up with Envy and then no one would attack either of you." She paused, lifting a brow to see if she was right.

"Unfortunately, together we are not even as strong as one of them." He inclined his head at her scoff. "I know it's hard to believe, but the politics of kings are... difficult. To say the least."

"A commoner like myself would have a hard time understanding any of it."

"That's not what I meant." He finally gave in to temptation and skated his finger over her cheek. "My brothers are so beyond anything humans have experienced before. Spirits have limits, just like everything else. But we are infinitely powerful and immortal. Nothing that we know of can kill us."

"Are you sure of that?" Her gaze searched his, and he wondered why she was suddenly so afraid.

"Many have tried to kill me. I've survived it so far." But he knew there was more to this. "What's going on in that head of yours?"

She turned her attention away from him, toward the town that was far in the distance. He could just barely make out the coils of smoke that rose from their chimneys. Why was she looking there, though?

"Their necks..." she whispered before shaking her head and looking back at him. "Gluttony, I've been thinking about their necks. They said it was you, but I've seen the wounds you leave. They aren't intentional, and that's very apparent in how rough they are. I don't... I think someone might be trying to impersonate you. Someone is killing these people, there's no doubt about that."

"How is there no doubt that it's not a creature?"

"One of the victims could barely speak. But she continued to say something about him. A man. She kept saying something about how dark it was and how he was so strong." Katherine shook her head. "It all lines up with you, but rather like shoving a similar puzzle piece into the same space. It lines up, but the picture is wrong."

"And all we're left with is a concerning picture indeed." Yes, her words were troubling. There were very few people who would try to harm him like this.

Gluttony didn't have a good reputation amongst the townsfolk. All anyone would really need to do was mention that they'd heard he was killing again, and that was more than enough to make people mistrustful.

Why were they killing anyone? It seemed like a lot of effort for very little reason.

He placed his hand on the small of her back and steered her back toward the castle. "You are still certain you wish to work?"

"Yes?" Katherine stared up at him, letting him guide her across the planks. "Why are you bringing that up now?"

"If those men were bothering you because they thought you were with me, then perhaps I will give them a reason to leave you alone. I'd like to come with you into town next time."

"That doesn't seem like a good idea."

"Oh, it's a fantastic idea." He wouldn't let her go alone. He needed to get her safely back in the castle so he could work this plan out a little better. "I prefer to know who my enemies are, and where they are. Rather than let them scatter my people like rats fleeing a sinking ship."

"Gluttony," she scolded.

"What?" He looked down at her with mock surprise on his features. "You don't agree?"

"I don't think you should risk it."

"Ah, but I cannot be killed." Wrapping an arm around her shoulders, he gave her a little squeeze. "And I have my best friend by my side. What could possibly go wrong?"

Chapter 25

S he didn't want to be friends.

Katherine realized that only a few days after their conversation. She didn't want to be friends with this strange and wonderful man who now drank from her neck when he wished. Just the touch of his lips against her skin made her entire body turn into a bonfire.

And he didn't know.

How could he? Gluttony was so certain everyone thought of him as a monster that he'd never noticed her shivers weren't shudders of revulsion, but something else entirely.

He thought she wanted to get away from him. He'd even mentioned it a few times that if he could let her go, he would. But she didn't want that. She wanted to stay in the castle with him. Wanted to keep working in his lab and hear his little pleased chuffs as if he were proud of himself for little details that moved him ever closer to discovery.

She was... Oh, she was so lost in all of this and Katherine had needed space. She'd asked for time away from the castle, just to get her head on straight. Because she was starting to really like him, and he only wanted to push her away.

He was reluctant to let her leave, as Gluttony always was. The few times she'd come home late, he'd been in such a strange mood that she wondered if he didn't know how to deal with worry.

After hours of arguments that had devolved into her threatening her own life if he came with her, he finally agreed. Though he'd given her a knife this time to put in her stocking. Just in case.

Katherine didn't think she would ever use it, even if those men attacked her. She wasn't cut out for violence, in any way, shape, or form.

Still, she kept her wits about her as she clomped down the boardwalk toward the town. At least now she didn't have to hide her limp so much. She'd forgotten what it was like to walk without making sure her gait was even. Now, she tried to find that rhythm again as she approached her hometown.

"Good morning!" A young man called out. His dark hair flopped over his forehead and his bright grin revealed rows of crooked teeth.

She didn't know this young man either. And she hated how it made her so nervous to even respond to him. But Katherine could still feel the dagger in her stocking, so she nodded back. "Good morning. I'm afraid I don't recognize you, friend."

"Ah, there's a fair few of us new to town." He winked. "I haven't seen you around these parts either."

Katherine made sure her hair covered the slight scarring on her face and knew that now, more than ever, she had to hide her limp. The men on the boardwalk before might have spoken of her. They certainly had known who she was, and there was only one rare factor about her visage. "I'm so sorry, I can't stay to introduce myself."

"Why's that?"

"Work!" she cheerily replied as she walked past him, hoping she looked like a normal person.

Who were all these people? Ducking her head low, she made her way to the almshouse in a rush. So many strangers in this town didn't sit right.

This town didn't get new folks. The people here had survived on their own for years, and if people were new to the kingdom, they stayed near the light bridge that connected them to freedom. It took years for a person to give up their hopes that they might escape.

So why were they here? There was nothing in this town for them to steal or take. She had few belongings that she called her own, and Katherine knew there were many people who were in the same situation as her. Anyone who came here looking for treasure, or even work, would be sorely disappointed.

The boards to the almshouse were loose. She stumbled and caught herself on the railing, but stared down into the water not to see dangerous features staring back at her, but concerned expressions on the souls of the lost. Almost as though they knew something she didn't.

Gulping, Katherine quickly made her way to the almshouse after that. Stumbling through the door, she closed it firmly behind her and caught her breath.

Palms pressed to the cool wood, she forced her heart to slow down. This was the safest place in town. No one attacked the sick or the dying.

Why had she insisted on coming here?

Because maybe something deep in her soul wanted to prove that Gluttony was a monster. This was the only place that blatantly screamed he was a monster. He was killing people. All the wounded in here were supposedly murdered by him, and she should hate him. Fear him, even.

A hand settled on her shoulder and she let out a shriek.

Spinning around wildly, she tried to put weight on her bad leg so she could reach the knife, but that only resulted in her falling against the door and losing her balance. She would have crumbled into a ball if Grace hadn't grabbed onto both her shoulders and held her where she was.

"Katherine!" Grace gave her a little shake, as though that might help knock her out of this state. "What has gotten into you?"

"I... I..." Eyes wide, Katherine couldn't stop the words from tumbling out of her mouth. "There are so many strangers in town, Grace."

Grace's features changed. Something hardened in her eyes as she dropped her hands from Katherine. "So they've bothered you as well?"

"Bothered?" Katherine shook her head. "Worse than that. They threatened me the last time I came to town, and it sounded rather personal. Almost as though they knew where I have been staying. Like they've been following me."

That tough expression was one Katherine had never seen on her friend's features before. Grace had always been soft and kind, even to the hallucinating patients they'd once had. The patients had all eaten a certain type of moss that caused them to believe everyone in the almshouse was hunting them.

Grace hadn't ever held anything against anyone. Her heart was pure as gold, and light as a wisp.

But right now? She looked like she wanted to hurt someone. She looked like she wanted to punch, and bite, and scratch until that fear deep in their bellies was gone.

"Listen to me," Grace said, stepping closer as though she didn't want anyone to hear what she was going to say. "Something is happening here. I don't know what. I don't know who these men are or where they came from, but they are dangerous. You hear me?"

"I have gathered that much."

"The things they are saying, Katherine, it's changing this town." She dropped her head and whispered, "I've been waiting for you to come back because you need to know—"

A deep voice interrupted them. Alexander, their boss.

"Katherine, I've been waiting for you to return." He stood in the hallway that led toward his office and also partially their surgery room. "Come with me, please."

"I was almost done speaking with Grace," she replied. "I'll follow you in a moment."

"Now." His voice whipped through the air, angry and almost mean. "I'm afraid I have no time to wait today. I'm actively in a surgery."

She looked at Grace and noted how her friend's face had paled. So much so that even her lips had lost all color.

What had Grace been about to tell her?

Apparently, there was no time for her to listen, though. Anger bristled through her. Katherine knew this was in part because she'd been allowed more freedom in Gluttony's home. Even a demon king would not have spoken to her like that, and yet she was expected to run to her boss's side because he snapped his fingers.

She was not a dog. He could not order her around however he

saw fit.

Squaring her shoulders, Katherine followed him into surgery. There was another woman laid out there, her body already growing cold with death. She'd smelled it so many times in her life, it was a wonder that it wasn't stuck in her nose.

The woman still wore her clothing, a rarity when they performed surgeries. But it was hard to mistake the gashes that had ripped her throat open. So many of them. Terrible, slicing gashes that were pale and bloodless.

Again, this was not the work of Gluttony. She knew that her people must think it was. With wounds on the neck and no blood in the body, surely that was the work of a demon. But it wasn't.

Katherine had seen what he did. She knew he didn't rake his fangs through someone's throat unless they moved on their own. Or at the very least, he'd never do that to her.

"Do you see this?" Alexander said. He pointed to the marks on the young woman's neck. "This is the seventh person that's come in today."

"I don't recognize her face."

"No. They're all strangers. I've never seen anything like it, but it's made me leery."

Alexander had once been a very handsome man. When Katherine was a child, she remembered overhearing conversations between the women of who would be lucky enough to be his wife. She'd even caught a few women arguing over who was worthy enough for a prize like him.

But time had not been kind to their resident healer. His once golden hair was now streaked with yellowed grays. His skin had sagged and sallowed, and the bags under his eyes were loose. He looked perpetually tired and even when he wasn't tired, he just looked angry.

And right now, he was more angry than she'd ever seen him.

Katherine needed to tread carefully. Licking her lips, she moved to the other side of the body and brushed the woman's hair out of her face. "It is a shame to see so many strangers in our town lately. They seem to not understand how things work around here."

"Shouldn't that change?" Alexander looked up at her then, his eyes burning with rage. "They see the problem. They understand our plight. You are quick to deny them when they are the ones offering a solution, Katherine."

She furrowed her brows in confusion. "I'm not sure what you're saying, Alexander."

"Is it true that you've been traveling to Gluttony's castle?"

She could have heard a pin drop in the silence that followed. How did she respond to that? So few people knew what she had done, and that was only because she refused to brag. Katherine hadn't made the deal with Gluttony to be a martyr to her people. She'd done it for... Well, she wasn't all that certain these days why she'd done it.

But she wasn't going to lie about it, either.

"Yes," she replied after a brief hesitation. "I have been going to his castle. I made a deal with him. My blood, and my blood alone, so that he would leave our people to their own devices."

"And you believed him?"

"I do."

Alexander pounded the metal surgery table with his fist. "That sounds like you still believe him, Katherine, and I thought you were smarter than that."

Her jaw dropped open before she could catch herself. "What do you mean? He's not doing this, Alexander. Look at the wounds! We have spent years treating women who came in after making a deal with him. The wounds don't look like that."

"He's gotten more bold, more hungry. He's eating our people, Katherine, and he's killed before."

One.

He'd killed one person. They'd saved all the others, and Katherine knew because she'd been there. And she couldn't imagine Gluttony killing anyone, even though she was certain he had done it before.

He didn't want to murder people. How did no one else see that but her?

"Alexander, I think there are a lot of people saying things that are simply not true. Right now, we have to focus on what we can see and what we can fix. That is our job as healers." She was botching this, but really, what did the man expect from her? "I do not believe, in this instance, that he has done anything wrong."

The man who had paid her for a rather significant amount of years lunged for her across the table. Though she flinched, Katherine couldn't pull away fast enough. Alexander's fingers pinched her chin and forced her to tilt her head down.

"Look at her," he snarled. "Look at this woman who could have lived until she was well into her eighties. Look at the life he has taken and tell me again that you believe him innocent."

Because he was so adamant, and because his fingers hurt, she looked.

This young woman had been beautiful in life, she was certain of it. Her skin was clear of any acne or scars. Her lovely dark hair billowed in pretty curls that framed her elven features. Lovely, likely a woman who many men had tried to win, and none of them had succeeded. Because she was here. Dead.

But those marks around her throat were not made by anyone's

teeth. She'd seen Gluttony's fangs up close and personal. She knew how wide they were and what damage they might do, and it was not that.

He could not tear holes that large. He could not rip through flesh like it was paper and leave it so mangled that it appeared she had been skinned.

"This was not him," she replied. "And if you were in your right mind, you would know it was not him. One of the creatures in the swamp, perhaps. Or those strangers who have come into our home and spread these lies."

He jerked her head to the side, now forcing her to look at him. At all that anger that simmered underneath the surface. "He has warped your mind. Some magic spell has bound you to him."

"I am sound of mind and purpose." Katherine placed her hand calmly over his, coaxing him to release her face. "I know you want to point fingers at the villain, Alexander, but I don't think we know who that villain is yet."

He watched her like she'd lost her mind. Staring at her with wide eyes and a mouth that opened over and over before he finally said, "I cannot have a woman who sees so little working for this clinic."

"Excuse me?"

"You are blind to those who harm others, and that makes me question why you are working here at all. Are you stealing blood for him? Draining more of these victims before they can die?"

She flinched away from him, staggering back from the table as her entire body rebelled at the accusation. Vomit rose in her throat at the mere thought. "What are you saying?"

"He's made you into a monster for him," Alexander muttered, before lifting a hand and pointing his finger at her. "It's not safe to have you around my patients. You are no longer allowed in this clinic. Nor are you allowed to step foot anywhere near it."

"You can't fire me, Alexander. I'm your best stitcher." Katherine tried her best to reason with him. "This is just a misunderstanding, and I can prove that these are not the same marks that he's left before."

"Get out!" he shouted. His voice rang out through the surgery room, echoing down the hall, and she knew that all the other people who worked here had heard him. "Get out, demon!"

Flinching, Katherine realized this could quickly turn into a dangerous situation. She did need to leave. She should run, but she couldn't because of her damn leg.

So she strode out of the surgery room with her head held high. As she left she looked for Grace, but her friend wasn't here any longer. The only people looking back at her were unfriendly faces filled with suspicion.

They would believe anything they were told, she realized. And this town was no longer safe for someone like her.

Chapter 26

"Envy?" Gluttony said, pushing his glasses up his nose as he looked at his newest experiment. "Get out of my lab."

"I'm just looking."

"No, you are not. You're touching." He sighed and spun around on the stool, watching his brother poke at everything he could get his fingers on. "You're leaving smudge marks."

"I am not." Envy lifted a vial up to the light, tilting it back and forth. "See? Perfectly clean."

"Still touching."

His brother heaved a rather dramatic sigh and then placed the vial back on the table. "You really are too finicky about these things. I can replace any vial I might break."

"But not what's inside it."

"Yes, yes, we all know how finicky you are about your things."

At least Envy put the vial down, but apparently he was taking this opportunity to talk.

Gluttony didn't want to talk. He was getting significantly closer to solving his brothers' problems, and that was all because of a small amount of lunar caustic he had left over from a while ago. He'd found the dust covered bottle in the very back of his lab and thought to give it a try.

The black mist had turned a pretty deep blue. Which meant, unsurprisingly, he was correct. The mist that had been used to attack both him and Greed was alchemical in origin, and he could figure out what it was made of.

Envy was only prolonging that process, however, and he needed his brother to leave.

Envy, apparently, had other opinions. His brother snatched another stool and set it in front of Gluttony, plopping down beside his workstation and grabbing yet another vial.

"Has she forgiven me, yet?" Envy asked, looking at the pale yellow substance through the glass.

"For telling her that she was less worthy because of her past injuries?" Gluttony snorted. "Oh, sure. She's forgiven you."

"Well, that's good then."

"I was being sarcastic." Gluttony pushed his glasses up again and turned back toward the vials, ignoring his brother's spluttering anger. "She will not forgive you without a reason to, and all you've done since then is hide or lurk around us. You need to actually apologize for it."

"I did."

"You haven't said a word to her since the whole ordeal." Gluttony rolled his eyes, trying his best to focus on his work and not on his idiot brother. "She's not a toy for you to play with. She's a woman who was extremely insulted by what you said. And has every right to be."

"I'm not good with women. I'm better with toys."

"Is that what you call your conquests these days?" he asked, while tilting a slight amount of ammonia into his vial. "I'm sure they appreciate that very much. They probably return to their mother and sing your praises about how the demon of envy thought they were fun to play with."

"Sarcasm doesn't suit you."

"Oh, it always has. You just don't like hearing that you aren't a very good person."

Envy stiffened beside him. "I'm a fine person. Besides, we aren't people, anyway. We're demon kings who rule our kingdoms because no one else could do it properly."

Yet again, another one of his brothers showcased the arrogance that had gotten them all in trouble to begin with. Instead of arguing, although he wanted to, Gluttony peered at his experiment and asked, "Do you really believe that?"

They sat in silence for a while as his brother thought over his words. And Gluttony found himself surprised at Envy's response.

"No, I suppose I don't. My kingdom had always been well off long before I ever got involved, and I inherited that. My councillors do most of the work for me, while I live in luxury until there are times when they need me." Envy shrugged. "It's not the same existence as the others, and I acknowledge that. I am less of a king and more of a glorified god they send out to their enemies when the time comes."

"Enemies." Gluttony coughed out a laugh. "What enemies do mortals make?"

"You'd be surprised." Envy's voice had darkened into a low growl. "They make more enemies than you or I could ever dream of. They spend their lives fighting and fucking and dying. It's all they care about. Those three things."

"You sound like you have more experience with their kind than you're letting on." Gluttony finally put down his experiment and turned to his brother. Removing his glasses to clean them, he asked, "I thought you were always the brother who avoided humans?"

"I take what others have," Envy replied. "So what makes you think I haven't taken mortals as well?"

They stared at each other while Gluttony tried to understand what Envy was telling him. "You clearly wish for Katherine to forgive you. Why? Because you wish to take her for your own?"

"I cannot lie and say that I haven't thought about it. You and her are so very comfortable with each other. It is tempting to want that for myself." Envy held up his hand before Gluttony could lash out. "But I have no interest in your pretty little broken doll, brother. I only wish to not be the person who has ruined that for you."

"Why?"

"Because there is change in the wind, brother. Change that neither you nor I can understand." Envy leaned forward, bracing his elbows on his knees. "Lust is no longer the same spirit. Neither is Greed. I have to wonder if this is a reckoning for all of us."

"We all knew it would come."

"We did. But we do not know what will happen if we cannot control ourselves." Finally, Envy looked back at him. "I fear what will happen if we do not adapt. You or I are not ones to change who we are easily. I see myself in you, Gluttony. What will happen if you cannot fix yourself and your need to consume? Will your kingdom be taken from you? Will you fall behind as the tides of change sweep everyone else to sea?"

"Are you worried?" Gluttony asked. "You seem so very much unlike yourself."

He had to admit, however, Envy's words struck true. They had seen two of their brothers change, and their kingdoms flourished because of it. Both of them now had a partner to rule with, and the women had made significant changes to their realms.

Lust worked harder than ever, and with more focus than any of their brothers had seen. His kingdom was already producing spells and magic for people to bring to their own kingdoms. Greed's kingdom was slowly piecing itself back together. The fractured desert had always fought, but now it appeared to be fixing those long open wounds.

What would Gluttony's kingdom do if he changed himself? He had a hard time imagining it.

"So you think this woman might be the one to change me?" he asked, before tossing his head in denial. "I doubt it. Katherine is a captive who made a deal with me to save her people. There is no love between us. Nothing other than an understanding that she is here to do her duty for her people."

"And yet, she keeps coming back."

"Because her people need her to."

"Because she wants to," Envy hissed. "How can you be so blind? I have seen her with you, brother. I've seen the way she even moves differently. As though you put her entirely at ease and no other person has ever given her that chance. You need to open your eyes or you will lose her."

"Why are you saying all this?"

"I am afraid!" Envy shouted, and his words echoed back at them. The truth ringing clearly in every word. "I am afraid I cannot change and I want to make sure that you are well. If I cannot fix myself, then

I will damn well fix you."

Gluttony stared at his brother, wondering if Envy had lost his mind. "Of all our siblings, you know I am lost the farthest in darkness. There is no saving me, Envy."

"You see yourself in a far different light than anyone else who meets you. I can save you, brother, and that starts with the woman I gravely insulted." Envy turned his head toward the door and then gestured for Gluttony to get up. "She's back. Go to her."

"I have work to do. Katherine knows this. I'll see her tonight when I... I..." Gluttony paused when he saw the absolute devastation on Envy's features.

"Don't waste so much time," Envy said, his voice pitched little more than a whisper. "Go to her, brother. We never know how much time we have with them until it is too late."

And Gluttony found himself standing. Perhaps it was the thought of losing her so soon, when he hadn't actually said everything that needed to be said. Or perhaps it was the strangeness in his brother's voice, but he couldn't remain here.

Not when Katherine was in his castle. Not when her footsteps echoed through the halls and the scent of her trailed through the air.

He wanted her more than he'd ever wanted anything in his life. This woman who was so lovely, but who had no idea just what she was.

Gluttony caught up to her halfway to her room. She was muttering to herself, words he couldn't quite catch, but he relaxed the moment he heard her voice.

"Katherine," he called out, rushing a bit to join her in the dusty, dark hall. "I wasn't expecting you to return so soon."

She whirled around and he saw the frantic panic in her eyes before she burst out, "Are you sure you're not killing anyone lately?"

Gluttony froze. Hadn't they already had this conversation? "I am not."

"You're not sleepwalking?"

"No." He scratched the back of his neck. "I don't sleep."

"Then I know I am right. Someone is impersonating you, trying to kill as many people as they can, and then get away with it." She shook her head, tiny furrows appearing between her eyes that he wanted to smooth out with his thumb. "But I cannot puzzle out why they're doing it. You're an easy target, certainly, but do they simply just enjoy killing? It's a gruesome way for someone to die. And yet, nothing seems to make sense."

He approached her, arms raised like he was trying to tame a wild horse. "I'm not following what you're saying, Kat."

"I'm saying there are so many new people in town. Ten? Twenty? More men than I saw, I'm certain of that. They're all swarming that town and bringing in these mangled dead bodies while saying you did it. It doesn't make sense." She tapped her lips before her shoulders rounded in on themselves. "I'm sorry. I can't figure it out."

"Someone clearly wishes for your town to rebel against me. It's not the first time it's happened." Gently, he reached for her hands and took them in his own. "It's not your job to fix this, you know."

"I feel like it is." She stared up at him, those big green eyes seeing far too much. "I'm the only one who can tell them the truth. You cannot defend yourself. They won't believe you. And every single one of them wishes to paint you as some kind of demon, and I just won't let them."

He squeezed her hands and tried to smile. "Kat."

"What? Don't use that tone with me."

"I am a demon." He tugged her a little closer, because how could he leave her so far away from him? She was a lioness, protecting him until the bitter end. "My brothers and I are all the villains in these stories. I've accepted it a long time ago."

She let him reel her in, but she didn't come into his arms as he'd expected.

Of course she didn't. His Katherine was not the kind of person to take comfort in a time like this. Instead, she braced her hands on his chest and stared up at him with determination and strength.

"Someone needs to tell them the truth," she said. "Someone needs to show them that you are not the monster they believe you to be."

"How are you so certain of that?"

"Because I have been here for a while now and I see how hard you struggle. How much you work to make sure that your brothers are safe even when they give you no reason to treat them so well." And then, as if she couldn't help herself, Katherine reached up and traced her finger across his bottom lip. "And I have seen how gentle you are. I know what it feels like to have these hands on me. To touch you as I wish and to know what it is like for your fangs to be in my neck. You are not a killer, Gluttony. I truly believe that."

Oh, and how that hurt. She had to know that he'd killed before. The rumors were rampant in his kingdom about the young woman he'd murdered in cold blood.

"You know that's not true," he whispered.

But he'd expected her to withdraw from him, and instead, she only took another step closer. Their hearts beat as one, thundering against each other as though struggling to touch through their ribs. "Tell me the truth of it," she said. "I want to know."

And for the first time since it happened, he wanted to tell someone.

"It is not a pretty story," he murmured. "That part of my life is not something I am overly proud of. Nor is the ending happy."

"I saw her body." Katherine didn't even stiffen when she said it. Just allowed the words to come out of her, so pragmatic and simple. "I was there when they brought her back to town. I remember her father crying and shrieking. I remember everyone in town believing that they should hunt you down."

"They likely should have."

"You didn't let me finish." This time, she put those gentle fingers over his mouth to keep him silent. "I remember what she looked like. How peaceful and serene her expression was. How her eyes were fluttered shut like she'd just closed them and how there were only two twin drops of blood on her neck. So pale and graceful she might have been asleep."

Oh, the words hurt to hear. He remembered how she'd looked. Gluttony had been the one to bring her back home after he'd done... what he'd done.

It still hurt to think about. It still killed him that he'd had to do it, and now, he had to tell this other wonderful woman. She'd look at him differently after this, but... It was the right thing to do.

And he was trying so hard to do the right thing these days.

Folding his hand around hers, he drew her toward his study. "Come. We'll want to be comfortable for this story, and I need a good few glasses of brandy before I say it."

Katherine squeezed his hand back and followed him with a small limp. "Take all the time you need. I'm just proud of you for telling me the story at all."

He wondered how long those feelings would last once she heard the truth.

Chapter 27

She wasn't sure if she should be sick to her stomach with nerves or so shaky on her feet. Was this a normal reaction to a man agreeing to tell her how he murdered someone?

Katherine trailed him through the hallway, mourning the loss of his heat and wondering what had happened between them that would lead him here. Gluttony clearly thought that whatever he had to say would change her. That she would look at him like he was the monster everyone said he was.

Didn't he know she was beyond that?

A resolve burned deep in her belly. She would prove to him that she was not the person he thought she was. She wasn't some pawn who listened to the town's whims. Katherine made her own decisions about him, and she'd already decided that he wasn't a nightmarish beast.

Now, more than ever, she realized there were layers to people. Just as there were layers to Alexander who had fired her over something so silly as to think that she had been brainwashed by the man in front of her.

How could she be? He strode down the hallway, his back rounded in despair as he led her to his study. And she already knew the room was more comfortable for him than anywhere else. He would linger in his chair, cozying up next to the fire that never went out before he told her a story that he thought would rip them apart. What monster was this? A man who was willing to own his own actions?

No, he was no monster. But he needed someone to prove that to him.

As she walked into his office behind him, a plan was already formulating in her mind. First, she would woo him. Flowers were always a good option, and he looked like the kind of man who wouldn't be insulted if she brought him handfuls of flowers. In fact, he might even appreciate the effort. Then she would tell him nice things about himself, all leading up to a quiet evening where she would kiss him again.

Because she wanted to kiss him. By all the gods and the seven kingdoms, she'd wanted to do it again since the first time they'd touched. She wanted to feel him arching against her, and moving at the same beat. She wanted...

He stood before the fire, his back to her and the red light turning him into a ghostly silhouette. The darkness that surrounded him was... eerily familiar.

"Spite," she said with surprise. "There you are. I haven't seen you in ages!"

The little spirit rolled out from underneath Gluttony's desk, pulling its tendrils away from him and slowly moving toward her. But it wasn't black anymore. Not at all. The little gray spirit looked like it was ill.

She gathered it up in her arms, holding it against her heartbeat as she looked it over. "What happened to you?"

The spirit didn't seem capable of speech, and it was Gluttony who responded. "It's changing."

"It's what?"

"Changing into something else." He gave the spirit a wry grin, and she thought he looked rather sad as well. "At least one of us can change."

She wanted to ask what he meant by that. Why would he need to change?

But he was already shaking his head again and turning away from her. "I killed her. You know that much."

With the spirit still in her arms, she sank into the chair on the opposite side of his desk. "I think everyone knows that. We all saw you bring her body into the town."

"She..." He took a deep breath. "She was the first person to walk into this castle and see me as something other than a demon. I still remember the first time she walked up that boardwalk. She was all confidence, Katherine. A swagger to her hips and a determined expression on her face. Larissa, she said her name was. And that she was going to be the first person to enter my castle in a hundred years."

That was right. Larissa was her name. Katherine nodded and held Spite a little tighter. "She was beautiful, I remember. Her father used to say that everyone would want to marry his girl."

"They all did." He huffed out a chuckle. "That was part of her problem, you see. She didn't want to get married. She wanted to leave this place, grow her own family in another kingdom, see what she could make of herself without her family name shadowing everything that she did."

A dark, bitter silence followed after that. Katherine knew better than to push him, so she remained quiet while he meandered through his dark feelings.

"At first, I refused. I couldn't stand to see such beauty wasted in a castle like this." Gluttony cleared his throat, and then added, "On a man like me. But she was persistent, like you. She didn't give me the opportunity to turn her away, and soon enough, she was joining me for dinner. She used to bring food up from the village, good bread and wine and cheese. Showing me everything that your town could offer, and then denying it to me if I did not comply.

"At the time, I was not feeding on anyone. I had tasted and devoured everything that I could and I'll admit, the boredom was beginning to drive me mad. I am Gluttony, Katherine. My purpose in life is to consume and to devour. There is nothing else for me."

She wanted to argue that there was so much more, and yet he didn't want to hear it. She knew that.

His shoulders lifted up and down in another deep breath. "Soon enough, we talked more about what I was. Who I was. She wanted to know everything about being a demon, and I was so tired of being alone. I wanted to talk with her. I wanted to know what she thought when I bared my very soul.

"And she liked it. She liked me. I remember the first time she kissed me." He lifted a hand and pressed his fingers to his lips. "I'd tasted hundreds of women in the thousand years of my life, but none of them had been so willing as her. She wrapped me right around her fingers and that was why, years later, after she'd finally given up on her dream of escaping, I was so surprised when she came here and offered me her neck."

Katherine frowned and couldn't stop herself from asking, "Why would she do that?"

"She knew the temptation. Larissa was a smart woman. She knew the only thing I'd never tasted was... her. The life that flowed in her veins. Through all of your veins."

To her immense relief, he finally turned back to her and sat down in his chair. The desk between them might as well have been an ocean. He looked so... defeated.

He wouldn't meet her eyes as he continued to tell her what had happened. "At first, that was our relationship. She came here with the expressed interest at having me feed from her. Even after her father betrothed her to a man from another village."

"I didn't know that."

"No one did." He shook his head, his lip curling in disgust. "Her father saw her as a trophy. A prize to be given away to the person he deemed most worthy of touching his offspring. But she didn't want to be touched by anyone but me. And I..."

He stopped talking.

Jealousy churned in her belly for a few moments before she had to thrust it aside. Spite tucked itself against her belly, and she almost could feel it wriggling into her body. She wanted to hear him say terrible things about Larissa, not that she was lovely and that she...

Katherine breathed, "She loved you."

Gluttony nodded. "In her own way. But I did not love her back. I am a demon, Katherine. The feelings of love and devotion are so far from what I am capable of. It crushed her. I think in some part of her mind she'd always thought I would save her from the marriage. That as their king, I could order her father to give her to me."

"It would solve a lot of her problems."

"But I couldn't do anything at all. I couldn't save her anymore than I could gift her freedom. She would have been nothing more than a blood slave if she stayed with me." His fingers tapped a rhythm against his knee, and she wasn't certain he was aware he was doing it. "I told her as much, and she disappeared for a while. I feared something had happened to her, but then... she came back."

Just like Katherine had. Just like he'd been so afraid that she wouldn't.

Gluttony saw the thoughts in her eyes and nodded. "Yes, that's why I've always been... nervous that you wouldn't come back. Because she almost didn't. Her father had beaten her bloody, and I was the monster who stood there, looking at this beaten woman, wondering if her blood would taste sour because of what had happened."

Her heart twisted in her chest. She knew that this was some kind of compulsion for him. How could she not? Katherine had always seen the way he watched her with hunger when it had been too long since he had fed. She understood the need drove him sometimes, but... that was cruel. Even for him.

He nodded. "Ah, you see now. I am not proud of the reaction, nor do I believe anyone else should be subjected to my dark thoughts. It took only a moment for her to thrust herself in front of me. I thought for a second that she had come seeking my help. And if she had asked me to hide her, I would have.

"But that was not why Larissa came to my castle that night." He swallowed hard, his throat bobbing with emotion. "She asked me to drain her dry. That I should have the last meal and to know what death itself tastes like. That she couldn't live like this anymore. Not in this kingdom. Not with her father. And not without my love."

"So she..."

"She wanted me to kill her," he finished for her. "She asked for it, and I did what she wanted without question. I should have stopped. I should have begged her to reconsider or to think for a few more moments, but I did not. I held her in my arms and I listened to the sound of her dying breath as I drank from her. And even now I remember how peaceful she sounded."

Tears gathered in his eyes, turning those red orbs glassy as he seemingly begged for her to understand what he had done. He wanted her to condemn him for murdering a young woman.

What a terrible memory to rule his life.

Slowly, Katherine stood. She set Spite down on the chair. The little spirit was almost liquid as it watched her walk around the desk and then kneel in front of Gluttony.

Placing her hands gently on his knees, she looked up into his eyes to make sure he understood what she was about to say. "You are not a monster for giving a woman release from this world."

"Katherine—"

"No, Gluttony. You've said what you've had to say, and you have given yourself too many years of torment. Now it's my turn to talk." She squeezed his knees. "She was an adult, not a child. Though perhaps to you, all of us seem like children after a thousand years of watching us live and die. But she knew what she was asking of you. Would she have changed her mind if you had stopped? Maybe. But she also might have reminded you that she was very ready for the end and that her life had gone in a very wrong direction."

"She wouldn't have—" Gluttony stopped when she lunged forward and pressed her hand over his mouth.

"You don't get to speak for the dead," she said with an angry snarl. "You might be a demon king and perhaps you now know what death tastes like, but you cannot speak for the souls of those who have passed on! Enough, Gluttony. You carry your past deeds like a weight on your shoulders and you should have put them down a long time ago."

He stared down at her and she could feel how lost he was. "I don't know how to put it down, Katherine. I've carried it for so very long."

Getting up onto her knees, she shortened the gap between them. Scooping the back of his neck, she drew him closer to her and breathed against his lips, "I will help you."

And because she needed to, because she felt like she would break apart if she didn't, she kissed him. A soft, quiet kiss. A lingering touch that was gentle and kind.

He parted his own beneath hers, the exhalation of his breath filling her lungs as she consumed his sadness. Drawing it deep into herself so he wasn't the only one who had to carry it.

And when she parted from him, she whispered against him, "I will carry it with you for as long as you wish to keep it. And then, together, we will let it go."

A shuddering, trembling breath shook through him before he crushed her to him. Not in a kiss or even for hunger's sake. He just held her. So Katherine slid her arms around him and held him back. She kept him close to her chest, tucked her head against his shoulder, and held on for as long as he needed her to.

She had no idea how much time passed, only that she listened to the crackling of the fire and the ragged sounds of his breath. And when he finally drew back, she thought perhaps his eyes were a little more red than normal.

"Thank you for that," he breathed. "I'm not sure you can understand how much I needed to hear it."

"Oh, I understand well enough." Skating her thumbs over his

cheekbones, she wiped away the last remaining hint of tears from his cheeks. "You don't have to be alone, Gluttony. Not unless you wish to be."

"I have been alone for a great many years."

"Then I have a lot to make up for." And she refused to stay in this office for any longer than necessary. She had a man to woo, and a heart to mend.

Standing, she held out her hand for him.

Gluttony looked up at her, suspicion already clouding his features. "Where do you wish to take me?"

"To rest." Katherine was decidedly pleased when he placed his hand in hers and allowed her to draw him to standing. "Stay the night with me, Gluttony. You said you don't sleep often, but I wonder if perhaps sleep is exactly what you need."

And so the demon king placed his hand in hers and allowed her to guide him from the room. Together, they walked through the dark halls, and it felt like perhaps they were a little lighter. Just like Spite.

He let her draw him into her bed, quietly and without any complaint. And as Katherine crawled in after him, he curled his body around hers. Like this was the most natural position for the both of them, and she had to imagine that it was.

Because, like everything they did together, it felt so easy to lie with him like this and drift off into sleep.

Chapter 28

Gluttony couldn't remember the last time he'd felt so rested. He didn't even dream. No nightmares to plague his rest, not even a single thought other than a peaceful, deep rest.

The one time he'd woken during the night, a tiny hand had smoothed over his chest. He'd come out of a dream that he couldn't remember in a slight daze. A warm body pressed against his side, hugging closer to him with a slight mewl that put a smile on his face.

As she drew closer, Katherine moved in her sleep like she didn't even know what she was doing. She just snuggled up to him, because she had known he was a little upset in his sleep.

Like she wanted to be near him. Even when he was angry or wasn't acting like himself. She wanted to cozy up to him and breathe him in and damned if he didn't want to roll her over and sink into her heat. Gluttony wanted to feel that acceptance all the way through his body until they were one piece. One person.

But he couldn't do that. She was still Katherine, and he was still... a monster. Even if she didn't want him to think that he was.

Rolling into the thin beam of sunlight coming through her window, he realized it was one of the rare sunny days in his kingdom. The people in the town were likely all rushing out of their homes. Running into the sunlight and cancelling all their plans for the day.

They would celebrate, as they always did. Pulling out kegs of wine and mead, breaking bread with each other, and visiting family they might not be able to visit on a normal day. But today, not a single monster would reveal itself in the light of the sun. They were safe. No matter where they went.

He lifted a hand into the light, turning his pale wrist back and forth. He didn't disappear in the sun, so perhaps he wasn't quite a monster either.

The door to the bathroom opened and a healthy wave of steam erupted from it. Katherine stood in the doorway, wrapped in nothing but a tiny towel. Her hair had turned dark red with the weight of water, tangled on her shoulders and stuck to the sides of her cheeks.

And she smelled divine. So perfect and so lovely, and he'd never seen her in this light before. Never noticed how there were a thousand freckles that danced across her skin in the sunlight. Never knew she would glow like that, as if a goddess herself had stepped into his castle to bestow him a rare gift.

Her cheeks turned a lovely shade of pink as she caught him staring at her. "Sorry," she said. "I thought you were going to stay sleeping for a while, so I just had a quick bath. I can go back in to change if you—"

But he'd noticed the scars that his brother had mentioned. The scars that were only silvery and barely visible on her face, but that danced down the entire side of her body. He could see the coiled tangle up her leg, and the mottled pattern on her right arm all the way up to her shoulder.

He wanted to see more of that pattern. He wanted to see more of her. And a flush of heat seared through him, turning his voice into a deep, guttural snarl as he said, "Don't move."

She knew what he was looking at. She had to know that he wanted to see all of it, all of her, and she should have run. But she stood there, patiently waiting as he rolled out of bed and prowled toward her.

If the hand clutching the top of her towel shook just slightly, he didn't mind. She had good reason to be frightened of him, but he would never, ever hurt her. He'd rather flay his own skin off than lift a hand to her in anger or rage.

Circling his pet, Gluttony used his own body to move her into the center of the room, where he could really look. Really see everything that he wanted to see.

And he saw the gooseflesh pebble on her skin as he stepped closer. Did she feel it too? This strange heat that passed between the two of them until he could hardly breathe at all?

"Gluttony," she whispered. "What do you want?"

You, he wanted to say. I want you more than I have ever wanted anything in my life.

But he swallowed the words and instead said, "I want to see."

Because he did. He wanted to know what had happened to her. He wanted her to bare her soul to him just as he had her, because right now he felt a little raw. She knew everything about him now. Every dark and twisted secret that he had hidden from the rest of the world.

Sure, there were more. Thousands of years of misdeeds and horrible decisions, but he didn't hide those. Any book or historian could tell her all the terrible choices he had made in his life. And he had owned up to all of them.

But he had never killed anyone in cold blood. At least, anyone other than Larissa. And now she knew his darkest secret, and she hadn't even flinched.

She stood before him in nothing but a towel and seemingly was fine with him looking at her. Seeing her. Touching her.

And oh, it made his cock hard. The trust she gave him, it was more than anyone else had ever done before. Not Larissa. Not the countless lovers he had in the past.

She was the only one who had ever made him feel like a man.

Katherine's hands shook again and then... she dropped the towel. The pale white fabric fluttered to the floor and revealed miles upon miles of pale, soft flesh.

He was so glad he stood behind her because he had to bite his knuckle to stop the groan at what she revealed. Soft, rounded hips that gave way to what was likely the most perfect ass he'd ever seen. More than a handful in each globe, and those tiny indents just above. He wanted to bite her. He wanted to leave his mark on her and then do it again and again until no one would ever question that she was his.

Her hair was long and covered most of her back from his sight. But those long, lean legs were an ode to a god's divine work. Yes, there were scars on her right leg. Burn marks that were both silvery and dark, showing where the fire had maimed her more than in other areas. And he could see how stiff the limb was, but it didn't matter to him in the slightest.

A throb started between his legs, his cock jumping at the sight of her, but he refused to stop looking. Not now. Not when he had her right in front of him.

He couldn't touch her, though. Not like this. He kept his hands in his pockets and slowly walked to her front.

Her breasts were so lovely, pink tipped and faintly tinged with a blush that spread down from her cheeks. A thin patch of hair between her legs hid what he most wanted to see, but he indulged himself in watching her stomach flex as she allowed him to look his fill.

And, oh, if it wasn't painful to look and not touch.

"You are beautiful," he said, his voice ragged with emotion. "Lovely, Kat."

"But my scars—"

"I do not see them," he muttered, still staring at her like he wanted to devour her whole. "I see only a stunning woman who I would like nothing more than to pleasure. To touch my fill until you cannot think or stand or utter another word. I want to ruin you, Katherine."

Her breath puffed out her lips before she whispered, "Then do it."

He almost groaned. "You don't know what you ask of me, Kat."

"No, I don't. But I want to know and I think I want to find out all of it with you." Katherine's eyes had widened, and she'd turned a darker shade of red. "Touch me, Gluttony. I want to know what it feels like."

She didn't know...

Oh, he did groan then. He wasn't responsible enough to show her what actual passion felt like! Gluttony hadn't been with a woman in ages. He didn't... couldn't...

Her body was bathed in a flash of bright red and he knew it was emitting from his eyes. She deserved so much better than him, but he was absolutely going to take this opportunity.

He needed her. Just as she needed him.

A slow breath steadied him as he took the few remaining steps between them and stopped just before her. His clothing brushed against her skin and he saw another wave of goosebumps erupt all over her body.

"I want to do this right," he whispered, leaning down until he could skate his lips over her shoulder and up to her neck. He blew on her, a cold breeze that pebbled her nipples against him. "I want you to be barely able to stand when I'm finished with you."

She shuddered again, her breath coming out in a ragged little sound that turned his whole body to liquid fire. "Yes."

"You deserve someone gentle. Someone who will guide you into this new realm of pleasure and passion." He lifted his hand and was ashamed to see his claws had already erupted out of the tips. "But I am not gentle, pet. I am not the man to guide you with soft kisses and slow touches."

Carefully, he circled her throat with all those claws, grasping onto her neck a little too tight and stealing her breath away.

Katherine gasped, likely feeling the way he could end her life with just a simple twist of his wrist. But then she leaned into him, her leg rising between them to brush against his hard, throbbing cock. "Do your worst, Gluttony. I want you in any way you will give yourself to me."

And though it went against every instinct, he wanted that. Oh, he wanted to feel her lose herself around him and he would have it. No matter how much self control it took.

A low, guttural sound rumbled in his chest as he scooped her up. One hand around her throat, the other around her waist. He twisted them both and walked her to the bed. With a swift movement, he tossed her onto the sheets and followed her down.

The softness of the mattress helped to dampen his weight as he shifted on top of her, grinding himself against her core for the mere moment he was given before he focused on her once again.

She'd never done this, he reminded himself. He could not fall upon her like a rabid animal, no matter how easily she arched up into him or what kind of moans escaped her mouth.

He chased the sound, plunging his tongue into her mouth so he could taste her. So he could feel the moans in his own throat as he cupped her breast with his free hand. She was so soft, so plush, so giving as he flicked her nipple with a sharp point of his nail.

She met his every move with ease. Coiling her body, turning into him and groaning against his touch. Her good leg came up and wrapped around his waist, tugging him closer so she could press herself against him. And he knew what she needed. What she wanted.

But his hands were claws and he couldn't touch her like this. He'd shred through her delicate, freckled skin and even though the thought of it was near enough to send him into a frenzy, he would not ruin this moment for either of them.

This was the first time he had the opportunity to taste her, and he intended to do so.

Sliding down her body, Gluttony took his time to lave her neck with his tongue, tasting the faintest hint of her soap. He chased a droplet of water that ran from her hair and between the mounds of her breasts. He got a little distracted there, because he wanted to taste the pink tips of her breasts before he did anything else.

She arched into him as he coiled his tongue around her nipple, and he let out a little growl as she raked her hands up his back.

"Yes," she hissed. "Gluttony, please."

She didn't know what she was asking for, he had to assume, but that only made this moment all the sweeter. This was his time to show her just how much she should want to stay with him.

So he continued, pressing kisses to her stomach and leaving little red bite marks in his wake. She seemed to move of her own accord, struggling to get closer to his touch. But she wouldn't convince him to go faster, not when she needed to be teased. Tormented.

Devoured.

He pressed his hand flat to the softness between her hips, holding her down so she couldn't buck up against him. Gluttony had to ignore the sudden pain in his cock as he caught the first scent of her.

But oh, the first taste would be infinitely better.

"Katherine?" he said, nudging her good leg to the side with his shoulder. "Look at me."

She glanced down at him, her bright red face revealed between the heaving mounds of her breasts. She looked divine, staring down at him, her eyes wide and her breath already catching in her chest. "Why?"

"Because I want you to watch."

He felt a strange shift in his body. Gluttony had always heard of a battle form and he'd seen his own, which was as monstrous as Wrath when he fought. But he had never experienced his battle form coming out when he was lost in the throes of pleasure.

He felt his body erring toward that madness, and when he opened his mouth, his tongue was infinitely longer. With one long lick, he drew that very long tongue up her slit.

And the taste of her. It nearly unmanned him.

Gluttony ground himself against the soft mattress, his eyes rolling back in his head as he heard her moan. He felt, more than saw, her flop onto her back as though she couldn't keep herself upright. And he couldn't stop himself from tasting her.

He flicked his tongue through her folds, and it was now so long he could touch every part of her while still toying with her clit. The thickness of his tongue pressed against her, and he took his time learning her taste.

Sweet and salty, musky with her desire. He lost himself in her for a while, in the taste of something new. He licked and sucked and devoured until he felt her legs quivering on either side of his head.

Drawing his tongue back into his mouth, he licked the slickness from his lips before uttering, "Katherine. Look at me again."

"I can't," she wheezed. "I don't know what you're doing to me."

"Look at me."

At the snap of his order, she stared down at him and watched his tongue unfurl. Her eyes widened, and her cheeks darkened as she watched him lower himself between her legs once more.

He met and held her gaze as he plunged that thick, long tongue inside her.

Chapter 29

His thick tongue plunged inside her, and Katherine forgot how to think. How to breathe. How to do anything other than endure through the blinding pleasure that coursed through her body, starting at his tongue and ending at all the fine points of his claws that he delicately raked down her sides.

He never drew blood, she belatedly thought, but that didn't matter. She wanted him to draw blood. She wanted to feel him groaning against her as he did when he fed, but this time, because there was blood mixed in with what he sipped from between her legs.

Tilting her head up, she stared down at him with a strange mixture of delicious pleasure and slight confusion as she watched that dark tongue plunge inside her. That wasn't a man's tongue. It wasn't the pink tipped tongue she'd seen him lick his lips with before.

This was a demon.

A true, monstrous demon who feasted upon her flesh and growled with the pleasure of it. His nails had grown so long, they looked like daggers tipping his fingers that never once gave her any threat in the slightest. He left little red marks as he glided his hands over her, but she quite liked how they looked on her skin.

Like he'd lost all control, and suddenly that's what she was imagining. The growls that came out of his throat were so compelling. He didn't see her as broken or scarred or even a woman who had a terrible injury.

He stared up at her with so much passion in those eyes she thought she might burst. And then he sucked. Hard. Drew her entirely into his mouth with that wriggling tongue still working magic on her insides and everything felt like it was a hundred times more.

More pleasurable. More sensitive. More clawing and aching pleasure that burst out of every part of her body. She writhed, bucking up against that hand that had held her in place for his attentions, but now she couldn't stop herself. She couldn't help but move and shift and seek out that singular moment she wanted to experience and had only experienced by her own hand up until this point.

But he stopped. Drew back with a snarl on his lips and surely an argument he wished to start. But she couldn't let him do that, not when she had been so fucking close.

So she looked into those red eyes and snapped, "Bite me."

His eyes widened, and for a hesitating moment, she thought he would say no.

But then he leaned down again, with slow movements, and oh so delicately bit the inside of her thigh. It wasn't the one she wanted. It wasn't the rasp of slight pain that then led to his losing control, but it was the start of something.

Katherine had long ago lost her patience with him. Though he had bitten the inside of her bad leg, likely because he thought she didn't have much control over it, she shifted against his teeth. A slight jerk that started from her pelvis and just barely scraped her thigh harder against his fangs.

But it was enough.

He jerked back, his eyes somehow even wider now as he stared at the thin red line he'd created. A single drop of red beaded up on the wound, slowly crawling down the inside of her thigh.

"Katherine," he muttered, his voice deep and guttural.

She would not let him run from this. This was part of who he was, how he had to be, and if he was the monster, then...

She wanted the monster.

Purposefully, she lifted her injured hip even though it hurt. She bent the knee and angled the cut so that the drop of blood changed direction. Slowly, the red line pointed where he had been feasting. And she felt it. The warmth of blood that trickled to the lips of her pussy and then...

Oh, then he shattered.

His growl echoed in the room as he lunged for her. The sound sent gooseflesh dancing all over her body, but then she arched into him as that dark tongue consumed her. He licked and sucked, his claws digging into her hips as he dragged her closer to him. He lifted her hips off the bed, crouched over her like an animal while he devoured her whole.

Katherine was limp in his arms, unable to even move as the exquisite pleasure burst over her.

"Gluttony," she gasped, the sound choked as she pressed the back of her wrist against her mouth. A scream built up in her as her inner muscles clenched, pulsed, ached for something more than just his tongue. But gods, it was thick. His fangs pressed against her outer lips, digging only slightly in and enough that she knew he had drawn more blood. Not enough to hurt, but enough to satisfy.

His deep groan vibrated through her clit and elongated the orgasm that pulsed into something almost like pain.

And when it finally subsided, she felt him withdraw. Limp in his arms, like she'd lost all the muscles in her body, she opened her eyes to stare up at him in shock.

That long, thick tongue licked the shine from his lips and he certainly did not appear to be a man who was satisfied. If anything, he appeared even more hungry.

His eyes were glowing. Bright red and terrifying, enough that a small part of her brain whispered she was looking into the gaze of a predator and she needed to be more careful. She should run screaming from the room, hide as soon as she could find a safe place.

But that prey part of her mind also knew that he would catch her. And another other part of her, the part that enjoyed a bit of danger, knew that when he did, it would be exquisite.

Still breathing hard, she licked her lips and watched him for any sort of reaction. He'd sat back on his haunches, her knees now draped around his hips and his hands still clutching her waist. Gluttony seemed frozen as he stared down at her.

"You still here?" she asked.

He nodded, although he didn't really seem to hear her. "I have tasted nothing so divine as you. Forgive me for a moment, Katherine. I do not know what I will do next if I do not get control of myself."

Oh, she didn't want him to get control over himself. She didn't want him to think and over-analyze and see too much into this moment because she had just seen what the gods saw every day and she wanted him to feel the same. She wanted to touch him, lick him, taste him just as he'd done for her.

And if he started to overthink this, then he would never let her. He'd hide himself away in his office for days on end while he tried to justify his actions to himself, when he didn't have to justify anything at all.

This wasn't supposed to be about her, after all. This was supposed to be about her reminding him that he was worthy and wanted and that his past did not define him.

"Lay down," she said, removing her good leg from around his hips.

"What?"

"Lay down, Gluttony."

Still dazed, clearly, he rolled onto his side. And the bed was so big they didn't have to rearrange all that much for him to be reclining and for her to move over him. Her hair fell between them like a curtain as she moved to his side. She sat awkwardly on her bad hip as she ran her hand over his cheek. Gently smoothing her thumb over the wrinkles that had formed around his eyes.

"Thank you," she whispered as she crawled over him. "Now it's your turn."

"Katherine, I didn't do that for you to—"

Shushing him with a finger over his lips, she hungrily stared down at his body. "That's quite all right, Gluttony. I know you don't do anything with the expectation for me to do anything in return. I've wanted to do this for a very long time."

Those bright red eyes flashed again, and he sat straight up. Their faces were only a few inches apart. She moved to sit on his lap, but froze as he reached behind his head and pulled his shirt off. All those muscles, that pale skin, the rippling twinges that followed his movements. All of it was for her to touch.

And touch she did.

Katherine didn't know if they'd ever do this again, and she was going to take advantage of every second that he gave her. With a soft sigh of pleasure, she planted her hands flat against the planes of his chest and pushed him back down. Her fingers danced over everything she could, digging into muscles and running over the warm skin that she'd thought would be cold or dead, like the rumors claimed. But no, Gluttony was warm and real and alive.

She leaned down and tasted him. Flicked her tongue over his nipple as he'd done to her, and his little arch against her, the grind that pressed his hot heat into hers, made her grin.

She knew what he wanted most, and it was the same thing she wanted. Desperately. Almost recklessly.

Katherine scooted back down his legs, taking her time to kiss and worship everything that she'd wanted to taste for so long. By the time her fingers played with the edges of his pants, he was panting and his eyes had bathed the entire room with a faint hue of red.

He watched her almost frantically as she curled her fingers in the waistband of his pants, giving it a slight tug before she loosened the ties. He didn't say a word as she eased them down his lean hips. He bit his lips just before she glanced down to see his cock.

And gods, it was massive.

Granted, she'd only seen a few of them while bathing, so maybe this was rather normal sized. But she didn't think the beast in front of her was normal at all.

He still hadn't lost control. He only hissed as she wrapped her hand around him, tugging experimentally.

"You don't have to," he ground out through gritted teeth. "If you don't want."

"What I want, Gluttony, is for you to shut up and tell me how to do this right." She leaned down and flicked the pink tip with her tongue. Just to see what he tasted like.

His thighs clenched. The hard muscles pressed against her sides as she met his gaze and did the same thing again. She licked that tiny bead of glistening liquid at the tip, the taste of salt flooding her tongue. But still, he was too controlled. Too much in his head.

If he would not tell her how to do this, then she'd do whatever she pleased. Katherine flattened her hand against his stomach as he'd done to her. His abs flexed against her fingertips and he shuddered, his eyes rolling back in his head. So she leaned down and sucked him into her mouth.

Katherine had no idea if she was doing this right. All she knew was that when she swirled her tongue underneath the head of him, he let out a groan that rivaled the sounds he'd made between her thighs. And when she sucked a little harder, drawing him deeper into her mouth, he bucked just slightly.

She wanted more. Needed more. Desired for him to lose all control.

Wrapping her hand around him, she squeezed a little harder, working him with her hand and mouth as her free hand reached below. Cupping him, using her fingers to stroke whatever she could, she froze when the sound that came out of him was close to pain.

And then she felt claws stroking through her hair until he had the mass wrapped around his fist. Using her hair like a leash, he jerked her away from his cock.

There it was.

The red light flashed out of his eyes and his fangs had somehow elongated. He licked his lips, that long black tongue sending a rush of liquid between her legs. He touched her lips with his other hand, and she knew they must be red and swollen already. "You look pretty like this," he growled. "Tighter, pet. Use your tongue more."

And she was all too eager to comply, even if she wasn't sure of the reasoning. Why did she suddenly want to please him and have him tell her that she'd done a good job? She'd never cared what someone thought more than she cared right now. She needed... No, she wanted...

Gluttony guided her back down, and this time she used both hands. Holding him tight and licking up the side of the shaft while watching for his approval. His nostrils flared, his gaze darted between the sight of himself sinking between her lips and her ass raised up behind her as she bent down to worship him. He watched everything.

She slid her lips down his cock, kissing and sucking until she finally took him deep into her throat. She swirled her tongue again, as he'd seemed to like, holding him tighter in her hands as his deep groans filled the room.

She'd thought he would be quiet. That he would stoically lie there while she had made all the noise she couldn't keep in. But she'd been wrong. Gluttony held back nothing, his deep voice never ending.

"That's it, pet," he growled. "Take me deeper. Deeper, if you can. That's it. Good girl. That's so perfect."

And when he grabbed her hand, drawing it back between his legs and lower to the sack between, she knew exactly what he wanted. She toyed with him, played with him, enjoyed it immensely even as he tensed. His lower back arched, his thighs were suddenly rock hard on either side of her as he bucked into her mouth. He hit the back of her throat a little hard, but she didn't care.

She took him as deep as she could until she felt him shudder. Felt the sudden flex of his entire body as he pushed into her convulsing throat. Then a pulse and a flood of his cum that poured down her throat.

And she swallowed as much as she could. Drinking him down until he gently pulled her away by her hair.

She watched him, licking her lips to make sure she was cleaned up. And still, he stared at her. His eyes were soft and his features relaxed in a rare expression that made her heart thud a little harder.

"Kat," he whispered, shaking his head, and then a brilliant smile lit up his entire face. "I fear you will break me, woman."

She grinned back. "Just returning the favor."

"And what favor was that? Trying to kill me?"

"I do believe they call it the 'little death' for a good reason." Crawling up to his chest, she laid down on top of him. "I know we have to face the real world soon enough, but... Do you mind if we stay like this? At least for a little while longer?"

His arms curled around her, holding her tightly to his still rapidly beating heart. "Of course, pet. Of course."

She knew they'd need to talk about this. What it meant, how it changed things, what was going to happen from now on, but she wanted to bask in him for a little longer.

Chapter 30

Gluttony had never been so happy. He hadn't thought it was possible to feel like the weight of the world was off his shoulders. After all, it had been there since he'd taken mortal form.

But the incredible woman who now shared his bed had proven to him time and time again that he was so very wrong. Instead, she had gifted him with all the things he'd never hoped to dream of. She had stayed the night in a bed with him. She'd given him every reason to fall in love with her. And now he.... Well, he rather thought that he might be.

Gluttony knew these were dangerous thoughts. He knew he couldn't keep thinking she would stay. No one ever had before her, and it certainly would not change just because he had bedded her, but... He could hope.

He filled his day with thoughts of what it would be like if she did stay. How they would be together every day. How he would surround himself with her scent and the lingering sense of her touch.

How light his home would suddenly be.

And that was the reason he whistled as he worked. The reason he meandered down the halls as though he were a hundred pounds lighter.

Even though it had been hours since he'd gotten out of bed, finally releasing her from his arms because it had been harder than he'd expected, Gluttony hadn't realized that she would walk with him for the rest of the day.

Not literally, of course. They'd parted ways as she jokingly said she should take another bath and he gloated a bit, considering he was the reason she needed to do so. But figuratively, he couldn't get her out of his head.

No matter what he seemed to do, she was always in the forefront of his mind. And while that wasn't all that different from the past few months of knowing her, it felt different now that he knew what she tasted like.

He wasn't even concerned about his body going into battle form at a rather inopportune time. Because that monstrous tongue had done rather incredible things to her, and she hadn't complained one bit.

In fact, he thought she might have liked his tongue. Even though it wasn't even remotely human at all.

Still jauntily moving through his home, he made his way to the lab. There were only a few more tests he wanted to make with his formula before he thought he had it. Most of the reagents he was now using had responded well. Though he hadn't tried to use the black mist he had created, at the very least to see it if would mimic what Greed's kingdom had created, he had a feeling it would work the moment he tried. This was, without a doubt, the solution to all of their problems.

Though he wasn't all that interested to know what his brothers had to say about it. For the first time in a very long time, Gluttony didn't care what they thought. He didn't want to be the brother who wasn't the monster. Nor did he care if they thought him to be a disaster.

They were lesser in his mind in comparison to Katherine. She liked him, and that was all that mattered.

Maybe that would change soon enough once he had to talk with his brothers again. Once he saw the disappointment on their features the moment they remembered what he'd done.

But for now, he felt a little better about himself, and he would cling to that feeling like the blessing it was.

Not even the massive shadow darkening his lab would ruin this for him. He refused to look at his brother, who was, yet again, touching things that he shouldn't. Instead, Gluttony made his way to his main workbench, sat down, and got to work.

"You're rather happy today," Envy mentioned as he strode closer. "Why is that?"

"I am allowed to be happy without explaining it to you."

"Yes, you are. But generally speaking, happiness on the face of a monster is a bad thing." Envy rounded his table and crouched in front of him.

It didn't take long for his brother to smell it. Rearing back, Envy's eyes flashed a deep green and his voice deepened as his emotion got the better of him. "You didn't."

"My personal life has nothing to do with you, brother."

"It does if you're fucking humans again." Envy dragged a stool in front of him and plopped down. His massive arms took up too much space on the other side of the table, and that meant that Gluttony had absolutely nothing he could do other than stare at his brother.

Sighing, he leaned back and pinched his nose. "Can I at least enjoy this for a few moments before you ruin it?"

"Not while I'm here."

"I'm not the only one fucking humans." He arched a brow. "We've all been doing that for many years. You cannot tell me you haven't indulged yourself in over a thousand years, Envy."

"Never with feelings involved."

"Oh, come off it." Gluttony tossed his hands in the air. "I don't think you understand anything anymore! You were just saying for me to fix it. I fixed it! Just like Lust and Greed, I am focusing on what I want. No, what I need. I'm with her. Enjoying every moment of her body that I can, as well as moments of her mind. The closer I get to falling in love, that's the hope, isn't it? That I will change for her?"

Envy stared at him with so much pity in his eyes it made Gluttony's skin itch. "Do you really think Greed changed for anyone other than himself?"

No. And he'd been there to watch the whole mess fall apart when Greed tried to change for Varya.

Still. He didn't like it being pointed out.

Hissing out an angry breath, he pursed his lips in disgust. "I don't like you pointing this out to me."

"I don't like being here as your babysitter, either. But we're both here and there's nothing we can do to stop that. So why don't you just be a good boy and send the poor thing home?"

"I'm not sending her home."

"Gluttony," Envy groaned. "You have to send the girl home. You can't do this, and you know it."

"Why not?" Gluttony burst out. He stood, raking his hands through his hair and pacing in front of his brother. "Why can I not do this? You know as well as I do, there is nothing wrong with me. The humans fear what they do not know, but that doesn't mean that I am in the wrong. We have needs. Urges. She understands that, and fuck, I think she might even enjoy the urges that I have. Why can I not enjoy that?"

"You know why."

"I don't!" He spun on his brother, glaring at him and wondering how much a fight between the two of them would destroy. "I don't agree with or understand with anything that you're saying. Why can Lust and Greed do this while I cannot?"

Envy's face shuttered, and then his eyes went a flat black like Gluttony had never seen before. "Because you eat people, Gluttony. You are the first of us to fall prey to that battle form. You know why Wrath is worried."

"I don't." Gluttony took a deep breath, steeling himself for the truth he knew Envy would tell him. "Wrath never said a word about anything. He just yelled at me, sent me away from this kingdom, and did whatever it was that he did here. That was all."

His gut sank as he met Envy's gaze. His brother looked defeated, and that was never an expression that Envy wore well. He was the brother who was never defeated. He took what he wanted, stole and maimed and killed if that was what it took. But he never looked like that.

"Gluttony..."

Another voice interrupted them, thin and reedy though it was. Spite coiled up his desk as it spoke, gathering into a ball in the center of the desk. "The battle form you wear is one that only those who have taken physical form can use. Spirits are not meant to have a physical form, and there was a time when many of us were like you. All of these kingdoms were overrun with spirits who thought they knew what was right."

Gluttony had never heard this before. "This is not information freely shared."

"No," Spite agreed. "It is not. But I was in Pride's kingdom long before I was here, demon king, and I know things that you could not imagine. You seven are not the first. You are merely the ones who have lasted in this form for the longest."

"This form?" He looked at Envy and saw his brother nodding in reluctance.

His brother sighed heavily before saying, "I have discovered recordings kept secret and safe throughout the centuries. Even Pride does not know all of it, some of the details I've kept for myself. But magic is in my blood now, and I know the truth of it. The battle form we use is not simply because we are angry, but because it is who we can become."

"So our predecessors..."

Envy nodded. "They succumbed to the madness that is in all of us. They feasted, they fucked, they did not care that the battle form is dangerous and soon they became it. True demons who roamed our kingdoms and devoured all that stood in their way."

"And that is where the name came from."

"Indeed. They called us demon kings long ago because they knew what we could become. Perhaps it is our bond that keeps us more human, or perhaps it is that deep down we know what we would end up as. But the promise of power has always been the reason why our kind became monsters and..." Envy shrugged. "We have all the power we need. Until you."

Knees weak, Gluttony sank back onto his stool and stared at his brother. Dumbfounded. "So this was why Wrath intervened. He thought I was... was..."

"Turning into something that none of us could control." Envy reached across the table and grabbed his hand. "Listen to me, Gluttony. These urges that you have, they are not natural. We feed the beast inside us as much as we want, but you are consuming people. Just as the demons of old did. Of all of us, I believe you are closest to becoming one of them, and I cannot... none of us can take that risk."

Nor did he wish to.

But he did not feel like a monster or a demon. He wasn't turning into his battle form regularly, nor was he losing bits of his memory.

A flash of this morning bloomed in his mind. He felt all the blood drain from his face and knew the moment both Envy and Spite had seen it. They both looked at him, strange eyes focused on his features.

"What?" Spite asked. "Why do you look like that?"

"You did something," Envy added. "Didn't you?"

"While we were..." He stuttered, not wanting to share those private moments with his brother, of all people. "I... changed."

"You what?"

"Not entirely," he corrected, stammering to make sure that his brother understood what he was saying. "I didn't change completely into my battle form, but pieces of me did. Parts of my body shifted in a way they never have before. It was uncontrollable. Strange, but I didn't... I didn't mean to..."

"You're already changing without attempting to do so." Envy's shoulders lifted and rose in a big inhalation. Perhaps his brother was trying to steel himself for what he had to do next, or perhaps he was just affected more than Gluttony could guess. "That settles it, then. You'll have to leave again."

"I'm not going anywhere."

"This is your life, Gluttony. You cannot take this risk when you are so close to losing everything. What if she is killed? What if you change when you touch her and then you rip her to shreds? I have read the recordings. I have seen the drawings of what we will become and I will not lose one of my brothers to that madness!" Envy stood abruptly, his chair tipping over and striking the ground with a loud bang. "You will return to Greed's kingdom. If that is what healed you last time, then that is what we will do again."

"I'm not going anywhere," he repeated, his voice slow and quiet. "This is where I belong."

"Then this is where you will die!" Envy thundered. "They won't let you remain like this. You have to know that, Gluttony. If you change into one of those monsters, none of our brothers will allow you to tear through this kingdom and ruin all that we have built. We will be forced to kill you."

"Then so be it." Gluttony was not phased by his brother's anger or declaration. In fact, it was rather... soothing to know it would end like that. "If you are to kill me, then it will be a great honor to know that such a warrior did so. I hope I will have enough control to make it easy on you all."

"You are a fool," his brother hissed before conjuring a portal and disappearing from the room.

Silence fell like snow, blanketing the laboratory with a white haze. Spite shifted from its position on his table, a pale gray like ash now. "Why will you not leave?"

"Because I know what it feels like to be held in her arms. And I would rather die than never know that bliss again." He smiled softly at the spirit, then pat it on the head. "She is beauty and kindness, all wrapped in a warm blanket. It would not be such a terrible way to die, knowing as I do that she is here with me."

"What if you kill her?"

"I couldn't." He had no question of that. Not a single speck of his body would ever lay a hand on her with the intent to harm. Even his battle form had manifested only to pleasure her. "My only fear is that I will scare her. And I do not wish for her to ever be frightened in my presence. She is very dear to me, Spite. I don't know when it happened or how it did, but seeing a smile on her face is the greatest gift anyone has ever given me."

Quiet footsteps echoed down the hall, approaching the laboratory as she did every morning. He could smell the coffee she carried and the breakfast rolls she must have made, even though they had both gotten out of bed long after breakfast.

Gluttony wiped the conversation from his mind. Perhaps he was a selfish man for doing so, but he stood with a smile and wide open arms for her as she walked into his lab.

Because he hadn't lied or embellished the truth. The grin on her face made everything disappear. It was a gift, every time, when she looked at him like a man and not a monster.

So he would steal whatever he could to keep her with him. Forever. As long as she would let him linger in her happiness and bask in the glow of her smile.

Even if that meant he would slowly descend into madness or lose himself, he would do so. Because to know happiness even once in his life was worth the risk.

Chapter 31

Katherine came out of a dream in a daze. Her heart sluggishly beat in her chest, and she didn't want to let go of it.

She'd been dreaming a lot lately. Every time she closed her eyes, Gluttony appeared in her room. He crawled up from the foot of the bed, all liquid muscle and lithe heat that blanketed her body in comfort and affection. He always wound his arms underneath her head, tilting her neck for his fangs that were so gentle as they pierced her skin.

Her entire body would flush with desire. She'd wriggle closer to him, wrapping her arms around his lean hips while she tried to keep herself still. She didn't want him to know how much she desired him. Grinding against him would only be an embarrassment as she revealed just how much she wanted him.

But it was hard.

Every night, it was so difficult to keep herself still while his tongue lapped at the wound on her neck that never seemed to close anymore. And every night she found herself growing a little more limp.

Katherine slept more, but she considered that to be a mere blessing to catch up on all the sleep she'd missed. She wasn't going back to that village. Not with all the shadows that watched her every move and all the people who wanted to hate her for what she had done.

They were ungrateful.

Thoughtless.

They didn't see what she could see, and that was all right in its own way. She didn't need them to understand her choices, because now she was here. Languidly lying in bed until the late hours of the morning, waiting for the telltale knock on her door as a demon brought her food.

This time, though, she had a hard time even tilting her head. Trying to swallow, she realized her mouth was so dry. And she was tired. So very tired.

Katherine felt like there were two people in her mind. One exhausted individual who was enjoying laying in bed and wanted to close her eyes for a little while longer. And another person screaming in the back of her head that something was very, very wrong. She needed to get help. This wasn't normal and if she didn't get up, then something very dire might happen indeed.

The knock came again. Gluttony rarely entered her room without announcing himself. He liked to give her a semblance of privacy, perhaps because he understood that she'd never had that luxury before. Not in the boarding house, and not even in her old home with her parents.

"Gluttony," she whispered, her tongue sticking to the roof of her mouth and lisping her words.

Did he hear her?

She needed him to hear her because she didn't know what was going on. She was fine. Just yesterday, she'd walked around this room with a determination to clean it and make it much more presentable. Had she been a little light-headed? Of course. But that was normal for her. She wasn't as distracted, and perhaps her hip hurt a little more than usual. Pain was so much a part of her life, it was hard to tell when something else was happening.

But something had absolutely happened. She could barely move at all.

Her fingers scratched at the bed even as he walked in. Gluttony's back was to her, giving her even more semblance of privacy. "Envy arrived again this morning, just thought you'd want to know. Ridiculous man, he won't get out of my fucking castle. I know he annoys you as much as he does me, so I thought perhaps we could commiserate together this morning. He's set up in the kitchen, certain that we'll come down there and have to talk to him, but I do not have any wish to do so."

Normally, she'd laugh with him. Normally, she would have the energy do something other than flop her head to the side to watch him.

When he turned and saw her, she knew how sick she must look. The plates in his hands clattered to the floor, and he lunged. Gluttony moved so quickly it was hard to track his movements. One moment he was at the door, the next he was frantically running his hands down her body.

"What happened, pet?" he asked, his eyes trying to see every part of her and his hands quickly following suit. "Where are you hurt?"

She must look terrible if he thought she was injured. She wasn't, but... Maybe something else was wrong.

"Sick," she muttered, and the single word emptied all the air in her lungs. She had to wheeze in a breath that rattled in her chest.

"You're ill?" His eyes widened even more, his face turning pale and ghostly. "I don't know how to help you."

She did. There were certain things she'd want to check. Her temperature for one, but he wouldn't know how humans normally felt. Then she'd want to pinch the skin on the back of her hand to make sure she wasn't dehydrated. There were a thousand things to do, and maybe he could bring her to the almshouse.

But the word was too hard to form. It took every ounce of her energy just to keep her eyes open and watching him. And somehow, he seemed to understand that.

Gluttony gently moved her hair away from her face, touching each strand with reverence. "My poor pet. We're going to fix this. I promise."

He scooped his arms underneath her, turning her into his shoulder with such slight movements that she barely noticed the difference between the bed and him. And then he was moving from the room, carrying her as though she weighed nothing through the halls.

Everything blurred as they moved. She couldn't quite guess where they were going, but then she noticed a small dent in the wall and thought they were heading to the kitchens.

Why there?

That made little sense. She wasn't hungry. Not at all. This wasn't hunger. It was a weakness that spread through every ounce of her form until she couldn't think or breathe or stay awake.

"Katherine," Gluttony murmured in her ear. "Stay with me."

Of course. That was the smart thing to do. She had to stay with him and not move and let him take care of her because she certainly couldn't do it herself right now. He would take care of her.

He always had.

Katherine blinked her eyes open. When had she closed them?

The warmth of the kitchen played across her icy skin. She hadn't even realized how cold she'd been until she felt the blast of hot air from the furnace. And oh, it was so much better now that she was here. Now that she was actually warm.

Gluttony held her in his lap as he sank down beside the fire. Katherine wanted to protest. The stone floor must be so hard on his knees. He could just lay her down on the stones. She was more used to the discomfort of it than he was. Just a few moments of sleep and she would be better.

"Gluttony." Envy's voice sliced through her mind, forcing her out of that dream-like state and into the present. "What have you done to her?"

"She said she was sick."

A hand picked up her wrist and let it flop back down against his chest. "Sick? That's what she said? You've nearly drained her dry, you fucking idiot."

But... No. That wasn't right. That couldn't be at all. She would have known if the dreams were real. If she'd actually whispered those words of pleasure and hope in his ears. She'd said too much in those dreams, about how she was so happy she'd chosen to stay here, and that if he knew how she really felt...

In what world did Katherine believe that was just a dream? Of course, he'd been coming into her room every night. After they'd spent the night together, after they'd tasted each other, why would he stay away?

She could pretend that she hadn't known what was wrong with her because of the blood loss, but that wasn't truthful. She had known. Why would he not come to her room and roll her into his arms?

Oh, she was a complete and utter fool. How could she forget that she was in the home of a demon king who only wanted to feed off of her? How could she ever think for a moment that she was in a normal castle with a normal prince who had somehow developed feelings for her?

Fluttering her eyelashes, trying to stay awake so she could hear more of this conversation, she looked up at Gluttony.

He was staring down at her. An expression of complete and utter loss marring his usually handsome features. Carefully, oh so carefully, he brushed her hair behind her ear. "It's not blood loss," he whispered, the words meant for only the two of them. "Is it?"

It was. She had seen it before in so many patients. They were cold and listless, struggling to stay awake. Sometimes it took every ounce of her strength to get food into them without watching them drown because they simply could not stay awake for it.

It would be a vicious fight for her to stay alive and well. But it would happen.

"Gluttony," Envy hissed. "You have to let me take her."

What?

No!

She didn't want to go with this brother who had seen her only as a broken little doll. Envy would do gods know what to her, and the last thing she wanted in the end was to be parted from Gluttony.

She wanted to be with him. He would take care of her, and she trusted him to do so. Not his brother.

And yet, she felt his arms quiver. He shook against her and then pressed his warm face against her icy neck. He breathed her in, pressing a slight kiss to the side of her throat. Right over the wound that never quite healed.

"Be safe," he whispered against her skin. "Be brave. Envy will not hurt you because he has no wish to harm me. You understand?"

No! She didn't understand. Why was he handing her off like a sack of grain or a wounded animal that only his brother could fix? She just needed rest, food, she needed...

Katherine couldn't fight as they handed her between the two brothers. Her head lolled against Envy's chest, so much broader and harder than Gluttony's. The faintest plush feeling of chest hair underneath her cheek felt so wrong when she knew what Gluttony felt like.

Then she heard the rumble of Envy's voice in his chest. "You're doing the right thing, brother."

There was no response from Gluttony. And she already knew he was taking it out on himself. He'd all but told her that she was precious to him, and he'd already harmed her.

Broken her.

Proven that she was just as weak as the rest of the village thought.

It had just taken him a little longer than most to find that weakness and to flaunt it against her.

She fought to keep her eyes open as Envy strode to the back of the kitchen. She felt his hands shift underneath her, making some kind of motion with his fingers, and then all she could see was a bright flash of green.

"Wait," she whispered, and in one last expulsion of energy, she rolled her head on his shoulder to look over it. Just enough for her to see past the bulk of the demon carrying her.

Gluttony still knelt by the fire, on his knees. He stared down at his clawed hands, his silhouette the picture of a man who had given up entirely. But he must have felt her eyes on him because he looked up and there was still hope there. Just the tiniest amount.

He had better hearing than most. So she whispered, her dry throat clicking as she said, "I will come back."

Envy strode through his magical portal and then everything blinked out of existence. For a few moments, she wondered if she'd died. Then, faint light filtered back in and she could see that they'd stepped into a gray room.

Gray everything, actually. The stone above her head had been meticulously polished and then carved with visions of snakes slithering over her head. They were so detailed she could see each individual scale and the pupils of the creatures that almost seemed to move and watch her as she was carried beneath them.

Envy wasted no time. He carried her to a corner, where he put her down on something plush and soft. It was warm and comfortable, and she was so tired.

The demon she did not know banged around in the corner for a bit before he approached and held something to her lips. "Drink."

Katherine did not know him or the substance he wished to pour down her throat. She stubbornly sealed her lips shut and did her best to glare at him, hopefully looking at least a bit intimidating.

She failed.

Envy rolled his eyes and kept the vial against her lips. "If I wanted to kill you, little human, I could have done it in a thousand ways already. I will not poison you."

He had a point.

Katherine opened her lips and the cold liquid seared as she

swallowed. But it was an almost instant affect. She could feel her entire body fill with strength for a moment, before it leaked out her ears like it had never been there at all.

"It'll help rebuild all that blood you have lost," Envy muttered as he turned from her. "There are more I will make, and you will take them every day. If you're so insistent on risking your life with Gluttony, then the both of you need to learn how to be a little more careful. Foolish idiots. You should not and will not continue to do it like this."

She swallowed, her mouth feeling a little more wet. "Water?"

"Yes, yes." He lifted a hand above his head, scraping over the vials above him before coming up with another greenish colored liquid. He held that out to her as well. "Drink this, and I'll get you water."

"What is it?" Her voice was still little more than a croak.

Katherine took the few seconds between his replies to look around. She thought maybe this was a bedroom. She was lying on a cot with so many pillows it was hard for her to guess how many there were. A workbench in one corner was covered with books and dusted with what looked like strange glitter. Until she realized most of the shelves above that desk held crystals and stone.

So not glitter. Shards of precious stone.

Everything else was rather sparse, if one considered carved walls sparse. It was beautiful here. Full of magical carvings and creatures that she hardly recognized at all.

The stone shapes moved, following their master around as he muttered under his breath. And Envy was far too large in this room. He took up all the oxygen just by existing and she wanted... well, she supposed she wanted him to leave.

"Here." He tossed one more vial at her, and it thudded onto the bed beside her. "Take all those and sleep. I'll be back with food and water."

And then he left her alone in this cold, stone room with no windows. Like he'd brought her to a tomb.

Chapter 32

He threw himself into his work. How could he be so foolish? He had known how fragile she was. Not because of her past injuries, but simply because she was human.

But it had seemed so natural for him to feed from her every night. And she'd enjoyed it. How could he ever forget the sound of her faint moans in his ears and how she'd twisted her body so he'd settled between her legs just right? She'd wanted him, and he had been so caught up in his own need that it was hard for him to think of anything else.

Like her safety.

Like how much he needed to control himself because he was a glutton for everything he could get his hands on, and that included her. He would break her if he had his way with her, and he had known that from the start.

He'd just forgotten about it. Like the fool he was.

Envy visited him once a day to keep him informed on her health, but every day refused to bring her back. There were too many factors for her health right now, and Envy had practiced magical healing for a very long time. He would make sure that she was perfectly well, but he would not return her until then.

And every day, Gluttony wondered whether or not she was happy. Envy's kingdom was... well, it was more than this. Every other kingdom was more than this. And his brother liked to take things that weren't his.

Gluttony tortured himself by imagining all the wonderful things Envy could show her. The halls of living carvings. The underground city that opened up into a giant cavern lit by a single hole above their head. How the clouds had come into his kingdom and almost every single person within it knew how to cast at least some spells.

Envy's kingdom was full of magic and sights that no human ever got to behold. He wouldn't blame Katherine if she wished to stay there. He wouldn't blame her in the slightest.

What did he have to offer here in this kingdom? Nothing but danger and gray days.

He got so close to solving all the puzzles with his alchemical solution. He was almost certain that he knew exactly what it was, and that was more than enough for him to feel some sense of pride. But all he felt was a sense of loss when he could not share it with her.

Then came the day that the portal opened in his lab. He stood as he always did, pulling off his glasses and rubbing his eyes that were surely surrounded by dark, bruised circles. He expected Envy to step through with another disappointing update, but what he saw in front of him was a vision in white.

Katherine wore one of Envy's white robes that so many people wore around him. It clung to her shoulders, scooping deep between those lovely breasts. And she was still so pale. But she was alive, and the portal closed behind her without a single word from his brother and he...

He almost fell to his knees in relief.

"Katherine?" he said, taking a shaky step toward her. "Are you well?"

"Well enough." She took a step toward him as well, almost as though she wasn't sure if he'd want her to. "Are you well?"

"I..." No.

He wasn't.

He'd fallen apart without her and had a thousand worries dogging every step. He wanted to touch her. He wanted to tell her that he would protect her for the rest of his life, but he didn't know how to do that when he also wanted to devour her whole. Every moment without her had felt like he walked on broken glass, and it had torn into his very being to know that she was not here with him. He wanted her.

Gluttony needed her.

Every part of his dark life had lit up with her here and the mere thought that he had almost ruined it made him want to gouge out his own eyes.

But this was not about him. He had been the one to hurt her, and now he would be the one to welcome her home.

Gluttony opened his arms wide, about to ask if he could hug her. But she took the choice right out of his mouth. Instead, Katherine launched herself at him and tunneled into his embrace.

He pressed his lips together, trying desperately to keep the emotions inside of him. Curving his body around hers, he held her close to his heart. Listening to the sound of her own breathing and feeling her ribs move every time, she snuggled a little closer to him.

"You are well?" he asked again.

She nodded against his chest.

And together, they stood like that for a little while longer. Just reveling in each other, and feeling that the other was alive. That they'd waited for each other, as impossible as that sounded.

"Envy's kingdom is beautiful, isn't it?" he asked quietly.

"It is cold," she whispered. "It is empty and cold."

That was not the kingdom he remembered at all. He knew the great spires and artistry made most people lose their minds. And yet, this woman saw something he did not. As was so often with Katherine.

Holding her a little tighter, Gluttony felt his heart squeeze. "I am so sorry, Kat. I did not think that what I was doing would…"

"I know who you are, Gluttony. I know what you do. I agreed to it, did I not?" She pulled back slightly, wincing at the movement. "I know what you want from me and I have never said no to it. We were both too careless. This is not entirely on you."

But it was. If he was not the man who desired to suck out every bit of her life, then neither of them would be in this situation. And even now, he saw the throbbing in her throat and he wanted to take from her. He wanted to feed and draw every bit of her inside of him. It was a need that he could not explain.

Instead, he swallowed hard and forced all that desire down.

"Come," he said, cupping the back of her head and tipping her back to look at him. "You must be exhausted."

"I have been sleeping for many days while your brother tutted over me like a mother hen." She smiled, but he could see how tired she still was. "I have rested for more than I wish to rest."

"And yet, I have already prepared something for you."

"What?" She looked up at him with those wide eyes and he knew he had done something right for once.

After all the time without her, he had known there were some things that he had to change. First, the castle needed to be fixed. He'd gone into town himself and chosen a few people who were returning from work. They were tired and haggard, and they were the desperate ones. Exactly what he needed, considering the town had not been all that receptive for his return.

He'd offered them a lot of money. Enough to get them across the light bridge and to another kingdom if they wished. And he offered them food and water while they cleaned his castle from top to bottom. So they had. They had spent hours upon hours slaving away while he worked in his lab, the only place he'd told them not to touch, and in the week that she'd been gone, everything was fixed.

He hardly recognized the place when he walked through it. They'd done a remarkable job, and he'd told them so himself. Then gave them more money than he'd promised and sent them on their way.

It was worth it to see the expression on Katherine's face. They walked through well lit halls, on plush carpets that had been taken out and washed. Tapestries that he hadn't seen for years now gleamed, so bright and lovely he'd forgotten that some of the threads had been imbued with magic to make them look like there were gemstones encrusted in each one.

It was gluttonous to have such luxuries in a castle that no one saw, but he had forgotten that he enjoyed being a glutton over more than just people.

"Is this the same castle?" she asked, laughing as she spun in a circle.

"Is this really the same place?"

"I thought you'd like it."

"Oh, I do." She turned to him with her hands pressed against her chest. "I'm so glad you aren't living in the past anymore, Gluttony. This place was keeping you in old memories. And look now! You can move on."

If only.

For now, all he wanted was to show her the room he had readied for her. Holding out his hand, he drew her into a side room that was filled to the brim with candles. They flickered merrily as he wandered and lit each one so that she could see it. Her head tilted to the side as she looked over the bed in the center of the room.

"A little small, don't you think?"

Ah, his fiery woman was back. He arched a brow in response. "Are you so eager to risk your life again? Perhaps you have forgotten what happened the last time we indulged ourselves."

And he swore her eyes flashed with passion. "I have not forgotten a single detail about that morning," she replied. "I know exactly what you feel like now, demon. And you will not frighten me away with a single episode where the two of us forgot that I am mortal and you are not."

He would not forget it either, but now was not the time for that conversation. Instead, he gestured for her to get up on the bed. "Come, now. I have been researching."

"And what have you been researching?"

"Hip injuries, mostly." He turned her, so she was facing away from him. And carefully he drew the robe down her shoulders.

It took every ounce of his strength not to fall upon her like an animal. The smooth curves of her shoulders drew his attention, as they connected to the swan-like neck with all the freckles he wanted to count. The faint outline of her shoulder blades, like wings hidden underneath her skin. He wanted to trace his lips down them, but first, he wanted to prove to her that was a better man.

And still, he could not stop the groan that escaped his mouth when the robe clung to her rounded bottom before falling to her feet. Those legs. Those long, lovely legs that he now knew the taste of. They would be his undoing.

"Gluttony?" she asked, her voice a little hoarse. "What now?"

"Lie down." Before he fell on her like an animal. Before he dragged his teeth and tongue over every crevice of her body while she screamed for mercy.

She sat on the edge of the raised bed, lying down before he caught her and turned her around. "No, pet. On your stomach."

He showed her the head rest he'd carefully made to ensure that she would have a comfortable way to breathe. And as she settled, he covered his hands with a slick oil mixed with lavender and peppermint. Both of which would help her stiff muscles ease, especially if he could follow the instructions without ruining this moment.

"In the books I read, they said manual manipulation is helpful." He dragged his slick hands down her back, watching the long, lean muscles as they spasmed underneath his touch. "Tell me if this is too hard, or not hard enough."

He pressed his thumbs into the knots he found all along her body. Focusing mostly on her back at first, he waited until she relaxed into his touch. Then he tried more of what he had read. Gently lifting her hand, he threaded their fingers together and drew her arm back to expose the wing of her shoulder blade. He traced his free thumb through the tense muscle there.

She let out a little moan, and he paused for a moment to make sure none of this hurt before he continued. Her fingers spasmed in his, and the now glistening expanse of her spine was a temptation he struggled to avoid.

He wanted to touch and taste and linger, but right now was about fixing her. About healing her. Reconnecting them together after he had almost lost her.

Gluttony took his time massaging her body. He released her hand to scoop her hair up, then threaded his fingers through the tangled mass. He held onto her head, massaging her scalp with the fine points of his nails before he dragged them down her spine to her hip.

This was where he spent most of his attention. Slicking his hands with more oil, he dug deep into the aching joint that never worked well for her. And never would, he had read. She had too much damage from too long ago. But he could help with the pain.

So he focused all his attention on her hips and legs, carefully moving her body and manipulating her until they were both breathing hard. She stared up at him with eyes half mast, allowing him to part her legs and stretch the muscles in whatever way he wanted. Limp and trusting, he couldn't help but look. And his entire body shuddered as he saw how wet and aroused she was.

He hadn't meant to tease, only to help. And yet he had riled them both up until neither of them could think straight.

Katherine laid on her side, her good leg resting against his shoulder as he stretched out her tight tendons. It gave him the perfect view of her glistening sex, how she was practically dripping for him.

And, damn, he was drooling for her.

Just a taste, he told himself, as he bent to allow her knee to hook over his shoulder. He bent down, gently running his tongue between her folds. She gasped, falling onto her back and drawing him with her as he stroked her. Just a taste, he reminded himself, even as he plunged his tongue inside her.

"Yes," she hissed, her back arching into him. "Yes, please, more."

Claws retracting without thought, he filled her with two of his fingers. No hesitation, no waiting, just shoving them inside her and feeling the way her inner muscles clenched around him. She hissed out a long breath, an aching breath, one that seared right through his cock. He rocked himself against the edge of the bed, trying without luck to ease the pressure that told him to rear up over her and find nirvana in her warm, silken sleeve.

But he didn't.

He focused all his attention on that little nub at the top of her sex, drawing light circles around it and then flattening his tongue until he coaxed more of those sounds from her. Curling his fingers, he found the point inside her that made her mewl like a kitten, her entire body coiling, tightening, holding onto him as she sought a release that had been denied to her for too long.

Sealing his lips around her clit, he sucked and tossed her over the edge. She clenched so hard around his fingers he feared he would lose blood to them, and oh, it made him growl against her.

He licked slowly after that, drawing her back down from the orgasm that left her panting and liquid on the bed. And though he was certain this wasn't the plan he'd had in mind, at least now she looked truly relaxed.

Looking up from between her thighs, he licked his lips and waited for her to look down at him. To see the demon she'd tamed.

Chapter 33

Katherine couldn't think. She couldn't breathe. She couldn't do anything but stare up at the ceiling in shock because he'd ripped all her sense out from between her legs and suddenly there was nothing but the feeling of that long, black tongue writhing inside her.

He was...

What was he? She forgot the words. Just that he had made her feel so incredible for such a long time and no one had ever done that before.

She hadn't even done that to herself. Katherine hadn't realized an orgasm could go on that long. Or had it been two? Had he somehow tied orgasms together into a long knot that refused to uncoil until he touched it like he'd massaged the rest of her body?

Finally, she looked down where he still crouched between her legs.

And the sight was obscene. He looked like an animal hunting its prey, those red eyes glowing and casting shadows all around him. His long tongue coiled around his lips the moment he caught her gaze, as it licked at the shimmering remains of her pleasure.

But above all else, her eyes widened as she realized he had changed in between her legs. Reaching down, she gently touched the tip of her finger to the horns that had sprouted out of his forehead. Long and coiling, they looked like an antelope's horns. Twisting just slightly around themselves, and sharp at the tips.

"What are these?" she asked, her voice a little raspy from all the screaming. "They're new."

"Envy said they might happen. The closer we get to madness, the more our battle forms come to light." Gluttony closed his eyes for a moment, wearing an expression of pain, before he looked back at her. "If they frighten you, please tell me. I will do my best to prevent them from…"

He didn't seem capable of finishing the sentence and she didn't think she wanted him to. "I like them well enough." She stroked a finger down one again, watching as he shuddered at her touch. "Nothing about you scares me, Gluttony. No matter what happens to you."

"You should fear me, at least a little. I am a demon, after all."

"Oh," she whispered, grasping his horn firmly and yanking him up to her. "But you are my demon. And I couldn't possibly fear you."

She kissed him, coiling their tongues together as she tasted herself on his lips. The earthy, musky taste made her want to touch him. To feel him. To know what it would be like if he sank deep between her folds. She wanted so much from him that it should frighten her and yet, it didn't.

Katherine couldn't be frightened of anything that came with this man. No matter how strange or otherworldly he seemed, he was still hers.

And hers alone.

Gluttony groaned deep in his throat, his fingers coming up to yank at her hair. He tilted her until he could skate his lips down her throat, and the twin tips of his fangs dragged down the long length.

She let out a little moan and moved to give him even more access. It was depraved how much she wanted him to bite her again, but she wanted it.

It didn't matter in the slightest that she'd just been taken to his brother's kingdom to heal from their little enjoyments. She didn't care that she'd nearly died because he could have drained her dry. Right now, there was a clenching between her thighs at the mere thought of him dragging her closer and sinking his fangs into her neck.

She wanted to know that a part of herself was in him. And maybe that was wrong or strange or beyond anyone else's understanding, but she had come to crave... this. Whatever this was between them.

"I shouldn't," he murmured against her throat. "I could hurt you so easily."

"Or you could enjoy yourself and stop when you know you have to." She pressed her palm to the back of his head, holding him against her. The silhouette of his horns filled her gaze and oh, she was being devoured by a demon and she didn't even care. "I trust you."

"I don't." The broken whisper fanned across her neck before he pressed a closed mouth kiss to her pulse. "I don't trust myself at all, Kat."

It broke her heart to know that things had changed so much between them. He didn't want to risk her health, but that meant... that meant...

He rose from the bed, standing right at eye level and all her thoughts scattered. She could see how hard he was. Impossibly long, and thick, and she'd forgotten that her immediate thought the first time she'd seen him was, how am I going to fit that all inside me?

But she'd taken him into her mouth and she'd be damned if she wouldn't try to fit him into other places.

"If you don't want to feed—" She let her words trail off meaningfully as she stared at what she really wanted. She wanted to taste him, to tongue him, to slide him deep inside her, where she wouldn't know where he started and where she ended.

Her eyes widened as he reached down and fisted his length through his pants. "Is this what you want, pet?"

She licked her lips, unsure if she could respond to that. What would another, more wanton woman say in this situation? "Yes."

"How do you want it?"

"Whatever way you will give it to me." And it was so wicked of her to admit the truth, but she wanted him inside her in whatever way she could have.

His hand moved languidly up and down, outlining the impressive appendage that would surely wreck her. "You have to earn it, then. You have to show me you are well and healthy. Prove you're taking care of yourself first. You hear me, pet?"

She nodded frantically, but she would have agreed to anything he said. "I am well and healthy. I've had a week's worth of potions poured into me for too many days. I am healthy enough for this, Gluttony."

His hand paused at the head of his cock, squeezing hard once before he released it. "That has yet to be seen."

"What?" she squawked as he walked away from her.

Was he... denying her? Again? He'd done this a few times now, and she was starting to think there was something wrong with her. Did he worry about her hip? She could move it to the side a little more, perhaps. She could figure out a position that would allow both of them to enjoy the moment, because she wasn't broken, she wasn't...

His hand slid underneath her back, easing her into an upright position. Gluttony left his arm behind her, holding her upright as he slowly slid a buttoned down shirt onto her body. One of his.

It still smelled like him, all warm, like he'd just taken it off. "How..."

"It's been warming by the fire," he said with a soft smile on his face. He was obviously still so uncomfortable and yet here he was, taking care of her. Making sure that he didn't put even cold clothing on her. Warm and cherished, she allowed him to wrap the shirt around her and then slowly button it. His fingers skimmed her oversensitive skin and goosebumps broke out all down her arms.

His smile never budged, not even when he saw those. He even ghosted his fingers over the slight bumps that had risen before he tugged the sleeves firmly down. "Comfortable?"

"As much as I can be when you have denied me even a hint of the pleasure I seek." She narrowed her eyes at him. "I'm going to start taking this personally. You realize I'm not some fragile, broken thing. Yes?"

"Yes." Gluttony leaned down and touched their foreheads together. He breathed her in, slow and steady, before he let all the air out. "I almost lost you, Kat. I was the fool who allowed you to skate too close to death, and I refuse to let that happen again. You are, without a doubt, a shimmering star in the night sky of my life. I will not make the same mistake again. Not with you."

"Envy gave me potions to take. He said they would help replenish the blood faster for when we—"

Gluttony placed his hand over her mouth, silencing her. "I don't want to hear it right now, pet. I only want to know that you are here, and alive, and that nothing has changed between us. It was a gift to me that you even allowed me to touch you."

"Gluttony, you know that I enjoy it when you touch me! It's not a gift if I'm getting just as much pleasure as you."

He didn't seem to hear her, or to listen to her argument. Instead, he just pulled her out of the room and down the hall again. "I know you haven't been gone for very long, but clearly I have been working in your absence."

"Yes, I can see that." Although, she wanted to continue with their conversation.

"Well, the castle is much cleaner than it was before. And of course, we have been focusing on creating more space and more jobs for people in the town. I'll need your help to ensure there are trusted individuals here and not the newcomers who apparently want to make people think I'm still murdering." He paused in the hallway for a moment, a dumbstruck expression on his face before he tugged her back into movement. "I'll also have to address the fact that people think I'm still killing."

"Are you going to start again?"

He cast her an angry glance over his shoulder. "Do I look like I'm going to start a murderous rampage?"

"Well, you apparently don't wish to feed from me anymore." As soon as she said the words, her stomach churned. It was a horrible thing to even think, but if he wasn't feeding from her, then their contract was null and void. He could do what he wanted and she...

Gluttony tugged her closer and wrapped an arm around her shoulder as they continued, although he did at least slow down his pace. "I am not interested in feeding from anyone else. But I am afraid that I will harm you. So no, Katherine. I have no intention of backing out of our deal. Not while you are alive. But I will not feed from you as much as before, either."

"Why is that?"

"You have reminded me that gluttony is so much more than just food." His eyes flashed bright red. "Gluttony is living in a way that is lavish and overdone. I wish to live like that again, as I have forgotten so much of that enjoyment in the later years of my life."

That... didn't settle well.

Katherine said nothing as he steered her down the now gleaming halls. Her mind churned over what he had said, and none of it seemed healthy. He would deny himself a taste of her blood—which was the reason why he had faltered in the first place—only to change his indulgences to yet another problem? This wasn't the right way to fix anything.

And he wanted her to find villagers he could trust? There were no such people. Even she hadn't trusted him until living with him for quite a significant amount of time.

Now, she wasn't certain what to think. This didn't seem like the Gluttony she knew or the man who had wanted so desperately to change. But she refused to leave him alone in this. Maybe he was trying out a new way to live, and perhaps this would be better for everyone involved. She had no idea. He was a good man, a kind man, and he had it in him to be better. She had to believe that.

They strode by an empty room, or so she thought, until she saw the pale gray mist that hid underneath the bed. The poor little spirit was rather melancholy in appearance, but a deep glow burned inside of it as she strode past. She saw it roll after them, sluggish and slow but reaching out for her to touch.

She would have picked it up if Gluttony hadn't thrown open the doors to his lab and brought her inside of it. "Here, I am so close I can taste it. But I wanted you to do the honors."

"The honors of what?"

"Discovering the final piece." He drew her to his personal table where there were only a few wisps of the black smoke left in a vial and two others remaining beside it. "There are only two possible alchemical substances it could be, and I want you to be the person to choose. Pick one."

She lifted one of the vials to her nose and had to control her own sneeze. "Bee's pollen?"

"Seemed unlikely at first, but..." Gluttony shrugged.

The other she lifted and peered into the glass. It took a few moments for her to recognize the ground herb, but it wasn't one that regularly grew in this area of the kingdoms. But then she noticed the pale yellow remains of a petal with a black center, and she knew exactly what she held.

"Henbane?" she asked, her brows furrowing. "This would make more sense than I wish to admit."

"Why's that?" Gluttony took a step closer to her, his front pressed to her back. "I have never heard of it before. Nor had I met anyone else who knew what it was."

"My mother used to grow it in a pot by the window. She said never to touch it, because it's very poisonous." Katherine tilted the vial a little, marveling at how well he'd ground it. "She said her people used to eat it in small doses. It will put a mortal into a trance so they can speak with the divine powers of the realm."

"Ah," he breathed. "So that is how they are using it to control us.

What happens when one of the divine is given their own herbs of power?"

Katherine shrugged. "I don't know the answer to that."

"Indeed." He took the vial from her, a small frown wrinkling his handsome brow. "Shall we, then?"

It was rather daunting to watch him pour the remaining black smoke into the henbane. If she was wrong, then they would have wasted the last specimen. She'd seen him use that smoke time and time again. Watched it change color a thousand times, or sometimes shattered the black jar in his hands. Gluttony would leap back, swearing whenever that happened and grumbling about meddling mortals.

But this time, nothing happened at all. The black smoke remained black. If anything, it darkened even further. It changed into a substance that made her heart feel bitter and cold.

There was something deeply wrong with that smoke. Something that made the hairs on her arms stand on end.

"There it is," he breathed, gently setting the vial down. "Henbane. So that's what they're using to attack us."

"Attack you?"

"A group of mortals has been using this to incapacitate demons like me. They throw this smoke at us, and if we inhale it, we pass out. Gone. Asleep. For hours on end and we cannot stop it." He eyed her with no small amount of appreciation. "You might have saved us all, Katherine."

"I did nothing at all." Wringing her hands, she stepped closer to him. As though her next words needed to be kept a secret. "Gluttony, henbane is a sacred herb of the dead. It can even poison the soul, so the legends say. It transcends life and death itself."

His expression turned troubled. "I need to speak with my brothers about this."

"Perhaps you should."

And then she froze when he looked at her again, his eyes flicking up and down her body before he nodded firmly. "And so will you."

She would what?

Chapter 34

He wasted no time. Namely, because Gluttony felt as though he couldn't enjoy her or her company until he proved himself worthy of it. If he could show his brothers that he was, finally, not the fuck up of the family, then maybe everything would change.

He'd deserve to have a woman like her. He'd deserve to wake up next to her. Not as the monster he was, but as the man he could be.

To her credit, Katherine didn't seem to mind that he'd dragged her back to his office. She followed him with a bemused smile on her face, keeping pace with him even though it made her limp even more pronounced.

He'd massage her again later. Gluttony would do anything to run his hands all over her body again, to drag his talons along her back and to feel the plump cushion of her hips.

He wanted her. Everything about her. Every inch of her body and soul, that was what he wanted. And this was the only way he could feel like he deserved even the slightest bit of her.

"Where are we going?" she finally asked before they'd reached his office.

"Calling my brothers."

At that, she yanked her hand away from him. Or at least, she tried. He was significantly stronger than his little mortal, and she couldn't force him to do anything he didn't want to do.

So he continued dragging her all the way into his office and then plopped her down in a chair. Crouching before her, he braced her hips with his arms as he forced her to look at him. "You deserve to be in this room just as much as them."

"Talking to a room full of demon kings is rather intimidating, don't you think?" Her wide-eyed stare proved just how intimidated she was. But that was silly.

Leaning forward, he bumped his forehead to hers and then leaned back to grin. "You're better than the lot of them combined. And they won't really be in the room."

"What do you mean?"

Gluttony leapt to his feet, making his way to the desk where the small crystal was hidden. He twisted the top of it, activating the magic that would be required to summon all six of his brothers at the same time. "It's magic. Something Envy came up with in his spare time. You know how he likes to dabble in spells. I'll tell you who each of them are, don't worry."

"I don't really want to—"

He didn't let her finish the thought. Instead, he moved behind her chair and dragged it over to his side of the desk with her in it. She gripped the arms until her knuckles turned white and let out a little squeak that only made him grin even wider.

Sitting down in his own chair, he looked at his desk and then nodded with pleasure. "Yes, this will do."

"Why will this do? You moved me like a sack of potatoes."

Gluttony reached underneath his desk and grabbed her hand in his. He curled their fingers together, linking them as he'd wanted to do from the first moment he'd seen her through her window. As he always should, no matter what difficulty stood in front of them.

"There," he murmured, squeezing her fingers. "Does it feel a little less intimidating now?"

Katherine's mouth slightly opened, and she watched him with a soft expression on her face. "Yes. That's much better, Gluttony. Thank you."

He must have glowed with pleasure. That was all he wanted, after all. He just wanted her to feel comfortable and not like she was out of place because she was everything he'd ever wanted. And now she was right where she belonged.

The first flickering blue image was exactly who he expected. Gluttony leaned closer to Katherine and murmured, "That is Lust and his bride Selene."

He tried his best to see his brother through her eyes. Lust with those shorter, curved horns that disappeared into the golden locks of his hair. He reclined at his desk, a billowing white shirt parted down to the short corset he had wrapped around his waist. His bride perched on his knee, draped over him in a stark contrast wearing a rather demure silk gown. Apparently, his brother hadn't been able to get her to wear the revealing clothing he would have chosen.

Another blue image glowed across the room from Lust. "Greed, and his new wife, Varya. They were who I stayed with while I was not in this kingdom."

Varya stood beside Greed's desk, her hip leaning against the wood. But she grinned at him and waved the moment she saw him. "You're looking well, Gluttony!"

"Well as I can be."

"Still eating people?"

He bared his fangs at her. "Only one, these days."

Varya's eyes widened, and she bit her lip while looking at Katherine. "My, my. How time changes a man."

Before his own little human could ask a question of Varya, another light blinked into existence. Gluttony quickly cleared his throat and said, "You already know, Envy."

"I do." Katherine gave him a little wave and then froze when the next demon appeared.

Gluttony's brows drew down in concern. He'd never really looked much at his brothers. They were just demons, like him. But he'd forgotten how Sloth drew the feminine eye. His brother wore a sheer dressing robe, revealing plains upon plains of glistening muscle. Oiled and sleek, he didn't even attempt to hide the golden scales that stretched over his shoulders and spun down his stomach in swirling patterns. Dark hair falling over his eyes, Gluttony could just barely make out their piercing blue color.

In person, Sloth was even more devastatingly handsome. He was perfection personified, as they all were, but unlike Lust, who had both women and men flocking to him at all hours of the day, Sloth had a deadly edge that only drew the most brave.

Or perhaps the most foolish.

"Sloth," he said quietly, ripping his gaze away from his brother to look down at Katherine's shocked expression. "Stay away from him."

"Why?"

"Because he has a harem of women to choose from every night, and he doesn't need to add you to his collection." Gluttony bristled when he realized she still hadn't looked at him. "Besides. I've heard he's a terrible lover."

That did it. Katherine flicked her amused gaze to him. "Really?"

"I'd imagine women would prefer a lover who enjoys partaking in the event rather than one who expects his women to do all the work." He eyed her hungrily. "Or perhaps one who couldn't get enough of them. Ever."

She bit her lip to hide a grin he knew was there. "Oh, I highly doubt he expects his women to do all the work, Gluttony."

Sloth interrupted them with a growled, "She's right, you know. I'd be happy to show your woman just how much I partake in the... event."

A snarl on his lips, Gluttony bared his teeth at his brother and pressed his hand against the arm of his chair, as though he could launch himself straight into Sloth rather than just the projection of him.

Though they all silenced the moment a dark figure appeared. Even with the blue light of the spell, Wrath was darkness personified. He suddenly appeared and all the oxygen was sucked out of the room. They all stared at him, waiting for their winged brother to turn around and face them.

Katherine's soft gasp was the only sound as Wrath finally spun toward them. And Gluttony saw the anger in his eyes the moment his brother saw Gluttony had brought a woman to their meeting.

Katherine shrank in her chair, melting into the fabric as though that might allow her to disappear from his anger. And he knew that Wrath was the most intimidating of them. They all were strange and inhuman, but he was the worst of their lot. Leathery wings, broken and dragging behind him. The scars that covered his body on full display without his cloak or shirt to cover them. And the stitches around his mouth from where he'd been silenced by his own people.

"Wrath," he murmured, squeezing her fingers and settling back into his chair. "Not as terrifying as he looks."

"Is that so?" she breathed. "Because he's looking at me like he wants to kill me."

"That's just how he always looks."

"Are you sure?"

No, but he knew that he'd never seen Wrath look like he didn't want to rip someone's spine out of their body. It was a very normal expression for him to wear. And his brother was surveying all the others, those red eyes so similar to Gluttony's own. Something that irritated Wrath horribly.

And finally, the last brother joined them. Pride blinked into view and he knew the moment all the humans went completely and utterly still that something was very wrong. Or perhaps it was that they were stunned to see such a creature existed.

Pride had taken an image that he knew the humans would worship. Golden skin, a face that was carved by the ancients. A perfect body that never once rebelled on him and, of course, massive white feathered wings that opened and closed with each of his breaths. He had modeled himself as their god, and as such, the humans had followed him without complaint.

"Cheat," he muttered. Then leaned down to whisper in Katherine's ear, "That is Pride. Our so-called king."

And that king turned his attention to Katherine with a laser focus before he snarled, "What is a human doing here?"

All sound in the room ceased. The discomfort stretched as everyone seemed to struggle with how to answer.

It was Selene who first spoke, even though Lust's hand spasmed on her hip the moment her mouth opened. "There is more than one human here, Pride."

He turned that glare to Selene and she paled under his scrutiny. "You and Varya are hardly human anymore, are you not? Enlighten me if the spirits inside you have suddenly left and then I will question your right to be here as well."

"Hey," Greed snarled, leaning forward on his desk and bracing an arm across it. "Our consorts have every right to be here. Mortal or not."

"Perhaps yours does, but she is a random mortal from a kingdom of peasants. Explain yourself, Gluttony."

Anger simmered in his chest. He could feel that battle form already pressing against his skin. He wanted to rage at his brother. Flip his desk and throw it through that stupid shimmering image of a man who thought himself a god. And he refused to bow before a man who could dare to insult the woman he... he...

Fingers squeezed his, and he was brought back to the present. To Katherine's eyes as she gave him a soft smile. "It's all right," she whispered. "Just tell them what you have to tell them."

And it was all right. Because she was here with him and because nothing would change that. No matter how hard he fought or argued with his brothers, they didn't matter.

This was his kingdom. And this was his woman. No one would take her from him.

He sat up straight and ignored Pride's rude interjection. "I have found what they are using to attack us with. The herb is called henbane and is a rather difficult herb to find in my kingdom. Likely why I have seen so very few attacks here."

Greed let out a grunt. "I'll have to ask where they're getting it here."

"It grows plenty in my kingdom," Lust murmured.

"The same in mine," Sloth replied. He even looked a little less relaxed at his desk. "How did you discover this?"

He looked down at Katherine and smiled. "The human you so wrongfully attacked was the one who discovered it. She told me about henbane and how her mother used it when she was younger. Would you care to share what you said to me?"

Katherine's eyes might have fallen out of her head, they were so big. She looked up at him like he'd asked her to spar with his brothers.

And, he supposed, in a way he had.

But she rose to the challenge, and he'd never felt more proud of her. She cleared her throat before leaning forward. "It is symbolic of the dead, an herb used to converse with the divine. In small doses, it causes hallucinations in mortals. But, I have no way of knowing what it would do to your kind. Apparently, it is rather like a sleeping agent. At least, according to what Gluttony has told me."

Pride seemed to bristle. "Why should we trust you—"

But this time, it was Wrath himself who interrupted their "king". The dark brother lifted a hand and all of them fell silent, even Pride.

Wrath's wings snapped open and shut before he spoke. "If this is an herb that is symbolic of the dead, could other herbs with the same symbolism have the same effect?"

No one knew how to respond. All the brothers looked back and forth between each other, but they had never considered it. Sure, they had reactions to certain foods or drinks or objects, but they had never fully researched why. They'd just avoided them.

Katherine cleared her throat again. "I believe it's likely. Considering the lot of you are unnatural in the waking realm, perhaps it is your greatest weakness? Items that are symbols of the dead also are what humans use in magic to walk the line between the living and beyond."

Selene leaned forward slightly, her eyes doing that strange thing that she did when she was casting spells. "It would make sense. The sorceresses have access to almost all of those items or plants. We could trial them to see what happens when they are touched or ingested."

Gluttony watched them all begin to murmur at the same time. Those with partners whispered amongst each other, while Envy and Sloth conversed quietly. Pride and Wrath remained silent, their eyes on Katherine as if they couldn't quite understand what she was.

And that unnerved him.

He gave them all a few moments to speak before raising his voice. "I have done as you asked. I discovered what weapon the humans were using against us, and I have gifted you not only that, but an entirely new situation to research. From now on, I consider my debt to you all repaid."

Pride glowered. "What repayment is that? There is no debt when you have besmirched our names. We are kings and gods. Now you have proven we are also the demons they call us. There is more repayment than simply discovering a weed that has been used to attack us."

Gluttony was ready to fight over that, but Envy spoke. "I will create a cure, brothers. Now that I know what it is, a cure should be rather simple."

"Good," Gluttony replied before reaching for the crystal on his desk. "Then have a nice evening, brothers. I know I will."

And with that, he turned the crystal's top in the other direction and made the lot of them disappear. He had no interest in speaking with them any longer.

"What did you just do?" Katherine said with a laugh. "Did you really just end the conversation like that? They're going to summon you right back."

"And I won't be in my office to be summoned." Swinging her up into his arms, he laughed with her as they made their way back down the hall. "I've missed you. Forget my brothers. Why don't we discover all the other changes I've made to the castle in your absence?"

It felt like the most natural thing in the world as she tossed her arm around his neck and kicked her good leg. "Can I suggest other changes?"

"Who is supposed to be the gluttonous one?"

She grinned at him and his entire world burst into bright light, like she was the sun itself. "I suppose it's all right if I'm a little gluttonous too."

Chapter 35

She planned to surprise him. Katherine knew that very little could surprise Gluttony after a thousand years of life, but she was determined that he would like what she had to bring him.

Besides, it was long pastime for her to empty her room at the boarding house. She'd only kept it because she'd been so afraid that he would send her back here and she wouldn't have anywhere to stay. But now, it was very clear that Gluttony intended to keep her, and she was... well, she didn't really mind that fate in the slightest.

When he'd fallen into one of his rare, deep sleeps, she'd snuck out of the castle with a tiny bundle of gray light following her. Spite hadn't been around very much lately, nor did it speak any longer, but it clung to her like a child did its mother's skirts. Even now, as she approached the boarding house, she probably looked like a madwoman.

Katherine held her arms around the tiny spirit that no one else could see. It whimpered, the pitiful noise grating on her nerves as it traced a tendril gently down her cheek.

"Everything is fine," she said quietly, opening the front door and making her way to her old room. "You and I are going to be just fine."

And she believed that. This time, her journey through the town had been relatively quiet. Though there were a few whispers and pointed stares, no one tried to talk with her. In fact, everyone ignored her. Like she didn't exist at all.

Such a reception was fine with her. If they wanted to fire her from her job, cast her off like she was dirty laundry, then that was fine with her. She wanted nothing to do with them, either. They were blinded by their own hatred, and Katherine had no business being around people like that.

It took a bit of maneuvering for her to get the key out of her pocket while still holding onto Spite. But she managed well enough and opened the room. It didn't appear that anyone had been inside, a small blessing considering she'd been gone for a while. Usually, if someone left their room for long enough, others would go through and see what they could keep for themselves.

Of course, she didn't have much either. Maybe that was why no one had bothered her things.

She set the pale little spirit down on her bed that had a fine layer of dust on it and started packing. She could fit all her things in a single trunk at the end of her bed, and Katherine should have been a little embarrassed at how quickly she managed to fold, roll, and stuff everything in its place.

But she left out a single book, which she waved at Spite. "This is a book on herbs for speaking with the dead. It was my mothers, and is the only thing I own that was hers. She'd lent it to a friend long before she died, before our house burned down. A few years ago, the old woman remembered it and gave it to me."

Flipping through the pages, she sat on the edge of the bed with a huff of disappointment. "I remember thinking this was so foolish. I didn't want to end up like my mother. Muttering about spirits and how no one else could see them. She seemed insane at the time."

Her heart squeezed and Spite slithered into her lap. It was getting a little stronger these days, but it certainly didn't look like itself anymore.

Setting the book on the bed, she gently ran her hand down the back of the spirit. "You don't look like yourself at all, little one. Is something wrong?"

It shook its pale head and seemed almost like it was ready to speak. But then they both heard a thud on the outside of the room. Katherine almost asked, "What was that?"

Why would she, though? She knew it was nothing good.

So much for getting through this visit without having someone causing an issue. Although, she supposed, that was unavoidable. She needed to find someone to help her carry this trunk back to the castle, and that wasn't going to happen easily. No one wanted to risk their own necks to help Gluttony's "favored".

Sighing, she settled the little spirit back onto her bed. "You stay here where it's safe. If someone comes into this room, hide. Run to the castle if you have to, but do not try to help me. Do you understand?"

It gave a worried little chirp.

Not at all like the Spite, she knew. The bitter little spirit was all too happy to cause trouble and mischief. But this version of it seemed... concerned. Worried. Fearful even as it plopped off her bed, made its way to her window, and then disappeared past all the people who had gathered there. They couldn't see it, and for that, she was very thankful.

Shaking her head, she took her time walking through the boarding house. She knew there was an argument waiting for her, but she didn't think they would actually hurt her. No one had put their hands on her before, but they might ban her from the town.

She had to be all right with this treatment. They would not accept her choices and she would not accept theirs.

Katherine lifted her hand to shade the sun that split through the mist as she walked out to greet her people. A whole crowd had formed in front of her window, and thus in the center of the town. So many faces she didn't recognize, and many more that she did. They were all gathered together, strangers and friends alike, to glare at her with hatred in their eyes.

"Why are you here, witch?" Someone shouted.

"I'm gathering my things."

"Leaving curses, more like," another person muttered.

It was hard to tell who was speaking in the crowd. They all seemed to mutter over each other until all she could hear was a garbled mess of fear and disgust. They didn't want the crippled hag to wander through their homes, leaving bad luck in her wake.

They'd never thought of her like this before. She might have come from an unfortunate family history, but she had never been some creature for them to look down upon.

Who had spread these lies? This venom that had infected her people?

Narrowing her gaze, she looked through the crowd and found them. The strangers who had infiltrated her town. They watched her with vivid eyes that saw too much. Eyes that expected her to fight or grow angry. To prove that she had turned into a monster just like the man they all hated.

But that was not who Katherine was. She'd never wanted to harm her people or make their lives harder. She just wanted them to see her as a person and to let her exist.

So instead of arguing back, she merely clutched the book to her chest, ducked her head, and started through the crowd. There was no other path for her to go. She had to walk through them to get out of the town, and maybe Gluttony would return with her to get her things later. The room was unlocked, so maybe she would be looted. But they were just things.

This was starting to feel like it could get out of hand, and she didn't think it was safe to stay a moment longer.

The first shove came from her left, thankfully. She placed all her weight on her good leg and stumbled. But at least she stayed upright. They learned after that. More hands shoving, pulling, pushing, moving her left and right until her bad leg eventually gave out.

She'd gotten a considerable way through them, though. So when she hit the planks, she was near the edge of the boardwalk. She stared into the green water, all the more colorful in the sunlight, and she saw everyone's reflection behind her.

Angry faces. Faces that had always looked at her with pity, but now, she only saw hatred.

She couldn't stay here. They were going to kill her, and in a very painful way. She just wanted to go back to Gluttony. Back to safety.

"Hey!" Grace's voice split through some of the others. "What are you doing? Shame on you! Let her through."

But as she turned to look over her shoulder, she saw hands on Grace's waist. They tugged her away from the crowd, away from helping her friend, and she knew this was going to get bad. Quickly.

A boot connected with her jaw. She bit through her tongue and the bitter taste of blood bloomed. She gasped and some of the warm liquid trickled down her chin. Who had kicked her? Why would they do that?

But apparently that's what the rest of the mob had been waiting for. They started kicking however they could, connecting with her ribs and her hips. Seeking out the soft places on her body that would hurt the worst for her. All her nightmares came to life.

"Witch!" they shouted. "Cripple! The gods did this to you because they knew what was in your heart."

Her heart had always been good. Always. No matter what had been thrown in her way and she wanted to argue with them. To say that they were the ones who had been poisoned, not her. Their souls were tainted black with jealousy and rage.

But she couldn't say anything with blood coating her tongue and her arms over her head, desperately trying to protect her face and neck from the boots that flew from every direction.

A low growl rumbled across the moors. She heard him long before she saw him. Everyone had frozen and Katherine peered through her arms to see a dark shadow surging across the water. Not the boardwalk where there were broken planks and meandering pathways, no.

Gluttony raced to her side in a straight line. Monsters be damned, they all fled from the sight of the enraged demon who sprinted among them. The water didn't even slow him down, but how could it? Even the moors flinched away from the horned beast that charged through them.

Her demon. Her monster, who hated to see her even get a paper cut, let alone endure a crowd of people attacking her. And she knew, in that moment, she could choose to save them. She could throw herself over the edge of this boardwalk and he would be forced to save her.

But...

She didn't.

She hesitated and in that split second, he attacked. He lunged for whatever flesh he could find. Hauling himself out of the moors and onto the town center with a powerful thrust of his body. His claws came first, slicing through the nearest man, who had been the last to kick her.

Katherine watched the man's eyes go wide as he pressed his hands to this throat. The blood that spurted out between his fingers was almost comical. Like she was watching a play rather than a man die right in front of her.

Gluttony went for the next in a blur. His teeth sank into the woman's neck and he ripped at her skin, gristle hanging between his teeth as she staggered away from him. And even in this moment she could see that the marks he left were not the same as the countless people she'd seen in the almshouse. It wasn't the same. Not even his claw marks were the same.

No one here would see that, though. All they would remember was the monster who stood among them, heaving with ragged breaths as he dripped swamp water onto the planks. He was massive. Far larger than she'd ever seen him with horns so tall they jabbed at the sky. His red eyes glowed and he could barely keep his mouth shut around the rigid fangs that gleamed in the sunlight.

Then came the screams. Countless screams and shouts as the villagers tried to run from him, but he was so fast. She noticed he didn't attack everyone, only the people whose boots she recognized.

Their blood splattered onto the raised planks until it looked like a river of red flowed through her town. He only slowed when people had run so far from him that he needed to choose who he chased after.

A group of strangers had remained, knives and wickedly curved blades now in their hands. One of the men she recognized from the boardwalk, and he stood tall and strong as he called out, "So the demon is here after all."

Gluttony grinned, blood dripping down his chin. "You asked for a demon the moment you attacked her. And thus, you have received one."

One of the men rushed forward, and then two others. But Gluttony didn't even flinch. Those long claws reached for them, dragging them closer and allowing their blades to pierce through his flesh. He didn't even react. He just leaned down and ripped out their throats with his teeth before dropping them dead to his feet.

The crowd still watched from a safe distance, and they all seemed to hold their breath as he pointed at her. "She is mine," he snarled. "Any who touches her again will face my wrath. I will not stop at merely killing you, for that is a mercy. The next person to touch her, I will drain dry. Slowly. In front of all your loved ones, as I make them watch you die in front of them. Do you hear me?"

She could hear the sounds of dragonfly wings as they returned after the tussle. The fluttering sound vibrated next to her ears. The faint burble of the moors behind her, and the chuff of a kelpie who had been drawn by the scent of blood. It was all there, but not a single sound of human life. Not even a moan from the people he'd harmed because he'd killed them so quickly.

She started shaking. Her fingers wouldn't stop moving, twitching, and then her hands followed like she didn't know where to put them because that river of blood was coming closer to her. Katherine wanted to move away from it, but that would put her right in the moors. The creatures behind her had already been drawn to the scent of blood.

Blood that she'd spit into the water herself. Blood that her own people had drawn because she had dared to have feelings for this man who had been the only one to step in and save her.

But he'd done so much.

Eyes wide, heart thundering, she lifted her head to see that no one was offering to help her now either. They didn't care. They just stared at two people they believed to be monsters.

Perhaps she should have hated them for that. Katherine wished she could get angry at someone, but the only person at fault was her.

She had started all this. She'd turned her town's life upside down, and she'd changed Gluttony, too. And she wouldn't apologize for any of it. She was sorry they were all hurting, but sometimes it hurt to do the right thing.

"Do you hear me?" Gluttony snarled, his voice pitched low and deep. His gaze sliced through the crowd one last time, so loud he made people flinch away from him.

Even the strangers seemed to back away. But not before Katherine saw the darkness in their eyes.

This wasn't the end of their attacks against him. She feared it might be just the beginning.

Chapter 36

He had a hard time coming down from the rage. He wanted to rip into more of them. To feel their soft flesh parting beneath claw and fang. Mortals were so easy to torment, so easy to destroy. All it took was one crook of his claw and they folded underneath the weight of his anger.

But he was not here to hunt. He was here to save someone, and that meant he needed to turn his back on those who wished to murder him.

To murder her.

His vision turned red again as he remembered what he had seen. Spite had found him in the castle, and though the little spirit could not speak, it had given him a sense of urgency and warning. So he had run. He'd sprinted through the swamp, darting past every creature that thought to stand in his way.

And they parted for him like waves on either side of his body. He knew if he had called them to fight with him, they would have swallowed this town up. But his Katherine had a heart big enough to save a town like this and he knew she would not want to see more of them harmed. So he stilled the anger in his chest. He bottled up all the rage and need for more blood, more pain.

Gluttony eyed the crowd one last time, knowing that they would not test him as he turned away from their hate-filled eyes. But he still listened and scented for any movement as he gave them his back, because he no longer trusted them.

They would feel his punishment soon. But for now, the death of their loved ones was punishment enough.

Katherine lay on the boardwalk, her hands planted in front of her. Propped up like this, she almost looked like one of the rusalki on their rocks, waiting for a young man to come into the water and save them. She was beautiful, even bloodied as her nose and mouth were.

But she was also shaking. Her hands trembled against the rotting wood beneath her and her eyes darted from him, to the bodies, to the blood. Always ending on the blood.

He had been too rough in front of her. His Katherine had seen death before. After all her years in the almshouse, he knew she had seen enough death to last her a lifetime. But he had forgotten how much it would affect her to see this. These were still her people, attackers or no.

So he crouched lower, pressing his own palm to the bloodied wood to make himself seem small. Less threatening as she watched him like a cornered, trembling mouse.

"Katherine," he said quietly, taking one small movement closer to her. Crawling, as it were, with one hand stretched out to her. "Katherine, you are safe."

Her eyes flicked up to him again, and he knew what she must see. A monster drenched in blood, long tangles of dark hair hanging around his horned head. He knew his face changed as well. His body bulking with muscles, while his face became blocky and more filled with fangs and sharpened teeth.

He tried to make himself small. Gluttony knew that right now, she probably didn't see him. All she likely saw was another person who was coming toward her, wanting to hurt and harm and maim. What they had done to her...

He had to close his eyes and grit his teeth to stop himself from spinning on them again. He could still feel their eyes. The scent of their blood was in the air, and it made him want to feast even more. It made him want to rip out their still beating hearts and offer them to her like some goddess on a bloodied throne he had built.

But he was not that monster. Not for her.

Gluttony was not just his battle form, waiting for the next fight to feast upon blood and organs. He was a man who loved a woman, and that truth burned through his chest so powerfully that it made his entire body ache.

He loved her.

Oh, he loved her more than the sun loved the moon. He loved her more than forever and wanted nothing more than to rot with her until nothing was left but them.

So he kept that hand outstretched, holding out his claws with hope in his eyes and a heart that pounded only for her.

And he waited. He kept his back to the daggers, pikes, and torches that people were surely ripping out of their homes as they prepared to fight a demon who had killed so many of them. He waited, knowing that he showed his weakness and they both might be in danger.

Because he did not care.

Let them try to kill him. He would gladly die if it meant she was safe and happy.

She took a deep, rattling breath. Her wild eyes locked on him and him alone. He wondered if she was feeling like a mouse trapped against the floorboards while a cat loomed over her. But no, not his Katherine. For all that she was different, for all that she had suffered, she had remained impossibly brave.

Her fingers looked so tiny against his as she slipped them into his grip and held onto two of his fingers. The most she could hold onto comfortably, he had a feeling. They were connected to each other again. Close enough so that he could feel her heartbeat through her fingers, and it was enough for him. At least for now.

"Can you stand?" he asked, his voice a low grumble. Though he tried to be softer with the tone, it was impossible in this form.

But she looked up at him with those big, wide eyes and he knew that she saw him. She knew who held onto her hands and she knew that right now, she was safe.

"I don't know," she whispered. Katherine winced and her gaze flickered away from his for a mere moment to look down at her bad hip. "They kicked me."

"I know, love." He held onto her fingers, squeezing them tight. "I know they did."

And oh, his heart broke all over again.

She would have given up everything for them. Katherine's heart was so big, she would likely forgive them even this. She'd look back on the memory with fear, but she would swallow it so she could be there for her people when they clearly weren't themselves.

He was not so forgiving.

Once he had her back in his arms, he turned his glare on the people behind them again. Baring his teeth in a wicked snarl, he slowly slid his hand down her palm. Seeking the pulse at the base of her wrist with his fingers, before bending again to slide his grip underneath her elbow.

It took so little effort to lift her, and that only made him even more angry. Because she was so delicate and bird-like and they had attacked her without hesitation. Like she was the monster they needed to expel from their home, when he was the one they wanted to hurt.

So they had attacked the person easier to harm. The smaller target because they knew her injuries would hurt him even more than if they had tried to carve out his heart. He knew what this was. He'd seen this tactic a hundred times in his long life, but it had never hurt so badly.

Like the monster he was, he curved himself around her. A beast with horns, claws, and a long, whipping tail behind him as he wrapped Katherine in his arms.

"Pet," he said quietly. "I need you to put your arms around my neck. Can you do that?"

She nodded and reached for him even as someone shouted her name in the crowd.

He turned with her, his gaze narrowing on an older gentleman who stood in the crowd. Everyone seemed to look at him with some level of respect, so he could only assume this was a man of power.

Katherine looked at the man too, but then she turned away and tucked her face into Gluttony's neck.

He softened. If this man had any power over the woman he loved, then he no longer did. Gluttony was the only one she sought out for reassurance, and he was the one who had saved her. Not this man. For the first time in a very long time, Gluttony felt... powerful.

He pointed at the stranger with a long nailed hand, his teeth peeled back in a snarl that surely revealed every glinting point of his sharpened teeth. "Keep your mouth shut," he said, his voice warped with fangs. "This woman is mine."

"Lust at first bite, I take it?" the man challenged.

He would not reveal the true depths of his feelings for the first time with a crowd before them. He had no intent on allowing this man to goad him or Katherine into saying anything they were not ready to say.

So he turned away from the man instead. He stepped off the boardwalk and ignored the gasps as he walked off the planks and into the swamp. The villagers of this town were not his problem, but the injured woman in his arms absolutely was.

He strode through the water that splashed against his now massive thighs and quickly disappeared from the sight of the village.

It was time for Katherine to meet the others in his kingdom. The ones that she'd feared most of her life, because he had encouraged those who were different to feast upon whatever they wished. Hunt the humans, he'd said all those years ago. Hunt them, and destroy them for all I care.

But now, he had one in particular who was his and his alone.

Someday he would introduce her to the loup garou and the other more terrifying beasts of his swamp. He would show her that there was nothing to fear in their monstrous forms, as long as he was with her.

But for now, he had one intent and one alone.

The rusalki were the softest of his strange creatures, although likely they would still terrify Katherine. They were... well, not the most beautiful of creatures when they were not attempting to lure men. How they appeared to either sex was rather different in most cases, but they were also quite magical on their own.

And they would be able to heal her. They would make her more comfortable.

Slogging through the water, he noticed when Katherine came back into herself. She jolted in his arms, her fingers curling a little more tightly around the back of his neck.

"Where are we going?" she asked, lifting her head from his shoulder and peering about them for the first time.

They were far from the walkways. Farther than any human likely had ever attempted to journey. They wouldn't have gotten far if they tried.

But this was a wonderland to him. The scent of peat and the earthy addition of bog water filled his lungs. Fireflies danced around them, mingling with dragonflies that rushed to get ready for the night. Wild lilies on their bright green pads floated around his knees. And in the near distance was a weeping willow whose tendrils brushed the water with delicate fronds. Tiny ripples fluttered out of reach as the slightest breeze knocked them into movement.

It was peaceful here. Beautiful. Not an ounce of humanity to touch it.

"Oh," Katherine breathed. "This is lovely."

"I have a favor to ask," he said as he strode more confidently toward the willow.

"Anything."

"Not of you, pet." Gluttony felt his lips twist into a smile, though. Because even injured and frightened, she trusted him to take care of her. And he would. For the rest of her days.

Ducking underneath the delicate fronds, he stepped into another world. The rusalki lived underneath the curtain of the willow. Their beds were carved into its giant trunk, although many of them still slept underneath the water in their algae covered beds. There were four of them lounging on the roots of the tree, weaving new crowns for their heads.

They did not have their faces on, though. The faces they wore for men were beautiful and lovely. Young women who had never seen a day of hardship in their life.

These were their true faces. Rotting and sunken in death, as they had died in the bog. Most were pushed into the water and drowned by their partners. Some because they did not love the man in return, others because they were pregnant and their partners did not wish to be fathers. Or to marry.

Rusalki were dangerous creatures who lived with hatred in their hearts. Their purpose was mostly revenge, and to drown all men who came near them. They dragged them into the depths, tangling them in their long hair as their slippery bodies escaped the men's reach. Once he drowned, they were rumored to feast upon the man's flesh.

One of the rusalki sat up quickly at his approach, her black hair tangling around her nude form. Her dark eyes flashed in those sunken sockets before she recognized him.

"Gluttony!" she said, and the others perked up.

Soon they were swarmed by countless women, their skeletal figures making soft creaking noises as they peeked over his arm to look at Katherine.

"What happened?" the first rusalki said, her eyes large and wide with emotion.

And Katherine... Oh, he'd thought she would tremble in his arms with fear. He thought looking upon those thin, emaciated faces, ghostly pale and ashen with death, that she would feel some ounce of fear.

But he had forgotten who he held in his arms.

Katherine's eyes filled with tears. Not in fear, but sadness as she choked, "They attacked me. I was one of their own, and they... They kicked me. They knocked me down and if Gluttony hadn't come, they would have..."

She couldn't say the words, considering the young women who stood before her knew exactly what would happen. They had not survived their fates, and they knew what death by drowning felt like.

Tutting, the rusalki reached as one to take Katherine out of his arms, but he refused. "She cannot walk," he grumbled, stomping through them to reach a small, flat section at the base of the tree. Then he settled her carefully, making sure she was comfortable on her rump before he took a step away from them all. "She needs healing."

"Healing," one of them said. "We do not heal."

"You do."

"Our magic is in death."

Gluttony took a deep breath, reminding himself that even though he was in battle form, he did not have to be the monster. "We both know you are lying. I'm calling upon our bond and the boon you owe me, ladies. Put her back together."

They all looked at each other, then back to him, then made a sound of a collective sigh. "Then we are no longer in your service?"

"You've never been in my service. The lot of you do whatever you want," he grumbled. "Fine. Yes. You can consider yourself free of all debts."

They clustered together, a menagerie of bony elbows and hollows between ribs. Then they turned again, and he heard one of them say, "We will care for her, demon."

And so he settled in the roots a small distance away, bracing his forearms on his knees as he watched the women cluster around his heart. For he had surely ripped it out of his own chest and given it to Katherine.

Because she owned him, he realized. Mind, body, and soul.

Chapter 37

The rusalki patched her back together as best they could. They hadn't been lying when they claimed their magic was more in death than life. Katherine had never been healed quite so painfully before. But they were kind. Their hands were gentle as they touched every one of her hurts and cooed over each bruise.

They knew what it was like for people to betray them. They knew the bone deep hurt that now lived inside her soul. A hurt a regular healer couldn't touch.

Bony hands held hers, squeezing her fingers through the pain and the anguish that they slowly ripped out of her being. Over and over. Tearing out pain with their fingers until she couldn't feel it anymore.

They snapped their fingers and claws at her, tearing at the air over the wounds on her body. She thought it mad before she watched her skin start to knit back together. Bruises disappeared after they ripped at her body and suddenly, she was well. Katherine had never been subjected to such magic.

And throughout it all, she watched Gluttony. He stayed frozen in place, his fingers pressed against his lips as the battle form slowly disappeared from his body. His horns were first. They slipped back into his skull, sliding down until they were little nubs and then nothing at all. His claws went after, sliding back into his hands in much the same way as his horns. Then his bloated body returned to normal, his tail last as it slowly disappeared and suddenly, it was her man seated there against the roots.

Though he wasn't anywhere near as large as he had been, she was still awed by how big he was. He was a massive creature who would stop at nothing to keep her safe and the ease that brought her? Katherine hardly knew how to deal with the feelings that blustered through her.

Finally, the corpse women stepped away from her and stared down. "We cannot heal your injured leg."

"It is an old injury."

"It is one that is filled with more pain than we can take." The woman in front of her, missing half her face, had tangled hair that was so knotted it was hard to tell how long it might be. But it still plastered down beyond her hips, tangling around her breasts and making her appear to have been dipped in a pool of ink. "We would take it, if we could."

"You carry enough pain."

"We do."

Gluttony stood, walking over to her with hesitant steps before he held out his hand for her to take. "We have places to go, pet."

She looked up at him with a new light in her eyes. He was more than just a man who wanted to keep her. Now he was the monster who had killed for her safety. And she knew that should terrify her. She should be afraid of what he had done, and how easily he had torn through her people like their flesh was butter.

But oh, all she saw was a man who was willing to risk everything for her.

She slid her hand into his and allowed him to help her stand. And then he gathered her up in his arms, tugging her against his chest and tunneling his hand into her hair so he could cup the back of her head. He held her. Just held her against his heart as he breathed her in.

"Katherine," he breathed into her hair. "You are well?"

"I am well." Or better than she was before. There would be a time for her to consider the betrayal of her people, but now was not the time.

Like she was in a dream, she followed him through the curtain of weeping willow leaves and out into the place where she had always dreamt of going. The moors put on a show of a lifetime. Thousands of fireflies blinked all around them. The darkness had fallen, but she'd never felt more safe as they hopped from stone to stone, the moss cushioning every step she took as she followed him up a small incline.

There, he released her hand and strode up to the top. She took a few moments to look at him. A dark figure standing in the center of a swamp, blinking lights swirling around him, basking in his magic. The moon silhouetted his tall, muscular form, and his long hair swayed down his back. He was a mythical creature, just like the villagers always warned her about.

The monsters of the swamp would call you deeper, the legends said. They would drag you into the farthest corner and devour you whole.

But oh, she wanted nothing more than for this man to do that.

"Katherine," he said, his voice deep and low. "I almost lost you."

"But you saved me."

"I could have lost you, though. So easily. Your people almost took you from me, and I do not..." He paused, and she watched as his expression shuttered.

No, that's not what she wanted from him right now. How dare he try to hide from her? This was not what she would do. Not in the slightest. He was hers and no one else's, and this just proved it.

She stalked up the hill, determination in every step, even if it made her hip ache yet again. Stopping in front of him, Katherine caught his hand. She pressed it against her heart, so he could feel the heavy thud of the organ caged behind her ribs.

"This beats for you," she said. And it felt like her soul took flight. Finally, she'd said it. She'd let the words free. "I want to be with you for as long as you will have me. You are not just a monster, Gluttony, you are my monster. And I love you."

He stared at her, apparently lost for words, but that only meant she had to keep going.

"I want you," she said, purging all the thoughts that had plagued her for so long. "I want you now and forever. And I think I've always wanted you, from the first day we met. You have consumed me, Gluttony. No one has ever cared about me like you do."

At least, she hoped. He was still standing there like he'd forgotten how to speak. Katherine could only hope she hadn't ruined this for the both of them, but she needed him to know. To understand that she would do anything for him. Everything.

He lunged. Or maybe she moved first. Either way, suddenly their lips were pressed together, and he was kissing her like she was the last woman on earth. He devoured her, tongue lashing at the seam of her lips until she allowed him to deepen the kiss into something so wondrous, so magical, that it made her heart stutter in her chest.

Gluttony glided his hand down her throat, over her collarbone, to cup her breast as he said, "I love you. I have loved you for such a long time, you beautiful creature who walked out of the moors and into my life."

Soon, they were tearing at each other's clothes. She had no idea how he'd gotten her dress down around her hips, but then again, she didn't know when she'd ripped his shirt off either. All she knew was that they were suddenly pressed heart to heart, and her nipples pebbled against his flexing muscles.

Gluttony growled into her mouth, his hand suddenly palming her breast, while the sharp point of a claw stroked over her nipple. "You are so dangerous, pet. One moment I am a man, and the next a ravenous monster."

"Yes," she moaned, tilting her head back so her neck was exposed to him. "That is what I want. My monster."

He groaned and then he was there. His teeth sinking into the side of her neck as he caught her limp body and lowered them to the ground. They curved around each other as he sank onto his knees with her in his lap. He drew deep at her neck and she felt the instant dizziness that she'd come to love.

"So good," he growled against her as his hand tunneled between them.

His claws delicately parted her folds, and she couldn't breathe with the feel of him there, at her neck, everywhere. His teeth in her throat and his finger pressing deep inside her. No claw, she didn't think, but it wouldn't matter.

Katherine ground herself against him, feeling the burning pressure of a second finger as he strummed her clit with his thumb. He played her body like a masterful musician who knew how to only play one instrument.

Her.

"I have wanted this for a lifetime," he said. "Your taste, the sounds of your moans, the whispers of your need ringing in my ears. I have wanted you for a thousand years, Katherine."

She couldn't speak. Shouldn't she say something sexy back? Something that would make her seem more ready for this? More experienced?

But then he twisted his fingers, pressing something deep inside her that made light spark behind her eyes and she squeezed them shut. Her entire body clenched at the movement he made, but it was so perfect she couldn't think at all.

"There it is," he said. "The sound that I so adore."

His deep hum of satisfaction made her quake, and then he did it again. His fingers pressing deep inside as his thumb played with her clit and she couldn't think at all. The coil inside her tightened, near to snapping, and she should be embarrassed by how wet she was so quickly, but she just wanted... needed...

"Beg," he said, his voice right by her ear. "Beg for me."

"Please," she whimpered. "Gluttony, please."

Katherine slammed her hands down on his chest and arched into herself as a blistering orgasm turned her world to white. She had no idea how long it took for her to wind down, but when she did, his fingers were still inside her, slowly moving in and out, scissoring to stretch her.

"Now, I will have you," he said, running his tongue up her neck. "You will taste ever more sweet from the inside out, love. And by the gods and all the seven kingdoms, I will know what it feels like to be inside a goddess."

"Gluttony—"

"Anything, love."

She felt pressure on her spine as he tilted her back. She bowed in his arms, her legs still spread around him, but now her breasts displayed to his mouth like a banquet. Gluttony dragged his teeth down her chest, hard enough to leave welts before he bit into her right breast. Right around her nipple, where his tongue swirled to mix the taste of her tightened bud and her blood.

"I need." She didn't know what she needed, only that she needed him. Inside her. Biting her. Everything she wanted, needed, desired.

"I know," he whispered, dragging his tongue over the bite marks. "I know what you need."

He lifted her effortlessly, and she barely even noticed that he moved her skirts over to one side, pillowing her bad hip as he fumbled with his own pants.

And then he was there. The hard head of him, so hot and velvety it made her choke. Notched against her entrance in a foreign feeling and yet one that was so enticing.

"Look at me."

She did. She looked up at him to see the horns had grown back. Slowly, that long, black tongue slipped out and licked his lips in one wide circle. "I want you," she whispered, her eyes dancing over all these changes and knowing without a doubt it was the truth. "Demon of mine, I want you to devour me whole."

She felt his thighs flex below her and then he was moving. Easing into the wet heat of her. She'd heard it would hurt and maybe it was a little uncomfortable, but she was so desperate for him that it was a pinch she hardly focused on.

Because he was inside her. He stretched her near to bursting, and it felt so amazing that she gasped.

"Pain?" he asked, his teeth bared as he froze.

"No." She clutched his shoulders, her fingers curving into claws that dug into his skin. "More."

Her pussy fluttered around him, gripping and squeezing until he groaned with her. And then he pushed harder, his cock sliding between her folds slowly until their hips met.

Katherine exhaled, feeling her entire body ease around him. The battle had been won, and he had conquered her so thoroughly that she would never look at him the same.

"Yes," he hissed through his fangs. "You are so tight, Kat. So perfect."

"Move," she ordered, because all she could say were single words. Lifting herself was nearly impossible without the use of both hips and she needed friction. She needed him to move for them, and he knew.

His eyes flashed red with approval, and Gluttony palmed both her hips. His abs flexed as he leaned back just slightly, enough to see underneath her skirts where he tunneled into her. And then he lifted her up until she almost couldn't feel him inside her and then dropped her.

The sudden slam made her throw her head back and the sound she made was obscene.

Fireflies burst into movement around them, a whirlwind of sparkling lights that filled her vision.

Another thrust sent her world spinning. His hands were on her, his cock inside her, and she was more than just Katherine. The pressure inside her had eased into pleasure only. But it wasn't enough. Not yet. She wanted more from him because he was her monster, and a monster did not stop until he was finished.

Throwing her arms around his neck, she drew him closer to her neck. Holding the back of his head against her, she whispered, "Please."

His teeth glinted in the light before he sank his teeth into her throat. And yes, this was what she wanted. This. This pain and pleasure mixing together as he started a pace that made every nerve ending in her body flare to life.

He slammed into her harder and harder, growling against her throat like she was being taken by an animal. His horns flashed in the moonlight, his red eyes glowing ever brighter. He was a demon, ruining an innocent on an island in the middle of the moors. His shallow huffs, mixed with grunts of pleasure, filled her senses. She could only think of him and how his broad back felt against her palms as she slid them down, leaving her own marks with her short nails.

"Gods, you feel so good," he groaned against her neck. "You taste so good."

And maybe it was madness. Maybe she had lost all sense, but Katherine leaned down and sank her own teeth into his shoulder.

A rush of blood coated her tongue and suddenly he lost all control. Gluttony plunged into her, in and out, shoving so hard that she felt the twinge of pain in her hip, but she didn't care at all. He could hammer into her for hours and she wouldn't complain.

He pressed his thumb into her clit, a little too firm, a little too hard, but then suddenly she was spinning out of existence. She clenched down on him, her orgasm hitting her so hard that she ground her teeth into his shoulder even harder.

He tossed his head back, and she felt him. She felt the pulse of his cock inside her and the warm rush of his release into her body. He pushed in one more time, a hard thrust that she swore she could feel in the back of her throat.

And then he held her. Shuddering. Hissing out long breaths as he tried to get himself under control, but she didn't want control.

Liquid in his arms, she gathered up the back of his head and drew him down to the unmarked side of her neck. And with a shudder and a twitch of his cock inside her, Gluttony leaned down and feasted.

In his arms, she was both goddess and banquet. Katherine realized the power in that. Because the shuddering demon in her arms was hers and hers alone.

Chapter 38

He hadn't thought...

By the seven kingdoms, Gluttony had thought no one could stand to be in his presence, let alone allow him to touch them like he'd touched her. She held him tightly in her arms, holding him close to her heart as they both spiraled down from the madness that had claimed them.

He hadn't even gotten her dress off, he realized. He should have laid her out on the moss, given her a fantasy night to remember, and made her dream of this evening for years to come.

Instead, he'd knelt on the ground and rutted her like an animal in his lap and she'd... enjoyed it? She'd liked it. He was certain of that. She'd whimpered in his ears with pleasure and he didn't know how to take that.

It was still almost impossible for him to consider that she liked him. That she wanted to spend time with him, and him alone. She'd given him the greatest gift of her body and time, and here he was with his teeth still digging into her neck as her blood sluggishly pooled over his tongue.

Carefully, he eased his fangs out of her neck. At least he could remove those and make her a little more comfortable. With a soft lap of his tongue, he soothed the aching flesh that was bright red after he'd...

Damn it.

He wasn't supposed to do that to her again, not when he'd nearly lost her yet again. He was supposed to be more gentle with her, be the man she needed, not the monster.

And yet, when he leaned away from her to skate his fingers over the wounds, she smiled at him like he'd lit up the sky.

"You are well?" he asked, tugging her dress up from her hips.

"I'm fine," she said with a chuckle. "Better than fine."

His brows must have creased in disbelief because she touched the wrinkles there. He was giving himself away a little too easily for his liking. Or maybe she just read him better than anyone else.

And he would not hide from her anymore. He would not pretend that he was a better man than he was, because he'd proven to her that he wasn't.

Again, he touched his fingers to the wound at her neck, frowning at the twin marks there. "I should not continue to drink from you. It is too dangerous for us to do this."

"I enjoy it."

"I'm telling you, Kat, it's too much of a risk. We need to be more careful with your life."

What would he do without her? Flashes of returning to the

loneliness that had nearly destroyed him made his stomach churn. He refused to go back to that darkness. Back to that life where he had drowned in that sadness. He couldn't. Gluttony already knew what would happen to him if he returned to that life, and it was not a life of happiness like this one. He'd return to the darkness and this time... he might never return.

She held his hand in hers, cupping his fingers and squeezing them. "Listen to me, Gluttony. I enjoy it when you feed from me."

"No one enjoys that."

"I like the pain." She shifted a bit in his lap, clearly uncomfortable admitting such a thing, and just that tiny movement gave him hope. "And I like knowing that you're enjoying yourself to the fullest. I don't want you to hide who you are just because you think I'm uncomfortable with what you need. I'm not."

Something warm bloomed in his chest. Somehow soft and heated at the same time, and it burned him from the inside out. Quietly he asked, "You enjoy it?"

"I do." Katherine smiled at him and his entire soul lit up. Taking flight as he realized that she accepted him. Even as monstrous as he was. "I enjoy it quite a bit, actually. I thought that was rather obvious."

But then she winced as she shifted, and reality came slamming back into his mind. He was still kneeling on the ground, half hard inside her, and her hips were stretched so wide over his that he was certain she was in pain. Again. Because of him.

"Shit," he muttered, drawing her dress all the way up and covering the mounds of tantalizing flesh that now wore the marks of his teeth. "You must be sore. I'm sorry, love. Let's get you up."

It was one of the worst sensations to withdraw from her comforting heat, but he did. He tucked himself haphazardly back into his pants as he stood with her in his arms, making sure that she could stand on her own two feet before he yanked his shirt back over his head.

He needed to get her back to the castle and into a warm bath. Somewhere comfortable. What had that book said about people who had these kinds of injuries? Heat was better for old wounds, ones that won't get fixed easily. And then he was supposed to add something to her food that would help with inflammation, of which he must have just given her plenty.

Her tiny hand pressed against his chest, still bearing the marks of her ordeal. Apparently, the rusalki hadn't healed every part of her body.

He followed the long, delicate line of her wrist all the way up to her face. She was still smiling. Even though he was panicking, she was a steady rock of patience.

"Gluttony," she said. "Come here."

"I'm—" He flapped his arms up and down. "I can't get any closer, Kat."

"Yes, you can." She stepped into him and wrapped an arm around the back of his neck, drawing him closer down to her. "Kiss me, you stubborn man. I can see you turning back into that sad boy, and before that happens, I'd like to taste you one last time."

He melted.

Gluttony swept her up into his arms with a groan before devouring her lips. He nipped and bit, kissing her like she was the last person in the world, and he was desperate for her touch. Because to him, she was. And he was. He wanted her more than anything in this world and to know that she was his? It gathered up every shattered shard of his soul and patched them back together.

All the anxiety and panic filtered out of his mind the moment their lips met. And the ease that she brought him, the relaxation that pushed away all that fear, it stayed with him even as she drew back to breathe.

"Wow," she whispered, before giggling again. "Look at that."

"Look at what?"

"You've got will-o'-the-wisps all through your hair." Katherine reached up and plucked one out of the long, tangled strands. And he watched the tiny creature struggle in her grip before she released it to float back through the air like a firefly.

He had never loved her more. Standing in the moors with his arms wrapped around her, watching her eyes as she followed a wisp through the air. She was so stunning. All that tangled red hair floating around her head like a cloud. Every freckle on her cheeks that he wanted to count a thousand times over, just to make sure he knew exactly how many she had. Without a doubt, he'd never adored a creature more than her.

Gently, he pressed their foreheads together and breathed her in. "Where did you come from? What goddess put you on this earth to teach me how to love?"

"I would like to think it was meant as a punishment," she teased. "Perhaps with a realization that you'd been wallowing for too long."

He growled a little, mockingly yanking her hips tighter to his. "Indeed. It was a punishment, certainly, because I have thought of nothing other than you for far too long."

"Soon there will be more to think about, I'm certain." Katherine cupped his jaw, holding him a little closer as her eyes fluttered closed. "But for now, I'm rather enjoying pretending it's just you and me. That there is no one else in this world but the two of us."

And, oh, if that didn't squeeze his heart and make his world spin out of orbit.

"Come," he breathed, lifting her into his arms as he strode into the bog. "I think it's time for us to return home."

Katherine tilted her head back, dangling in his arms like she had no question that he would carry her safely. "Home. I like the sound of that."

So did he. But only when she said it.

They talked about nothing and everything as they meandered back to his castle. He took the long way to show her all the secret hiding places of the dangerous creatures of his kingdom. She even got to see a baby kelpie. The little calf snorted at them and then tripped on a thick patch of moss. The sound of her joyous laughter made even those beasts pause.

He showed her the kingdom that she'd never seen before. The kingdom that was filled with so much dangerous beauty, just like her. And though Katherine would likely never see herself in the same light, he knew just how dangerous she could be.

She held the reins to the most dangerous creature in this kingdom, after all.

Him.

Once they got back to his castle, he made quick work of bringing her to her room. He set her down on her feet only once they'd crossed the threshold, and even then he was loath to no longer have her in his arms.

She giggled at him, then pretended to get angry. "What, you're making me stay in my own room still? After everything we've done?"

He backed her into the bathroom, forcing her to move or be trampled by the wall of his massive chest. "Pet, I moved all the most comfortable furniture into this room for you. Unless you want to go back to sleeping on straw, we're staying in this room. Together."

"You've been sleeping on a straw bed?"

"I would sleep on a dirt covered floor if that would ensure you more comfort." He held onto her wrist so she wouldn't trip and then turned on the faucet to fill the tub with steaming hot water. "Besides, this room has the best view."

And then he was given another one of her soft looks. The one where he knew she was thinking how much she loved him, and now that he had a name for it, it made everything so much better.

Tucking his finger underneath her chin, he tilted her face up to look at him. "Now you're going to spend a good long while in this bath. Do you understand? Soak those muscles that I overused."

"Or what?"

Baring his teeth in a snarl, he made sure she stared at his fangs before answering, "Do I need to remind you that I have use for a body that is healed and comfortable, but less use for a body that is hurting? I will make you stay in that bed until you heal yourself, pet."

"Are you threatening to withhold sex from me if I don't get in that tub?" Katherine crossed her arms over her chest, eyeing him up and down before snorting. "I'm willing to accept that challenge."

Bracing his arm on the wall behind her head, he caged her in between the tile and his body. He gave her another growl that he hoped was intimidating, but thought it was a little more suggestive than he had planned. "I have waited a thousand years for you, Katherine. A thousand years. And I won't claim that I didn't touch anyone else during that time. I won't even suggest that I didn't enjoy myself before you. But now that I have you, there is no one else. There will never be anyone else. So if I have to dunk you into that water and hold you underneath it so that you are well, I will do so. You are mine, pet, and I will keep you happy and healthy. There is no other way."

Her mouth fell open at his words before she licked her lips and nodded. Eyes darting to his mouth and then back up, he already knew what she was thinking before she even said it. "And if I wish for you to join me?"

Gluttony coiled one of her curls around his finger and gave her hair a little tug. "As tempting as that is, I do not know how to behave myself around you. This is about healing. Your body needs rest, Kat, and your mind likely needs time to process what happened. I'm not giving you an excuse to hide."

At that, she seemed to wilt in front of his eyes. All the memories came rushing back, and he knew it had to be a lot to think about.

Excluding what they had done, her people had betrayed her in a fashion that would be difficult to forget. She was, without a doubt, needing time to think about this. Time to herself.

And he... Well, he didn't want to leave. He didn't want to take any more time away from her because he wanted her. In any way he could get. He wanted to bask in her presence, even if it became more of a torment.

Gluttony had to stand back and keep his hands by his sides as she stripped. He'd seen her like this before, of course. Bare to his hungry eyes was how he preferred her. But this time, he had no intention to touch.

Although he held out his hand to help her into the bath. She was strong and capable, but he knew the slippery surface of the tub was dangerous for her hip. Especially when he noticed the strange hitch in her step that wasn't normal. Even for her.

Usually, she would cast aside his help and give him a glare for even offering. But right now, in this soft bubble they had created, she allowed him to help. She sank underneath the water, a quiet sigh on her lips, and he watched the blush rise up from her chest and burn into her cheeks.

He crouched on the other side of the tub, one of his arms braced on the side and his fingers toying with the steam. "Comfortable?"

"Yes." She rolled her head to the side to look at him, a soft smile on her lips. "Why are you doing all this for me?"

"Taking care of you?"

She shrugged, but he knew that was her real question. What kind of a life must she have lived before him that she couldn't understand why he'd want to do this?

Gluttony swirled his fingers in the water, waiting for her response. But she didn't give him one. Instead, she just watched his movements with a faint hint of amusement in her gaze.

Finally, he relented. "You have been so kind to me, Katherine. More so than anyone else in my life. You have a heart of gold, even for people who wish nothing more than to harm you. You've met my brothers with bravery and a thoughtful nature that made my heart beat in my chest. And you have returned to me. Every time you left. Every dark secret I've told you hasn't scared you away, and I must be honest, that still startles me. You should run."

"And yet, I have no plan to." Her hand lifted out of the water, wet and glistening as she traced her finger over his lips. "I would miss you if I was gone."

Oh, she had no idea how much he would miss her.

Gluttony pillowed his head on his forearm and spent the next hour with her. Not inside the tub, just listening to her tell stories. Watching the expression on her face as she grew more animated and splashed water on the wall with each of her movements.

He'd never been more in love. Not once.

Chapter 39

She'd never been so in love with anyone in her life. Katherine practically floated through the next few days. They rarely were without each other, and if they were with each other, then they couldn't keep their hands from wandering.

Her hip hurt worse than it ever had before, and she couldn't care less. Envy's potions were helping, as well. She needed to ask Gluttony to send a message to his brother and let him know that they worked. Even though Gluttony rarely feasted from her in a way that she wanted, he was still biting her. The tiny pinpricks covered her body, and she loved to see them in the mirror.

Even now, wringing out her hair from yet another bath, she could see the faintest hint of them. The newest ones were more red than the others. Touching her fingers to the one just underneath her jaw, she grinned.

Her reflection looked like a different woman. A woman with a bigger heart and a delighted soul. Every inch of her was well pleasured and happy.

Blowing a kiss to that smiling woman in the mirror, she wrapped her towel a little tighter and made her way into the bedroom.

At this point, she just slept naked. Gluttony came into her room at all times of the night. He was busy doing something, though she had no idea what. He claimed it had something to do with his brothers, so she could only assume it was more alchemical solutions to whatever weapon had been created to attack the demons.

And yet, all of that felt so far away. She didn't even think about the attacks on his brothers or the strangers in her town. They were in their own little safe bubble in this castle. So far away from reality that it was hard to think of anything else at all.

She was safe here. He was safe too, and together they would keep each other alive.

Sighing, she coiled the long mass of her hair on one side of her shoulder and eyed all the blankets. They were still tangled from their escapades this morning. A blush burned her cheeks as she thought about that entertainment.

Of all the men she could have picked, she'd had to go and get herself a demon. Both in and out of bed.

Pressing her hands to her lips, she tried to contain her mirth, but she just couldn't. All that happiness bubbled out of her into laughter that filled the room. And she didn't care who heard her. If Gluttony wandered past, maybe he would think she was mad, but did it really matter?

He made her so happy she couldn't contain it.

The shadows to her right shifted, where he used to stand while she was asleep. The curtains moved as well, letting the thin light of the moon play across the features of a man who had been waiting for her to notice him.

"You shouldn't do that, you know. You might scare someone." Katherine mockingly placed her hand on her chest, but he would know he hadn't startled her. She'd long ago started searching for him in the shadows. Even when she didn't notice him at first, she always could feel when it was him.

Gluttony stepped out of the darkness near the curtains, his eyes already gleaming red. "But not you."

"Rarely me."

Katherine let out a little squeal of delight as he lunged for her. Though she pretended to run, she didn't get very far before his arms slid around her waist and his face tunneled against her neck. His warm breath played across her throat, and he inhaled her deeply.

"I need you again," he grumbled against her skin. "Damnable woman, you've tunneled your way into my very being. Just a few hours without you and I'm useless."

"Useless?" She rocked against him, pressing her behind to the hard cock that pushed back against her. "I could find some use for you, if you need one."

"Don't tempt me."

"And why shouldn't I?" Katherine turned in his arms to pin him with a stare. "It's just you and I here in this castle, and I desire you more than anything else in the world. You are mine, Gluttony, and I will not deprive myself of you."

He groaned, and she watched his throat work before he gathered her a little closer. Grinding himself into her core, he muttered, "I thought I was the monster, and yet here I have created one."

"You sure do complain a lot for a man who is now, finally, well satisfied in all aspects of his life." Roping her arms around his neck, she tugged him down for a firm kiss. "Now, are you going to do something about this burning need or do I have to take care of it myself?"

He nipped at her lips, sharp fangs drawing the faintest pinpricks of blood. "Hush, woman. I'm trying to be understanding of your injuries. You've only just begun this adventure, and already I've abused your poor womanhood more than I should have."

She made a face. "Womanhood?"

"What would you prefer I call it? Sheath? Hidden wonders?" He grinned.

Katherine made a different face of disgust. "None of that."

"Then what would you suggest?"

She backed him toward the bed, fully aware that he was allowing her to move him around to where she wanted him. But it still gave her a sense of control. Of power.

So when his knees hit the bed, she pressed her hand to the center of his chest and pushed. "You may call it my pussy."

"Sounds rather cat-like." Obediently, he fell onto his back, bouncing until she crawled on top of him. "I have better words."

"Do you now?"

He caught the back of her neck and jerked her down on top of him. With a nip at her ear, he murmured, "Warm. Wet." Another nip that sent a trail of gooseflesh down her spine. "Mine."

"These are good words." Goodness, was she already breathless? He did things that startled her every time they were together. Even now, with his cock pressed against her belly and all those hard slabs of muscle at her disposal, she wasn't quite certain what to do.

She wanted all of it. All of him. Every inch of his body against hers and she didn't know what to ask for.

But her man certainly did. He knew what he wanted from her, how he wanted it, and how he was going to take it. Gluttony curved around her, dragging them until they were both lying on their sides, her back to his front. Her bad leg beneath her, she had a lot more mobility this way. And he proved just how much mobility she had.

Leaning over her, he breathed into her ear, "I have words for you to say as well, Katherine."

"Oh?" She had a hard time focusing when his hand opened the front of her towel. Icy air played over her chest, tightening her nipples to painful points long before he closed his fingers over them.

"I want you to tell me exactly how you feel." His deep voice made her body react in ways she'd hadn't expected. Just the sensation of him wrapped around her, with only his fingers playing at the tips of her breasts. It was... enthralling. "I want to hear you describe what you want me to do, and how you want me to do it."

She whimpered. "I don't know if I can do that."

"You can."

"But I'm—" What if she was terrible at it? What if she voiced it in a way that made him feel like she was too inexperienced or that she wasn't... good enough?

"Stop thinking so much, love." His fingers twisted and that blissful bloom of pain was everything she needed to focus on him and him alone. "Or perhaps you would like me to tell you what I want to hear? Just this first time. We'll do it together."

Frantically, she nodded, needing him to tell her what she could do to make this better for him. Anything, she would do anything.

His hand slid from her breast down to her stomach, and the smooth glide made every muscle in her body clench as she waited to see what he would do. Knowing that it would feel good but also anticipating what would come.

Gluttony touched her so lightly between her legs that she almost didn't feel him. Just the faintest, feather light touch. "Your pussy," he said, amusement tinging his words a little lighter. "I want you to tell me how badly you need me to touch you here. How wet you are at just the thought. Are you wet for me, love?"

She frantically nodded because she could already feel the slickness.

He hummed low, and the sound made all the hairs on her arms stand up straight. "Let's see, shall we?"

Gluttony cupped her thigh and stretched her leg up, exposing her to the cold air even as he draped her leg over his hip. It left her open, slightly tilted into him as his hand moved back to play with her. "Ah, yes, pet, you are so wet for me."

He toyed with her clit, those light, feathering touches driving her insane. She wanted more from him. Needed more. And even as she tried to rock against his hand, she knew he already had her trapped. He was in control, no matter how much she wriggled against him.

"What do you want?" he asked. "Or do you want me to tell you what you want?"

He didn't know what she wanted. Or maybe he did. But if he did, then why wasn't he doing it?

Katherine made a sound like his growls. "I know what I want, Gluttony."

"Then tell me."

Damn it, the words stuck like they always did. But this time she would not be bested by her body freezing. Grinding her teeth, she bit out, "I want your fingers inside me."

"Good girl," he praised, his lips ghosting over her temple right before he sank two thick fingers deep inside her.

And oh.

Oh.

She was so full, pulsing around him with hot, hungry squeezes echoing through her entire body. He moved his hand in and out, the slow glide of his movements so delicious and not nearly enough. He licked her ear, that long black tongue snaking down to coil around her neck. And she knew he was changing into his battle form. That demonic presence had always made her feel so hot and ready for him.

"What else do you want from me?" He loomed over her suddenly, his presence so much that it blotted out even the shadows behind him.

He was her personal darkness. Her nightmare that was hers to command if she so wished.

And she wished.

Like he'd unlocked some key inside her, she gripped his hand and squeezed his wrist. "Harder."

He bared his fangs, the thin moonlight glinting off their tips. "And?"

"Bite me."

"And?"

She let out a little frustrated mewl, arching into his touch. "I want to feel your hard cock inside me."

"Oh," he murmured, and she felt him moving behind her back as he drew her towel up over her hips.

When had he gotten his pants off? Because suddenly she felt him. Notched at her entrance and so hot he was almost boiling. The hard head of him nudged at her, pressing but never actually sliding deep inside her.

She pushed back against him, but he'd already locked her in place.

With her leg stretched over his hip like that, she couldn't move unless he let her. Unless she begged him to move and she was so close to doing that.

But then he pressed his finger down on her clit, gently massaging the small bud that ached so much for him. Her eyes rolled back in her head and she turned into a heaving puddle of woman in his arms until he finally, finally, whispered in her ear, "I want you so much it feels like dying."

"Then fuck me, demon."

"I intend to do just that. But first, I want to make you scream."

With a swift, sudden movement, his finger circled her clit with the perfect pressure. The perfect tension. She was coiling, spiraling, spinning out of existence and came so hard that every muscle in her body clenched. At the same time, he pushed inside her with a hiss at the tension and oh.

Oh, she'd definitely never felt like this before.

The sudden fullness in her body at the same time as her orgasm made her come harder and longer than she had yet. Every fiber of her being unraveled as she came, and came, and came. She might have begged for mercy through some of it, as he shoved harder and deeper into her with every thrust.

His grunts echoed in her ears and when she came back to herself, he was pounding into her. Thunderous in his movements and growling in her ear before he sank his teeth into her neck.

She'd only had a few seconds of rest. Only a few seconds of being a real person again before she splintered into another blistering orgasm that was somehow even stronger than the first.

"Need you so much," he snarled against her throat, gulping down mouthfuls of blood between the words. "Too quick. So sorry. Going to—"

The deep, guttural groan that followed those words lit up her entire world. She loved it when he lost control. She loved the long nights where he pet and stroked her body until she couldn't formulate a single word, and she equally loved these quick sessions where both of them lost all sense until they unraveled in each other's arms.

And as she caught her breath, certain she had died for a few minutes there, she listened to the soft sounds of his swallows until he yanked himself away from her neck.

Gluttony let her leg drop down, his hand smoothing over her hip as he made no attempt to withdraw from her. Long claws danced down her arms, and goosebumps rose at every one of his touches. She knew he loved to watch those appear.

"So responsive," he murmured as he leaned up on his arm, staring down at her with a soft smile on his face. "You are lovely, pet. More than I ever dreamt of."

"You are too kind, Gluttony." She stroked her hands down his face, watching as his eyes rolled back in his head and for once, she couldn't stop herself from asking, "When was the last time someone touched you with kindness?"

He turned his head into her palm and kissed the center. "Only you, sweet. Only you."

And though it made her heart squeeze, it also made her feel a little special. He was her first, after all.

In a way, so was she for him.

Chapter 40

Gluttony worked to get his home in a better state for her. Katherine deserved the best. She should have a castle full of silks and beautiful stained glass, not the haunted house he lived in.

But that took a lot of time and effort. There were few people who were willing to come work for him, less and less as the time went on. So Gluttony found himself doing a majority of the work. Which, surprisingly, he didn't mind.

The new blisters on his hands were as expected, he supposed, and he was quite pleased that his body could still work so hard. After all, he had spent a thousand years not doing... anything at all.

Or perhaps it was just his natural desire to be a glutton for punishment. He did very much enjoy the aches and pains that came with fixing his home.

It also gave him an option to leave the castle more as he traveled farther and farther from it. Not so far that he couldn't return if he needed to, he was very aware that there were people looking at attacking his castle at any point. But so far, they were allowed to remain in peace while they remained far away from anyone else.

He knew this was a gift, and a rarity that would likely be broken soon enough. And in the meantime, before they were attacked, he wanted to make sure that Katherine was as comfortable as possible.

Today, he was returning with an armful of silken sheets. They had destroyed theirs. The memory made his head spin, and it was far pastime that he gave her sheets better than ancient homespuns.

Whistling as he entered the castle, he started toward their bedroom to surprise her. She'd be so happy with the color, as well. His Katherine preferred brighter colors, he'd found out. She enjoyed light splashes of yellow and rose, bright patterns and vivid hues that whirled through the mind's eye as she walked by them.

The sheets he'd found were a bright shade of green, the same color as her eyes. The merchant hadn't been all that interested in selling them to a demon, so Gluttony had taken matters into his own hands.

The moment the man turned around, he stole the sheets and ran.

As a true royal did.

But he only made it halfway to their room before he heard a horrible sound. The wrenching sob broke his heart. He'd never heard her cry like that.

Gluttony couldn't remember if he'd ever seen her cry at all. Katherine was stronger than most, and she took what life gave her without an ounce of complaint. Even after all she'd endured, she still found ways to smile.

Sheets forgotten, he dropped them onto the floor as he charged through the hall, seeking out the sound in every room that he came across.

"Katherine!" he called out, nearly frantic now to find her. "Katherine, where are you?"

Why wasn't she responding?

His thoughts spun out of control. What if the people from the village had come while he was gone? What if they had attacked her instead of him, as they had the last time? He might find her curled up in a ball on the floor somewhere, incapable of being fixed because he was the fool who thought she needed better sheets.

But then he heard it. The soft shuffle of movement from a room just beyond and he burst into it so quickly that the door slammed against the wall. Dust rained down on their heads, falling like snow on top of his hair and down around his shoulders.

He was frozen in place by the sight in front of him. His heart stopped in his chest and every muscle in his body locked.

Katherine sat on the floor, her crimson skirts pooled around her like blood. Her hair fell in a waterfall down one side of her shoulder, shielding the little soul she held in her arms. Tear tracks had left red marks down her lovely cheeks, and those pretty green eyes had turned to chips of glimmering emerald as she cried. She didn't even look up at him. Not once. Instead, all her attention was on the soul that leaked down to her lap until she gathered it up again.

"Oh no," he muttered, before walking into the room.

Spite. The poor little spirit should never have stayed here. It should have gone back to the town where there were plenty of emotions for it to feed on. And in truth, he'd thought it had returned to that darkened village.

He hadn't seen it in such a long time, and he'd been the fool who assumed it was fine. That it had gone back to the feeding grounds that were so close.

He'd never thought it would come to this.

Crouching beside Katherine, he placed his hand on her shoulder and gently squeezed. "When did you find it?"

"It was just lying there in the corridor." She sounded more than upset. Hysteric, perhaps. Her words were a little too loud and too frantic. "I thought maybe it was just resting, because Spite hasn't been itself for a very long time, you know? I thought maybe it was just pausing for a little rest and then when I leaned down to touch it, it just..." she hiccuped. "It didn't move, Gluttony. Not even a little. It didn't even flinch when I picked it up and you know how little it likes to be held."

Again, he squeezed her shoulder. Taking a deep breath, he readied himself to tell her about the end of spirit's lives. "There was nothing here for it to feed on. I wondered why Spite had remained when it knew how easily it could get food in the town. There is so little of its emotion to find in this castle."

She sniffed. "Was it too weak? Is this our fault?"

She looked up at him with those big, water filled eyes and he felt his own soul fracture. "No, sweet." Gluttony smoothed a tear off her cheek, chasing the droplet with his thumb. "No. We could have brought it back to the town, perhaps. And maybe it was too weak to return to its usual hunting grounds. But Spite chose to be here with us."

"I don't know why." Katherine sniffled again, looking down at the little creature. "It should have gone home. It could have left at any point."

He couldn't understand it either. But he'd seen the life wasting away from Spite. The dark cloud of a creature had slowly turned into something pale and lifeless. A fraction of what it had once been. Even its ability to speak had left.

He reached out with his hand and gently pressed his fingers into the white mist. Perhaps, if he was lucky, he could usher its death along. Gluttony had consumed spirits before, and though that wasn't part of his life anymore, he could do so again if the creature wished. It was a fitting end to a creature who had fed off of others. To be eaten wasn't a dishonor amongst their kind.

But when he touched Spite, there was still the faintest thrum of magic. A power that wasn't like the creature he had touched so many times before.

A surprise.

Eyebrows raising, he stared down at the little spirit and muttered, "It cannot be."

"What?" Katherine asked. "What cannot be?"

He reached for the spirit, letting the liquidy mist pool through his hands as he scooped up the spirit into his grip. He was less gentle than Katherine, so it didn't slide away onto the floor. Instead, he made sure that it was carefully cupped, but firmly trapped.

Lifting the spirit to his eyes, he peered into the mist and said, "It shouldn't be possible."

"What shouldn't be possible?" Katherine snapped. "You're acting like you've found some wonder of the world."

"Because I might have." Slowly, he stood and started out of the room.

"Where are you going?"

"To the lab." Because he wasn't actually seeing what he was seeing. It should be impossible. Spirits were spirits, that's all they were. Only he and his brothers had changed, and that was unusual in its own right.

Although Greed would disagree. Considering he had given two spirits physical forms, and that alone was supposed to be impossible. So there were deviations to the rules, but this rule was one that wasn't supposed to be possible at all.

Katherine trailed along behind him, wringing her hands every time he looked at her before finally breaking through her silence the moment he deposited the spirit onto his table.

"What is going on?" she asked, rounding the table so she was right in front of him. "Are you going to answer me or not?"

"Not," he muttered, grabbing his glasses and sliding them onto his nose.

Apparently, that was the wrong question. Katherine snatched his glasses off and dangled them out of his reach. "Explain, demon."

He sighed, pinching his nose before resolving himself to answering questions while he did his investigative work. "Spirits are born a certain way. We are spirits of an emotion, this much you know. But it has been rumored that a spirit subjected to a certain amount of emotion can turn into another."

Her brows swept together in a frown. "Explain better."

"That's what I'm trying to do," he grumbled before grabbing his glasses back from her. "A spirit of justice who loses a war repeatedly will eventually become a spirit of vengeance. A spirit of hope who only sees death and dying will eventually become a spirit of despair. It is a very rare phenomenon to happen, and usually only happens to spirits like myself and my brothers. Stronger spirits who have been around for a very long time. Spite is a very young spirit."

He glanced down, frowning at the creature, who was now nearly as white as snow. He had to admit, this was the most likely circumstance.

440

This little spirit had done a lot of work here. It had tried very hard to break both of them with its spiteful words and had managed with Gluttony many times over. But it had never broken Katherine. And it had spent a lot of time with his lovely human.

"Or at least, I thought it was a younger spirit," he muttered. Peering down at the mist, now actually able to see better with his glasses, he searched for the little specks of darkness that should be in the mist.

"What are you doing now?" Katherine asked, her hands coming into view to help hold the spirit, even though it wasn't moving.

"I'm looking to see if there's any remaining part of its original essence," he muttered, prodding the white mist with one of his metal rods. "If it isn't changing, and it's dying instead, there should still be specks of darkness. Shadows of its former self. We could save it, perhaps, if we gave it enough food. There isn't enough here. Don't get that into your head, Katherine. Neither of us are capable of enough spite to feed this spirit."

He felt more than saw her pout. She would do anything to save it, he knew, but that didn't change their situation. Even if they ran to the town and set it loose, Spite would likely die. There just wasn't enough food.

However... "Do you see any darkened spots?" he asked. "I want to be certain that what I'm seeing is what is actually happening."

"I only see a white mist," she said, meeting his gaze over the weakened spirit. "So, what does that mean?"

Pulling off his glasses, he set them on the table and leaned back in shock. "Then it's changed."

"Into what?"

He almost shrugged and said he didn't know, but... he did. And he knew exactly why it had changed. "Spite spent a lot of time with you, didn't it?"

"No more than it did with you." Katherine frowned. "Maybe a little more time. It was always popping up when I didn't think it was around. Why? Is that important?"

Very, actually. He leaned forward and huffed out a breath. "You devious little monster. It knew that being around you more and more would likely force it to change. That's why it was always lurking around you, and I bet it was around you more than you were aware of. It was soaking in your emotions, your essence, trying to force itself to change."

"Why?" Katherine shook her head, as though dislodging those thoughts. "And what did it change into?"

"Compassion," he replied with a quiet laugh. "It changed into a spirit of compassion and I think that is entirely because of you. Because it knew you had so much of the emotion that you could live with it. Be its host. It would experience life in an entirely new way if it possessed you, and it knew that I wouldn't say no if it wanted that."

Of course, this was the spirit's plan the entire time. A spirit's life was infinite as long as there was a source of its emotion to feed off of. But they were still spirits. Unable to experience life like the humans, nor were they able to truly enjoy living.

They only got a taste of it. Every now and then, the emotion would change to a slightly different flavor, but they weren't actually living. Spirits were on the outskirts of both life and death. Living in an in-between that was both unique and exhausting.

Spite had wanted to live. Perhaps it had been this emotion for a very long time and now it realized just how imperative it was to experience life. And now, as weak as it was from changing, there was only one other option to save its life.

"It wants me to be its... host?" she asked. "That can't be right,

Gluttony. Spite never mentioned possession or anything along those lines. It cannot want to live inside me."

"It does," he murmured, nudging the little spirit until it rolled closer to her. "Otherwise it will die. If you don't allow it to live inside you, with you, experience living through your eyes, then it will die here and now. It didn't want to ask because it didn't think we would agree to it."

"Well, I don't even know what it would do to me!"

He hated this part. But now he knew how his brothers had felt. "It will make you immortal," he replied, meeting her gaze. "No wound will remain. No sickness will take you. Life will be forever, with you at my side, frozen in the same state you are in right now."

And for a time, they stared at each other. Katherine's thoughts played across her features, like he was reading the pages of a familiar story. Disgust, fear, denial, and then finally acceptance as her gaze flicked down to the tiny spirit. "And doing so will save it?"

"It will." He reached across the table to cover her hand with his. "Immortality is no easy choice, Katherine. Don't rush this."

She straightened her shoulders. "Choosing to save a life is the easiest choice to make, Gluttony. No matter the cause or what might happen, I would do anything for those I love. So what do I do next?"

And who was he to deny her? He got to keep her forever and she... well, she would find out what it truly meant to be a god.

Chapter 41

Katherine took the weak spirit in her hands and stared at what used to be Spite. There was only the faintest grey mist between her fingers. The color was so light she almost couldn't see it at all.

"Compassion?" she asked quietly, her voice filtering through the mist like a breeze. "I need to know that you actually want to do this. I don't want to hurt you anymore than you already have been hurt."

And with one giant move of energy, the mist rippled in her hands. It was trying. So hard. It wanted to tell her that this was all it wanted, because apparently Gluttony was right.

Spite had fought its entire life. Fought for food, for attention, to turn people's will toward something dark and angry. It had done all it could to feed and affect her village. But in the end, it was still just an emotion. A spirit of something ephemeral that lived between the living and the dead.

It wasn't a life she would choose to give to anyone. And this would be the ultimate act of compassion in giving this tiny spirit a way to live on. A way to experience life through the eyes of a human, which it had been watching for likely centuries.

Meeting Gluttony's eyes one last time before everything changed, she smiled. "Will this hurt either of us?"

"It might hurt you." He looked troubled, his brows drawing down in fear. "When Greed's wife did this with a spirit not so weak as this one, she was ill for a week. He waited on her hand and foot because he knew how dangerous it was. She made it, though."

And so would she. Katherine had no fear if Gluttony was the one taking care of her.

"All right, then." She held the spirit a little closer to her face. "How do I do it?"

"Breathe it in," he answered. "Varya consumed her spirit, swallowed it whole because Greed hadn't done this in a very long time. He forgot what we did when we possessed bodies. And we did, when we were the same age as these spirits. Trying out a real form before we decided to create our own."

Breathe it in. Like smoke.

A memory filtered through her mind. Before her mother had disappeared, Katherine could remember falling very ill. She'd been so congested that it made it difficult to breathe. So her mother had brought out a bowl of steaming water and draped a towel over Katherine's head. Breathing in the steam had been uncomfortable, but it definitely helped the congestion. And throughout all of it, her mother had rubbed her back.

The memory of that calloused hand rubbing against her shoulder blades and reminding her that she wasn't alone calmed her. Even at her weakest. Even when she wanted to lie down and just let the sickness take her, her mother had been there. Kind and quiet, a strong presence who reminded Katherine that she was loved and taken care of.

With that in her mind, she leaned a little closer to the mist of the spirit and inhaled. She breathed it in deep, feeling the coiling zap of its magic stretching through her entire body. It spread like roots of a tree, digging into her lungs and into her very being.

For a moment, it hurt. She stiffened, her face twisting with a wince that made Gluttony lunge forward.

But it wasn't terrible. It wasn't awful. It just was what it was. Pain was no stranger to a woman who lived in it for years now, though her hip was nothing compared to this pain. But she endured. She would survive it, if only so she knew that the spirit could live through her.

If anything was worth suffering for, it was for compassion.

And the moment she thought that, the pain eased. Gluttony held onto her shoulders a little too tightly, his grip so strong she had to blink and look up at him in surprise.

"You are well?" he asked, searching her gaze for the truth as though he thought she might lie to him. "What hurts?"

"My lungs," she wheezed, tapping a finger to her rib cage before taking a slow, deep breath. "I think I'm all right, though."

"It might take a few moments to start hurting."

"It won't." She didn't think, at least.

Katherine watched how worried he was and she reached up to trace a finger over the furrows between his brows. She didn't want him to worry.

The thought was soon whisked away from her, the feeling pouring into the strange spirit that lived inside her. And strangely, it didn't feel bad. It only made her smile and that compassion inside her bloom again, whisking to the spirit and feeding it.

"I think it just needs to feed," she said.

"How is it doing that?"

"Every time I feel compassion, it seems to soak up that feeling."

Gluttony shook his head, almost in disbelief. "Well. That's something I wasn't expecting you to say. What an experiment. I'll have to share this with my brothers, you know. Just in case any of them find their..."

He stammered over what to call her, and Katherine realized they hadn't had this conversation yet. The poor man was probably wondering what they were. Partner, wife, beloved? So many words for the same thing.

"We are what we are," she said softly, tucking herself against his collarbone where she was most comfortable. Pressing her cheek to his shoulder, she breathed him in with a chuckle. "I don't care what you call me, Gluttony, as long as I am the only person in your life."

"I would never dare to even look at another." His arms came around her tightly. "You are the moon in my sky and the stars on the horizon. One look at you and I forget that I'm a monster, Kat. One look at you, and I remember why life is so worth living."

And oh, that made her heart bloom. She could feel the spirit lighting up inside her as well. This was what it had wanted to experience. To experience the feeling of love, true love, was so hard without a physical body.

Gluttony held her for a few moments, his nose pressed into her hair as he rocked them back and forth. Katherine soaked up every ounce of his attention as though she would never get it again.

"Do you want to spend a quiet day together?" he asked, his voice a low murmur. "I think, after all that, it would be rather nice to have a few moments with nothing but each other."

"Isn't that what we do every day?" she replied with a laugh.

"Perhaps. But that doesn't mean I want it to change."

He drew her from the laboratory with careful hands and a quiet countenance that made her wonder if he was watching her avidly to make sure she wasn't about to fall apart at the seams.

She didn't feel like herself. Katherine wouldn't lie and say that everything was fine. There was another presence in her body, and though she didn't think she would ever be able to converse with it, she was very aware that it was inside her.

Compassion wanted to experience life, but in a very quiet way. This was a tired spirit who had been used and abused and the mere idea of being Compassion terrified it. So many people could use compassion in the wrong way and that was so scary that it made the poor thing tremble in her chest.

She could literally feel it when she touched a hand to her ribs. The faintest vibration from the spirit inside her that shook her ribs. How strange it was to know that there was something living inside herself.

Not a child. Not a life that she would ever bring out into the world again. It was a spirit who now shared her body.

That was something she'd have to think about for a while yet, she had a feeling. How did one settle into realizing that there was... well. So much different. So much that she was now going to have to think through and realize that her life had changed yet again.

Gluttony twined their hands together and squeezed her fingers before drawing her into a room she'd not been in before. "Come on, pet. Let's get your mind off of it."

That would be lovely. She needed to stop thinking, perhaps. And this room was a perfect way to do it.

Katherine had never been in here before, but it was a rather cozy and small library. The walls were ringed with shelves that were filled to the brim with books and cozy loveseats that had cushions clearly worn by many people throughout the years. There was the perfect leather seat waiting for them by the window, and it was the largest one she'd seen still intact in this castle.

The metal lines that crossed across the glass did nothing to stop her from seeing the family of kelpies outside the window. A mother and three foals, an impossible feat considering kelpies usually only had one child. The sight drew her to the window as though she were under a spell, pressing her hand to the glass and watching the happy family kick their heels in the sky and canter about.

They were so precious, even with their sharp fangs glinting in the dim light of the day.

Her heart squeezed in her chest and she remembered that this was why she'd given up her life. This was why she was willing to take any risk for this kingdom. Because she loved it so much. Even the dangerous monsters who lived in the shadows. She could still see the beauty in their kelp covered hair and ignore the blood that coated their hooves. She didn't care what they ate or hunted. She only cared that they existed.

And that was why she'd come to this castle in the first place and put herself in danger with a man she had been so certain was a demon.

Now, here she was, standing in front of a window watching the beasts of the swamp when she should be screaming at them to leave and then rushing to the town to tell people to run. And she wasn't flinching at all when a demon walked up behind her and wrapped an arm around her waist.

In fact, she leaned back into his warmth as he rested his chin on her shoulder and held up a book for her to look at.

"Shall we?"

She glanced down and snorted. "These are children's stories."

"They are fairytales," he corrected. "And they are all quite good. I'm particularly curious to hear what you have to say about the story of the beast and the young woman who is forced to stay in his castle."

"Sounds familiar."

He bit down lightly on her neck, but hard enough to make her arch back into him for a moment before he was pushing her toward the loveseat. The leather one that looked out the window, so she could still watch the kelpies as they played.

Gluttony sat down first, then imperiously waved his hand for her to join him. When she tried to sit beside him, he grabbed her by the hips and made her sit down on his lap. With both his arms wrapped around her, Katherine was reminded of just how safe she would be for the rest of her life.

She leaned into him, enjoying the heat of his body as she watched the outside moors come to life. Night drifted into the sky like someone gently tucked the world into bed. The sound of Gluttony's murmuring voice relaxed her muscles as he read to her from the book of fairytales, spinning webs of wondrous adventures and women who overcame all the odds to beat back the nightmarish hoards that attacked their homes. Stories of women who were warriors and who fought tooth and nail to get what they wanted while kings bent a knee to them.

His low voice sent goosebumps dancing down her arms and she wouldn't have it any other way. He kept her warm, safe, tucked into his body with his chin resting on her shoulder while he read story after story.

The wisps burst to life outside their window. Skittering in giant waves of light that seemed to make patterns on the other side of the window.

It was almost a perfect moment. She didn't know what else could make it better, only that she was so in love with every single moment of this. So in love that it made her heart ache.

Tracing her fingers lightly over Gluttony's forearm, she interrupted him mid sentence. "I love you," she blurted out.

"I know you do."

"I don't think you know how much." It was bursting out of her, like she was too full of the emotion. "I love you very much and if anything happened to you, I don't know what I'd do. I don't think I could keep just going on."

"You could." He set the book on her lap and used his free hand to trace her jaw. "And you would. For centuries, now that you are immortal as I am. There has never been any question in my mind that you were the princess in my story. The avenging queen who came riding to my castle to tell me that I was a terrible king who had forgotten the use of my kingdom. You have changed the way I view everything, Katherine. And soon I will use you to help me decide how to make this kingdom a better place. How to convince my people that I care again."

She searched his gaze, hoping this was the truth. She wanted nothing more than that.

"Do you mean it?" she asked, quietly. "Do you really mean that you want to change this kingdom so that we all may live better?"

"Of course I do. I have wanted to do it for many years, but I was lost in the how and the why." He pressed a soft kiss to her forehead.

"But you are resting today, Katherine. You have done the impossible and taken a spirit into your form. You are changing now, whether you want to believe that or not."

"I can feel the changes already happening." She wiggled in his lap, trying to face him more directly. "But now, I want to know what I can do with it. How can I help my people? What plans we must make to do all this—"

Gluttony tightened his arms, pinning her to his body. "Listen to me, my dear love. You are going to rest and not push yourself while you discover what it means to be the host of a spirit. And then, tomorrow maybe, we will talk about this."

Wilting against him, she knew there was sense in what he suggested. Even if she didn't want to listen to him. "Fine," she muttered. "Where were you in the story?"

"The queen had just cornered the king with a sword to his throat."

"Oh, right. This is my favorite part." Tilting her head against his shoulder, she leaned into him and let herself soak in the sound of his voice and the music of crickets outside.

Because while there was a lot they could fix, right now, she could bask in him.

Chapter 42

Gluttony awoke many mornings later with a pit in his stomach and a sense that something terrible was going to happen. It wasn't a sensation he got often, and one he had learned long ago to pay attention to.

Such an unfortunate feeling when he woke with Katherine in his arms. Yet again. His beauty had never once disappointed him in the morning, because she knew how much he enjoyed waking with her cuddled in his arms. Sometimes, he even woke with her reading a book on her side while he'd wrapped himself around her in his sleep.

He'd counted his blessings for too many days. Round and round the world went, bringing them closer and closer to the next moment that would test their happiness. And he was no fool. He knew there would be another moment.

Lying there with a naked goddess draped across his chest, he knew today was that day.

Gluttony carefully slipped out from underneath her, arranging her body so she would be comfortable in his absence. This was something he had to pursue on his own. A feeling he had to chase, even if it felt like the world was ending while he did it. But it was not something she could help with him, and he knew better than to involve the innocent.

Getting dressed felt like he was preparing to meet his end. And maybe he was. Maybe he was the sad soul who walked toward the end of his life after only just been given a blessing of a woman.

He followed the feeling through the halls as if he were stuck in a dream. But it wasn't a dream when a portal appeared at the end of the hall and his brother stepped through it.

Envy.

Though usually put together well enough, this time his green-eyed brother was disheveled. His hair stuck up in all directions, his shirt was on backward, and he was breathing hard. As though he'd cast a spell too quickly and drained more of his energy than he should have.

"Gluttony," Envy wheezed. "You're still here. Good, that's... good."

"What happened?"

His brother stared at him, hesitating as though what he was about to say was too terrible for him to even voice. "I heard... A rumor."

"About?"

"Your kingdom. There are people here who wish to start an uprising and they have... Well, it sounds like they've gotten a pretty good foothold. The spies I'd sent out said it sounded like they were going to attack the castle very soon and I wanted to make sure that it didn't happen today. I wanted to..." Envy blew out a long breath and ran his hands through his spiky hair again. "You know why I'm here."

Of course he did.

The brothers didn't get involved in other kingdom's affairs. Envy wasn't here to cause trouble for Gluttony or to help him fight. The only reason that Gluttony himself had helped Greed was because he had been forced to be there through it, and he'd wanted to feed. Otherwise, he wouldn't have helped. It was against the code they had created long ago.

Unfortunately, there were other people involved in his life now. There were more people who needed to be looked after.

Namely, one.

"You're here for her," he breathed. "Of course. Thank you, brother. Keep her safe until all this unfolds. If something should happen permanently to me..."

"I will keep her safe."

"Thank you."

Gluttony would make sure that she was set up well. She could have everything that he owned and more. He'd give her the kingdom if he thought she might want it, but after everything that was going to happen soon... Well, she might not want to be here for a few lifetimes, at least. But then she could come back.

That's what he would do. He would pledge his kingdom to her, but only after all of this had boiled over. Envy would be sure to see it happen. If anything happened to Gluttony, he thought Katherine might fight tooth and nail to free him. Eventually, at least.

For now, there might be centuries of pain waiting for him.

He couldn't fight his people. He knew that. There were people here who had instigated the attack, and those people he would kill for what they had done to his home. But the people who fought with them?

They were right.

That's what stung the worst. They'd been his people for centuries now, and they knew that he deserved to be punished.

Perhaps he was no longer a monster, but he had been one for a very long time. He had been the creature who plagued and tormented them for years upon years. He was the one who had haunted their nightmares and the creature who had devoured his people whole. And before that, he had drained them dry. He had eaten and consumed until there was nothing left.

Perhaps he deserved this. But Katherine did not.

Envy strode forward and clapped a hand to his shoulder. They stared into each other's eyes, two monsters who knew that they were going to eventually get what they deserved.

"I will take care of her, brother." Envy enunciated each word carefully. "She will be well cared for in my kingdom."

Katherine's voice sliced through the quiet moment. "Your kingdom of stone? I have no interest in going back there, Envy. And your brother should know better than to make decisions for me."

Oh, she was mad.

More mad than he had ever heard before. He could almost feel it searing through the air as she strode into the room. She'd put on one of her most simple gowns. Just a plain brown thing did nothing for her coloring, but she had never looked more beautiful to him.

For this was the avenging queen he had claimed her to be. She strode into the room with a single purpose, and unfortunately, the battle in her eyes was all for him.

"How dare you?" she snarled before shoving his chest surprisingly hard. "You know that I will stay with you. I plan to be with you, for all time. If they come for you, then they come for me. That is the promise we made to each other, you insufferable man!"

"I will not risk your life—" he started.

"It is not yours to risk." Katherine drew herself up straight and tall, the muscle in her jaw jumping as she ground her teeth and glared. "It's my life. My choice to risk it if I wish. You do not decide for me, demon. And that is the end of it. Do you hear me?"

He wanted to fall on his knees before her and beg for her forgiveness. He wanted to kiss her boots and tell her that he would do anything for her. His queen. His everything.

Instead, he merely bowed his head. "Understood."

Envy looked back and forth between them with wide eyes. "Have you both lost your mind? You realize what an attack on a demon looks like, don't you, madwoman? They will not only come with pitchforks and fire but also with sword and bows. They will burn this entire castle to the ground with you in it. They do not care in the slightest that you were once one of them."

"I understand that. I have already been the target of their cruelty once before."

Gluttony couldn't take his eyes off her as she glided across the room and stopped in front of him. She stared at him, her face screwed up and her eyes squinched as though she were staring into the sun. "You are not alone any longer, demon king. Do I need to remind you of that again? I am here for you, with you, and always will be. Through hardship and pain."

His throat tightened, and though he tried to swallow the emotions down, he couldn't, really. Not when she looked at him with those big eyes that made him want to sink into their warm gaze. "I forgot."

"Don't do it again." She turned her glare to Envy, who even took a step back. "Is there anything we can do to prevent this from happening?"

"We could give Gluttony over to them." His brother pointed at him before turning a little pale at the sight of Katherine's anger. "They aren't going to stop until they have him. That's the point of a mob, little human."

"I don't care that it's the point of a mob. They are humans. They can be reasoned with." She looked at him, that glare burning through his chest. "Well? What about you? Do you have any good ideas?"

He thought Envy's idea was a rather good one. They wanted Gluttony, and they weren't going to stop until they had him. So he might as well join them.

Which... "At the very least, we should prevent them from getting to the castle. So, I suppose, it would be best if we met them at the village."

"It's a start," she muttered before clapping her hands. "Let's get on with it, then. We can talk about our plan along the way. If the two of you can't come up with something, then I surely can."

And so he found himself walking down the boardwalk with his brother and the limping love of his life, knowing that he had to do something drastic. But without the emotional response that he deserved this, Gluttony was more focused on why they were attacking now.

Of all times, why now? There were plenty of strangers in town to instigate it, but where had they come from? And why were they so focused on a demon king, when there were countless slum lords and shitty mayors doing more work than him?

This was the answer he needed to discover.

"No, I'm not going to allow them to rule themselves," he rejected.

"Well, what about offering them free passage to other kingdoms?"

"Then this kingdom would die and there would be no one left living in it."

"You could at the very least offer them restitution for their troubles," she muttered. "Maybe a few free passages a year? Something along those lines."

He grunted and saw Envy watching the road with a more calculated expression. His brother knew where this ended, just as he did. Bloodshed, fire, and the death of good people on both sides.

In this case, the only death he feared was hers.

The closer they got to the town, the more he could hear their anger. The town that Katherine had grown up in was the largest in his kingdom, and it wasn't that big. Spread out over miles upon miles, there were few places where people could live outside of this one. Most couples only had one or two children, and thus did not replace themselves very often.

His kingdom had been dying for a very long time.

Fire bloomed in the distance. Countless sparks of light that illuminated in anger and rage. There were so many people waiting for them in the town center, nearly a hundred of them all ready to destroy and conquer.

And they all turned as one the moment they realized he was there. He watched their eyes go wide and their faces pale as he stepped out of the shadows, all darkness and red eyes. Likely the creature they expected from a storybook, not the king who ruled their kingdom.

One man stepped forward, and though he was shorter than the others, he watched Gluttony with a spark of bravery that was admirable, if foolish.

"So the monster comes out of his hiding place," the man called out. "You are the one we are hunting, demon. You make this too easy for us, and I have to wonder why. Are you here to kill us all?"

"I am not." He stepped further away from his companions,

hoping that the distance would make them harder to notice. "I am here to reason with you."

"Reason?" the man scoffed. "The time for reason is long past, demon. You have haunted our home for far too long."

Katherine's voice soared through the air. "This is not your home, stranger! Perhaps you should be the one we question."

A slight rumbling started in the crowd. Others might have thought the same, but hadn't been brave enough to say it. Who was this man who appeared out of the night with so many others?

Gluttony hummed low in his throat, "I have wondered the same thing for many nights now. I do not know you. Nor do my people know you. So, where have you come from?"

"Does it matter?" the man said, and he swaggered forward as though he didn't care that Gluttony's claws were sharp and his reach was long. "You are the monster who has destroyed so many lives. We are here today to take back this kingdom."

"There is none other who can rule it."

"We can rule it. It will be the first kingdom ruled by mortals and mortals alone. We will make this place a haven for all who wish to run from the demons that have plagued our homes for much too long." His voice lifted at the end, a shout of triumph and a roar of confidence. The people behind him echoed the words, shouting along with him in a wordless cry that echoed throughout the kingdom.

And this was when Gluttony realized something was terribly wrong.

Greed's kingdom had been overrun by men and women who thought they could do the same. These people were strangers here, and yet they had easily incited this coup.

He looked over at Envy and said, "Get her out of here."

Katherine shouted a quick, "No!" before his brother scooped her up.

He knew, if he survived, that Katherine would want to kill him for this. She would yell and scream and likely hit him over the head with a book if it was within reach. She would accuse him of trying to take his own life while protecting hers, but... Well, he wasn't all that worried about dying.

It would be a good reprieve from everything that had happened in these long years. A painful reminder of why he had taken this form in the first place. But Death? Ah, he would not meet Death in this lifetime or the next.

Envy dragged her away as Gluttony allowed his claws to come out of his hands. Already he saw the world through a tinge of red. "Who are you, stranger? Really?"

The man seemed all too pleased with this new development. "You see how the monster prepares himself to fight? He never wished to speak with us! He only wanted to look like he was more human than before. He only wanted to pretend."

"I want to know who you are and where you came from." He pointed a long claw at the man and then gestured to the people behind him. "I will pull them all apart. One by one. Finger by finger to discover where you came from and what your plan is. But you are in the wrong kingdom, stranger, to play games like this."

The man just grinned. "Why's that? Do you believe your people to be so weak as to not be able to kill you?"

Gluttony arched a brow. "No, my people are strong. But I am endless, and I will find out who you are long before you kill me."

The man faded into the crowd, that grin on his face never budging. "We'll see about that, monster. After the bloodbath ends."

Chapter 43

Katherine fought and spat and kicked at Envy as he dragged her away from the town. No one even saw her, because he had somehow cast a spell over them that made them invisible. She couldn't even see her own hands as she scratched at his arm around her waist, desperately trying to get back to the man she loved.

Gluttony shouldn't have to face them on his own. He shouldn't have to deal with the townsfolk who had clearly been affected by these strangers.

Though some part of her wondered if Gluttony had recognized those men. There had been something in his tone, some wandering words and long pauses that made her think he had known who they were. What they were. Clearly Gluttony has his suspicions about what was going on here, and that frightened her.

He'd walked into a lion's den with no one to help him but himself.

And though she knew he was strong and powerful, he still shouldn't have to do it alone.

Because he was always alone. He had always been alone. In his feelings, in his home, and now in his life. No longer. He didn't have to suffer now that she was here and she would damn well not let a demon king take her away from him.

"Let go of me," she snarled, still wriggling like some kind of she demon who had been released into the wild. "Envy, you don't know what you're doing."

"I know exactly what I'm doing." He grunted when she stabbed her elbow into his gut. "Listen to me, woman. Gluttony will take care of the situation, but he doesn't need you there to distract him."

"Is that why you're taking me far away from it? Is that why you said you would keep me in your kingdom?" She twisted harder, kicking her heel back and connecting her sturdy boot with his shin. "You can't lie to me, demon. I know all too well that you are the embodiment of envy. You want to keep me for yourself and you'll stop at nothing to steal me from Gluttony."

"That is not—" He let out a long groan when she finally reached her good heel up and connected it hard between his legs.

That did it.

Katherine felt his grip loosen as he wheezed out a breath that really did sound quite awful, but she refused to feel bad about it when the man was trying to kidnap her.

Envy staggered to the side, bracing himself against the railing before he glared at her. "I am not trying to steal you from my brother. There is no reason for me to do so, you ridiculous, foolish—"

"Woman?" she finished for him, drawing herself up so her shoulders were square. "It's in your nature, Envy, and I don't begrudge you for it. I know what you're doing, even if you do not. But I will not be taken from him. He needs me."

"He can take care of himself. He's a demon!"

"Just like Greed took care of himself? In the same way that all of you gathered together to make sure there was some understanding of a substance you'd never seen before, but could knock you out like you were nothing more than a mortal?" She jabbed her finger at him. "You are all afraid, and the fact that you would let your brother go off to fend for himself in a pack of wolves is despicable."

His glare turned a little colder, a little harder. Chips of emerald stared back at her and she wondered, for a brief moment, if maybe she'd gone too far. "You know nothing about me or my family."

"I know well enough to see there are some great flaws that you refuse to take any ownership of." She flattened her lips into an unimpressed line. "Now I'm going to go back there, and I will slap reason into all of them. Including your brother."

She turned around, and likely would have made her escape if she hadn't frozen in startled realization that they were quite a far distance from the town. Somehow in her struggles, she had missed that Envy must have been moving like the wind. They were nearly half a day away from her home, almost back to the castle where Envy had left his portals.

If she hadn't caught him in that instance, he might have actually succeeded in kidnapping her.

An iron arm banded around her waist and hauled her back against an equally hard chest. "I'm doing this for your own good, woman. Now shut up and let me save you."

"Save me?" she shrieked. Katherine twisted in his arms again, struggling to kick him in the balls one more time, because he damn well deserved it. Maybe this time she would make enough contact to see him weep. That would make her feel a lot better about the entire situation.

"Stop moving," he snarled.

"Never."

"This is what Gluttony wanted! He asked me to make sure you were safe in case anything went wrong."

"He knew them!" Katherine screamed the words as a last resort. Envy had to listen to her. He had to hear the fear and conviction in her voice.

And for once, she was right. He froze, his arms nearly trembling around her as he held himself still.

"What did you say?" he rumbled. "What do you mean, Gluttony knew them?"

"Or at least he had his suspicions." Katherine cleared her throat and kicked her feet where they hung high above the ground. "I know your brother better than anyone. The way he spoke to them, the way he suggested that there was something more afoot, Gluttony has an idea who those strangers are. And I think it has something to do with the substance you had him researching."

"You are certain of this?" He eyed her, and she wondered if he thought she was lying. "How would you know?"

"Because I've taken more than a few seconds to get to know your brother. Put me down, Envy."

He let her slide down his body before he stared at her with too much intensity in his gaze. Finally, he grunted, "If what you're saying is true, then there is a larger problem than myself or my brothers have considered."

She nodded. "Your problem is in every kingdom. Not just Greed's."

"Exactly." He tapped his finger to his lips, and she watched a snake tattoo slither up the long column of his throat and coil in a circle around the thick muscles as he swallowed. "It would suggest we have missed the true issue here."

Katherine was so tired of demon kings who refused to see what was right underneath their nose. "It suggests that you are completely and utterly without thought or reason. If one kingdom had a rebellion that was starting to boil in it, why would others not feel the same? You have ruled our world for a thousand years. Has no one ever tried to change that before?"

He shrugged in response, but she could see how troubled he looked. "There have been many rebellions, but they are always contained within the kingdoms themselves. No rebellion has ever spilled over between multiple kingdoms."

"Maybe it has something to do with when the light bridges appeared. The history books say the kingdoms never used to be able to connect with each other, but now they can." Katherine tossed her hands up in the air. "I don't care, Envy. I don't care about any of this. I want to get to my man. Gluttony is in danger while we're talking about the possibility of a rebellion you already know is happening. This is a waste of both our time."

If he wouldn't let her go, then she would carve her own path. She didn't care if that meant wandering right through the swamp. She'd do it. Thigh high in the muck and the mire, through all the dangerous creatures that she'd always been warned about.

No one and nothing would stand between her and the man she loved. No old wounds, no terrifying creatures, not even this demon king in front of her.

Envy's eyes hooded, darkening with interest as he surveyed her.

"You really would do anything for him, wouldn't you?"

"Without a doubt."

"Even give your life?"

She met his gaze, so he knew how true her answer was. "Without question."

"Fascinating," Envy muttered before he rubbed a hand over his lips. "This is the first time I've wanted to steal you, little human. What does it feel like for Gluttony to know he has a human so devoted to him?"

"Terrifying, I imagine." She gestured between the two of them. "Clearly, since he told you to kidnap me before I got involved in anything."

He hummed low underneath his breath before nodding. "I suppose that makes sense. Humans are a rather expensive and delicate pet to keep."

Somehow, it made her even more angry for him to call her by that name. Gluttony used it as a way to express his affection for her. He only called her pet because he adored her and wanted to keep her safe and happy. This demon? He called her that as an insult. Proof that he still thought she was lesser than him simply because she wasn't a magic practitioner or whatever it was that he might actually respect.

Scoffing, she turned away from him and started toward the edge of the walkway. "I'm going to help him."

"You're going to die," Envy replied. The words were blunt and sharp-edged. "They want to kill him, but he cannot die. You can."

"He had me consume a spirit," she hissed. "I am as immortal as you."

"You aren't, actually."

She froze at the edge of the boardwalk, her toes hanging off the rotting wood. "What do you mean by that?"

"Possession is a delicate process. The spirit inside you can keep you alive indefinitely, but you are still mortal." Envy stood beside her, his eyes on the moors and not on her. "We are spirits taken flesh. They could cut Gluttony's head off and he would likely grow a new one."

"Speaking from experience?"

"Not personal experience." Tiny wrinkles appeared between his eyes. "But there is one of us who has endured all of it and wears the scars to prove it. We are impossible to kill, Katherine, but you are still a mortal. You stand before me, all flesh and blood and bone. I could cut your head off or stop your heart and there would be nothing you could do to stop me. And it would end. Your life would stop and the spirit would leak out of your body, off to find another. Mortal wounds will always affect you."

And maybe that should have been the only warning she needed. Maybe she should have felt the shiver of fear and the worry that death would find her. But Katherine didn't feel that at all.

She just shrugged. "Then I will be more careful."

"You aren't afraid of death at all, are you?"

She thought about his question, letting it mull in her mind and roll over like a stone in the sea. But it was a stone that had been in her mind for many years. She'd already worried it smooth, the sharp edges of anxiety and fear turning into a quiet acceptance. She'd lived with that fear for such a long time that it no longer had any bite.

"No," she finally replied. "I have lived my life hand in hand with pain. I know what it feels like to come close to death, and I know what it feels like to live a life only half awake. I've been held back from so many things because I cannot do them while watching other people do them with ease. When I was younger, I thought this made me half a person. Less whole than the others. But now I know I am just as much a complete person. Life can be lived with modifications to the fullest extent. Perhaps even more than people who are already whole, because I live in this world and see it for what it really is. Not for what it can give me."

His gaze softened a bit, and his eyes flicked down to her hip as though he had any right to even look at it. It wasn't for him to see. It wasn't for him to pity her. She had an injury from when she was a child, but she was still a person.

Maybe Gluttony was the only one who could see her in the right light. It was all the more reason to love him and throw herself into keeping him safe.

He deserved it. He had never once looked at her hip as something that made her weak or lesser.

Turning her attention to the swamp, she nodded once. "I'll go straight through the swamp. There are creatures there, but I have met some of them before. Perhaps that meeting will be enough for them to let me through."

"You'll need help."

"I can do it, Envy."

"I have no doubt of that, but there are still creatures who will try to attack you, and you are not very good at fighting." Amused, he held out his hand for her to take. "I cannot interfere in the politics of other kingdoms. I'm sure you understand why we do not do so."

"I don't."

"Because if I interfere, then it will make me want to take this kingdom for my own. I have saved it, therefore, part of me exists inside it." Envy's eyes burned that glowing green. "I would take it, and I would keep it."

"Right," she muttered. "That would be a big problem. Anyway, Envy. Nice chatting with you, but I don't have the time for this."

"Then allow me to give you a gift, Katherine. A guide to help you should you need it."

Though she was a little suspicious of what this demon would call a gift, she nodded. "Fine. Just hurry up."

Envy rolled up his sleeve, and she saw ink drip down from his neck. It seemed to rip off the snake and coil down his arm, down to his wrist, where it bloomed into wings that opened as if the bird were already flying across his body. He reached for it and then pulled the ink off his skin. With a flick of his wrist, a falcon with shimmering black wings edged in green burst into life out of his hand.

It soared up into the sky with a screech of anger that echoed across the swamp, and she swore she heard the entire world go still at the sound of its wrath.

"What kind of magic is that?" she whispered.

"The magic of a demon king." Envy grinned at her, his teeth suddenly a little too sharp. "It will watch over you. Should you find yourself in trouble, that falcon will fight for you. And if it believes you cannot win the fight, then it will summon me. So stay away from the kelpies, dear girl. Perhaps they will ignore you, but perhaps they will not. Gluttony will have my head if you die."

Well, she couldn't argue with that.

Katherine gave him a brief nod and then leapt off the boardwalk into the murky waters below.

Chapter 44

Gluttony grinned with blood splattered teeth up at the young man who thought he could contain a demon. "You haven't done much research, have you?"

The man before him was the same one who had been so outspoken in the crowd. The same man who very quickly ordered everyone to follow what he said to do, and corralled the entire crowd into creating a barrier that Gluttony could not punch through without more bloodshed. And then he'd placed iron shackles on Gluttony's hands, which would have done nothing if not for the inscriptions on the inside.

They actually could contain a demon, shockingly, and that meant someone with magical abilities was helping them. Gluttony could still fight all of them with his hands behind his back, but he wanted to know more about this young man and where he had come from.

So he let them hit him. He let them punch and kick and do whatever it took for them to feel better. The purging of their emotions was swift, but he saw the regret on so many faces. He could see the horror on women's faces as they backed away from what they had done. And what their men were doing.

Those were the people who did not escape his notice. The people who were willing to realize that they were in the wrong. They had stepped away from the dwindling crowd, returning to their homes and closing the doors tightly behind them.

That had angered the strangers. They stirred the fires of rage again, calling out to the villagers that there was something wrong with this demon before them. That after all he had done, surely they had to realize he was not like this for a good reason? Gluttony was barely even responding to their kicks. What kind of monster couldn't even feel pain?

And that had been enough for many of his people, unfortunately. The next thing he knew, there were more punches raining down upon his head. But he healed quickly, and they realized it very fast. In just an hour, they had cut him in so many ways that he couldn't count the amount of times he'd been sliced.

Still, this was fine. He deserved a little punishment for his neglect and he would not deny them that. If causing him pain made them feel better about their daughters and all the other things that had happened? Certainly, they could. He would not deny that it was a good option. After all, Gluttony had used pain many times in his life to solve his own issues.

But now it was just him and the stranger. Just this man who had dragged him into someone's root cellar and left Gluttony alone to address the crowd. As though he was already their king.

The man dragged a stool in front of him and then dropped down onto it. Pulling a knife out of his back pocket, he started cleaning the drying blood out from underneath his nails. "I have done research, demon. So have the others. We know more about your kind than you would likely be comfortable with."

"Rumors and legends," Gluttony spat. "No one would tell you the truth, even if you tortured us."

"We're going to put that to the test, now aren't we?" The man looked at the knife in the air, his threat a little too obvious. "Now, you will address me as Nikolai. I enjoy hearing a demon say my name when they're in pain."

"A demon?" Gluttony tilted his head to the side, eyeing this Nikolai through the red haze cast by his eyes. "You have met another of my kind? I find that hard to believe."

"It is not so hard to believe. There are many of you, after all."

"Fewer than you would think." Although he had the sudden urge to reach out to Greed and make sure his two spirits taken flesh were well. Loyalty and Passion were more people than they were spirits at this point, but that didn't mean this man hadn't gotten to them.

"That's part of the problem with you demons. You think you are completely untouchable when there are many ways for us to touch you." Nikolai pointed at the shackles with his knife. "We know how to contain you. And we know how to knock you out with a gas that will make you pass out even if you're on a horse."

"Ah," Gluttony breathed. "I had a feeling you were one and the same. So you have people in Greed's kingdom as well. I did not expect the rebellion to have spread like poison so quickly. You are the messenger, I take it?"

Nikolai watched him with far too cunning eyes. This was a man who knew how to control a lot of people. And if Gluttony was right, he was the cause of a lot of trouble in many of the kingdoms.

But surely this was not the ringleader. No one running such a detailed, intricate coup would go to each kingdom on their own.

This was just one of many people who were likely sent out. Trusted individuals. So, Nikolai perhaps knew who the real person was that threatened Gluttony and his brothers.

Nikolai leaned forward and grinned, his teeth a little crooked. "There are more of us than ants in an ant hill. You can stomp us out and send all the poison you wish into our mix, but we will never disappear from your kingdoms, demon. We are the pest you cannot get rid of."

"No pest is impossible to get rid of," Gluttony muttered. "Soon, we will find out where you came from and who your leader is. And we will extinguish them with flames unlike anything you have ever seen before."

"Is that so?"

"It is." Gluttony leaned forward, too close for Nikolai's comfort because the man backed away from him, nearly falling off his stool. "Let me tell you something to bring back to your leaders, something that no one else has told you. We are not just demons. We are gods with powers that are so far beyond your understanding. I am the weakest of us, little man. But all I need is a single drop of your blood and I will turn into a monster from your nightmares."

Nikolai laughed, but the sound was at least a little nervous. "I am not afraid of you. Nor am I afraid of death. My purpose is to spread the news that you can be beaten. Your own kingdom will do the rest for me."

"Will they?" Gluttony nodded at the door behind him, the one at the top of the stairs that led up to the crowd, who were already heading back to their homes. "It appears you are in here alone, stranger. And no one will hear you scream when I am done with you."

"You will never find our leader," Nikolai said, still stroking that knife like it gave him any protection at all. "Because you will be long gone before you piece together who it could be. You see, I'm going to cut you up into little pieces. One by one. Your fingers, your toes, and I'm going to keep them with me. Spread them out around all the seven kingdoms. And if that doesn't work to contain you, then I will bury you under the ground so deep that no one will hear you scream. And all those incantations that are pressed into your iron shackles will surround the coffin I put you in."

"What a relaxing reprieve from stressful duties," Gluttony bit through his teeth. "But you know that the moment I get out—and I will—I will track you to the very ends of this earth and return all your favors in kind."

"I don't think you'll be able to do that in my lifetime."

"Then I will find your children. Your brother's children. Whoever shares your blood will fill a tub for me and my bride to bathe in." Gluttony's eyes burned red, and he knew the entire room must be awash in it. A pain spiked through his forehead as his horns grew and a tail burst out behind him. His claws, though hidden, were already long. "I will gift your life and all the lives of those who come after you to the one woman who matters. She will have a say in whether or not I bless your lineage with life or death. And trust me when I say this, if you keep her from me, then she will only choose death."

"Your bloodthirsty bride will be dead long before that happens," he hissed. "I will watch her eyes bulge in fear and then I will drag her through the streets until her blood coats the boardwalk. She will know why it was a foolish decision to love a demon."

And though he had always been able to remain calm and collected, something in Gluttony snapped. He refused to listen to anyone speak ill of his woman, let alone this sniveling child who thought he could threaten a queen.

Baring his fangs, Gluttony managed to form the words to say, "I'm going to kill you now. Painfully. Slowly."

"I'd like to see you try, demon."

He lunged forward with a single-minded attempt at murder. Nikolai knew what he was doing, however, and that made sense, of course. The man stuck his knife in between Gluttony's teeth, the sharp edges cutting through his cheek like he was a dog gnawing on a stick. If it took his jaws powering through metal to kill this man, then that was exactly what he would do. The mortal thought he had caught easy prey.

Gluttony was the predator here, and it was time for the humans to remember that.

Blood poured over his tongue and pooled down his throat. It coiled in rivers down his neck and still he did not stop. He chewed, and bit, and gnashed, and soon the human before him looked a little pale.

Nikolai's biceps bulged, the muscles in his neck straining as he tried to hold the rabid creature at bay. Once he pulled the knife back, only to saw at the other side of Gluttony's face. But the demon would not be stopped. No one would prevent him from biting into the flesh of this man. Eventually, Nikolai would break. Eventually, he would become distracted or weakened and Gluttony would rip his lower jaw off before he stopped.

A shriek echoed from outside, and the piercing cry of a falcon. No natural creature made that noise and he was quite certain he also heard an echoing call for people to run. On the tail end of the word, a scream.

Nikolai flinched, and that was all Gluttony needed. Wrenching the blade out of the other man's hands with his teeth, Gluttony spat it onto the floor and grinned at him. He knew the expression was likely elongated by the sliced cheeks that made his smile even wider. "Come on, stranger. It's time for me to feed."

Nikolai tried to run, but he didn't get very far. Gluttony lunged forward, snapping the chains that connected him to the wall. Though the manacles held strong, the chains had not been enchanted.

He grabbed onto the other man by the base of his neck, where his throat and shoulder met. Gripping it with all the strength in his jaw, he sawed back and forth until a thick chunk of meat tore off.

He met Nikolai's horrified gaze as he chewed, and then swallowed.

"You... You..." The gurgled mess of the man's voice was nothing like it had been before. Nikolai pressed his hand to his throat, trying to contain the gushing blood that billowed more and more out of it. "You can't..."

"You can enchant the shackles, but not the chains," he snarled. Gluttony hardly recognized his own voice. The battle form had overtaken him. "Now run, stranger. I wish to hunt."

Nikolai turned toward the stairs, only to have the door at the top open. And there, standing in the light that spread in rays around her as though it wouldn't dare mar her lovely skin, stood Katherine.

His Katherine. The one who shouldn't be here, but who he was no more surprised to see than he would have been surprised to see the moon rise on the horizon.

Nikolai staggered toward her, only freezing when she stepped deliberately into his way.

Her gaze hardened, and she looked the stranger up and down. "You're covered in blood."

He nodded.

"Strangers have no place meddling in the minds of the innocent." She shifted to the side. "Go. But don't think this is a mercy. I'm not sure you'll make it out of this kingdom alive without a kelpie chewing on your flesh."

Nikolai jerked past her, not even noticing that Katherine grabbed the keys from the back of his pocket. He was a dead man walking, and even that poor soul knew it.

And oh, Gluttony had never loved this woman more. He'd never wanted to kiss her more, but the moment Nikolai left the cellar, he could feel all the pain that sizzled through every inch of his body.

Apparently, there was a limit to how much his spirit was willing to heal.

One step to the side, and he was suddenly down on his knees. Staring up at her like the goddess she was. Like the gift she had become.

"Katherine," he said quietly, and his voice was different. Changed from what it had been before.

Right, his mouth. The cut open lips and ghastly smile he was probably subjecting her to. Not to mention the amount of blood that coated him from head to toe and the bright red marks that would eventually become bruises.

But his beautiful, compassionate bride didn't care about that at all. She walked down the steps quietly, and a falcon landed in front of the door. Guarding them. He recognized Envy's magic and, for once, wanted to thank his brother for at least having the thought to do that. Katherine had not returned on her own.

"What did that monster do to you?" she whispered, stopping in front of him. She cupped his cheek gently, and he could see the smudge of blood on her palm as she wiped at the liquid on his cheeks. "My love. You didn't deserve this."

As he stared up at her, he wondered what she saw in him that no one else did. Did she see a brave man? A king who wished he was better than he actually was? He hoped that was what she saw. He wanted her to see that.

Carefully, he leaned forward and pressed his cheek to her stomach. He would have lifted his tired arms and wrapped her in them, but he was still tied up. So he knelt at her feet with his hands behind him.

"Just a moment," he whispered against her soft flesh. "Just a few moments, and then I will face them."

"You have no one to face," she said. "They are the ones who must face you. But my love, you cannot see them like this. You cannot let them think they have defeated you."

He should heal. She was right. They would only think him weak, and right now, he had to be strong. Strong enough to prove that he was worthy of being their king.

But he was so tired. He just wanted to rest for a few moments and then maybe he could convince his powers to heal him one last time.

"A few moments," he whispered against her belly. "Just let me rest."

"We need to get you free." Katherine drew away from him, and he felt like he'd lost something. Some marvelous creature who had always been the only thing that mattered.

And without her, he felt... empty.

His arms fell forward, and the metal clanked onto the ground with a rough thud. And then she was there again. Kneeling in front of him, her arms coming around him first, then encouraging his own arms to wrap around her.

"Come here," she whispered, turning her head to the side and baring that swan-like neck for him. "Feed, my love. And then we will remind them that you are their king for a reason."

Perhaps he was still a bit of a monster, because he scraped his fangs against her neck and then sank them in deep.

Chapter 45

Her poor monster.

Gluttony had been used, abused, tossed aside, and beaten. The cuts on his cheeks... They had sliced a permanent smile into him and it made her stomach turn to even think about it again.

He should never have been exposed to that level of punishment. Every ounce of him was lovely and wonderful and kind. How could they not see it?

Because they hadn't wanted to. Their kingdom was falling apart at the seams and it was so easy to blame an absent king when they had just as much part in it. She did as well. Her people had plodded through their lives, so certain that someone else was to blame. They never had to look any deeper if they believed that. They never had to think that their own people could have fixed many of the issues if they'd just cared enough. If they'd just tried a little harder.

But she'd seen that realization on their faces when she walked back into town. They had seen her limping into view, emerging out of the mist like some kind of mythical creature pulling herself out of the swamp, and they had looked away. No one could meet her eyes, no one but Grace, who had stumbled toward her.

Twin black eyes had turned her friend's usually beautiful countenance into one that proved something horrible had happened to her. And Grace was the one who linked their arms together, and the two of them had walked through the crowd. Quietly. Calmly. Without inciting more violence or anger, as they seemed so likely to do.

No one had tried to stop her. A few of them had even pointed her in the direction of this root cellar, one that had clearly been built to withstand a kelpie or other monstrous creature's attack.

"Go to him," Grace had said, standing outside the door with the falcon. "See if he's..."

Neither of them wanted to admit that there could be a chance their king was dead. Even though Katherine knew it wasn't possible for him to die. There was still that fear that she might find him headless, or just a body.

Instead, she'd found a man with a carved out smile, covered in blood and bruises, but who looked at her like she was the most beautiful thing he'd ever seen.

And now, Katherine held the back of his head as he drank from her neck. The sounds were rougher than usual, more audible as he gulped mouthful after mouthful of blood. She wasn't light headed yet, though, so he could take all that he needed.

Her blood would heal him, she thought, and if it didn't, at least he would go out to that crowd without the edge of hunger and rage. He would be comfortable, at ease, a man who could make them feel guilt for the monstrous things they had done.

He was alive.

Running her fingers up his cheeks, she felt for the giant wounds that were slowly closing. And though it was perhaps morbid, she kept her fingers against them until she felt them seal. The blood that stuck to her fingers, however, that would remain in her mind for many years to come.

Gently, she tugged at his jaw, smoothing her fingers down his neck as he growled at her.

"Gluttony," she whispered. "You have to stop."

He clutched her to him a little harder, holding her against his body a little too tightly as he started to coil around her. Like a snake who wanted to consume his prey whole.

"No, my darling." Katherine didn't feel an ounce of fear from his movements. She just patiently waited for him to come back to himself. "You cannot feed off me any longer. You will hurt me."

His fingers spasmed against her back, and though he was still holding her too tight, he at least slowed in his drinking.

"That's it," she whispered. "Come back into yourself, Gluttony. You are the king of these people, and we have to prove to them why you are king. You cannot be wounded. You cannot be weak. You have to be the Gluttony I know, so that we can tell them what you will do now."

And so, slowly, he drew back. She felt him lick her neck, but knew those wounds were too deep for any healing to be done. Even the spirit inside her seemed to realize that the marks he had left needed to remain.

She wanted everyone to see them. She wanted to show the signs of his feeding and wear them with pride. She would prove to them all those bodies in the almshouse had not ended up there because of Gluttony.

Katherine stood, using his shoulder to brace herself until the dizziness faded. And then he joined her, every inch a king, even though he was covered in blood and dirt. Without a word, he held out his arm for her to take and the two of them made their way up the stairs into the dim light of the sun.

A small crowd had formed, all standing at odds with Grace, who seemed ready to fight anyone. The black eyes made her look rather menacing.

But everyone froze when they saw who approached them from the cellar. Surely they had seen the man missing parts of his body leave this shadowy place. But perhaps they thought that Gluttony would also consume her.

Either way, they were looking at two united people. Not a victim and abuser.

Grace turned to her first, her voice low and quiet. "Katherine?"

"Yes?"

"You all right?"

She met her friend's gaze first, then turned her attention to all the people in front of them. "I am more than well. I have come to collect the man I love, and now I am going to take him home."

Low murmurs spread through the crowd. Love? How could she love a man like that? A creature who had tormented their kingdom for such a long time?

She glared at them all. Each and every one until they fell silent, their faces burning with embarrassment. But she could see their eyes on the wounds at her throat. She knew what they were thinking and where their fear came from.

Carefully lifting her fingers, she skated them over the wounds on her neck, drawing even more attention to the punctures. "These are the marks of the man who loves me. The man who I have committed myself to."

"The monster you have fallen under the spell of, you mean?" Alexander's voice cut through her crowd, her old boss meandering through them all with a challenge in his voice. "We have all seen what he can do to young women in his thrall. We know the cost of what he asks for."

"There is no more cost," Katherine called out. "I have pledged myself to him, and he to me. Gluttony will no longer seek out your wives or daughters. He will only feed from me, and this is something he has vowed."

"How can we believe that?" Alexander scoffed. "He lies and cheats, just as those strangers he killed have said. And now he chases off the truth seekers because he wants to weave his web of darkness around us once more."

She wanted to slap that stupid expression off his face. She wanted to hit him so hard that he saw stars and then maybe remembered that Katherine had never once lied to him. That she'd worked hard, for years, proving her worth and value in the almshouse while he had ignored all the options that might have eased her pain.

But Gluttony spoke, and every single one of them fell silent to hear his words.

"I have not been a good king," he said, his voice a low rumble. He wiped the blood off his cheeks to reveal the still red marks beneath. "I can admit that. I have always known that I was failing you, but I believed in staying away, that I was doing you better service. Your women came to me seeking money or safe travel, and I provided

491

whatever they asked for in return for their blood. You called me a monster. I gave you space. You blamed me for this kingdom's ruin, and I took that blame without question."

Faint murmurs rose in the crowd, mostly from women who had taken his payments.

"I do not wish to prove anything to you," Gluttony continued. "That will take years of improving this kingdom and listening to what you have to say. Reparations will be made for all that I have done to you and your kin. Trust me when I say I do not wish to brush our history aside. I know what I have done, and I will make amends for that. But I am still king. I am still the demon at your doorstep, and I have but one question for you. What use you will find for me? Shall I be the demon king who protects you, or would you prefer that I stay in my castle and you in your homes as we have done for many years now?"

And then he stayed silent. Katherine stood beside him, her arm linked with his, and she waited for her people to decide if they even wanted him anymore.

They shouldn't, she knew that. He had tormented their nightmares for a very long time, and even if he hadn't, Gluttony had done little for them. Food was scarce. Money even harder to come by. They were a hard people who worked until they dropped.

But they were also good people, and she knew that to her core. She had seen all the good they could do and how supportive they were to their neighbors and friends. She could only hope that they would extend that courtesy to a person they had always thought was a monster.

Finally, when no one spoke, she did for them.

"We have all been afraid of him for such a long time. I know you have good reason to be scared. But I am here to tell you that there is nothing to fear. He has been a good man, a supportive friend, and then someone so much more after I had stayed with him for even longer. I trust him with my life. And I believe without question that he wishes to make this kingdom better. I believe we can do this with him." Katherine glanced up at Gluttony and smiled, even though his expression was one of sincere worry. "I believe in him. So very much."

He smiled down at her as well, the soft expression making his entire face light up and change. He was so handsome when he did that. So little like the monster with red eyes that every legend made him out to be.

But no one stepped forward. No one said a word until Grace cleared her throat.

Even though there were a hundred eyes on her, Grace didn't wilt in front of their angry gazes. "If he's good enough for Katherine, then he's good enough for me," she said. "I'd rather have a demon on our side than against us."

A few other murmurs played throughout the crowd before another woman begrudgingly admitted, "He was rather gentle when he gave me all that coin. He could have killed me, but he really just took a few sips and then sent me on my way."

"He did the same for me," another woman said, even though her husband hissed at her to stay quiet. "When our boy was sick, I asked for money and offered my blood. It didn't even hurt, I just... I didn't tell anyone."

More and more women spoke up, quietly agreeing that they hadn't been harmed at all when they'd entertained Gluttony, but they hadn't wanted anyone to know that they had sought help. Sometimes it was because their husbands hadn't been doing well at work, others because they were on their own and hadn't made rent.

And Gluttony quietly listened to all of them. He stood there, listening to every story and appearing to really listen. He even nodded his head at a few women, who flicked their gazes at him before looking back to the ground.

Countless women, all who had sacrificed themselves so that they could make ends meet. And their king, who stood before them beaten and bloodied, but who had helped them. Even when no one else could.

Katherine sighed, knowing that this was the moment when she needed to make sure everyone was very clear about what was going to happen next. "Our king has been helping us even when he did not know how. Surely some of you can understand that."

And there were plenty of people who could. Mostly women who had been helped, but some men who were also able to see reason.

Alexander stood firm in his hatred, however. "What of all the bodies in my clinic? All the people who had their throats ripped out and their lives stolen from them?"

Perhaps Gluttony had a calm, reasonable answer for this. But Katherine refused to stand for this slander any longer.

The angry words burst out of her. "Are you still so blind? You're a doctor, by the seven kingdoms! We have seen the wounds from Gluttony's feeding countless times in our lives. You can see the wounds on my own neck now, fresh from a feeding. You know that none of those wounds in your clinic were caused by him. But there were countless strangers in our mix, encouraging us to violence and rebellion. Don't you think it's more likely they were the ones hurting us just to make sure we actually did what they wanted?"

Again the murmurs. Again, the shifting. And then she saw a few people drifting away from the crowd. Back toward their homes.

Finally, Grace spoke again. "I think I speak for all of us when I say we'd rather have our own demon than none at all. Stay Gluttony. Continue to be our king, and perhaps we can work together to make this kingdom better."

He nodded at her before lifting his voice to a booming tone. "One last thing."

They all froze in tandem.

"I will no longer feed from anyone other than my bride." He wrapped an arm around Katherine and she felt her face turn bright red. "If you need my help, I am pleased to do so. I will happily assist my people who need me to step in, but I will not feed from any other. This woman saved you all, and she saved me as well. We all owe her a great debt."

Katherine could not be more embarrassed and proud if she tried. Biting her lips, she grinned at him with all the love in her heart blasting out of her being. She'd never been more proud of him. Never been so certain that she had made the right decision in her life.

He looked down at her and then gently touched the tip of her nose. "You are the queen this kingdom has been looking for, my love. Now, let me put you on a throne."

Chapter 46

Gluttony grinned at the sound of Katherine's moan echoing through his ears. They'd holed up in his castle for a long time after their painful adventure. They assumed everyone needed a little space, and that had led to a ridiculous amount of time doing... this.

She reclined in his arms, her back pressed to his chest. Though her hands clutched at his wrists like she could push herself away from him. Or closer, he supposed, considering the things his hands had just done.

He had never been more happy than this moment. His woman, sweaty and limp in his arms, the powerful knowledge that he'd just given her so many orgasms he'd lost count at seven. All in front of a giant window that showed their kingdom spread out before them.

Breathing hard, Katherine tilted her head on his shoulder to peer up at him. "Are you quite finished yet?"

"With what?"

"Murdering me." She wriggled in his arms, arching against him to press her bottom against him. "And you have yet to enjoy yourself at all, husband of mine."

"Ah, well, sometimes the enjoyment is merely in listening to your cries."

Gluttony lifted one of her hands up to the sunlight. A bright day had blessed their kingdom for once, and he watched as the sunlight sparkled off the stone of her ring. The clear crystal cast rainbows on the wall, and he watched them dance over the window.

It was a human custom, she'd said. And he was more than happy to have her wearing his mark for all to see. More than just the wounds on her neck that never quite healed. Thanks to Envy's magic, she was never too bothered by them either. But now there was an additional mark, one that wasn't made in blood and violence.

Although, he supposed he had killed a few traders for her ring, but he hadn't told her that. His soft hearted wife was certainly too kind to continue wearing the ring if she knew he had murdered people to get it.

Besides, he still didn't trust strangers coming into his kingdom. Not after what the last strangers had done.

"Wife," he said quietly, letting the word roll over his tongue. "It has a nice ring to it."

"I suppose it does. It sounds as lovely as husband, although I think I might call you my prince." Katherine pressed a kiss to his neck.

"Prince?" He craned his neck to look at her. "Why prince?"

"Because you're the prince in my story, Gluttony. The fairytale ending, just like the books we read together. My demon prince."

Her little signs of affection had bloomed throughout his chest and turned him into a different man. He'd never thought such affection would soften him, but oh, it did. He would do anything for one of her kisses or soft smiles.

With a soft smile, he ran his nails up her thighs. Goosebumps rose in their wake, and he knew how much she loved to be touched like this. Feather light, almost as though she couldn't feel him touching her at all.

And he just liked to touch her. Any way and any time that he could. It reminded him that she was real, and that none of this had been a dream.

She was right in front of him. Right here. Nothing would change that, even if people came to his castle to attack them. She was his forever, no matter the cost.

"Gluttony?" she asked, shifting in his arms until her hands were placed over his wrists again. "Do you mind answering a question that might be a little uncomfortable?"

"Now?"

"Well, it's on my mind."

He nuzzled into her hair, breathing in the scent that was so uniquely her and so comforting. "Anything, my love. You know there is nothing you could ask that I am not willing to share."

"You said when your brothers met their partners that they..." She paused, swallowed hard, and then charged forward into the question like she was afraid of what he'd say. "They changed what spirits they were underneath. I know you all still refer to them as Lust and Greed, but you said they are no longer those spirits or... emotions."

"They are not." He had an idea where she was going with this, but he wanted her to ask it. "Lust is now Love, and Greed is now Benevolence. Both of them were changed once they started to spend more time, a considerable amount of time, with someone who thought differently from themselves. Us demon kings are not known for asking for others' opinions very often and, apparently, that has been holding us back for a very long time."

"Ah." She traced patterns onto his wrists and up his forearms as she thought about what he said. "Are they happy as different spirits?"

"I think happiness is subjective. They are who they are, and they are happy in their current lives." He hummed low in his breath, trying to find the right words to describe it to her. "If you take someone out of their life here, a mortal, put them into this castle that is so different from what they previously lived, and then ask if they are happy, are they?"

"It depends on the circumstances and what their life is like. Some people will be happy, others won't. There's just not enough details there to know if they're happy or not."

"The same goes for my brothers." He curled his arms around her a little tighter, hugging her close to his heart. "The same goes for me. I am happy because you are here. Because we are working on making this kingdom a little better, day by day. Because you have woken me from my slumber when I was slowly rotting and allowing this castle to crumble along with me."

"So they are happy, then?"

"I believe they are. Some days, they are probably less happy than others. There will always be a part of our spirit that remembers what we used to be. Changing from one spirit who has lived that way for over a thousand years into another... It's hard not to still have the old thoughts. They're just duller."

"Oh," Katherine said quietly. She hugged his arms around herself as well, unconsciously drawing him even closer to her before she sighed. "I wanted to ask if you had changed, but I also don't want to pressure you to do so. I love you the way you are. And I have loved you for a very long time. I know that there are circumstances in your life that make it very difficult for you to change. And I don't want you to think that I love you any less, or think less of you for not doing what your brothers did. I just..."

She trailed off, her words falling like drops of water on a still lake. He could almost see the ripples moving through her mind.

She didn't want to make him feel bad, but she also felt a little bad about it herself. What was it about Selene and Varya that had changed their demon kings? Was Katherine lacking in some way that she couldn't get him to change who he was?

All those thoughts and more likely played through his wife's mind, and he'd have none of it.

"Kat," he said with a warm chuckle. "Are you trying to ask if I have changed? Or if you have affected me as much as their partners affected them?"

"I wasn't going to be so blunt about it."

"And yet you are worried that you haven't done enough to convince me to change?"

"Well..." she grumbled. "There aren't many of you with partners, and the other two have already changed their emotions. You can't blame a woman for being a little disgruntled about it. What is so different between the two of us that makes you stay the same? Is it the blood? Is it the feedings? I don't..."

All right, that was enough of her spiraling.

He scooped her up into his arms and lifted her, rolling so he could stand with her wrapped around him like a little monkey. Together, they strode toward their massive bed in the corner that was completely covered in red silk and velvet. It was her favorite place in the house, she said, and this was where they would have this conversation.

Gluttony tossed her onto the springy mattress, doing his best not to snicker as he saw her bounce hard in the air a few times before she caught herself.

She glared up at him through the wild tangle of her hair. "Was that necessary for this conversation?"

"Absolutely." Prowling up from the bottom of the bed, he crawled over her and forced her down onto her back. "I want to look at you while I tell you all this."

"Why do you need to do that?"

"Because I enjoy watching your expressions change and I think it's best that you cannot hide from me by looking out that window." He tucked a finger under her chin and forced her to look at him. "Katherine, I need you to really focus and not let that anxiety whisper too much in your ears."

She set her jaw and nodded firmly.

"Brave pet," he muttered, leaning down to kiss her once because he couldn't not. "You are afraid that I have not changed, and I have not told you about these changes because I thought you had seen them already. You've already watched a spirit change into another being. That is my fault. I should have mentioned it while it was happening."

She blinked up at him, and he had the wonderful experience of seeing her rare expression of confusion. "What?"

"I've already changed, you ridiculous woman," he said with a chuckle. "You should have been the first person to realize that."

"What do you mean, you've changed?"

"I think it likely started the moment you walked into this castle. My spirit was more than ready to take up something new. I was hardly the remnants of the Gluttony I once was, anyway. Just a shadow of an emotion and then in you walked, the dream I had always had for myself and yet never was allowed to touch. Not even if I wanted to." He traced his fingers down the side of her face, following the outline of her jaw. "You made me dream of another life, another being, long before you even realized you loved me."

"Gluttony," she whispered. "Why didn't you tell me?"

He felt his cheeks flame a dark red before he gathered his courage to respond. "My brothers changed drastically. Lust to Love is a singular difference of how he learned to see the virtue in finding out who a person really is. Greed changed to Benevolence because he realized that taking from his people only hurt them, and it felt better to give." Again, the blush deepened. He could feel the tips of his ears flaming. "I apparently am still learning."

"I don't understand what you're trying to say."

He sank against her body, allowing her to take his full weight as he rocked his hips against hers. A distraction? Absolutely. And perhaps he needed to know that she was a little distracted so he could get the words out.

"I did not change all that much," he murmured. "There are opposites of who we are. The opposite of gluttony is abstinence, and I am not interested in stopping what I desire. I enjoy food, and drink, and..." He eyed her neck. "You."

"You know I wouldn't ask you to stop feeding off me, even if you were someone else."

"I know that. I do not need it to live. I merely desire it. So apparently I have yet to learn how to change all that much, because I have good reason to suspect that while I am no longer Gluttony, I still wish to enjoy the finer things in life." He took a deep breath, quite certain she would judge him for what he was about to say. "I believe I am Restraint."

"Restraint," she repeated, running the word over her tongue before searing him with a brilliant smile. "I like it. And I think that's quite a lesson for someone like you to learn. To devour everything without question or end, that consumes everyone and everything in your path. But learning how to have restraint that means you are capable of knowing when to stop. And when to see that you've had enough. That is impressive, Gluttony. Or do you wish for me to call you something else?"

Oh, the wave of relief nearly made him limp. Gluttony had been so worried she would judge him or say that it wasn't enough. He'd been so afraid that he couldn't be enough for her and to know that she saw the use in what he had learned? It just made him love her even more.

He had never known that love would consume him like this. That he would get eaten up by it and spat out as something new. Although, he supposed he should have guessed this would happen. He'd seen his brothers. He'd seen what happened to them when they finally gave in to the beauty of what their women could give them.

"No, don't call me anything else," he murmured, leaning down to drag his tongue down her neck. "It's a relief, I'll admit. And here I was, thinking you wouldn't find the value in a man who hadn't changed all that much."

"Oh, but I liked you exactly as you were. Don't you remember?" Katherine shuddered in his arms, already spreading her legs for him because she knew what he wanted now.

But then she palmed both his cheeks and drew him back up her body. She held onto him with a fierce grip, staring deeply into his eyes. "I loved you before you changed, and I will love you long after. If you change again in a hundred years, I will still love you. There is no storm I will not weather with you, and no form of you that I will not love. You are the other half of my soul, Gluttony, and I don't ever want you to question that."

This woman... how he loved her. More and more every day. She was the light, the wonder, the best part of his morning and the peace at night.

Rising over her, he kissed her with every ounce of love in him. Perhaps a little too passionately, a little too hard, but it didn't matter. She always took the love he had to give, no matter what way, shape, or form he gave it.

And when they both breathed heavily, he drew back with a sharp inhalation. "I need you, Kat. Now and forever."

She slid her hands down his spine, squeezing the muscles there, and then drew him into her. "And I need you, my love. My life."

Epilogue

Are The portal opened beside her husband's desk, and neither of them even flinched. Katherine had set herself in a comfortable armchair nearby, a book on her lap that described all the magical properties of a kelpie mane. She didn't believe an ounce of it, otherwise her people would have been using the magical hair to stitch wounds closed for ages now.

Of course, it would have been impossible for them to even brush the water horses without Gluttony's intervention. So perhaps there was some merit to closing wounds with a kelpie lock and then it staying closed forever. Apparently, it was rather good at healing human skin.

How someone had found that out, she didn't want to know.

Gluttony was at his desk, where he had set up a small amount of alchemical substrates. Because nothing was flammable or explosive, he'd deemed it acceptable for them to work in his office.

After all, he was trying to figure out a way for them to mine the peat without encroaching on the homes of the natural creatures who still wanted nothing to do with the humans. It was all a work in progress, of course, but Gluttony was fairly confident they could find some kind of trade. And if the humans were able to make a specific kind of food for the creatures that they couldn't get anywhere else, that was the first start toward healing the wounds that had plagued them all for a very long time.

But the portal opened regardless of their work, because Envy always thought everything was about him. Gluttony's brother hadn't come to visit them after the whole fiasco had happened, and Katherine was glad for it.

She wanted nothing to do with the brother who had almost kidnapped her. Nor did she think she was obligated to make amends.

Gluttony had different ideas, of course, but he'd feuded with his brother for centuries. He was used to arguments like this. She, however, was not.

Envy stepped through the portal and adjusted the fine suit he wore. The crushed black velvet was unlike anything she'd seen before, with silver threading traveling in swirling patterns of magic.

"You're dressed up," she said, then turned her attention back to her book, lest he think she was paying attention to him.

"I have other situations to deal with rather than just this one." He clearly wanted her to ask questions about that, but when she didn't, he sighed and snapped his fingers. "Are you going to give me back my falcon, or not?"

"You haven't asked a single thing about us." She snapped her book shut with a slam and glared at him. "The last time you saw the two of us, Gluttony was surely about to be attacked and you dragged me off to be kidnapped and then sent me through the swamp on my own!"

He waved a hand in the air. "My spies have already filled me in on everything. You're both fine. I'm not worried about you."

"You should have been! Your brother might have died!"

Even Gluttony gave her a strange look for that. "I can't die, Kat."

She was going to murder both of them and prove them wrong. "Oh, the two of you are just ridiculous. You do understand what I'm saying. I know you do. Envy, you should care more about your brother's wellbeing and you shouldn't be such an ass about everything. Ask him how he's doing before you barge in here making demands!"

Although Envy gave her a strange look, he turned to his brother and asked, "How are you doing, Gluttony?"

"The same as always," Gluttony replied, clearly trying to hide a grin. "I have changed into Restraint, but you may refer to me by my original name, as our brothers have set the precedence for."

"Wonderful. Restraint is a good choice for you." Envy turned to her with no small amount of exasperation. "Are you happy now, harpy?"

She ground her teeth together so hard she could hear them creak. "Not in the slightest."

"Well, clearly you cannot be satisfied." Envy sent a glare over to his brother. "Good luck with this one. I think she's going to run you ragged. Now may I have my falcon back? I have use for it soon and I know you've been overfeeding it."

Gluttony rolled his eyes. "One cannot overfeed a creature made from magic."

"You can and you have." Clearly annoyed now, Envy looked back at her and snapped his fingers. Again. "Give it back or I will take it back by force."

Katherine stood, wandering over to the window of Gluttony's office to summon his damned bird. "You know, one of these days you're going to find a woman as well and she's going to make you realize what an ass you are. In fact, I would hazard a guess that she's going to make your life a bit of a nightmare. I hope she leads you on, and then I hope you feel horrible for all the things you've put everyone else through."

Envy snorted. "First of all, no woman has ever been able to deny me. Second of all, there is no woman in this realm that would make people envious enough for me to waste my time. There are countless beauties, but there are no diamonds large enough to put the world on its knees."

The falcon flew in through the window with a shriek. And Katherine was rather horrified to see it careen into Envy as he absorbed it. Literally. The magic hit him like a bolt and he didn't even flinch. It just turned into ink that splattered across his face and neck, then sank into his skin and somehow disappeared.

Unnerving. This man was incredibly wrong and uncomfortable to look at sometimes.

Envy sighed and cracked his neck. "That's better."

"You're going to find someone," she called out as he strode toward the portal. "Mark my words, demon! And she's going to make you regret every choice you've ever made."

He looked over his shoulder at the last second, eyes glowing bright green. "Impossible, Katherine. She'd have to be perfect, and that doesn't exist."

"Maybe it does," she murmured as he stepped through the portal and disappeared. "Stranger things have happened."

Follow me on socials or Amazon to keep your eye out for the next book. You'll certainly turn a little... green with envy.

emma hamm

ACKNOWLEDGEMENTS

As always, this book wouldn't be the same without my incredible beta readers. Nic, you're a legend and I swear none of my books would be anywhere near as good as they are without you. You're the best person I've met on the internet!

A quick thank you to my parents and fiancé for listening to me prattle on and on about vampires and how to turn someone from a Glutton into a Saint (HA!).

And finally, for all my animals that allow me to swing them around in little circles and hug them way way way too tight. Thanks guys.

ABOUT THE AUTHOR

Emma Hamm is a small town girl on a blueberry field in Maine. She writes stories that remind her of home, of fairytales, and of myths and legends that make her mind wander.

She can be found by the fireplace with a cup of tea and her two Maine Coon cats dipping their paws into the water without her knowing.

For more updates, join my newsletter!
www.emmahamm.com

the demon prince

Milton Keynes UK
Ingram Content Group UK Ltd.
UKHW020242060424
440528UK00018B/126/J

9 781963 862010